Jonathan

Delighted that you joined us in Spain and I hope that you enjoy the read!

With kindest regards and best wishes

Hugh Robertson

22 / 1.6

Published by Alresford Publishing

Copyright © 2014 Hugh Robertson.
All rights reserved

Hugh Robertson has asserted his right
under the Copyright, Designs and Patents Act 1988
to be identified as the author of this work

ISBN-13 978-1-49603-131-0

Also available as a Kindle ebook
ISBN-13 978-1-84396-296-0

This work is registered with the
UK Copyright Service. Registration No. 284677965.

*As Time Goes By*
**Lyrics and music by Herman Hupfeld**
Copyright © 1931 Warner Bros. Music Corporation, ASCAP

This is a work of fiction. Names, characters, businesses, places, events and incidents are either the product of the author's imagination or used in a fictitious manner. Any resemblance to actual living persons is purely coincidental. It is acknowledged that there is a historical basis for this novel and the events it portrays or refers to, but it does not purport accurately to represent such or the persons involved in such.

This book is sold subject to the condition that it shall not, by way of trade or otherwise, be lent, resold, hired out, or otherwise circulated without the author's prior consent in any form of binding or cover other than that in which it is published and without a similar condition being imposed on the subsequent purchaser.

Pre-press production
www.ebookversions.com

Edited by Kelia Revitt
kelia@downtown.demon.co.uk

Cover by coversbykaren.com

Photograph of crown by
dbking on commons.wikimedia.org.

# THE FOOLS' CROWNS
Volume Two

# TRAITORS' GAMES

*Hugh Robertson*

ALRESFORD PUBLISHING

The man who pauses
on the path of treason halts on
a quicksand and the first step
engulfs him.

William Shakespeare – Henry V Act 1 Scene 1

# Foreword

The following background is to assist
any reader unfamiliar with the first volume in
this series of novels, *King or Pawn?*

Lord John, or Johnny Johnstone, as he was known in the international art world, in which he was a successful dealer, was sitting with his controller in the British Security Service, officially known as MI5, Lt Colonel 'Tar' Robertson. With the agreement of Sir Vernon Kell, the Head of the Service and its founder, he had recruited his lover, Lady Celia Ffrench-Hardy, the daughter of a Marquis, to work with the Service. He had yet to reveal to her that he was a long term serving officer in the Service.

He and Celia enjoyed a close relationship with the Duke of Windsor, who had been the King before he abdicated, and was previously Prince of Wales for many years. Through that friendship they had also become close to the woman the Duke wished to marry, the American married divorcee Mrs Wallis Simpson. Tar had wanted to see Celia to hear first hand of her experiences acting as a 'go between' on behalf of the German Ambassador to the Court of St James, Joachim von Ribbentrop, the then King and Mrs Simpson. The bisexual Mrs Simpson had not only been von Ribbentrop's lover but had also seduced Celia.

On reviewing Johnny's previous reports about Celia, Tar had originally formed the impression that she was a spoilt, self-indulgent and promiscuous young woman from an immensely wealthy aristocratic family.

She had inherited a fortune in her own right on the death of her doting grandmother who was herself the heiress of one of America's richest railway tycoons. Celia had her own fully staffed fine house in exclusive Hyde Park Gate, and was chauffeured around in her powerful Lagonda saloon. She was a party girl whose natural beauty had caught the eye of the Prince of Wales, as he then was, when she 'came out' as a debutante and was presented at Court.

It was natural for her to become one of the King's chosen circle with whom he indulged his hedonistic and selfish pursuit of pleasure, including a love of night clubs, sport, and in fact anything that gave him pleasure. Judged against the rigid mores of Tar's stern Presbyterian upbringing, there was nothing to choose between the King and his set of friends when it came to decadent excess.

That self indulgent excess was in itself most unfortunate when so many so many of his subjects in both Britain and the Empire were experiencing true poverty. Only months after acceding to the throne on the death of his father on 20th January 1936, the King's actions threatened the very fabric of the nation and the Empire.

The King would not accept that as the constitutional monarch he could not do as he pleased, and marry Mrs Simpson. To do so would be entirely contrary to the rules of the Church of England of which he was head and styled Defender of the Faith. There was strong political opposition both in Britain and the Empire. The government of Prime Minister Stanley Baldwin had made it clear that they would resign, and no other political party was willing to accept that the King could marry Mrs Simpson and remain on the throne. The Archbishop of Canterbury had made the Church's absolute opposition abundantly clear and even openly expressed his doubt as to the King's sanity and ability to rule.

The British press had observed a self-imposed embargo on the affair of the King and Mrs Simpson. By contrast, the foreign press had been running with the story in lurid, and at times salacious detail for months. The British press were divided with regard to the King's position. The King was aware that he could expect strong support from some of the popular press.

The King had also relied heavily on his belief that his popularity with the people as a whole would persuade the government and the Church to find a solution that suited him.

He failed to understand that the reasons for such strong opposition to his marrying his lover on the part of the government, were not solely those of which he was told.

Tar Robertson had been instructed to maintain surveillance on Mrs Simpson and also Lady Celia, who was known to be intimate with von Ribbentrop and a friend of Wallis Simpson. The telephones of the King's brother Albert, Duke of York, second-in-line to the throne, and of the King's personal country retreat, Fort Belvedere, were intercepted as was the telephone in von Ribbentrop's permanent suite in the Grosvenor House Hotel. There were strict instructions that the Prime Minister be kept fully informed of all developments. That task had fallen on Sir Vernon.

# Prologue

Tar had decided to meet Celia and Johnny on neutral ground and had booked a private room at the Savoy. He had arranged for a light lunch to be served.

Johnny ushered Celia into the room where Tar was waiting for them. He was wearing a well-cut three piece suit, a white shirt with a starched stiff collar and his old school tie. Tar stood and greeted Celia. 'Lady Celia – thank you not only for agreeing to meet but also, importantly, agreeing to help us, as has Johnny. I do not believe in formality between colleagues as we shall be once we get down to business. Please call me Tar – everybody else does. In case you are wondering, my nickname spells out my initials. I was given it at prep school and it has stayed with me ever since.'

'Very well, Tar, I shall do so, provided you call me Celia,' responded Celia, smiling warmly.

Drinks were offered, but both Celia and Johnny followed Tar's example and asked for water. They had settled themselves in the comfortable armchairs. Tar lit Celia's State Express 555 cigarette which she had taken from her gold cigarette case and fitted to an elegant holder.

Tar then asked, 'Celia, I know that you are a close friend of the Duke of Windsor and Mrs Simpson; also that you have been enjoying a relationship with Joachim von Ribbentrop for some time, and have been to Germany as his guest. Could you please tell me about these relationships, and the reason that you have indicated to Johnny that you would be willing to assist in the observation work in which he will be engaged?'

Whilst Tar's tone was warm and friendly, Celia could see that his eyes of palest blue were penetrating as he held her in a steady gaze. Instinctively she knew that this was a man that it would be hard to bluff. She decided to be totally frank. She told him of her friendship with the former King and how that had started. She said that she did not want to go into detail about the King's sexual inadequacy that had prevented them from becoming lovers. Tar was keen to break down any barriers or modesty on Celia's part. 'Precisely what is the inadequacy of which you speak?'

Celia glanced at Johnny, who gave her an affirmative nod. 'The King, who was Prince of Wales at the time wanted to go to bed with me. He was very persuasive and I was flattered, quite apart from finding him very attractive. I agreed and visited him at Fort Belvedere. We had dinner, danced a little and then started kissing. He took me upstairs and undressed me, then he undressed himself. I was not particularly experienced then but I could immediately see that although he was erect, his penis was very small, in fact, abnormally so. Also, he was totally without body hair.

'We kissed some more and he petted me intimately but when he tried to enter me – well – he just couldn't. Then suddenly he had a climax and it was all over. He was very upset and looked as though he might burst into tears so I cradled him as you would a child or sick animal and that seemed to comfort him. He then did a strange thing. He took my right nipple in his mouth and started sucking rhythmically – it was as though he was being breast fed. It certainly was not sensuous in any way whatsoever. When he finished he said that he always did this with Thelma – you know, Thelma Furness his close friend. I found it odd.'

'Yes, I can understand that you did. Was that the only time that he had any overtly sexual relations with you?'

Celia laughed at the formality of Tar's question. 'Oh yes, absolutely. It is now a bit of a joke between us, and when we are dancing he often asks me to go to bed with him and I point out that it did not work out when we tried. He treats it as a joke. Wallis, that is Wallis Simpson, told me that she took lessons from concubines when she lived in China and learnt tricks that mean she can satisfy him. To quote her, she says that she can 'make a match stick feel like a cigar'. Part of her secret lies in muscle exercises. She is a very sensual lady.'

'We can come on to her later, Celia. Tell me about von Ribbentrop.'

'He is a charming man, obviously much older than me but a super lover. What the King lacks in the equipment department, Bubbles – my nickname for Joachim – more than makes up for.'

Celia laughed nervously, but noted that Tar and Johnny had not reacted at all. She continued, 'He is very flattering and knows how to turn on the charm – I imagine that he was a very good salesman when that's what he did in the champagne business. We were having an affair without commitment. In my case it was purely physical and I assumed the same on his part. I now realise that he was using me, and had picked on me because of my closeness to the King and in due course also Wallis – she was a bonus for him and I introduced them.

'I was flattered to be invited to the Berlin Summer Olympiad, and to meet Hitler and leading members of the German government. Later I was invited to attend the Nuremburg Rally and again met Hitler. Yes, I was impressed by what I saw – it would be hard not to be. But I also met some Germans who were not so impressed, and mulling it over I have come to the conclusion that what I saw was a front – like a huge stage set designed to convince the world that Germany is a great nation again, and all of its people worship their Führer. I now believe that it is not worship and devotion to their leaders on the part of the majority of the people, but fear of what is now shown to them as an invincible state controlled by the Nazi party. I am sorry, that was rather a long speech.'

'Not at all, not at all. Now then, tell me about the role that von Ribbentrop asked you to play.'

Celia then outlined the messages that she had conveyed to the King and Mrs Simpson, effectively offering them the German Crown as well as the British if a non-aggression pact could be reached between the two nations. On Hitler's orders, two state crowns which replicated the British Imperial crowns were made for the King and his Queen to be, each boldly incorporating the swastika symbol of Nazism. She told of the crowns being taken to Fort Belvedere by von Ribbentrop to demonstrate the commitment of the German government.

She also decided to be open about her lesbian relationship with Wallis, who had seduced her at the Fort when the King was in bed with a gay lover. She could see that Johnny was looking pale and shocked when she described how Wallis Simpson had joined her and von Ribbentrop in bed.

Tar already knew something of the story in part from the observations of Johnny's purported manservant, Charles Harvey. In the capacity of manservant Charles had picked up valuable below stairs gossip from the house servants. He had also become close to the Duke's housekeeper, Elizabeth Beauchamp. Charles was also an agent in the Security Service. Tar had witnessed the King and Mrs Simpson trying on the German crowns as he had watched through binoculars whilst concealed in the garden of the Fort.

'Very well Celia, and of course you Johnny, I wish you to carry on as if we had never met. You must give no hint that there is any change in your views or feelings. I know that that will be hard for you Celia – I am aware of your relationship with Johnny on whom it will also be hard. Celia, I wish you to be as close a friend as possible to Mrs Simpson. I detect that you are uncomfortable with that relationship sexually but you will have to ignore that. You must become her confidante – her trusted companion. I believe that she is lonely now and soon she will be even more isolated.

'I also wish you to keep the relationship with von Ribbentrop alive. Remember that we have reason to believe that Mrs Simpson is passing secrets to von Ribbentrop. He bought her a Kodak Petite miniature camera disguised as a gold powder compact. The German Embassy regularly buys appropriate film.

'Johnny, you must nurture your relationship with the Duke. Finally, it is essential that you remember that this surveillance is not focused on the question of the King's wish to marry an unsuitable person, but it is to detect and monitor what for want of a better word is espionage. The Duke when King may have been naive in his leaking of information to his German cousins and carelessly leaving top-secret documents around. Personally I have doubts.

'However, we have no doubts about Mrs Simpson – she is a cold-blooded spy. Celia, you have seen the German military machine at first hand and met that nation's leaders. Can you tell what its purpose and intent are?'

Without hesitation she responded with just one word. 'War.'

# Chapter 1

Von Ribbentrop was sitting opposite Adolf Hitler and giving an all-round report on his view of British opinions, with regard to Germany and its Nazi government. It was obvious that the Führer was displeased as he said, 'Joachim, in my opinion Canaris and the Abwehr have been well nigh useless in identifying prominent and powerful British who are sympathetic to our cause and aims. Most of the information they have served up is in the public domain. The military side have only done a little better in their more direct approaches. So far as I can see the positive contacts that they have identified are retired senior officers living in Hampshire. This makes your efforts ever more important.'

'I have to concur, mein Führer.'

Von Ribbentrop could not resist a dig at his enemy, Heinrich Himmler. 'In fairness to Canaris and his men, and the military, the State Security Service under Himmler has done no better.'

To von Ribbentrop's delight, the Führer nodded agreement. Hitler then went off onto a tangent and mused, 'The British are a strange lot. They deprecate their politicians and appear to be indifferent to issues that we Germans take seriously. But if they see even the hint that an outsider is being critical, they will turn on him ferociously. That is why I think that the ex-King, the Duke of Windsor, is so important to us.'

'I agree, mein Führer'

'What is his state of mind?'

'I have asked Lady Celia who is in the Duke's inner circle. She is close to Mrs Simpson and she gets information through Lord John Johnstone, who is also very close to the Duke.

Indeed he is accompanying him to Austria as we speak. She reports that the Duke is by turns relieved that the crisis has broken and excited at the prospect of life with Mrs Simpson, but then deeply morose as he sees himself going into a lonely exile. He will not see Mrs Simpson for five months.'

'You report that he is to stay in Austria with Baron Eugene de Rothschild and his American wife. That will be at their castle at Enzesfeld, not far south of Vienna.'

Hitler then seemed to be almost thinking aloud as he spoke. 'Infernal Jews. Nothing we can do about the damned Rothschilds – we need their money. Why is it that the purest politics is besmirched with having to consort with Jewish usurers like the Rothschilds and opportunist wealthy American industrialists? We even had to rely upon affluent American politicians such as Senator Prescott Bush?'

'With respect, you know the answer, mein Führer. Without their money the Nazi Party would not now rule Germany, and we could not afford to re-arm quickly.'

'Oh, I know, it just pains me. Anyhow, we digress. What are you doing to get close to the Duke?'

'I am planning to go and see him – on a private basis, of course. He will almost certainly be skiing in the Tyrol. Otherwise I shall engineer a meeting in Vienna – I do not think that I should go near the castle. The Rothschild family's international intelligence and information exchange is a match for that of any Government.'

'Well,' laughed Hitler, 'that's how they made a great fortune, by being the first in London to know of the victory at Waterloo.'

Von Ribbentrop continued, 'I have liaised with Admiral Canaris, and he is arranging for observation on the castle whilst the Duke is there. It will not achieve much except that we shall know immediately if the Duke moves on. The castle telephones are also to be intercepted. The Duke and Mrs Simpson will undoubtedly be in touch.'

'What of Mrs Simpson, Joachim? You must be missing her!' laughed Hitler.

'I certainly miss the intelligence she was providing. As to her other attractions, there are plenty more fish in the sea. We are watching the villa in the hills above Cannes where she is staying, and are hopeful that we can insert an agent into the household in the guise of a domestic servant. Whilst her hosts, the Rogers, have a chauffeur, she of course does not, but she has her car there and I am sure that she will want to be independent.

'We have an extremely handsome young driver on tap. She will be like a cat on a hot tin roof after a few days and I believe she will find him irresistible. When it comes to her physical needs she is a voracious and predatory animal. He has now met the local girl who is acting as her lady's maid, and has planted the seed of the idea that he go to work for Mrs Simpson.'

'Good. I assume that she is no longer privy to any information that is useful to us?'

'That is so, mein Führer, but it is important that we are aware of what she is doing. One difficulty for her is that she left England with no money. Lord Brownlow, who is still with her, will raise this with the Duke, but in the meantime has personally made a substantial sum of his family money available to her. My bet is that when her maid shows her the picture of the young man who would be her driver, she will jump at it. His name is Didier Pascal, by the way.'

'Thank you for the update, Joachim. This may all seem a little trivial but I can assure you that it is at the heart of my plans to conquer our enemies to the East. We must neutralise the British at all costs. Now, Joachim, please be on your way, I have a speech to edit. Thank you again, and keep up the good work.'

Von Ribbentrop was greatly relieved that Hitler had been in a benign mood, and left with a spring in his step.

Wallis was already feeling the strain. She was close to the Rogers and regarded them as great friends, as evidenced by their hospitality to her at the expense of their own peace. The beautiful villa had been carefully chosen for its tranquillity. That was now shattered by the international press corps who were laying siege to it, and only kept at bay by the police guards. However, the Rogers' kindness and friendship could not satisfy the inner craving that was beginning to gnaw at her.

Her ladies maid was a pretty little thing but essentially a simple country girl. She would not be worth seducing. Wallis' growing need was for a sophisticated lover of either sex. With the press at the gates, there was presently no prospect of her slipping into Cannes incognito. There she knew that she would find a solution to her problem in a matter of moments at the Carlton Hotel. Some of the world's most sophisticated and beautiful courtesans frequented the cocktail bar of the hotel in the winter. In the summer they were to be found on the terrace facing the Croisette, as the elegant promenade was known. Even if she could leave the villa, she did not want to be tied to the Rogers' car and driver.

Von Ribbentrop had immediately returned to London following his meeting with the Führer. As always, he was astounded at the interest that Hitler took in items of minute detail. This was manifest in his wanting to be told the names of individuals who were to play only supporting roles. Now, as often in the past, he wondered whether this was a strength or a weakness in a nation's leader. He decided to contact Celia and start briefing her on the first message that she must take to Mrs Simpson. As he had official engagements every evening for the next few days, he invited her to lunch. As usual, it was to be at the Grosvenor House Hotel.

When Celia arrived, looking as elegant and seductive as always, he could not help wondering why he had earlier decided that on this occasion they would not go to bed together. They were sitting almost formally as the butler poured their drinks. Von Ribbentrop had correctly surmised that the butler was an agent of German intelligence. He had been surprised to receive the assurance of Admiral Canaris that he was not an Abwehr agent as not only he but British intelligence had believed.

He was aware that some time ago, orders had been given that 'sleeper ' agents were to be embedded in British and French society. The training to become an impeccably efficient apparently English butler was lengthy, but ultimately worth the effort. To the British ruling classes it seemed that the best servants were effectively invisible. This provided ample opportunity for a sharp-witted agent to pick up sensitive and often vital information from overheard conversations.

'Well, Bubbles darling – Wallis is kicking her heels in France and the Duke of Windsor, as we must now think of the former King is rattling across Europe in the Orient Express. I wonder how they feel?'

'Oh, I think that you can guess that easily enough Celia. That is why I should like to take the opportunity of explaining to you the nature of the first message that I wish you to give to Wallis. If I may, I shall do so over luncheon.'

'Most certainly – actually I am famished. I went for a hack in Hyde Park early this morning and met some old friends by pure chance. We had a damn good stretch and really covered some ground. Afterwards we chatted for longer than I realised as our horses cooled down. As a result I decided to skip breakfast when I arrived home. There is nothing like a lively time in the saddle to give a girl a roaring appetite you know, Bubbles,' said Celia, giving von Ribbentrop an arch look.

He decided not to take the hint. 'Right, my beautiful young lady, luncheon beckons.'

He stood and formally helped her to her feet. After they had finished their main course he explained, 'As you know, Wallis is very insecure. It is a manifestation of her childhood. She married Ernest Simpson because he appeared wealthy and sound. In fact, he got into financial difficulties, and the Prince of Wales, as he then was, bailed him out for a very substantial amount of money. I do not know whether she deliberately seduced the Prince to achieve that end. I can only surmise that she did – why else would he have done so?'

'I had heard some gossip to that effect. Knowing her I bet she did.'

'She is now broke, except for a temporary loan from Lord Brownlow. The Duke of Windsor will make provision for her, but in her mind she will want financial independence. That I shall provide. A Swiss bank account, of which I shall give you details, has been opened in the name of a nominee for her, and an initial sum of one hundred thousand pounds has been credited to it by the German government.'

'Gosh, Bubbles, that is an awful lot of money.'

'I can assure you that she has earned it. I shall also be giving you an official letter for her. It is signed by the Führer himself as a mark of respect. The letter will confirm that the deposit is made in respect of intelligence services rendered. It will also state that her future efforts will be similarly rewarded.'

'Surely that is potentially very incriminating?' asked Celia.

Von Ribbentrop laughed, and replied, 'That remark, Celia, is what I think you British would call a bullseye. I want her to have some dirt on her shoes to ensure that she does not change allegiance. You are also to tell her that she should not reveal the payment or even the existence of the account to the Duke of Windsor.'

'Now then, what were you saying about a lively time in the saddle giving you a hearty appetite?'

Celia had decided that she would forego lovemaking with Bubbles that day, and report directly to Tar Robertson as soon as possible instead. 'Oh, Bubbles darling, you are so sweet to ask. Lunch was delicious but I really must be off now.'

'Perhaps another time then.'

'Oh, rather,' responded Celia, to a slightly crestfallen von Ribbentrop. She rightly guessed that the talk over lunch would have put von Ribbentrop in the mood for a vigorous session in bed.

After leaving the hotel, Celia was driven straight home where she telephoned Tar. She caught him just as he was going out. She explained that she had had a most interesting lunch and would like to meet him as soon as possible. He invited her to come to his office at 4.30pm.

When Celia entered Tar's office, after exchanging the usual pleasantries Tar invited her to bring him up to date. 'What I am about to tell you makes me a sort of accomplice to spying on Great Britain. I trust you implicitly but in the future you may not be available to support my role. Tar, will you please make a careful note of what I will now tell you and make a copy. I should then like you to sign the note confirming its accuracy, and your express instructions for me to proceed as I have been asked.'

'Very well, Celia,' replied Tar looking steadily at her with his piercing ice blue eyes. After Tar had slipped carbon paper between two sheets of ruled foolscap on his desk and noted the time and date of the meeting, he nodded to Celia. Celia then repeated the conversation that she had had with von Ribbentrop as near to verbatim as she could manage. When she finished, Tar was smiling widely.

'Well done, Celia. This is absolutely brilliant! Von Ribbentrop has done what we could never have achieved. In entrapping Mrs Simpson in Germany's interests as he sees it, he has trapped her for us as well. You must follow his instructions to the dot, save that as soon as he gives you the letter and account details you must bring them here, so that we can copy them. I shall now conclude my notes by recording my direct order for you to act as requested by von Ribbentrop. I shall also have one of my assistants witness my signature.'

'Thank you, Tar.'

'No thanks are necessary, Celia. You are now a fully fledged double agent. Congratulations!'

# Chapter 2

After boarding the Orient-Express train at Boulogne, the Duke of Windsor informed his party that he was tired and accordingly was going to retire. He asked Detective Sergeant Storier to look after his Skye terrier Slipper whilst he was resting. The Duke and his party were occupying a whole darkened coach immediately behind the engine. It was separated from the rest of the train by the luggage van, in which armed French police were stationed. They were to keep guard and prevent anyone gaining access to the Duke. There were reckoned to be as many as 60 reporters and photographers on the train. There were very few other passengers.

After the Duke had retired into his sleeping compart-ment, which was one of eleven compartments occupied by his party, and closed the door, Slipper became very agitated and started to bark furiously. The Duke's compartment door opened and he called for Slipper, who immediately ran to him, scuttled through the doorway and leapt onto the bunk. The Duke smiled and shrugged as he closed his door again, and climbed back into the bunk with his dog curled up by his feet. Despite the noise of the engine as the train pulled away from the platform and then the clatter as it ran through the marshalling yard points, the Duke fell into a deep sleep almost immediately.

At each border crossing, the police guards in the luggage van changed to those of the country through which the train was to travel. Johnny thought to himself that his being with the Duke was probably a waste of time if he was going to sleep through the journey. He and the Colonel chatted for a while then both dozed fitfully. Neither went into a sleeping compartment.

The British detective sergeants took it in turns to stand in the corridor at the very rear of the carriage throughout the journey. They were very conscious of the fact that if anyone reached their carriage they would have first had to overcome the police in the luggage van. Both were well aware that if there were to be a shoot out, they would almost certainly be at a disadvantage with only their service revolvers. The valet, a former professional soldier, was also armed, as were the Colonel and Johnny.

The Duke slept as the train raced along, and it was 3 pm when he came out of his compartment and went into the bathroom. After he had washed, shaved and dressed, he invited the Colonel and Johnny to join him for a spot of lunch. He seemed in better spirits and clearly the rest had been good for him. It seemed to have eased at least some of the tension which had built up as the crisis had deepened. After lunch the Duke suggested that they play poker. None of them were fully concentrating on the game. The Duke's competitive side made him take risks unnecessarily, and Johnny recognised the signs that he was becoming frustrated.

'Sir, I believe that we shall be stopping in Salzburg at about 5pm for a few minutes. That would give an opportunity for you to stretch your legs and enjoy some fresh air.'

'Good idea, Johnny. We could all do with that, and Slipper could have a walk. He must be bursting, poor little bugger,' laughed the Duke.

Inwardly Johnny heaved a sigh of relief – a disastrous mood change had been averted.

As the train came to a stop in Salzburg, armed police formed a tight cordon around the special carriage, and also further up the platform where a crowd had gathered. The Duke and his party stepped down onto the platform. Although onlookers were kept well away by the police, they applauded and cheered the diminutive figure. The Duke acknowledged them with a smile, and doffed then waved his black bowler hat. He was wearing a dark overcoat with a Persian lamb collar and a red muffler. After he had acknowledged them, some in the crowd started to sing the British National Anthem. It was obvious that few knew the words and were humming the simple tune.

The train guard checked his pocket watch and waved his green flag. The driver, who was leaning out of the engine's cab, reached up and pulled the whistle lever. The short blast was a sufficient reminder for the passengers to re-embark. As he mounted the step into the carriage, the Duke turned towards the crowd that was now cheering again, and waved his hat above his head in a flamboyant gesture. As the train doors slammed shut the whistle sounded and the train pulled away in a cloud of steam.

They were now on the last leg of the journey, and the good mood of the Duke and his companions continued. Discussion turned to hunting, and there was a spirited debate about the relative pleasures of hunting over different types of terrain.

In Vienna preparations were being made for the Duke's arrival. The British Minister in Vienna, Sir Walford Selby, and Doctor Stubl, the Police President of the City, were at the station with a large detachment of police. It was arranged that the train would come into the platform adjacent to the grandly named Imperial Waiting Saloon so that the Duke and his party would not have far to walk. The opinion of all the security advisers was that he was at greatest risk when walking in the open. Reporters and photographers had been excluded from the station, so the only members of the international press corps who would see the Duke were those who had travelled on the train. As the train came to a halt the police formed up in two cordons as had been done in Salzburg.

The Duke was dressed in the same fur collared dark overcoat, distinctive scarf and bowler hat. As he stepped down from the carriage, the Duke again raised his hat high and waved it exuberantly. Sir Walford stepped forward.

'Your Royal Highness, welcome to Vienna. May I present Doctor Stubl, who is responsible for the police presence here, your escort to Enzesfeld Castle and the security at the castle itself.'

After shaking hands with Dr Stubl and speaking to him in German, the Duke turned to Sir Walford. 'Any messages for me Sir Walford?'

'There are, Sir,' he replied handing the Duke a bundle of letters and telegrams. The Duke crammed them into his coat pocket.

The party then left the platform, and were crossing through the ornate and rather grand Imperial Waiting Saloon on the way to the Baron's car when the Duke suddenly stopped. 'Let the photographers come along. They had a very tough journey and they deserve some pictures. Let's turn back.'

As the Duke came back onto the platform, to the obvious concern of Dr Stubl, he gestured for the photographers to be allowed through the cordon. He then stood and endured the cross fire of many flashlights, and by turn smiled, waved and looked serious. He then said loudly in German, 'Well I guess, gentlemen, that is enough.'

He smiled again, waved his hat and went back through the waiting room and out to the car, which he entered with the Colonel and Johnny. The car was preceded by police motorcycle outriders and a police car, and followed by two more cars. The police had thrown up another cordon, this time across the road, to prevent the eager press men in the street from following the Duke. Their orders were to hold them all back for at least five minutes. The Duke's luggage, which included his skis, was being unloaded from the train onto the platform. As the little cavalcade drove off the Duke turned to Johnny.

'I have stayed at Enzesfeld before you know. The Baron is a splendid fellow and his American-born wife, Kitty is utterly charming. The castle is really more of a hunting lodge. It was originally built in the 12th century. Since then it's been knocked about in various conflicts, and even razed to the ground. It is now extremely comfortable as you would imagine, and very isolated, sitting on a rocky outcrop in the middle of a vast estate.'

As he spoke he was idly flicking through his messages. His eye was caught by a telegram from Buckingham Palace. His former Private Secretary advised him that the Austrian government had confirmed that a detachment of police had been despatched from Baden to guard the 40-room castle. He was asked to pass the telegram to his Equerry, the Colonel, who would need the various police contact details to arrange security cover if the Duke should wish to leave the Castle. The former Secretary also provided the contact details and address of a prominent Viennese ear specialist, Professor Newmann. The Duke was impatient to reach the castle where he intended to telephone Wallis before he did anything else.

'Wallis, my dear love, how are you?'

'I am fine, darling man, but missing you so much. The Rogers could not be kinder but I have insisted that Perry head back home, I think that he plans to visit you on the way. As you know, our policeman and the brilliant driver left for England a few days ago, so it is just us and the press men at the gates. The police believe that the number of press people is beginning to reduce, and that there will only be a handful in a day or two. Sorry, my love. I am talking too much. How was your journey?'

'Oh, it was fine if you do not mind so many hours cooped up in a train. There were no dramas. And how about you? George, the driver, was full of the fact that you had quite a time going through France, even down to leaving a restaurant through the kitchen window.'

'Oh, it's true darling! It really was quite amusing, if a little undignified. Tight skirts are not designed for such antics. I think mine host saw rather a lot of what is normally private ground!'

They both laughed. 'When we meet you must give me all the details.'

'I most certainly shall, but, of course, if Perry Brownlow comes to see you he will be able to tell all. David, dearest, I must go now my love, we are having a very late and lengthy supper. Do call me again before you go to bed. I shall wait up by the telephone so that no one else is disturbed.'

'Very well, Wallis. We shall soon be 'WE' again, eh? – it is so grand to hear your sweet voice. I send you a big kiss and a warm embrace.'

'Hmm – thank you, darling David. Until later then.'

After so many hours travelling, the Duke could not wait to have a bath and change into fresh clothes. His valet advised him that the Baron had indicated that evening dress would not be worn this evening. Casual dress would be appropriate for the informal late supper the Duke and his two colleagues would be sharing with him and the Baroness. The valet laid out a grey suit in a fine Prince of Wales check, a set of clean underwear, a soft collared cream silk shirt and a dark blue woven silk tie. The combination of the talk with Wallis, the warm bath, and changing into clean clothes gave the Duke a feeling of well being as he joined his hosts and the fellow guests in the great baronial salon where drinks were being served.

'Aha!' he cried, as his gaze fell on a large oil painting of Windsor Castle hanging on the dark wood-panelled wall, 'now that I am the Duke of Windsor, perhaps I should return and claim my castle, eh?'

Although the Duke laughed, Johnny recognised that there was the seed of longing in the apparent joke. From what Johnny knew of the attitude of the new Queen Elizabeth and her husband the King, whom she so strongly influenced, he thought that the Duke was living in cloud cuckoo land. The only way that he would ever lay claim to Windsor Castle would be if he were put back on the throne. That would take what Johnny believed to be an unholy alliance or Britain's capitulation in a war with Germany.

# Chapter 3

True to her word, Wallis waited by the telephone after her hosts, the Rogers, had gone to bed. When the Duke telephoned he sounded relaxed, and they chatted affectionately. Wallis told the Duke that she was taking on a driver so that she would be able to leave the villa without inconveniencing her hosts by taking their car. She did not feel the need to mention that Didier Pascal was a devastatingly handsome young man with a muscular sculptured physique and a glint in his eye. As soon as Wallis met him, she knew that she could seduce him without any difficulty, and that he would be able to satisfy her now desperate need.

She had explained that although his employment would start immediately, he would not be taking her out in the car until the press interest had died down some more. She had explained that she would like him to take her car into Cannes once every day and park at the rear of the Carlton Hotel. He should then go into the hotel and simply sit in the bar and nurse a soft drink for an hour or two. Wallis wanted to establish a pattern in the hope that the press would become tired of following her car when it appeared that her driver had its use for his time off. In the meantime, she explained to him that she would require him to assist her in improving her French.

The Rogers always retired for a two hour siesta after lunch, and Didier could give her her coaching in the drawing room of her suite which was in the opposite wing of the large villa. He knew immediately that the French lessons would involve more than improving her accent, which was atrocious.

After the call from the Duke ended, Wallis summoned her maid Laurenne and asked her to help her undress. As Laurenne did so, Wallis thought about the following afternoon when Didier was to give her her first lesson. She absent-mindedly stroked Laurenne's cheek and then tilting back her head kissed her full on the lips To her surprise, Laurenne immediately revealed that she was not only experienced but enthusiastic. In what seemed like a few frenzied moments they were both naked and entwined on the bed. When Laurenne first felt Wallis' sex she drew back from their kiss with a start. Wide-eyed she exclaimed, 'Ooh, Madame!'

Wallis chortled and Laurenne swung round into the classic sixty nine position. Wallis was soon grunting with passion as Laurenne expertly brought her to the climax that she had been craving. After they were both satiated and lying quietly in a loose embrace Wallis asked Laurenne how it was that she was so experienced. She was pleasantly surprised when Laurenne explained that she and Didier had on occasions worked together as a professional escort couple.

Laurenne also explained that she and another girl of her age were regular performers at lesbian parties held in some of the back street clubs in Cannes. Wallis realised that the playground of Europe's idle rich was a place that catered for all tastes, however jaded. She decided that her time alone in Cannes was going to be far more entertaining than she could have imagined.

The day after their arrival at Enzesfeld castle, Johnny bade the Duke and their hosts goodbye, and was driven back to Vienna where he was to return across Northern Europe in the same train that had brought them from Boulogne. As he settled into his private compartment he thought to himself that by the time he returned to London, he would have had his fill of trains. He had often heard people talking of the romance of long train journeys. He now thought that such a notion was deluded.

At least without the security restrictions under which they had travelled to Austria, he could move about the train and enjoy the luxury of the near legendary dining car cuisine. He promised himself a fine bottle of Burgundy that evening. He rang for the steward and asked him to bring some refreshments and the wine list. He intended to make the best of the journey and had packed an Agatha Christie novel to help pass the time. He smiled as he opened her 1928 novel *'The Mystery of the Blue Train'*. He had yet to discuss arrangements with Celia, but believed when they visited Wallis in Cannes that they would travel on the legendary train from Calais to the South of France.

Le Train Bleu, as the French called it, also boasted a magnificent dining car. The train was most popular between the months of November and April. That was when many wealthy travellers wished to escape the Northern winter and enjoy the warmer Mediterranean climate. Johnny made a mental note to make their bookings as soon as he returned to London.

Lord Brownlow, Perry Cust, was not enjoying quite as luxurious a journey. He had taken an express to Lyon where he changed to a relatively slow train to Geneva. He then had to travel to Vienna. It was a cold and rather bleak journey and in stark contrast to the mild south of France. He had a number of letters from Wallis to the Duke, and numerous messages of affection that she had pressed him to pass on.

He was fond of the Duke, and regarded him as a good friend despite his short comings. Having spent so much time with her he was less sure of Wallis. He certainly would not tell the Duke of his misgivings, but he was almost convinced that she was a consummate, manipulative actress. It had not escaped him that by having him issue her press release she had diverted a large amount of potential blame for the former King's abdication away from herself. He did not find her attractive, but he could see that she had a sexual magnetism which she had honed to perfection. Whatever it was, it was rare for any man not to do her bidding.

Whether she truly loved the Duke was impossible to say. She played her emotional cards very close to her chest. She would be a superlative poker player he thought – possibly pretty handy at chess too. His eventual arrival in Vienna would go unnoticed and he would be met by the Baron's car. He was an old family friend of the Rothschilds, and he was looking forward to seeing Eugene and Kitty as the Baroness was known. He prayed that the Duke would be in a good humour and not brooding about the next five months of enforced separation from Wallis. Above all, he hoped for a few days rest before returning to London and his duties as Lord in Waiting to the new King.

He was also very aware that he had been neglecting the family estates. There would be long meetings with his Factor and a myriad of decisions to be made on his return. He hunched deeper in his seat, and pulled his coat collar even higher as his breath steamed in the compartment. It was bitterly cold even though he had set the heating matrix at its highest.

The new King was feeling his way with care. His courtiers were tirelessly explaining the finer points of detail that he must master. Elizabeth, the Queen Consort, was the rock on which he could rely totally. She had intelligence and charm aplenty. She was also very tough. It was she who asked or prompted the awkward questions and was unafraid to speak her mind.

'I h h have h h had a telegram from Perry Cust. He has left the Simpson c c c creature in C C C C Cannes, and is h he he heading for A Au Austria t t to visit D DDDD David. He ww w ill then r re re return as my my L L L Lord-in-W W Waiting.'

'I think not darling,' replied Elizabeth firmly. 'He has been too hugger mugger with David and the Simpson creature. You must replace him. If he cared about serving you he would have come straight back from the South of France.'

'I c c c cannot just sa sa sack him. Protocol is th th that h h h he must r r r resign.'

'Leave that to me, darling.'

At that moment Sir Alexander Hardinge, Private Secretary to the Sovereign, entered the room and bowed. Before the King could say anything, Elizabeth smiling sweetly spoke up.

'Alexander. Lord Brownlow has tendered his resignation as Lord-in-Waiting. Please be good enough to publish such in the Court Circular. A replacement appointment will be announced in a few days.'

Lord Hardinge, who was a very good friend of Perry Cust, was shocked and surprised. He already knew enough of the Queen not to challenge what she had said, and knew that he would have to comply with her instruction. The King cleared his throat as if to speak, but before he could Elizabeth spoke again.

'Alexander. A point of clarification, if you will. The King received a note from the Duke of Windsor just before he left the country, in which he stated that he required that his wife when he marries should have the style 'Her Royal Highness'. I understood that such was entirely in the King's discretion. Is that so?'

'Your understanding is absolutely correct, Your Majesty. At the Accession Meeting of the Privy Council, His Majesty appointed his brother a Royal Duke. By virtue of this the Duke of Windsor cannot sit in the House of Commons or speak on political matters in the House of Lords. In due course the King, advised by his Privy Council, will decide the terms of the Letters Patent which will be formally granted to the Duke. Those Letters Patent will also define the status of any wife or child of the Duke.'

'Thank you, Alexander, that is very clear to me – do you agree, darling?'

The King nodded his agreement as he lit yet another cigarette. The Queen would have her way and both her selfish brother-in-law and the shameless hussy that he would marry would suffer.

When Perry arrived at the castle, he was delighted to accept a warm glass of gluhwein from the Baron. 'And look who we have here!' The Baroness dashed over and gave Perry a long kiss, and the Duke's face lit up with one of his infectious smiles.

The rigours of the miserable journey were soon forgotten, as the friends sat around drinking and chatting amiably. Perry had given the bundle of letters to the Duke as soon as possible after he arrived. The Duke had taken them to the library where he quickly skimmed through them. When he came back after about 20 minutes he was still in good humour, and insisted that Perry regale them with his description of their adventures in France. Perry edited his account and focused on some of the more amusing or memorable moments. When the dressing gong sounded, the little group which had by then been joined by the Colonel, all went upstairs to dress for dinner.

The Duke could not resist a telephone call to Wallis in which after thanking her for her letters he swore undying love and devotion.

Wallis was feeling rather tired after a 'French lesson' with Didier Pascal, who had proved to be every bit as attractive in the buff as she had hoped. He was also a tireless and inventive lover. She reassured the Duke that all was well with her, with the exception that she was missing him desperately. After her lengthy session with Didier she felt that she owed the Duke a little white lie.

After the call she asked Laurenne to assist her in the bath and luxuriated whilst the pretty young girl washed her meticulously with a giant sponge. When she had bathed, Wallis lay on thick towels on her bed whilst Laurenne gave her a deep massage. She was soon aroused again but knew that there was no time for pleasure before dinner. She rolled onto her back and smiling at Laurenne she reached under the girl's uniform skirt and gave her a quick caress.

'You must come and help me after dinner my dear.' Laurenne made a moue and gave a mock curtsey. They both laughed as Wallis then sat up and removed her turban-like head dress. Dinner time, and the show must go on.

# Chapter 4

The Duke was noticeably more relaxed and Perry found that being in his company was not as challenging as in the recent past before the abdication. However, his obsession with Wallis and his constant wish to talk about her was tiresome. Perry found that the best way to deal with this was to suggest that the Duke should telephone her. Heaven knows what the cost of the calls would be, but whatever it was it was worth it. The only time of day when Wallis had asked him not to call her was between 2.30pm and 4.30pm in the afternoons, when she had informed him that she would be taking a siesta. The Duke had commented that she had never done this before but accepted the restriction.

Perry had raised the question of Wallis' finances. The Duke immediately called Wallis to assure her that he would have funds wired to her and he would repay Perry's loan. It was agreed that since she did not have a French bank account the funds should be sent to the Rogers' bank. Once she could leave the villa and go into Cannes, she would open an account at the same bank and her funds could be transferred.

The Duke had had some unsatisfactory conversations with his brother, the new King. He was upset and annoyed that he would not receive a stipend from the government-funded Civil List, but would receive an allowance from the King's own funds. That meant that his sister-in-law, Queen Elizabeth, would have some influence on his finances. He had called Sir Alexander Hardinge and asked him to contact the Prime Minister on his behalf.

He was shocked when Hardinge, whom he had regarded as a close friend, responded, 'I am sorry, your Royal Highness, but I have express instructions from His Majesty to the effect that I may not assist you.'

He had then contacted Walter Monckton who had agreed to intercede on his behalf. Again he was disappointed when he was told of the response.

'I have spoken to Mr Baldwin, who told me in no uncertain terms that neither the government nor the parties in opposition have any intention of voting that you should be provided for out of the Civil List. I am afraid that that door is firmly closed.'

'The bastards!' responded the Duke. In reality, he was extremely wealthy, having at his disposal the accumulated revenues of the Duchy of Cornwall to which he had been entitled as Prince of Wales for so many years. Also Sandringham House and Balmoral had been inherited by him personally on the death of his father, and he knew that the new King would wish to purchase them. What really riled him was the thought that he was being spitefully treated by both his own family and the government.

He took to telephoning the King every day, repeating the arguments that had so far fallen on deaf ears. The King was becoming exasperated with the persistent and as he saw it, pointless calls. They were upsetting him.

'My dear,' said the Queen in a tone of voice that brooked no argument, 'enough is enough. David has made his bed and he must lie in it. I will not have you upset by these pathetic begging calls. Even your brothers have now refused to speak to him. George has called him the "Puke of Windsor", although I fancy the hand of Noël Coward in that one. You must give instructions that you are unavailable when he calls.'

'Yes, m y my my d d ddear,' he replied, relieved to have the decision taken for him.

'Whilst we are on the subject of David and his cronies, we have dealt with Brownlow, and now we must do likewise with Alexander Hardinge.'

'B b bb but h h he is a g g ggood m m man,' responded the King.

'That he may be, but he was close to David for far too long for comfort. I have sounded out Lord Wigram and although he had officially retired, he is prepared to serve again in the dual capacities of permanent Lord-in-Waiting and your Private

Secretary. He will be an extra Equerry. I am sure that you would agree that he is a very sound pair of hands, and he served your papa very well.'

'I a a ag agree,' said the King, nodding agreement, but he then asserted himself, saying as he lit another cigarette, 'I shall keep Alexander Hardinge as my Principal Private Secretary, but Lord Wigram can have the honorary title of Private Secretary.'

The Queen was determined to purge the Royal Court and household of all who had been close to or supported her brother-in-law, whom she totally despised. However, she decided to humour her husband and bide her time so far as Alexander Hardinge was concerned, and she did count his wife as a friend. 'Very well my dear, as you wish, but Clive Wigram will be my eyes and ears.'

Wallis had just finished a long conversation with Celia. She had not mentioned Didier or Laurenne but Celia could sense that Wallis was noticeably less tense. She knew her well enough by now to guess that she had found some outlet for her voracious sexual appetite.

It was arranged that Celia and Johnny would be travelling to Cannes the following Tuesday in the Blue Train. It was a firm arrangement as Johnny had bought the tickets. Wallis looked at her watch, and realised that it was almost time for the routine pre-luncheon drinks with her hosts. She went to her dressing table and checked her makeup that was impeccable as ever. Today she was wearing wide legged cruise style trousers with a blue and white striped matelot top, a red scarf knotted at her throat and a jaunty beret. It was an outfit that David had particularly admired when they had cruised the Eastern Mediterranean .That had only been a few months ago but it seemed like a lifetime.

Drinks were served today in an open conservatory that caught the sun and was out of sight to the now dwindling group of press men.

'I say, Wallis,' said a beaming Herman Rogers, 'you sure look the part today – all we need is the yacht.'

Wallis laughed and kissed him lightly on the cheek, with her hand on his upper arm.

'Well Herman, I just thought that "when in France" you have to run with it.'

'The usual, Wallis?'

'But of course, my dear – you are so kind.'

He mixed her perfect Manhattan and had just handed it to her when her hostess arrived.

'Well Wallis, you are looking more relaxed every day – I think that the South of France suits you'.

'Oh it does, and you have both been so kind to me. I have some news have just spoken to my good friend Lady Celia Ffrench-Hardy – I have mentioned her to you. She and Johnny Johnstone – both old friends of David – are coming down on the Blue Train and should arrive here on Wednesday. You will love them. He is an international art dealer and just so, so amusing.'

'We shall look forward to meeting them. As they say, Wallis, any friend of yours is a friend of ours.'

The conversation was light and humorous as they finished their drinks and then went through to the dining room for a light lunch.

'Well Wallis, siesta time for us my dear,' said the ever-affable Herman Rogers.

'And a French lesson for me,' responded Wallis, as they left the dining room and went upstairs to their suites. As soon as Wallis had closed her door she turned to Laurenne who was waiting for her, 'Laurenne my dear – help me out of this outfit and into my wrap.'

'Oui, Madame,' she replied with a smile, and started to undress Wallis. When Wallis was standing in just her brassiere and embroidered knickers, Laurenne reached out to either side of the waistband.

'No my dear – I shall keep these on. Now run along and send Didier to me.'

Laurenne bobbed a curtsy and left the suite. Wallis had slipped into her silk robe and was tying its sash when Didier came into the suite and locked the door. 'Get undressed,' ordered Wallis in a harsh tone that was very different to the way she had spoken to Laurenne.

When Didier stood before her naked she spoke again, 'Now do not move,' she ordered. She then walked around him as if inspecting him minutely. She stopped in front of him and reached out with her right hand. 'Now come here,' she ordered and she drew him towards her as she walked backwards towards the bedroom.

Celia had arranged to meet up with von Ribbentrop on Monday evening, when he would give her the papers which she was to take to Wallis. The reports that he received from Germany were simply that Wallis had not yet left the Rogers' villa and was amusing herself with the German agent, Didier Pascal, and his friend, her maid Laurenne.

Knowing her as he did, von Ribbentrop guessed that it would not be long before she would feel the urge for a change and would venture into Cannes. He had vivid memories of times that he had spent in that decadent place. The combination of so much wealth, and people who had everything material that they could wish for, meant that every vice was catered for. The call girls working the Carlton Hotel and the Croisette were spectacular, but it had been in the darker backstreets where he had found true pleasure. Only in the days before the nightlife in Berlin was purged by the Nazis had he come across such a choice of depraved pleasures. He did not allow his mind to dwell too long on these memories. Of one thing he was sure, however, Wallis would find her outlet.

The Duke had never seen Perry so angry and upset.

'David, you will not believe it! I have just spoken to Alexander Hardinge in London. It is in today's Court Circular in *The Times* and the *Daily Telegraph* that the King has accepted my resignation as Lord-in-Waiting. How, I ask? I have had no thought of resigning! To cap it all, they have appointed Clive Wigram in my place and also as a private secretary to the King.'

'I am so sorry Perry – neither you or Alexander Hardinge deserves to be treated like that. This will be the Queen's doing. I always reckoned that behind that simpering exterior, there lurked a very hard woman.'

'What really rankles is that all I have done is my duty.'

'That, my dear fellow, is the root of the problem. You served me. She hates me. Bertie is too weak to stand up to her. She is now ruling the roost. Bear in mind that I cannot even telephone Bertie now – my own bloody brother.'

'I must return to London and try and sort this out.'

'No Perry, it is pointless. You will find nothing but a closed door. You must resign yourself to the fact that so long as she is in Buckingham Palace you will not be welcome at Court. The Queen is like a lioness guarding her cubs, but in her case that includes her husband.'

The King had just finished his weekly audience with the Prime Minister. He liked and respected Stanley Baldwin, regarding him as a safe pair of hands. He had been genuinely sad when Baldwin informed him in confidence that he would soon be resigning the leadership of the Conservative Party. He planned to do so the following May. His successor would be Neville Chamberlain, who came from a long line of politicians. He seemed competent enough but the King's instinct was that Chamberlain lacked Baldwin's cunning and astuteness. 'Still,' he thought, 'only time will tell.'

# Chapter 5

Celia entered von Ribbentrop's suite in the Grosvenor House Hotel in London's Park Lane. She had been dropped off by her chauffer at the rear entrance. As usual the doorman recognised her Lagonda sports saloon, and had leapt forward to open her door. He raised his top hat as she stepped out of the car and greeted this regular visitor.

'Good afternoon, Milady.'

Amongst the discreet staff it was common knowledge that the beautiful young heiress was a regular visitor to the German Ambassador. His suite was known to be no more than a love nest as he played host to a number of attractive women. It was a puzzle to the staff that these women seemed so available to the Ambassador. The chambermaids avidly confirmed that there was plenty of evidence that they did not call just for a drink and a chat. There are no secrets in a hotel. The staff and management know everything that goes on.

'Celia, my dear,' von Ribbentrop stepped forward smiling as his butler took Celia's coat, hat and gloves, 'how delightful to see you.'

'And you, Bubbles darling.'

He was formally dressed in a black waistcoat and tail coat and striped trousers. His shirt had a starched wing collar and he wore a dark tie.

'Tell me, Bubbles, why are you in morning dress – surely not in my honour,' laughed Celia.

'I am afraid not, Celia. I have just returned from a formal meeting at the Foreign Office. It was by way of a briefing for the Ambassadors of European nations.'

'Well, you look very elegant.'

'Thank you. I am told that the German Diplomatic Service is to have its own uniform soon.'

'Well, so you should. When I was younger and Daddy was in the Diplomatic Service he had a rather smart uniform. I remember a feathered hat as well.'

'I am not sure about the hat,' laughed von Ribbentrop, 'now, a drink perhaps – champagne?'

'Absolutely, and thank you'

After they had settled with their drinks he asked Celia whether she was staying for the evening. She knew precisely what he meant. He was giving her the choice of attending to business then leaving, or having supper and going to bed with him.

She and Johnny had discussed what she should do if given this choice. With some reluctance they had come to the conclusion that she should stay for the whole evening. To do otherwise might make von Ribbentrop suspicious.

'What do you think, Bubbles?' Celia laughed and eyed him archly.

'Right, you little minx – I think that you are teasing me. We can soon see about that.'

He leapt out of his chair with surprising agility, and taking her hands drew her out of her chair and into his arms. She could immediately tell that he was aroused and she felt the familiar sensations herself.

'Come on, Bubbles – let's not waste any more time.'

She half-wriggled out of his arms and kicking off her shoes, ran into his bedroom. Von Ribbentrop was clearly in no mood to take things slowly, and throwing her onto the bed he pushed up her skirt and petticoat. He had thrown off his morning coat but was otherwise still fully dressed as Celia frantically undid his button fly and drew him out. He pushed her flat onto her back and mounted her. This was not making love. It was pure animal sex. They both loved it.

As they lay getting their breath back some minutes later Celia started to laugh. Von Ribbentrop wondered why at first, then seeing the direction of her gaze joined in. He reached down, and after wriggling managed to restore some of his dignity and button his trousers. Celia jumped off the bed and dashed into the bathroom where she washed carefully. When she went back into the living room, von Ribbentrop was again fully dressed and immaculate.

Over supper he went over precisely what Celia was to say to Wallis. When they had finished their simple meal, washed down with a fine flinty Sancerre, von Ribbentrop led the way back into the living room, and opening the lid of the writing desk took out a stiff envelope and a velvet box. The envelope was simply addressed to *"Wallis"*.

'Celia. I want you to have this.'

He opened the box and there nestled a gold powder compact.

'That looks just like the very one that Wallis has!' exclaimed Celia.

'Yes it does, but actually it is different. I considered it best that the camera be disguised in case someone looks in your handbag – I have also had it engraved with your initials. Now, let me show you how to use it.'

Celia was a keen photographer and quickly grasped the way the miniature Kodak Petite camera worked, and also how to load and unload the film.

'I want you to take a picture of Wallis with the bank confirmation document in her hand. Ideally, please do so from an angle where it is possible to read what is on the document. It is deliberately in unusually large bold print.'

'I shall do my best.'

'Well done – I have every confidence in you.'

With that he led her back to the bedroom where they stayed for the next 2 hours. As Celia left the hotel she marvelled at the sexual stamina of von Ribbentrop given his age .She ached pleasantly in every limb. He might be a cad and over 20 years her senior, but there were few young men who could keep up with him.

The same doorman was on duty. As he saw her approaching he blew hard on his whistle and pointed to her car. As she came through the hotel door which his junior colleague held open for her, he raised his hat. 'Goodnight Milady,' he said as he handed her into her car. She flashed him a dazzling smile. 'Lucky bastard, that kraut,' he muttered to himself as her car drove off. The winter ache in his leg was the result of a shrapnel wound. He had no love of the Germans.

Celia had telephoned Johnny the previous night on her

return home. They had agreed that it was too late to meet, and had arranged for him to join her for a late breakfast at 10am. In fact, Celia did not feel at all tired, but she baulked at the idea of any intimacy with Johnny whilst she could still feel the after effects of her long session with von Ribbentrop.

The next morning when she and Johnny were alone in her breakfast room, Celia repeated what she had been told to say to Wallis. She also handed over the envelope and showed Johnny her camera.

'Right, I shall be going from here to see Tar and hand over the papers for copying. You have an appointment at Bishopsgate Police Station in the City at noon.'

He laughed at her shocked expression. 'No, you silly goose, you are not in trouble. They have a rifle range in the basement and Tar has arranged for you to have an intensive course in pistol shooting.' He raised his hand as she was about to interrupt.

'Let me continue. The villa in Cannes is certainly under German surveillance and possibly they have an agent on the inside. From the reports that we have had from our chaps it's a bit of a wasps' nest. We must be prepared, and both of us will be armed.'

'Johnny, surely that could get us into trouble with the French authorities?'

'No darling. The Foreign Office has made arrangements, and we shall be officially allowed to carry arms.'

'Gosh, it is all getting quite exciting.'

'Hopefully not, hopefully not,' he replied.

'Spoil sport,' she retorted. As she said it, the thought dawned on her that what had started out as a bit of a lark had now become serious, possibly deadly serious.

On the way to Bishopsgate police station, Celia's driver, Timms, who was a former City of London police officer, answered Celia's question about their destination. He explained that Bishopsgate itself was a major road that effectively divided the City of London,'The Square Mile' and financial centre of the Empire – some would say the world – from the East End of London. The East End as it was known was generally an impoverished working class area with high unemployment. He went on to explain that the area of

Bishopsgate was one of the ancient Wards in the City. These were constituencies from which were elected the City's Aldermen and Councillors.

As they passed behind Liverpool Street Station, Timms laughed as he told her that next to the police station was an infamous old pub called Dirty Dick's. It was deliberately kept filthy. He said that it was now more of a tourist attraction although still popular with police officers just off duty. There were also local 'characters' who hung around there in the hope that visitors would buy them drinks. They played on the seedier side of London's history, the underworld and hunting ground of Jack the Ripper.

As the elegant Lagonda drew to a halt outside the police station, Celia climbed out and looked at its unprepossessing facade with the familiar blue light hanging over the entrance. She looked striking as ever and was beautifully dressed. A young constable who was standing behind the Desk Sergeant caught sight of Celia as she crossed the broad pavement. 'Blimey Sarge – there's a real looker comin' in.'

The old Sergeant, who reckoned he had seen all there was to see in life, was unimpressed, until Celia strode up to his desk and announced in her perfect clipped tone that she had an appointment with a Mr Brownlow. The Sergeant checked his log for the day and asked, 'And your name, Miss?'

'Celia Ffrench–Hardy, Sergeant.'

He checked his log again, then smiled. 'Righto Milady, please take a seat and he will be with you shortly.'

She had only just sat down on the extremely uncomfortable wooden settle that was fixed to the wall opposite the Sergeant's desk when Mr Brownlow came out of a side door and introduced himself. He was smartly dressed and looked more like a stockbroker than an arms instructor. He was also younger than she expected. Probably he was only in his early thirties. Nodding to the Sergeant, Celia followed Brownlow out of the side door and then down dimly lit concrete stairs. He unlocked a heavy steel door and they entered the firing range. It was a low oblong space with an angled firing point covered in hessian matting and then what looked like a cinder floor that ran down to the target butts. The lighting was only bright over the butts which looked to be about 25 yards away from the firing point. The underground range had a dank smell of damp with an acrid edge of burnt cordite. Behind the firing point there was a large plain table on which there was a pistol and a box of ammunition.

Celia loved guns. She loved the smell of the oiled metal. She loved the precision with which they were crafted. She loved the acrid smell of burnt cordite.

'Right, Milady. The pistol you see is a Beretta model 418.It is light and fires a 6.35 mm bullet. It does not have great stopping power, neither is it accurate over any significant distance – like most pistols. It is best to think of it as a close protection weapon of last resort. The golden rule is, "Never draw a weapon unless you are ready and need to use it". Now, please pick it up.'

Celia was amazed at how light the pistol was and certainly small enough to fit in a handbag. For the next two hours Brownlow drilled Celia through every procedure from cleaning to stripping, loading and then firing the little pistol. She was an excellent pupil. He set up a target 10 yards down the range and explained the principles of pistol shooting in action. Her experiences shooting with her father both pheasant in England and grouse on the Scottish moors easily translated to this weapon. The results were impressive.

At the end of the session Brownlow explained that Celia would be provided with a pistol, ammunition and cleaning kit shortly after the English Channel crossing. He mentioned that Johnny would be receiving a similar package, save that in his case the pistol of choice was a Webley Bulldog pocket revolver. He explained that this was also a short range weapon but with much greater stopping power than the Beretta.

Celia thanked him for his time. She then asked, 'You know Johnny?'

'Oh yes, our families are old friends. Brownlow is the name that I use in the service – it is less conspicuous than my actual surname – Cust. I am William – Billy – Cust, by the way.'

'Gosh, so you are Perry Cust's...'

'Cousin,' laughed Billy. 'I work for Tar Robertson.'

# Chapter 6

Celia was at Johnny's house and they were running over their plans. She had handed over von Ribbentrop's envelope addressed to Wallis. A plainclothes motorcycle despatch rider had collected it and set off on his Norton 500 to deliver it to the Security Service technical team. They were based just north of London, in a nondescript building. It was in the grounds of the Metropolitan Police College.

Johnny explained, 'Von Ribbentrop will naturally have suspicions that his letter and its contents may be tampered with. It is quite likely that he will have told Wallis himself if they have spoken, or will get a message to her, to the effect that there will be a tamper proof seal that she must check. The boffins, as we call them, will find any seal and ensure that after they have copied the contents, it is replaced intact.'

'This is the miniature camera that he has given me,' said Celia, handing over the compact which Johnny picked up in his handkerchief.

'Why are you doing that Johnny?' she asked, looking puzzled.

'When you bring back the camera containing the undeveloped film and give it to von Ribbentrop, he will have it checked for fingerprints. The only ones on it should be yours and his.'

'This is all very cloak and dagger,' laughed Celia.

Johnny glared at her. 'Celia,' he said in a severe tone that she had not heard before. 'People's lives may depend upon our doing things properly. There is a lot at stake. The Nazis are ruthless in the extreme. Bear in mind the number of their own followers who have been purged and their treatment of Jews and gypsies. You witnessed their brutality when you were in Nuremburg, didn't you?'

'Sorry Johnny – I really do understand. It just all seems a little unreal?'

'That it is not, my dear girl. As of Tuesday, when we board the Golden Arrow at Victoria Station at 10.30am and set off to Dover, we are on duty. We do not know who might be following us or what their orders are.

'We join the boat train – the Canterbury – 98 minutes later for the Channel crossing and then in Calais we join Le Train Bleu. It will take us to the South of France overnight. On my recent marathon train journey to Austria and back I read Agatha Christie's thriller *"The Mystery of the Blue Train"*. It's quite a gripping story, although I find her hero, the plump, smug Belgian Hercule Poirot pretty tedious. Then, most Belgians are which is probably why she cast him in the role . here it is – tell me what you think.'

'I quite like a good mystery but I hope that I will not end up like a cat on hot bricks after reading it.'

'No worries on that score, my dear,' laughed Johnny, 'the plot is one of her most convoluted and preposterous. As for her schoolgirl French, it is painful! However, it does carry a hint of the romance associated with the great Train Bleu. Oh, and by the way, Billy Brownlow will be shadowing us on the journey. He's a very sound man. Do not be taken in by his youth and charm, he is a tough nut.'

'Like you, my dear,' responded Celia with a laugh.

'Charles Harvey will leave London with my car on Sunday morning, so please have your maid do your packing early that morning. It is much warmer there of course, but I expect that the evenings may be cold.'

'Poor Charles – I doubt whether he is keen to be apart from Elizabeth from what you have said. A regular pair of lovebirds, are they not?'

'Charles is committed to the Service for another couple of years – I am afraid that he has no choice. Quite apart from watching out for us, it will give him the opportunity to meet Wallis again, or more importantly, for her to get to know him. Tar's plan is to wangle them into the Duke's household, which will provide permanent surveillance once they are married and become mobile again. At the time of the abdication the Duke joked with Elizabeth Beaumont about she and Charles becoming members of his household in due course.'

'It is all really quite complicated, isn't it,' mused Celia, as she stared thoughtfully into her drink.

'Elizabeth is very fond of the Duke and intensely loyal to him. Charles will have to convince her that his being in the Security Service whilst a part of the household is in the Duke's best interests.'

After a strenuous session with Didier Pascal, Wallis was relaxing as they lay smoking.

'I am so excited – two good friends of the Duke and mine will be arriving on Wednesday. He is an English Lord and she an English Lady. All of these titles baffle me, so do not ask anything about them,' she laughed.

Didier had been admiring his reflection in the cheval mirror that he had moved nearer to the bed before he commenced the 'French Lesson' with Wallis. Whatever he was doing, Didier's focus was always on himself and the way he looked. His physical pleasure when making love came second to the image of his muscled, sculpted body and outstanding profile. The extent of his concern for Wallis' pleasure was limited to the generous salary that she was paying him. The fact that she seemed insatiable sexually and he could match her appetite was a bonus, as were her extraordinary skills as a lover.

The same could be said of his loyalty to his German spymasters, although in that case he was streetwise enough to know that there was more than money at stake. Termination of that employment might involve a lot more than hard cash. His interest was pricked. Who were these people who were friends of this Duke, who had been King of England, and this weird American woman?

'Wallis,' he asked in his delightfully accented English, 'these friends, the Lord and the Lady. Are they very important people in England?'

'Well, I guess they are,' she drawled back. 'They are aristocracy, with wealth and power within their families I think.'

'We were rid of our aristos in the revolution,' he replied, 'but you would not think so along the Cote D'Azure where so many claim to have French titles.'

'In the good old US of A we do not have any titles, but there sure is a pecking order. You tell a Rockefeller that he is not an aristocrat and he'll spit in your eye.'

'What are these two people like?'

'Well, they are attractive and fun and appear to play at everything, but they sure are tough. They play to win.'

'I will remember that,' he replied, really none the wiser He would report the conversation anyhow. The fortunate thing for Didier was that the instruction to take the Buick into Cannes each day suited him and his German contacts very well. He would make his report tomorrow at the Carlton Hotel. Wallis had put out her cigarette and reached for him.

'Just once more this afternoon,' he thought, as he moved Wallis into a position where he could admire himself in all his tumescent glory.

Charles Harvey was in his Mayfair apartment with Elizabeth Beauchamp, whose extended leave of absence from Fort Belvedere had become official as soon as the dust covers were in place. Charles had just poured himself his customary early evening single malt whisky and he had handed a small glass of amontillado sherry to Elizabeth.

'My dearest, I am so sorry to have to accompany Johnny on this trip to the South of France so soon after we have come together. However, there is a possible benefit in that I shall meet Mrs Simpson again. We should keep the Duke's service in mind as a couple.'

'Charles, I have a very serious question to ask you. You may be assured that I shall be sworn to secrecy whatever you tell me but I must ask.'

With a sinking feeling in the pit of his stomach, Charles waited for the question.

'Tell me honestly, what is your relationship with Johnny? It is more than just friendship. I am used to managing a close knit team and that is what I think you and he are. . .well?'

She had never looked more beautiful to him, and he knew that what he told her now could shape both of their futures.

'Elizabeth, I accept your promise of secrecy. Both Charles and I are officers in the British Security Service – popularly known as MI5. Our present task is to protect the Monarchy and that means specifically the Duke of Windsor for us at this time. There are what can best be described as 'dark forces' at large in Europe. By his abdication and continuing relationship with Mrs Simpson he has placed himself at great risk. Our job is to protect him.'

'Do I have your promise that no harm will come to him by your hand or Johnny's?'

'Yes, my dear, you most certainly do,' he replied, looking her straight in the eye. Knowing him well now, his unflinching gaze convinced Elizabeth that he was telling the truth.

'Then, in that case I need never ask you again about that side of your life.'

On the Friday afternoon, Johnny, Charles and Billy were sitting in Tar's office.

'Right chaps. I know that you are all set, but a final briefing. Both the Duke and Mrs Simpson are under surveillance. The Duke is on a lighter rein – even the Germans recognise that they dare not infiltrate the Rothschild strong hold. However, they are watching and monitoring. Mrs Simpson has not left the Rogers' villa, but we have observed her car doing so every day like clockwork. It is driven by a very handsome young man, Didier Pascal, whom she has taken on as her driver.'

'And the rest, no doubt,' muttered Johnny. Tar raised his hand and continued.

'Young Didier is reputedly a lazy layabout who has made quite a good living as what can best be described as a gigolo. Cannes and Monte Carlo are full of rich bored widows. Local gossip is that Didier is very well equipped and has been literally passed from hand to hand as it were. However there is more to it than that. One of his conquests or clients, whatever, is a German Countess. She took him with her when she went back to Germany for a family visit. He stayed in Germany for over six months before returning with her. The strange thing is that he was not with her whilst she was in Germany. He disappeared.'

'That's not surprising, surely? Her family would hardly welcome her much younger French sexual playmate, whatever his attributes.'

'Perhaps not in itself. However, a Frenchman of his description was enrolled in a German espionage and sabotage course – it was organised by the Abwehr.'

'Source of information?' asked Billy.

'Abwehr, I bet,' said Charles. They were all aware that the British Security Service had solid contacts within that organisation.

'Correct. So gentlemen, we believe that he is a plant in the Rogers' house. Wallis will be enchanted with her new toy, at least for a while, so will not think above his waist, and he is potentially dangerous.'

'How far may we take this?' asked Johnny. Tar thought for a moment, then looked each one of them steadily in the eye.

'If you perceive a danger to Mrs Simpson or any of our team, you must do whatever and let me be clear, whatever is necessary to eliminate it? Am I clear, gentlemen?'

They all confirmed so.

'I have a question about Celia, Tar.'

'Carry on Johnny.'

'She has had some training with Billy, who was very impressed, and I have already expressed my views as to her character. Should we not bring her into this information?'

'For the moment, no. See how the land lies at the villa. Her role is to act as von Ribbentrop's messenger and hook Mrs Simpson. Von Ribbentrop hates Himmler and his gang – the feeling is mutual. However, he will have cleared the dirty money thing with the Führer, so I think that Celia should not be at risk. However, we cannot be sure of her safety, or indeed yours, Johnny. Himmler is so jealous of von Ribbentrop that he will do almost anything to scotch his plans, and those plans include Celia. Any suspicion that she is in danger, get her out. That's why your motor will be there, Johnny. Your task is to get her out in one piece.'

'Understood, Tar.'

Charles, Billy, your task is to hold the fort and thwart any pursuit. I want her back in London with that evidence for von Ribbentrop. Oh, and for us,' laughed Tar, in an attempt to break the tension.

'Where are the Abwehr in all this?' asked Billy.

'Let me just say that we have some common interests at this time,' was the noncommittal reply that Tar gave.

'Very well gentlemen, bon voyage, and good hunting.'

# Chapter 7

As Celia and Johnny settled into their luxurious compartment on Le Train Bleu standing in the Gare Maritime in Calais, Celia gave one her infectious laughs and said, 'This really isn't a blue train Johnny.'

'You silly duck,' he replied with a smile, 'why else would it have the name? The whole train used to be first class and the carriages were in blue and gold livery. Now there are just the two first class sleeping cars, and it will be the Fleche D'Or, the French Golden Arrow, that takes us to Paris. After that our carriages are taken south by the Cote D'Azure Pullman Express.'

'So, first stop the Gare du Nord in Paris, then around the city to the Gare de Lyon, then off to the south.'

'Quite the little Bradshaw, Celia, or should that be Baedeker now we are on the Continent?'

'Now who's being silly. This is fun. What happens after Paris?'

'Well, I suggest that before then we go along to the dining car and have a spot of tea. After Paris we shall be having drinks and then a five course dinner. The food is excellent, even though other things have changed as a result of the depression and so forth. Mind you, these compartments are jolly comfortable.'

'May I call for some water now?'

'Of course, there are only ten compartments in each carriage so the steward will not be too busy I imagine. Allow me.'

Johnny pulled the gold-tasselled cord, and very quickly an immaculately turned-out steward knocked on their door and entered the compartment. Johnny duly asked for some water. As the door closed, Celia could not suppress a giggle.

'But he looks just like someone out of a caricature with his oiled hair and thin moustache. He could only be French.'

'Celia,' intoned Johnny with mock schoolmasterly severity, 'do you intend to keep up this ridiculous commentary until we reach Cannes?'

'Possibly not,' she shrugged, 'but then, I have never been made love to on a train, so that may keep me quiet.'

'That would be a change, you little minx,' laughed Johnny.

'Did I tell you that I took part in one of the Blue Train Races?'

Celia shook her head.

'We had two Speed Six Bentleys owned by 'Bentley Boy' Woolf Barnato. We raced the train from Calais to the South of France. We just won, but it was damned close – I have never been so tired, but it was tremendous fun.'

Celia laughed indulgently 'Oh you boys and your toys – speaking of which, when do we receive our pistols?'

'The armourer is on the train and will bring the pistols to us. Don't worry, everything is in hand.'

The steward had brought the carafe of water, and Celia had had a few sips when Johnny looked at his watch and said, 'Time to pop along to the dining car for a cup of tea I think. I expect Billy to be there. Are you coming?'

'Oh yes, I would love to see it. I shall pop into the bathroom on the way then catch you up.'

They left the compartment. The caricature steward was standing in the corridor at the end of the carriage, and he threw open the door into the next carriage as Johnny strode towards it. When Johnny entered the dining car he immediately saw Billy, who was every inch the English gentleman traveller with his immaculate tweed suit and Brigade of Guards tie. Although he reckoned that it would not fool a professional watcher, Johnny stopped by the table at which Billy sat and asked, 'Excuse me, but are these seats taken?' – as he spoke, Johnny indicated the two empty seats opposite Billy.

'No, they are not,' smiled Billy.

'Thank you,' replied Johnny, and as he sat down in the aisle seat he added, 'I say, what was your regiment?'

'Grenadiers – the name is Brownlow,' came the reply.

'Ah, I was in the Coldstreams – Johnny Johnstone.'

They shook hands. They then set about naming friends and relatives that might be known to each other. They were still engaged in this very English ritual when Celia arrived. Both rose from their seats and formal introductions were made.

Celia played the game and asked, 'Are you by any chance related to Lord Brownlow – Perry Cust?'

'But yes, he is my cousin – I am Billy Cust. Do you know him well?'

'Oh yes, family friends and all that. We had some super times at Belton House.'

After they had gone through this ritual for a little longer, Billy spoke quietly whilst apparently pouring his tea.

'There are three German agents on the train. Two followed from London and the third joined at Calais. They are in second class sleeping cars and we shall keep an eye on them. If they show signs of heading your way we shall deal with them. The armourer joined the train at Calais and is in the same carriage as you. When you return to your compartment, please tell the steward that you have a friend in the carriage and he is likely to call on you. He will do so whilst the train waits in Paris before heading south.'

'These are scrummy sandwiches,' said Celia in a loud voice, 'every bit as good as those at The Ritz.'

'Yes they are. What do you think, Brownlow?' asked Johnny.

'Excellent.'

When they had finished their tea, the three shook hands and went their separate ways. Once back in their compartment Celia locked the door and drew the curtain over the window. She turned to Johnny, and placing her hand flat on his chest asked in a low voice, 'Well Johnny, are you going to take steps to keep me quiet?'

'If I must,' he laughed as he gathered her into his arms.

Didier had parked Wallis' car behind the Carlton Hotel as usual, and entered through the rear doors. He walked through to the reception hall and then sauntered into the small cocktail bar. He was not impervious to the lingering looks of appraisal that he received from every woman there. He certainly did not look like a salaried chauffer. Thanks to the largesse of some of his wealthy patrons he was beautifully turned out, and looked like a matinee idol.

One elderly American lady turned to her companion and said, 'That young man is the spitting image of the young Rudolf Valentino!'

'Let's hope that he performs better between the sheets!' laughed the other lady with a wink.

Didier greeted his contact, and after shaking hands he told the waiter that he would have his usual soft drink. His contact, or more precisely, controller, was drinking champagne. Didier repeated his conversation with Wallis. His contact made a careful mental note. He then asked whether Wallis was becoming more indiscreet as time went by. Didier confirmed that he seemed to be gaining her confidence. He then commented that her physical demands were exhausting and he should be paid more. His contact quietly but firmly put him in his place.

'Look you little shit – you have always screwed for money. From what you previously told me at least this one knows what she is doing. You will have to keep your wits about you when the visitors are there. You understand?'

Didier was shaken by the vehemence of the other man, and quietly confirmed that he understood perfectly. His contact left, and Didier turned his attention to a prostitute who had perched on a stool by the bar showing her exquisite legs and derriere to perfection. He sauntered over and taking the adjoining stool, turned on his charm. By the time he left to return to the villa he had her name and telephone number in his pocket.

He did not realise that his contact, the controller, had been watching the whole time. A negative note would be made on Didier's file to the effect that he should not be trusted where there was any possibility of his making a sexual conquest. The contact had been provided with photographs of Johnny and Celia. He had reached the conclusion that Didier would be wild for her. That in itself could create a problem.

The armourer had been and gone. Both Celia and Johnny now had their pistols and ammunition. The armourer had explained that he was two compartments away, and would stand guard until the train reached Cannes the following day.

After he had gone, Celia turned to Johnny and said, 'I say, we seem to have a lot of people guarding us.'

'That is only to be expected in the circumstances. You are carrying something which might be seen as potential political dynamite. The Germans want to make sure that you get to the villa safely and fulfil your instructions. So do we.'

'Actually Johnny, who precisely is "we"?'

'Officially, "we" are the Security Service but often referred to as MI5. Since 1931 we have had full responsibility for counter subversion. That came about when we successfully revealed that the Police Special Branch had been infiltrated by Soviet intelligence.'

'Does that mean that the Service keeps tabs on people like Oswald Mosley?'

'Of course, but actually he is lower priority than many others. He is visible in every sense and regarded as a misguided patriot, but obviously a centre of infection nevertheless.'

'What about people like Unity Mitford?'

'Oh, your crazy friend. In herself she poses no security risk, and frankly, an obviously deranged girl's opinions, if she has any, carry no weight. Remember she comes from a strange stable.'

'Ha, you can say that again – Debs is really the only one of the sisters with her feet on the ground in my opinion.'

'Sir Vernon Kell, the Head of the Service, has had some real battles to keep its independence. He is a great man and he has attracted some brilliant people. Tar Robertson, for instance, is incredibly shrewd and intuitive, as is Maxwell Knight – you have not met him but I am sure that you will. He's an extraordinary fellow, as much a naturalist as a security agent.'

'I am going to dress for dinner now, Johnny. I hope that you were right and it is not too formal.'

After a sumptuous dinner with excellent wines, Johnny sat back savouring his cigar and a rare Armagnac. Celia had opted for a Kummel on the rocks.

'Well Celia, you are having the golfers' tipple,' joked Johnny after she had ordered it.

'I really do not care. I just love the clean fresh taste. The trouble is that like all good things, it is very moreish, darling,' she responded with a wicked glint in her eye.

'You could wear a man out if you are thinking what I believe you are.'

'Spot on darling, and I have every intention of doing so. You have my permission to finish your cigar and Armagnac.'

'Permission indeed. If we were in private I would put you over my knee for being so cheeky.'

'Oh, yes please.'

The last part of the journey into Cannes was tediously slow after the train had barrelled south through the night, non-stop down the Rhone Valley after leaving Lyon. After departing from Marseilles early in the morning, it stopped at all the major resorts on the Cote D'Azure, including Juan les Pins and Antibes, before reaching Cannes. As they came out of the station they were delighted to see Johnny's Hispano-Suiza gleaming after Charles had cleaned off the dirt accumulated on the long drive from London. Charles saluted smartly, and only when they were in the car did Johnny ask him for an update.

As they drove up towards the villa, Charles gave his first impressions. The Rogers were a charming couple, gracious hosts with no apparent vices. Wallis was still charming when it suited her. The below-stairs gossip was that she was enjoying sexual relations with Didier Pascal, whom she had employed as her driver, and who gave her what were euphemistically called 'French Lessons' in the privacy of her suite in the afternoons. The other staff had noted that when Wallis retired for the night, her pretty young ladies maid, Laurenne, was often with her for well over an hour.

'So not much new there then, eh?' laughed Johnny.

'No, but interestingly it was Laurenne who introduced Didier. He was a cert for Mrs Simpson. He is devilishly handsome with an athletic body and – I apologise, Celia – but Herman Rogers' manservant, who interrupted him in the shower, says that he is hung like a horse.'

'That should keep Wallis happy,' said Celia, 'actually it will only keep her happy for a while. She will soon be on the hunt for something else.'

'She will find that easily in Cannes from what I hear – there is no, er, "speciality" that is not catered for in this town,' laughed Charles.

'You make it sound seedy,' commented Johnny.

'It is. Behind the glittering façade, vice of every sort flourishes. It reminds me of Cairo. Back to Didier. He seems to have wangled his way into the job. Mrs Simpson will not be paying him anything like what he could be making as, shall we say, a freelance. So why did he want to become the sexual puppet of a depraved middle aged woman?'

'I think you know the answer perfectly well, Charles. He is an agent. I shall ask Tar to contact his oppo in the French Deuxieme Bureau – their version of MI5, Celia – and run a check on him. Good work Charles, Good work.'

The group of press men by the high gated entrance to the villa had dwindled to less than 10, and they took little notice of the Hispano-Suiza as it swept past the two gendarmes on duty.

# Chapter 8

Didier was watching the courtyard of the villa when the Hispano-Suiza returned from the station with Celia and Johnny. Charles had been right. When Didier saw Celia he caught his breath. She was exquisite, tall, and beautiful with a stunning figure and legs. She was the most attractive girl he had ever seen, and he knew that he must have her. Didier decided there and then that he would seduce her come what may. In making his decision he was totally overlooking his controller's instructions.

'Celia, my dear!' cried Wallis, as she almost ran across the salon and embraced her. Johnny was left high and dry for a moment or two but caught Herman Rogers' eye, and they both smiled. After a few moments Wallis stepped back from Celia and holding her by her arms said, 'You look so well and that's after a long journey.'

'Oh, well it was pretty comfortable and we kept ourselves amused,' laughed Celia.

'I am forgetting myself,' said Wallis. She made the introductions to her old friend Katherine and her husband Herman. Herman Rogers then said, 'Now would you like a drink now or to go to your rooms and freshen up first?'

Johnny looked questioningly at Celia.

'I should like to freshen up first if I may,' replied Celia.

'Then I shall too,' agreed Johnny.

Herman Rogers led the way, and as they left the sweeping marble staircase he took them to adjoining suites in the guest wing.

'This is the wing where Wallis has her suite too,' he explained, indicating another door on the landing. 'I shall leave you now and look forward to seeing you downstairs as soon as you are ready.'

Celia had just taken off her coat when Laurenne entered her suite. They spoke French together. Laurenne explained that for this day she would act as Celia's maid as well as looking after Wallis. Another maid was due to start that evening. Celia could see what Wallis would be attracted to in Laurenne. She was a pretty little thing and could only be French by the way she carried herself and her movements. She helped Celia take off her suit and blouse and asked whether she was going to have a shower. Celia was delighted to say that she would – thank goodness for having American hosts. Laurenne followed her into the bathroom and took the remainder of her clothes as she stripped off.

The shower was excellent, and Celia felt the inevitable dust of travel being washed away. When she turned it off she stepped out and Laurenne wrapped her in a giant fluffy white bath sheet. Unlike Celia's English maid she did not then stand back and leave Celia to dry herself. Instead, she started to gently pat Celia dry.

'Do you dry Mrs Simpson like this?' asked Celia.

'But of course, Milady,' she replied smiling.

Celia returned the smile and in that instant knew that the below stairs gossip was right. Laurenne was definitely having sex with Wallis. She reached out and gently ran her fingers down Laurenne's cheek as they both smiled at each other. When Celia had dressed in fresh clothes she thanked Laurenne and left her suite.

As she did so she was very surprised to see a youngish man come out of what she knew to be Wallis' suite. She disliked the look of him on first sight. He was beautifully dressed and handsome in a flashy way. However in her eyes he looked narcissistic, but there was more and his shifty eyes held a menace – she felt a pang of unease in the way that he looked at her. She did not think for one moment that it was chance that brought them onto the landing at the same time. He stood to one side and gave a little bow as she headed for the staircase. She ignored him, noting his almost reptilian smile that verged on a smirk. Just then Johnny appeared from his

'Celia my dear – wait for me,' he said as he strode across the landing, barely giving Didier a glance. It was obvious from the way that Johnny took Celia by the elbow that he and Celia had an intimate relationship. Didier suddenly felt a wave of jealousy and a hot, irrational anger sweep over him.

Wallis kept everyone amused over the late lunch, once again recounting her marathon journey across France. Johnny told her about the spiteful way that the new King and Queen had treated Perry. Wallis reacted angrily.

'That would be Elizabeth's doing! David has told me on a number of occasions that she rules the roost and is utterly ruthless. The King will not even take David's telephone calls now. Your William Shakespeare recognised the animal when he brought Lady Macbeth into his play. She was Scottish too.'

'I say,' said Johnny, 'I think that is rather harsh, Wallis. I know and like the Queen. Yes, she has to be tough but everyone recognises that she is protecting her husband.'

'Well Johnny, from where I am sitting she seems nothing but spiteful.'

'Well Wallis, we clearly will not agree on this one,' laughed Johnny, in an attempt to lighten the atmosphere.

When lunch was finished, Katherine Rogers stood and her husband came to her side.

'Celia, Johnny. Herman and I always have a siesta in the afternoon and Wallis has her French lesson. Will you amuse yourselves for an hour or two?'

'Of course we will,' replied Celia, 'Johnny, let's go down into Cannes and have a walk along the Croisette.'

'Capital idea,' he replied, and they all left the dining room.

Wallis was the first up the grand staircase and turned off towards the guest wing. The Rogers followed, and behind them came Celia and Johnny who had stopped to ask one of the staff to have Charles bring the car round. Celia and Johnny were just in time to see Wallis enter her suite. Celia gasped as she recognised the young man whom she had previously seen on the landing. He was in full view in Wallis' suite. He was stark naked and fully aroused.

'Well Charles, you were right on both counts this morning,' said Celia as they drove away from the villa. 'The girl,

Laurenne, is a pretty little thing and I am sure that she is happy to accommodate Wallis Simpson's desires. There is a sleazy young man in the villa and he was standing naked in Wallis' suite just a few minutes ago. He was all too obviously ready to give her her French lesson,' laughed Celia.

'I am pretty certain that he will be the German plant in the villa, do you agree Charles? ' asked Johnny

'Absolutely. The question is, for which arm of their intelligence services does he work? If it's the Abwehr we should have no problem, but it's a different kettle of fish if he is one of Himmler's crew. Are you both armed?'

'Yes we are,' replied Johnny.'For what it's worth London still says that he is Abwehr.'

'I suppose you have your favourite Webley?' laughed Charles.

'There is nothing wrong with the Bulldog,' responded Johnny, 'at least it has stopping power, which is more than I can say of Celia's Beretta.'

Johnny continued, 'If this Didier is one of Himmler's lot, he could be very dangerous. You never know what that many-headed creature's people are up to. I sometimes doubt if he knows. However in my briefing before we left London it was made clear that it was the Abwehr who were getting a man on the inside.'

'I agree Johnny. We must be damned careful just in case.'

After a brisk walk along the Croisette, Celia and Johnny went into the Carlton Hotel for a cup of tea and to kill the time until Charles would be picking them up. Instinctively Johnny chose a corner table where he had a good view of the whole area, including the lifts and the bottom flight of the staircase. Johnny excused himself, going to the concierge's desk, and said that he wished to make a call to London. He was directed to a telephone booth after he gave Tar Robertson's private number to the concierge. When they were connected he came straight to the point.

'The woman has hired a French man as her driver and is receiving one to one French lessons every afternoon. Please ask our French friends to check him out. The name is Didier Pascal.'

Johnny returned to Celia. He and Celia appeared to be chatting amiably and could have been any couple who had stopped for refreshment. Didier's controller had been alerted by an agent outside the villa that the two recently arrived guests were apparently heading into Cannes. They were followed into the town, and when they entered the hotel he received a call to that effect. He spotted them immediately when he strolled out of the left hand gilt-framed lift.

He took a seat and ordered tea in impeccable English. Johnny's instincts told him that this man was not what he seemed. He might look every inch the English gentleman but something was not quite right. Johnny checked his wrist watch and gestured to a waiter for the bill. When he had paid, he steered Celia towards the entrance to the hotel, passing close to the man he had been surreptitiously watching.

He then took a bold step and, stopping by the man's chair, smiled and said, 'I say, your face is awfully familiar – should I know you? I am Johnny Johnstone and this is Celia Ffrench-Hardy?'

The man's face did not register surprise as he stood up.

'I really do not know – Bernard O'Reilly,' he replied smiling. His voice had a hint of an Irish lilt.

'I am so sorry to have disturbed you,' apologised Johnny, and then smiling to O'Reilly he led Celia out of the hotel.

Once they were in the car Johnny said, 'Right, Charles. That chap in the hotel – the one I spoke to as we were leaving. I am sure that he is a German agent. Irish by birth I would say, but otherwise pretty much the well-to-do Englishman. He is calling himself Bernard O'Reilly and I assume that he is staying at the Carlton.'

'Are you planning anything?' asked Celia.

'Oh, I think that Billy Brownlow should have a look over his room. I shall call Billy when we are back at the Villa whilst the others are having a cup of tea.'

'Charles, I want you to keep an eye on young Didier. Note his movements. If there is a pattern we must have him followed. We need to know to whom he reports. Celia, I do not want you to pass on von Ribbentrop's letter and the bank papers until we have a clear idea of who he is working for and reporting to, and what the gigolo is up to apart from looking after Wallis in the afternoons.'

'Righto, Johnny.'

When Celia and Johnny joined their hosts and Wallis for tea, Celia could not resist asking Wallis, 'So Wallis, how is your French coming on?'

Wallis gave Celia a calculating look as she said, 'Just dandy,' and laughed. 'You should have some lessons too, my dear – I am sure that you are a little rusty.' Wallis smiled knowingly at Celia. The Rogers appeared to be oblivious to the undercurrent running between their woman guests, but Wallis' meaning was not lost on Johnny who quickly changed the subject.

'As a small gesture of thanks for your kind hospitality, I should like to invite you out to luncheon. Katherine, is there a particular restaurant that you and Herman like?'

'You really do not need to do that, Johnny – we are just so glad that two good friends of Wallis are here to keep her company. If you insist, and I can see from your expression that you are determined, then La Vielle Auberge, which is quite close by, is quite an experience. It is a former monastery and best enjoyed at lunchtime on a sunny day.'

'Excellent, I shall be delighted to take everybody there on the first sunny day,' replied Johnny, before saying, 'Herman, would you mind awfully if I used the telephone for a quick local call.'

'Of course not – use the one in my study so that you have some privacy.'

'Thank you, that is most kind – if you will all excuse me I shall make the call now.'

Johnny closed the study door and took a seat in front of the writing table. He turned the telephone around and he took his pocket notebook out, flipping over the pages to find Billy's number. After picking up the handset he asked the operator to put him through to Billy's number. He was in luck and Billy answered almost on the first ring.

'There is a man who I believe to be staying at the Carlton using the name Bernard O'Reilly. Find out what you can but do not approach.'

'Roger,' replied Billy and hung up.

As a precaution, neither had used the other's name. Johnny did not think that the Villa's telephone had been tapped, but certainly he could not be sure. Unfortunately he felt that he had no choice but to pass on O'Reilly's name. He re-joined the others and thanked Herman.

'When do you think that the gentlemen of the press will lose interest and stop besieging us here in our villa?' asked Herman.

'My guess is that they will leave one or two local stringers to keep a watching brief,' replied Johnny.

Wallis then mentioned how she had instructed Didier to take her car into Cannes at the same time every day, park behind the Carlton and then spend two hours in the bar.

'Do you think that I can risk being smuggled out in the car now that the press must be bored by Didier's routine?'

'You can but give it a try,' said Johnny.

'Where will you go in Cannes?'

'Probably the Carlton for a KT.'

'Well, you must be careful – shall I come with you?' asked Celia.

'No, I will give it a try on my own and I will have Didier to keep an eye out for me.'

'Bloody brilliant,' thought Johnny. 'Wallis is going to be swanning around Cannes with her gigolo driver, who is himself a potential significant threat.'

'Actually Wallis, I insist that my man Charles accompanies you. He can sit in the front with your driver. He's a good man and he knows how to handle tricky situations.'

'Darn it! If you insist. . .'

Before Wallis could finish, all the others said, 'We do.'

She gave in gracefully. She was damned if she was going to be saddled with a chaperone for long. Didier had told her about some of the more interesting diversions that Cannes could offer. Judging by his skills she eagerly anticipated exploring the seedy side of the fashionable town.

# Chapter 9

Von Ribbentrop was not a happy man. Celia had duly travelled to Cannes with the documents and message for Wallis, but it seemed that she had not immediately passed them on to her. He had ordered that the German agent in the villa, Didier Pascal, should encourage Wallis to confide in him. Von Ribbentrop knew her well enough to judge that in the intimate time after lovemaking, Wallis was invariably utterly indiscrete.

The report from Didier's controller, Brendan O'Reilly, had confirmed that Wallis was making good use of the young man's body. It was for Didier to gain her confidence. Otherwise a back-up plan would be needed. If necessary, Wallis would have to be tricked into using the secret Swiss bank account. Obviously that could not happen when she was holed up in the villa as a virtual prisoner.

The Führer had asked to see the evidence that Wallis Simpson had been compromised. Von Ribbentrop had explained that such evidence would only be available after Celia's return to London. Hitler was clearly angry that so far as he was concerned there was a delay. Von Ribbentrop did not like to dwell on the prospect of Hitler's reaction if the plan failed.

Von Ribbentrop's agents, watching Schloss Enzesfeld where the Duke of Windsor was staying, had followed him into Vienna. There he had visited the eminent ear specialist Professor Newmann. When paid a visit by two security agents, Professor Newmann was quickly convinced that in the interests of the safety of his family and himself he should confirm the date and time of "Mr Windsor's" next consultation.

Von Ribbentrop decided that it would be easier to meet the Duke in Vienna, rather than trailing him around on the skiing trip that he was thought to be planning with his old friend and former Aide de Camp, Fruity Metcalfe. Von Ribbentrop gave instructions for travel arrangements to be made for him to go to Vienna, arriving the day before the Duke's appointment. He also contacted the German Ambassador in Austria as a courtesy and asked that it be noted that he was paying a private visit. The ambassador undertook to deal with all matters of protocol. An appointment was made for a Herr Schmidt to attend Professor Newmann immediately before Mr Windsor.

'Wallis – it is wonderful to talk to you, I am missing you so much.'

'And me you, David darling. How are you bearing up today?'

'Oh, not too bad. The Rothschilds are delightful as ever – it just is not like being in one's own place. Kitty is wonderful company through it all. Bloody cold – I make a point of taking Slipper out for walks, but the poor little chap isn't too keen on the snow.'

Wallis felt a pang of jealousy at the way the Duke referred to Kitty. She tried to put the image of the pretty and younger Kitty out of her mind as she responded, 'It's hard to imagine you in the middle of a white wilderness. The weather here has been pretty good although I cannot really get out to enjoy it. I know what you mean about being a long-term guest. I thought you were going to go skiing in the Austrian Tyrol?'

'That's the plan, but I have to get this damned ear sorted out first. I have seen a professor in Vienna and he has prescribed drops which I get my valet to put in every night. The professor was a charming fellow – Jewish of course, but then I am told that most of the top medicos and academics in Austria are.'

'Well, they sure are clever. Oh David, I am so fed up with being a prisoner here. As I have said in my letters I feel so trapped, and I cannot wait to have the protection of being your wife.'

'Speaking of protection, I decided to knit you a jumper.'

'Are you serious?'

'I most certainly am. I learnt to knit when I was on those

interminable tours. I found it therapeutic. How's your French coming on?'

'Just dandy, David darling. I have a two hour session every afternoon whilst the Rogers have their siesta. It suits me better than trying to sleep. By the way, Johnny and Celia have arrived. I think that they may end up settling down together. He's a lucky man – she is such a looker, and a clever girl too.'

'Excellent. Did I tell you that Fruity Metcalfe is coming over to visit me? I have asked if he can manage a long visit – we can then go skiing together which would be fun. He will have to arrange leave of absence but knowing Fruity, he will manage it somehow. I had better go now and dress for dinner.'

'So must I, darling man. I love you so much. Kisses for now.'

'And to you, my darling.'

Johnny and Celia had decided that for the sake of appearances, they should each sleep in their own suites. They did not know the Rogers or how they might react to their obviously sleeping together. Celia was tired after the journey and announced that she was going to have an early night.

As she was leaving the salon where they were all sitting, Katherine Rogers said, 'Oh by the way, the new lady's maid has been delayed until tomorrow so Laurenne will look after you this evening.'

'Oh – that's fine, if it's ok with you Wallis?'

'Of course it is – I shall not be going up for a couple of hours.'

Celia entered her suite and kicking off her shoes sank back into a deep and comfortable armchair. There was a knock on the door and Laurenne entered.

'Milady, you look so tired.'

'Yes, I really am. I feel as if I ache all over.'

'Let me give you a lavender massage. It will relax you wonderfully.'

'That sounds like a jolly good idea.'

Laurenne reached down and drew Celia out of the chair and then turned her around. She quickly undid the buttons on the back of her dress and soon Celia was in her underwear. Laurenne fetched two of the giant bath sheets from the bathroom and a bottle of lavender oil. After spreading the bath sheets on the bed she indicated for Celia to lie down on her front.

'Milady, you must take off your underwear or it will be ruined by the oil.'

'Yes, you are right,' said Celia, lifting herself so that Laurenne could slide her silk knickers down. When Celia was completely naked, Laurenne rubbed oil between her hands then started to massage Celia's back and shoulders. Gradually she worked downwards until she was massaging the base of Celia's spine. Laurenne then went to the foot of the bed and after massaging each of Celia's feet, individually drew them apart and then knelt between Celia's legs.

'Now you must totally relax,' said Laurenne, as she slid her oiled hands up the inside of Celia's thighs.

Celia moaned with pleasure as the French girl's nimble fingers worked their spell.

Later, when Johnny slipped into bed next to Celia he commented, 'My dear, you smell just like those lavender farms we passed through in Provence.'

'And you, my dear, smell of Armagnac and cigars.'

'Touché,' he laughed as he stroked her silky smooth skin.

'I had a wonderful massage when I came up. The maid Laurenne really knows what she is doing. Sweet girl, but what she sees in that creepy driver I do not know.'

'Well you did mention one attribute that you fleetingly saw when Wallis went into her suite,' laughed Johnny.

'Oh you men just do not understand. It would take more than that thing, I can assure you. And now I must go to sleep.'

Johnny leant over and kissed her then lay back and soon fell asleep himself.

Laurenne meanwhile was having a rather painful experience which seemed to be giving Wallis a great deal of pleasure. Wallis was perspiring with the effort of what she was doing, and the girl was whimpering.

'So, you gave Lady Celia one of your massages you little hussy, did you?'

The girl gave a sob and confirmed that she had.

'For that, I want you and Didier to put on a show for Lady Celia and me. You understand, and I do not mean anything tame.'

She was not sure whether Celia would wish to watch and possibly even participate but the idea appealed. She decided that the girl had suffered enough and releasing her stepped back. As Laurenne turned her tear-laced and flushed face towards her, Wallis beckoned her to follow to the bed where Wallis lay back ready to be pleasured.

The next morning was bright and everything looked fresh in the clear Provençal light. Johnny stood in the morning sun and admired the view from the balcony outside his suite. Beyond the darkly wooded hills and far below, the sea was a contrasting sparkling blue, stretching unbroken to the horizon. Johnny was enough of a romantic to want to share this moment with Celia, and quickly went to her suite. Shaking her shoulder gently, he leant and kissed her temple tenderly.

'Come on sleepy head – I want you to see this.'

'Oh you beast,' she said as she sat up, knuckling her eyes and stifling a yawn, 'I was having a super dream and you spoilt it.'

'Tosh, my dear, now come on and look at this.'

'Slave driver,' she replied, pulling on her silk wrap. As soon as they were on the balcony she snuggled up to Johnny as he made an extravagant gesture, swinging his arm as if to encompass the whole panorama.

'Yes, it is beautiful. Truly beautiful, but I am cold. I don't have a thick cashmere dressing gown and leather slippers like you.'

'Well, if you will pad about barefoot in your wispy night attire, what do you expect?'

'Pompous pig,' she retorted and skipped back through the French doors, which she closed as soon as Johnny went to follow her.

Later, Celia joined Johnny in his sitting room. They were both dressed smartly but informally.

'I think it's time that Wallis got out, and I am going to suggest that I take us all to lunch at the restaurant that Herman mentioned – you know, the former monastery,' said Johnny.

'That sounds fun. What about the press?'

'I shall contact the Chief of Police and ask him to arrange an escort and a couple of guards at the restaurant. Billy will also be riding shotgun, in case our German friends become too interested. Now, let's go down to breakfast.'

Over breakfast, it was agreed that lunch would be at the old monastery and Herman would book it. Johnny said that he would contact the Chief of Police in Cannes.

Later in the morning, after she had received instructions from Wallis with regard to the clothes that would be required for lunch, Laurenne slipped across the inner courtyard behind the kitchen and up the stairs to Didier's rooms above the garage. She told him that the Rogers and all the guests including Wallis were going out to lunch. When Laurenne told him that the party would be going in the Rogers' car and that of Lord John, he was furious.

'Where are they going?' he demanded.

'I do not know, but I have been told to lay out one of her smart outfits. She has also said that she wants us to put on a show for Lady Celia, who might even join in.'

'Excellent – that is no problem. When does she want it?'

'Tonight, I think.'

'Find out when you help her dress for the lunch.'

'I shall, and I must run now.'

Wallis hummed to herself as she carefully applied her make-up. This was going to be a dandy day, she reckoned – her first escape from the villa, an interesting lunch and then an entertaining evening.

The latest report received by Heinrich Himmler revealed that neither the former King of England or Mrs Simpson were engaged in any activity of interest. He noted that von Ribbentrop was utilising the Abwehr network of Admiral Canaris. He disliked Canaris and did not trust him. As a consequence, the Admiral's every move was watched and analysed – Himmler took a perverse pleasure spying on those who were apparently colleagues. So far as he was concerned, he trusted nobody, and for one reason or another hated most people. His attempts to find sympathetic senior officers in the British services through General von Manheim had failed.

Whilst he accepted that the General had genuinely tried to carry out Himmler's brief, he had failed. He had not forgotten, nor would he forgive the unpleasant and acutely embarrassing incident as he had left the General after lunch. He had enjoyed reading the details of the agonising torture and death of the young SS soldier who had been stupid enough to burst out laughing when Himmler was overtaken by his habitual chronic flatulence.

Unfortunately, the General was very highly regarded by the Führer, who believed him to be a brilliant strategist. The General had presented the Führer with innovative campaign plans that had appealed to Hitler's view of the way that Nazi Germany would fight in the future. Himmler would bide his time until the General's star waned and then he would strike, just as he would with Canaris.

He sat quietly contemplating the moves that he would make, once the former King and his woman were together. It was then that he would strike.

In the meantime he was content to allow Ribbentrop – he refused to even think of him as 'von' Ribbentrop – to get on with his plans and toady to the Führer. He pressed the bell under his desk and when the attractive young secretary had settled with her notebook on her knee, Himmler dictated an order to be given to his senior officer in the South of France.

' *"The agent, Didier Pascal, who is controlled by Abwehr foreign (Irish) agent Bernard O'Reilly, is to be questioned vigorously to ascertain what he has learnt from Mrs Simpson. He is then to be disposed of in a manner that will not raise any suspicion of our involvement."*

'Have the order despatched at once,' Himmler instructed.

Maxwell Knight sat down with Tar Robertson. 'We have just received details of an instruction direct from Himmler to his station chief in the South of France.'

'How did we get it?'

'It was routed through London and crossed the desk of our man in the German Embassy, Wolfgang zu Putlist. It reads. . .' Knight then read the message.

Tar laughed, 'Bloody Himmler – he cannot leave well alone. The Germans have got their man into the villa and by all accounts on intimate terms with the Simpson woman. He is perfectly placed but the impatient and jealous sadist Heinrich Himmler wants him grilled, then disposed of.'

'I agree, it's absurd. We are on the ground there too. Should we intervene?'

'No, because that will blow our cover, and possibly your man in the Embassy. We must warn our people but instruct them to keep out of the way. I shall get on with that. Billy Brownlow is on the outside so I shall contact him now.'

# Chapter 10

Johnny was called to the telephone and Herman invited him to take the call in his study. It was Billy who went straight to the point.

'Orders from Himmler to interrogate the gigolo and then dispose of him. We are to keep out of it.'

'Understood. Plans confirmed for later. Locals will keep press at bay. You watch our friends.'

'Noted. I have information on the Irish gentleman. Dangerous piece of work. He should have been hanged. Hates us. French have confirmed that the gigolo is just that and preys on single women on the Riviera. No charges – probably the victims are too embarrassed to report – but believed he steals and blackmails. Their comment that even by Marseilles criminal standards, where he hails from, he is scum.'

'Come to the glorious South of France, playground of the rich and privileged and mingle with truly vile people,' laughed Johnny.

'Anyhow, thanks for the info, and bye for now, old boy.'

Brendan O'Reilly was puzzled. His finely-honed instincts told him that something was awry but he could not work out what it was. The Simpson woman – the whore, as he thought of her paradoxically, reflecting his strict catholic upbringing – was currently posing no problem. The sleazy Didier was inside the villa and cosied up with her and would pick up any information that was forthcoming. So why was he so worried?

A reflex action born of years of living in danger made him pat his jacket to feel the reassuring bulk of his shoulder-holstered Luger 9 millimetre pistol. He looked at his watch and noted that Didier should be in the hotel bar.

Looking the picture of elegance, he left his room and walked along the thickly carpeted corridor to the lifts. On entering the bar he noted with annoyance that Didier was sitting next to the beautiful prostitute with whom he had struck up a conversation a few days previously. Brendan took a seat where the bar was in full view, then loudly summoned the barman.

Didier heard him, and looking around caught Brendan's eye. There was no mistaking the look of anger, and Didier quickly told the girl that there was someone he had to talk to but would telephone her later. He took his drink and went and sat opposite to Brendan, who spoke to him quietly in impeccable French.

'Look, you stinking little shit, I pay you good money to look after one woman. Here you are playing around with a prostitute. If I catch you at it again there will be trouble, and when I say trouble, you will be badly hurt – do you understand?'

Didier was shocked at the vehemence in Brendan's voice but it was the look in his unblinking pale eyes that churned his bowels. Brought up in the slums of Marseilles he knew what the eyes of a killer looked like.

'I am sorry,' he stammered, 'I am bored just sitting here every day.'

'Be bored boy, or I'll have your balls off – and that's a starter.'

Didier stifled a yelp as Brendan reached under the table and gripped his testicles hard. That grip, added to the look in Brendan's eyes, was enough to convince Didier that he was better off obeying his orders. Blinking back involuntary tears and overcoming the nausea caused by the Irishman's vicious grip, he reported that the Rogers and their guests were all going out to lunch later, but that he would not be driving Wallis. She would be going in the car of Milord John. He described the Hispano-Suiza and confirmed that it would be driven by the intimidating Charles Harvey.

Brendan dismissed Didier and noted that the prostitute had already left the bar. He rightly guessed that she had sensed his venom and beaten a prudent retreat. The working girls in the

South of France stayed beautiful, and alive, by being alert to the slightest threat.

Brendan finished his drink, then leaving the hotel took a leisurely stroll along the Croisette. He stopped at an unprepossessing bar and took a wicker seat at the edge of the pavement. A waiter with the traditional ankle-length black apron was at his side in a moment. He ordered his coffee – a noisette, with just a splash of milk in the small cup of strong coffee. He would rather have had a large cafe au lait but he was ever conscious of his weight now that so much of his life was sedentary.

The waiter returned and placed the coffee on the zinc-topped table. Just then, the man that Brendan was due to meet arrived. He was one of the Abwehr agents stationed outside of the villa. He was instructed to ensure that the Hispano-Suiza was followed and the actions of the passengers noted.

Wallis still felt almost childishly excited at the prospect of leaving the villa. She checked her appearance one last time, then went downstairs to join the others. They went into the rear courtyard where the two cars stood with their drivers. The Rogers climbed into their car. First Celia and then Wallis slipped into the rear of the Hispano-Suiza. Johnny joined them, joking that it was a good thing that the two women were so slim.

'Now, you know the drill, Wallis. Head down on Celia's lap until I tell you that it is OK to sit up.'

Wallis gave a throaty laugh, 'My dear, that will pose no problem.'

Celia joined in the laugh as Charles started the engine and eased the car out of the courtyard. Two of the villa gardeners swung open the tall iron gates and the two cars swept under the archway and turned towards the hills away from the sea.

Johnny looked over his shoulder and noted that the French police car was behind them but keeping some distance. There were other cars following but they were kept back by the police car and were almost out of sight.

'Righto, Wallis – you can sit up now.'

It turned out to be only a ten minute drive through hilly, heavily-wooded country. The two cars swung into a courtyard within old stone walls. The police car pulled across the entrance blocking it and the four police officers climbed out. Johnny was pleased to note that, as well as their holstered pistols, two of the police were carrying sub-machine guns. The party walked across the worn flagstones and then through low, but very wide oak double doors.

Moving out of the startling bright light in the courtyard, it was a shock to be pitched into what initially seemed like total darkness. As their eyes adjusted, they saw a line of waiters all dressed from head to toe in black except for their white collars. One stepped forward.

'Welcome to La Vielle Auberge. Please come this way.' He led them through a long low-ceilinged room, lit only by the sunlight shafting through the arrow slit windows in the thick stone walls. They were seated at a large round oak table with a single fat church candle burning in a large pewter candlestick at its centre. Large pewter chargers were in front of each guest. Mozart could just be heard in the background.

Another waiter appeared with filled glasses, which he placed before them. Celia realised that none of the party had spoken since they had arrived at the auberge. Herman Rogers broke the silence.

'Welcome to this awesome place. They only serve Kir Royale as an aperitif and there is no menu to choose from, neither is there a wine list. The welcome that we received is the only thing that will be said by any member of the staff. Enjoy the experience, and good health and happiness to us all.'

He raised his glass and they toasted each other. The meal was deliciously simple and the wines impressed even Johnny, who regarded himself as something of a wine buff. When coffee and brandy had been served, Herman announced rather theatrically, 'And now for a big surprise. Please follow me.'

They left the table and followed him down a long flagstoned corridor lit by flickering wall sconces. They turned a corner and gasped. Facing them was a wall of glass and behind that a large straw laid cattle byre. In the byre there were pigs, cows, sheep and goats. The shock was that all of the animals were garishly fully made up with eyeliner, rouge and lipstick.

'Oh my God!' exclaimed Wallis, voicing the thoughts of not only herself but also Celia and Johnny.

'Now look at this,' said Herman as he led them to a side window through which they could see a sloping meadow with grazing animals. All of these animals were fully made up as well.

'And that, dear people, is my surprise of the day,' said a smiling Herman.

'What kind of perverted people would dream up a stunt like this?' asked a bemused Wallis.

'I think that it is utterly fantastic, Wallis,' replied a laughing Celia. 'When we ladies are on show we slap on cosmetics, so why not do it for the animals?'

The party returned to the villa. Wallis reckoned that this was going to be one hell of a day. She was now looking forward to some lively evening entertainment.

Katherine Rogers had suggested that after their long lunch, a light supper would be appropriate. Wallis replied that she would be happy to literally have a snack. Celia and Johnny agreed, and Katherine sent for her chef and gave instructions accordingly. They were to have a Salade Gourmande announced Katherine, adding that it was her favourite.

'I shall love it if you twist my arm,' laughed Wallis.

Katherine replied, 'We first had it in a restaurant called Greuze just by the Abbey in a town called Tournus – a bit north of Lyon. The young chef is wonderful – Jean Duclous. I sent our chef there to try it and some of his other dishes, and it was well worth it.'

'That's a long way to go for a salad,' quipped Wallis with a smile.

'But worth it. You will see – foie gras, langoustine and – oh well, just you see. I bet you that you will say that it is the best salad you have ever had.'

'I am going to have a little rest and possibly a very short French lesson.'

'That's fine Wallis – Herman and I will have a short siesta. Celia, Johnny, what will you do?'

'I fancy a good walk to settle lunch .What about you, Johnny?'

'Excellent idea, let's run along the coast a bit and find a good spot to set off from. Put on some good walking shoes – I will let Charles know that we will be ready in say, 10 minutes?'

'Yes, that's just perfect.'

Wallis had sent for Laurenne who had helped her to undress and put on one of her silk kimonos.

'Send for Didier, my dear, and then come back in an hour please.'

'Oui, Madame,' Laurenne bobbed and left the suite.

Didier had expected a summons, and quickly crossed the courtyard and ran up the back service stairs. He knocked quietly on the door to Wallis' suite and then went straight in locking it behind him. Wallis beckoned him over.

'We have not much time this afternoon, Didier, but that is a good thing because I want you at your peak for this evening's performance. I wish you to pleasure me but we will not have intercourse and you will have no release. Just think, tonight you may even get to sleep with Lady Celia.'

Wallis could see that Didier was very excited at the prospect, and reaching for him she stroked him through the fine cloth of his trousers.

'Oh you poor boy,' she laughed.

He hated her at that moment. He knew what he had to do, and his encounter with Brendan left him in no doubt that he had no choice in the matter. He opened the kimono and started to lean forward.

'No,' commanded Wallis, 'get your clothes off, now.'

Didier did as he was told. Wallis was thrilled at the sight of him.

'C'mon,' she said huskily.

The light supper was every bit as delicious as Katherine had promised. Afterwards Katherine excused herself.

'I have the beginning of a migraine I think – it may have been triggered by the contrast between the very bright sunlight and the dark restaurant. I should be OK tomorrow if I lie down now.'

'You go on up my dear, I shall not be long either. How about you, Celia?'

'Well if Johnny and Herman are going to have their backgammon needle match I think I shall have a long luxurious bath and an early night.'

'Shall I ask Laurenne to send for your new girl?' asked Wallis.

'No thanks Wallis – I am happy to be on my own.'

Celia went over to Johnny and kissed him on the top of his head.

'Good night darling, I am off for a bath and an early night. May the best man win,' she said. Johnny gave her a quick smile, as did Herman before they both turned their attention back to the board.

As Celia and Wallis went up the stairs, Wallis took her hand and said very quietly, 'We have had no time together. Come and see me after your bath. It would be fun.'

'Oh,' she paused, 'yes, I shall Wallis, you are right. I will not have a long soak and will be with you in about 45 minutes.'

Wallis squeezed her hand, 'That's just fine, my dear.' She blew Celia a little kiss as she went into her suite, where she immediately sent for Laurenne.

'Laurenne, go and fetch Didier now. Make sure that nobody sees him on the back stairs.'

Laurenne returned with Didier a few minutes later.

'Right you two, go and get ready for your show and wait in the second bedroom. Use its bathroom now and do not make any sound until you hear me clap my hands twice. You are then to come in here and then do as I say. You will of course be naked, and Didier, I expect you to be fully aroused. Do you understand?'

'Oui, Madame,' they chorused, and went into the second bedroom.

Wallis quickly prepared herself for Celia, and after applying her strategic perfume as she always thought of it, slipped on a revealing negligee. Celia arrived promptly, and Wallis locked the door. They embraced, and Wallis had quickly slipped Celia's robe off. She stood back and admired her.

In spite of her reservations, Celia, as usual when with Wallis, was quite aroused already, and when Wallis moved closer it was only a matter of a few moments before she was whimpering with pleasure. Wallis steered her towards the large bed in the main bedroom and Celia lay back with her legs wide apart. To her shock, at that moment Wallis gave a chuckle and clapped her hands hard twice. Before Celia could move into a more modest position, Laurenne and Didier came into the bedroom. Both were naked except that Laurenne had a deep leather collar to which a chain was attached, the other end being held by Didier. He was totally and formidably aroused. His gaze fell upon Celia and his smile become a leer and he visibly twitched.

'Oh no,' exclaimed Celia, 'Wallis, stop this now.'

Celia's voice had a menacing tone that Wallis had never heard before and she realised that she had overstepped the mark.

'Ok darling – do you wanna watch them?'

'No, I bloody well don't. He gives me the creeps. Poor Laurenne.'

'Ok folks – show's over. Laurenne and Didier, scram.'

Within a few moments they turned to go. As they left, Didier was glaring at Celia venomously.

'Do you want to stay darling,' asked Wallis in a much softer tone.

'Actually Wallis, I think that I really will have that early night I promised myself.'

'No hard feelings?' asked Wallis, in a tentative tone.

'Of course not. It's just him, I think he is horrible.'

'I know what you mean honey, but you've seen the equipment, and boy does he know how to use it.'

'I am very glad,' laughed Celia, who had now regained her composure, 'but I have no wish to sample it, and he has seen rather a lot of me too! I'll be off now.'

They kissed and Celia left. When Celia had returned to her suite she decided to lock the door. After pottering around she put out the lights in the living room with the exception of one small table light. It really only gave out a soft background light. She had her bedside light on as she snuggled into the very comfortable bed. A few minutes later she thought she heard something in the living room, and slipping out of bed went and stood listening. Her attention was caught by a noise at the door and moving closer, she thought she saw the handle turn.

'Perhaps it was Johnny,' she thought. She could not shout – the doors were heavy and she would have to bellow so loudly that she might bring the whole house running. She was about to open the door when another thought struck her. What if it was Didier? That venomous look he had given her flashed into her mind. Celia went to her handbag and took out the little Beretta pistol. As she had been taught she checked that it was fully loaded. With the safety catch on she placed it under her pillow.

She was no longer in the mood for reading so she turned off her bedside light and lay in the dark, with only the glow of light from the living room framed by the door. She tossed and turned and sleep just would not come. She tried to remember which Gilbert & Sullivan operetta had the patter song which included tossing and turning like this when sleep would not come.

'Please let me go to sleep,' she thought –and then she froze. She was not sure but she thought she heard a sash window opening. It could only be the second bedroom – the living room had French doors onto her terrace. She reached under her pillow and took the pistol, slipping off the safety catch. She climbed out of bed and thinking of ridiculous nursery games, pushed the large pillows into the bed so that at a first glance she would appear to be in it.

Billy Brownlow had drilled into her that with so low a calibre pistol she had to be close, and should aim first for the body to bring her assailant down. Any coup de grace was another matter. She stepped into the shadows away from the bed but with a full view of the doorway, 'What is taking so long?' she wondered.

Then she knew. Silhouetted in the door was a plainly naked Didier Pascal. With a low growl he stepped towards the bed. Celia had seen how strongly built he was and knew that in a fight she would not stand a chance. He was still silhouetted in the light from the door as she stepped towards him. Sensing her presence he spun around and seeing her he snarled. She fired first into his chest and then his groin. Even in the poor light she could see the shock and horror in his eyes.

She fired again into his chest, and he suddenly doubled up and fell to the floor on his knees as if praying. He gave a choking cough, and a gout of blood ran down his chin and onto his chest. Slowly he seemed to sit up and to reach towards her and then rolled backwards.

'Is this how long it takes a man to die?' thought Celia dispassionately.

As Didier took his last gurgling breath, his bowels voided. The stench was appalling. It brought Celia out of her almost trance-like state. 'Christ!' said Celia to herself, 'what the heck do I do now?'

# Chapter 11

Celia's initial panic shocked her back to reality. She could not handle this on her own. She slipped out of her suite, remembering to lock the door. She knocked quietly on Johnny's door. After a short wait during which she knocked again, constantly looking over her shoulder fearing that someone else might come onto the landing, she heard the key turn.

'My God, Celia – what the hell's the matter!' exclaimed Johnny, as he took in that her face was white as a sheet and there was blood finely sprayed across her nightdress. 'You look as if you'd seen a ghost!'

As he quickly reached and pulled her through the doorway, the dam burst and she collapsed sobbing into his arms. He held her tightly for a few moments then freed one hand and locked the door.

'What is it?'

She was now wracked by gulping sobs but managed to blurt out, 'I killed a man. Wallis' driver. He was going to rape me!'

'Where is he?'

'In my bedroom.'

'Right. You must be brave. Charles and I shall deal with this. You must stay here. Let's get you out of that nightdress and into one of my shirts. Then into bed and wait for me. OK?'

'Yes, Johnny,' she replied very quietly. When she was in bed, he took her key and his own after calling Charles on the internal telephone.

'Charles. Get dressed and up here as quickly as you can. We have a heavy disposal job on our hands. Have you a waterproof groundsheet or similar in the car?'

'No Johnny, I haven't.'

'Ok, have a look around the garage, there might be something there. We shall need some rope and later on, cleaning stuff. See you shortly.'

Whilst waiting for Charles, Johnny got dressed in a heavy navy blue fishing sweater and dark trousers. He put on his soft-soled tennis shoes. He then went and unlocked his door. As soon as he heard Charles tap quietly on the door, he waved to Celia and switched off the living room lights. He then slipped out onto the landing, locked his suite door and opened Celia's.

As they opened the door, their senses were assailed by the stench of violent death. By the dim light of the lamp in the living room they could see the naked body of Didier slumped just inside Celia's bedroom.

Charles then left to fetch the tarpaulin and rope. Johnny went into the second bedroom where the window was not fully closed. Didier's trousers and a sweater were in a crumpled pile on the floor and next to them a pair of espadrilles. Charles closed and locked the window and scooped up the clothes and shoes.

Charles was soon back with a tarpaulin and rope that he had found not in the garage but the gardeners' shed. Working silently, they lifted the corpse onto the tarpaulin and straightened it out as best they could.

'Right,' said Johnny. 'I suggest that we parcel him up as he is and ditch his clothes elsewhere –there is nothing remarkable about them. They, the tarpaulin and rope can go in the sea separately after we have dumped the bastard's body.'

'Do you reckon the sea for him too?' asked Charles.

'I think better not. There's no tide to speak of in the Med and we don't want him washing up whilst he is still recognisable. That would bring the gendarmes straight here.'

'Do you reckon we keep him in the boot of the car until morning, then you and I go out, dump him and then the rest of the stuff in the sea?'

'It'll have to be. There is no reason for us going out at this time of night. We need an excuse for going out bloody early in the morning.'

'How about that you decided to go down to the sea and buy the freshest possible fish for a breakfast treat?'

'Well done. It's a bit thin, but good enough. We must not forget Celia's night dress, Charles.'

'That's no trouble – I will put it in the boiler.'

'Right, let's get him down those service stairs and into the car.'

Didier was surprisingly heavy and they had to stoop and rest a few times on the steep stairs. Luckily, they did not encounter anyone then or as they slipped across the courtyard. Charles opened one of the garage doors just wide enough for them to squeeze through with the body. Once it was in the capacious boot, Johnny slipped back into the villa and fetched Didier's clothes and shoes. With the boot locked they left the garage and quickly slipped back inside the villa.

Charles whispered to Johnny, 'I know where all the cleaning stuff is kept. You go ahead and I will join you in a few minutes.'

As Johnny reached the top of the service stairs he realised that someone was on the landing. He eased the door open a crack. Laurenne was standing by the door to Wallis' suite. She was in a negligee and her long hair was down. She seemed uncertain and hesitant, but then as if she had suddenly plucked up courage she knocked on the door. The door opened, and there was Wallis.

'What is it, Laurenne?'

'Oh Madame, it is Didier. I am so upset. He is in a fury and earlier he ordered me away from his rooms. I think that what happened earlier with Lady Celia has driven him mad.'

'Oh, well, my dear, in you come and I will try and cheer you up.'

'Oh thank you, Madame,' replied the girl as Wallis reached out and drew her into the suite. The door closed and there was the unmistakeable sound of the key turning in the lock.

'Thank God for that!' thought Johnny, as a wave of relief spread over him.

Charles arrived with a bucket, cloths and some cleaning materials. They slipped into Celia's suite, and after closing her bedroom door and checking that the curtains were fully drawn, put on the lights.

'It's not too bad,' said Charles, as he quietly half-filled the bucket in the bathroom.

'Celia will have to say that she was sick in the night and I asked you to come up and clear up, Charles. I shall tell Katherine Rogers that Celia was greatly embarrassed, hence my getting you involved. That will account for the wet carpet. Katherine will tell Celia's maid to keep her trap shut. Celia will give the girl a nice cash present, and all will be forgotten.'

Charles laughed quietly, 'You should do this more often, Johnny.'

'Not bloody likely!'

When they had finished, all that there was to show for Didier's death was a dark patch of wet carpet and a bucket half full of dark stained water.

It was still dark when Charles formally reported for duty. He was in his smart chauffer's uniform. Johnny was smartly but casually dressed. They went down the service stairs together and whilst they spoke quietly, they carried on a polite conversation. Just as they reached the ground floor hallway a door opened. Through it came the Rogers' butler in his checked dressing gown, pyjamas and carpet slippers. His hair was on end and clearly had not received its usual attention with pomade and brushes. Johnny immediately addressed him.

'Ah Henri – just the fellow I wished to see. Spur of the moment but I am going to give everyone a surprise for their breakfast. Please tell the kitchen that I am off to meet the fishermen and I shall bring something special back from this morning's catch.'

'Mon Dieu!' thought the butler, 'I thought the Americans were crazy but these English!'

'Of course, Milord. Some of the best fish can be found in the smaller villages away from Cannes.'

'Oh, jolly good, and thank you. I say, did you hear that Charles?'

Charles replied in a resigned tone, 'Yes, my Lord.'

When they were in the car Johnny burst out laughing. 'I think that that was a pretty damn fine Bertie Wooster, Charles!'

'Yes, it was, Johnny. Just remember that I am not bloody Jeeves.'

Charles had swung the villa gates open and the gendarmes on duty said that they would close them. They saluted Johnny as the car drove out. 'If only they knew,' he thought.

They drove down nearly into Cannes then turned right, almost doubling back on themselves into the heavily wooded hills. They came to a stretch of road where there was a series of bridges over deep, rugged gorges that looked bottomless in the growing light.

'One of these will do,' said Johnny, and Charles swung the car into the entrance to a woodland fire beak track where it could not be seen by any other passing motorist. 'We'll keep him in the tarpaulin, but take the ropes off here.'

They quickly untied the ropes and then manhandled the unwieldy bundle onto the bridge. They tipped the body over, and stopped for a moment as it cartwheeled through the air before crashing into the dense undergrowth a hundred feet below. Back in the car they both felt a sense of relief as they drove away, heading for the sea. They were confident that the foxes and other creatures of this wild place would soon leave Didier unrecognisable.

After dumping the tarpaulin and rope in a dirty-looking deserted inlet that appeared and smelt stagnant they carried on along the winding coast road, until they came to what had once been a passing place on the cliff top road, but was now big enough for a few cars to stop and take in the dramatic view. Charles bundled up Didier's espadrilles and sweater with his trousers, and threw them as far out over the sheer cliffs as he could. The bundle unwound as it fell and the separate items disappeared from sight in the gathering light. 'Fishing time, Charles.'

Brendan O'Reilly was vexed. Where the heck was that whoreson Didier. 'I'll strangle the little swine,' he thought as he waited in the bar of the Carlton Hotel.

His thoughts were black when the beautiful young prostitute who had clearly caught Didier's eye entered the bar. She looked around and almost flinched when she saw Brendan. A thought entered his head in an instant. He turned on his easy charm and rising from his chair and said,

'My dear – come and sit with me and what would be your pleasure?'

He ordered her lemon frappé and then giving her a lingering admiring look, asked with a smile, 'And for what would a beautiful girl like you come to a gentleman's room for an hour or so?' She told him her price and that that was for nothing fancy.

'If the gentleman fancied tying the beautiful girl up what would be the price?' he asked, still smiling. She told him. 'Very well my dear, now drink up and come with me.'

The barman had watched the familiar scenario unfold, and wistfully thought that if he had the elegant Irishman's money he would now be in the lift taking the beautiful girl to his room. When they were in Brendan's room and he had locked the door, he told the girl to undress as he sat in the armchair by the French doors that opened onto the ornamental balcony. She did so slowly and seductively, and when she was finally naked but for her suspender belt stockings and high heels she struck some poses that were as provocative as they were erotic.

She was wasting her time. Brendan preferred boys, pretty boys, not pretty girls. He was happy to abuse girls for pleasure but the posing and posturing gave him no pleasure. 'Lie on the bed for me my dear,' he said smiling all the while. As she complied he went to the large mirrored armoire and took out four silk ties and a silk handkerchief. He went to the bed, and moving around it expertly tied each of her wrists and ankles to the bedposts so that she was spread-eagled. His smile vanished. She was puzzled. He was still in his immaculate three piece suit.

'Now tell me. Have you been seeing the handsome young man you saw me speak to in the bar the other day?'

She had seen the threat of violence in the way that Brendan had intimidated Didier. 'Of course not.' The first blow to the side of her head felt like a pile driver.

'Think again bitch!' came a very different voice to that of the smooth gentleman in the bar. The voice was thickened by a strong Irish accent.

'Yes I have seen him, but only twice for a drink.' The second blow to the other side of her head set her ears ringing.

'It's true!' she cried.

'What did he talk about? His work?'

'He said that he was a chauffeur to a very important person.'

'Did you ask him who?'

'No.'

'Lying bitch!'

He stuffed the balled up silk handkerchief into the girl's mouth. Her beautiful eyes were as wide as saucers as she watched him. He took a gold cigarette case from his inside pocket and opening it selected a cigarette. He then took a gold lighter from another pocket and lit the cigarette. He drew on it hard, then as he came to the side of the bed the girl realised what he intended. She wet herself as he held the burning cigarette to her nipple. Her gagged scream was silent as smoke rose from the hissing flesh.

'This is what we gave the Protestant bitches in Ireland and the Commies in Spain. It always works,' he laughed. She strained against the restraints and arched her back as he slowly walked around the bed, and then after drawing hard on the cigarette held it to her other nipple. She was in agony but he had not finished yet.

'Now, bitch, you will really feel a little holy fire.'

He moved down the bed, and drawing again on the cigarette reached between her legs with it. She convulsed, screaming silently, and mercifully fainted. She came out of her faint into a world of pain and horror when he dashed cold water in her face. 'Now bitch, when I take the gag out of your mouth I want the truth. Understand? No shouting or God help you!' From experience he knew that he had broken her.

She nodded, and he took the gag out of her mouth. She spoke between sobs. 'He told me that he works for a disgusting old woman who is going to marry the former King of England. She has boasted to him that she will be Queen one day and maybe quite soon. That is all he told me.'

He undid the girl's wrists and ankles and counted out the amount that she had previously mentioned. 'Get dressed bitch, and keep away from him or I will find you – understand?' The terrified girl nodded. 'The same if you tell anyone about our little time together.'

She nodded again, convinced that he could and would find her. She had had beatings from customers and a pimp before, but never had she been so intimidated. She left the room walking with difficulty, a broken girl. Brendan had heard enough to confirm that the Simpson woman was as indiscreet as suspected, and still harboured the regal dreams that she had publically denied.

'Time to leave Cannes,' he decided, and he packed. He called for a porter to be sent up to collect his luggage, and he left a substantial tip for the chambermaid who would have to clean up the mess the girl had made. He was a perfect gentleman after all.

# Chapter 12

Bernard O'Reilly left the Carlton Hotel by taxi. He was cautious by nature .That caution had first been honed by his experience fighting the hated British occupiers of his beloved Ireland. In Ireland he had justified his actions by his belief that he was a freedom fighter, striving to overturn the rule of a brutal foreign power. He had become almost impervious to the brutality of all involved, and any qualms that he might have had at the outset had soon evaporated. He became a feared member of his Republican unit.

His colleagues were at times sickened by the treatment he meted out to prisoners. He was particularly brutal in dealing with suspected informers or British undercover agents. His torture of women was regarded by even hardened colleagues as bordering on repulsive. His commanders were concerned that some of his activities were so extreme that they were counterproductive, and when partition came he was removed from the active list much against his wishes.

He came from an affluent middle-class background which by most standards would be regarded as privileged. His father was a martinet and believed that corporal punishment was an essential part of forming character in a boy. He did not spare the rod. When Bernard was sent to be a boarder at a Catholic seminary at the age of thirteen, he found the regular floggings at the hands of the monks and senior boys were no worse than he was used to at home. He looked forward to the day when he would be a monitor and able to thrash younger boys. He had been at the school only three months when he was seduced by one of the priests.

After the initial shock he realised that he relished his

regular sessions with the priest. It became known in the seminary that he enjoyed homosexual relations and he became the willing and promiscuous plaything of a number of priests and older pupils. He realised that as a consequence, the beatings stopped and he occupied a special place in the school. By the time his fourteenth birthday came, he had recognised that his willingness to offer illicit and illegal sex had brought him power.

His undoubted academic ability marked him as a prospect for the priesthood, but instead he chose another path. After school, he declined the opportunity to study at Trinity College Dublin, and went straight into the family business.

To all outward appearances he was a typical young bachelor who enjoyed hunting, shooting, fishing and, of course, parties. He was popular with the girls in the county set. After all, he never molested them or pressed for sexual favours. As a consequence, he was regarded as a gentleman in comparison to many of his peers.

The other side of his life was very different. He had become a member of an active nationalist unit, where he built a reputation for sometimes sickening ruthlessness in an organisation that was not known for being squeamish.

He found sexual gratification where he could, until he had a long affair with a young parish priest in a village near his family home. The young priest was plagued by guilt and welcomed the thrashings and indignities to which Bernard subjected him.

When Bernard's father died, he inherited the business which he quickly sold. He purchased a generous annuity for his mother and moved her out of the family house into a pleasant cottage. He was now a very well-off young man and free to indulge himself. Beneath the elegant and charming façade, Bernard O'Reilly was an unbalanced and dangerous man.

Johnny and Charles decided not to report Didier's demise to London but merely to say that he had left. Billy confirmed to Johnny that Bernard O'Reilly had suddenly left the Carlton Hotel later on in the morning of Didier's disappearance being discovered.

Billy first went to the hotel bar. The barman was polishing

glasses when Billy slid onto a stool by the bar and ordered a small beer.

'Have you seen my friend – you know, Mr O'Reilly – the very elegant gentleman who was often in here?'

'Yes, he was in here earlier, but that rather suspect young man he usually met has not been in which is unusual – he never misses a day.'

Billy palmed a note which he slipped to the barman. 'Did Mr O'Reilly leave suddenly?'

'In a manner of speaking he did,' said the now-smiling barman, 'he picked up Lisette, one of the best-looking working girls in Cannes and took her upstairs.'

'Where could I find her?'

'She has an apartment quite close by. She does not work from there, just concentrates on the hotels or visits some of her regulars in their homes. I can give you the address.'

'Excellent, and thank you.' Another note passed over the bar and into the barman's pocket before Billy paid for his drink, and the barman jotted down the address on his order pad. As he tore out the page he gave Billy directions and said, 'Tell her that I sent you – my name is François.'

'Thanks again, François.'

Billy followed the directions without difficulty. It had turned into a cold and blustery day and he turned up the collar of his heavy Crombie overcoat. Lisette's apartment was above a small but smart dress shop. Billy rang the door bell by the dark green painted door. The door opened a little, and Billy could hear the rattle of a safety chain.

'Who is it?'

'I am a friend of François at the Carlton and he gave me your address. Can we talk?'

'What about?'

'I am sorry, but I am freezing out here. May I come in please?'

'But Monsieur, I am in my dressing gown – I was not expecting any visitors.'

'Please do not worry about that.'

He heard the chain rattle some more then the door opened. Lisette had obviously been crying. Her eyes were puffy and red-rimmed. She was still beautiful and her dressing gown did nothing to detract from her figure. Billy pulled off his right glove and held out his hand.

'Billy Brownlow – but do please call me Billy.'

His disarming smile struck a chord with Lisette who gave a half smile, and gestured for Billy to put the chain on and follow her up the steep staircase. The living room to her apartment was small but well-furnished, with a comfortable sofa and an armchair. One wall was taken up with book shelves.

'You are a reader,' commented Billy, as Lisette took his overcoat and hat.

'I love to read and study. I am particularly interested in philosophy.'

Before Billy could respond she said, 'The way that I earn my living is immaterial – it does not touch my heart or my soul.'

'It is none of my business, but why are you so upset?'

'I was badly hurt earlier by a man at the hotel.'

'I think that I know who it was.'

Billy then described Bernard O'Reilly. 'That is him,' said Lisette in a quiet voice.

'He has left Cannes. I doubt if he will ever return. Now, tell me the whole story.'

Lisette did, starting with her first meeting Didier and ending with her torture by Brendan. She even included the detail that she had wet herself. Lisette drew her dressing gown to one side and showed Billy her burnt nipple.

'The swine – the utter swine!' was Billy's shocked response.

He had learnt all he needed to know but he was loathe to leave Lisette, who was obviously deeply traumatised. 'May I have some water?' he asked.

'But of course – I apologise for not offering you anything before.'

An hour later Billy left and was reasonably satisfied that Lisette was over the worst of the emotional shock. The physical pain would take longer. He had given her his contact details for the new apartment that he was moving to, which was very close to hers. His parting words were, 'You must call me at any time day or night if you are afraid or just want to talk.'

'Thank you for being so kind.' She stood on tip toe and

gave him a peck on the cheek. As Billy walked away, they both knew that they would be seeing each other again and not on a professional basis.

'What's going on in Cannes?' roared von Ribbentrop into the telephone. 'You are telling me that Didier Pascal has simply disappeared into thin air? Do you think that I am an idiot? Find out, I need to know!'

Bernard O'Reilly did not take kindly to being shouted at, nor the inference that he was an idiot. He couldn't care less what had happened to the little reptile Didier. He had served his purpose and thanks to the tart he had passed on exactly the information that von Ribbentrop had asked for. He did not think that the girl would report what had happened. Even if she did, the lazy Cannes' police would assume that she had been paid handsomely for allowing the attack. In that town of perversions nothing would surprise them. Nevertheless, he would keep clear of the place. He decided that a few days at the Hotel Eden Roc was a just reward. He was bound to find a playmate there.

There had been deep concern at the villa when Wallis reported that her driver had simply left, apparently witout telling anyone – his friend Laurenne was as puzzled as anyone. Wallis suspected, but would certainly not tell anyone else, that he had stormed off in a fit of pique after Celia's rejection of the show the previous night.

Johnny voiced the opinion that Didier was a young man who lived by his wits, and had probably found his life in the Villa too boring and constricting and left on impulse. The Rogers were not particularly interested – he was not a member of their staff and their butler had confided that he was greatly disliked amongst the other staff, and not trusted. It was decided that there was nothing to be done save that if he returned, Walis would dispense with his services.

Heinrich Himmler was deeply displeased. He never shouted, but his menacing tone struck fear into the listener. 'You have failed in your duty. You were ordered to sweat the Abwehr's French agent and then dispose of him. Now you say that you have lost him!'

'Someone must know where he is,' blustered the now-terrified agent in Cannes.

'You have 48 hours to find him, otherwise you will be recalled and dealt with here for dereliction of duty. Do you understand?' Himmler did not wait for a reply and put the telephone down.

Von Ribbentrop was fuming, but totally frustrated. He had just learnt of Himmler's order with regard to the Abwehr agent in Cannes. No wonder Didier Pascal had missed his rendezvous with O'Reilly. Himmler's men had obviously carried out their orders.

He had berated Wolfgang zu Putlitz for not informing him sooner but knew that in reality he was powerless, even though the Führer himself was taking an interest in the Abwehr-run operation. No doubt Himmler would be toadying up to the Führer with the information his people had extracted.

Von Ribbentrop nevertheless drafted a cable to Hitler, which he passed to his personal aide to take to the encryption room before being sent.

Tar Robertson and Maxwell Knight were sharing a moment of quiet satisfaction. Once again the many-headed hydra that was the various German intelligence agencies was tripping over itself. Billy's report of the information obtained from the call girl, coupled with a report by Wolfgang zu Putlitz in which he described von Ribbentrop's impotent fury, were very satisfying.

'One day,' mused Tar, 'the jealousies within the Nazi regime will cause an implosion.'

'Do you think that they are any greater than in Britain?' countered Maxwell.

'I mean, look at the Government – it's rife with rivalries and vendettas. When Baldwin stands down as he has indicated, it will probably be Neville Chamberlain who steps into Number 10. Seems a dedicated servant of the nation, but whilst he might be politically shrewd he lacks the spark to be a leader. If war comes he will not last.'

'Now that we have sorted out the areas of responsibility in the British intelligence services I am confident that we can do better than the Germans,' was Tar's response.

'Time will tell Tar. Time will tell.'

Wallis was in a vile mood and it was contagious. The sudden disappearance of Didier was not only puzzling apparently to everyone in the villa, but for her it meant sexual frustration. She had become addicted to Didier's ministrations. His absence meant that she would have to venture out but, of course, she no longer had a driver.

'Tell you what Wallis,' said Johnny, 'we are here for another week. Please feel free to make use of Charles if you need a driver.'

Wallis thought for a moment. Unlike the Rogers' driver who was a permanent fixture and liable to gossip with his easy-going master and mistress, Charles would be off soon. 'Why thank you, Johnny. That is very kind. May I take you up on your offer this afternoon?'

'Of course you may. Just give me a time – do you want to use my car?'

'No, no, that is too kind. Mine could do with an airing. Would 2.30pm be OK?'

'Absolutely. Please excuse me. I shall instruct Charles and I have a couple of calls to make.'

After lunch Celia said that she was going to rest for a while. Johnny insisted that he keep her company. The Rogers went for their usual siesta and Wallis entered her car in the garage forecourt.

'Where to ma'am?' asked Charles.

'Oh, I think the Carlton Hotel please.'

Billy was in the bar of the hotel, having been told by Johnny that Wallis was being driven into Cannes by Charles, and since she did not know the town would almost certainly go there. There were few people in the bar and the three elegant prostitutes at the bar could not be missed.

Charles dropped Wallis off and she warned him that she might be an hour or two, certainly at least an hour, if he wished to go a have a coffee. He thanked her and closed the car door as she walked into the hotel. She went straight to the bar and sat at a table where she could survey the room. Her gaze immediately rested on the three young women sitting at the bar. François the barman took her order. He was delighted that she had ordered a cocktail so that he could show off to the girls.

He lusted after them in vain. He was below medium height with a paunch that strained his black waistcoat. His only distinguishing mark was his magnificent bushy moustache that almost made up for the bald dome of his head. The only way he could have one of the girls would be to pay, and an hour's pleasure would cost more than a week's earnings including tips.

One of the girls looked around to see who had ordered the cocktail, and noted the beautifully dressed, heavily made-up, rather mannish woman. Her smile was returned by the woman. She slid off her stool and walked over to Wallis. She asked if she could join Wallis, who replied in French with her appalling accent that she was welcome to. 'Are you American?' the girl asked in perfect English.

'I sure am my dear – and where did you learn such excellent English?'

'From my first lover. It is the best way to learn, or so they say.'

'Was he English?'

'Yes, she was.'

Wallis raised an eyebrow and smiled warmly. Placing a hand on the younger woman's wrist Wallis looked her in the eye and said, 'Perhaps we could have some fun after finishing our drinks?'

'Of course we can. My apartment is the best place I think. It is just behind the hotel. There will be a donation of course.'

'Naturally, my dear. My name is Bessie. What is yours?'

'Your name is Wallis – your picture has been in the newspapers for months – I am Leonie.'

'OK Leonie, let's saddle up and go to your place.'

As they left the bar, François caught Billy's eye and then gave an expressive French shrug. Billy paid for his drink and said, 'It takes all sorts François.' The barman and the remaining two girls were laughing as Billy followed Wallis and Leonie out of the rear entrance of the hotel at a discrete distance.

# Chapter 13

Von Ribbentrop had arrived at Professor Newmann's Vienna consulting rooms in good time. He sat in a waiting room which could have been in any European city. He wondered why it was so hard to relax in these places even if you were not a patient. There was the usual array of magazines on the antique table in the centre of the room and chairs against the walls. He chose an upright carver chair in preference to one of the lower armchairs.

At the appointed time the attractive receptionist bustled into the room and asked him to follow her. She moved as if there were some emergency, and von Ribbentrop found himself instinctively moving quickly behind her. 'Why?' he thought. 'Medical consulting rooms discomforted all visitors,' he told himself wryly.

He was shown into a panelled room with a large leather topped partners' desk and two wing chairs in front of it. Professor Newmann was a small very neat man in old-fashioned formal attire, even down to a starched wing collar. A gold pince nez perched on his nose gave him an almost owl like appearance. As the Professor rose and started to extend his hand, von Ribbentrop firmly asserted his authority. He spoke in a commanding tone.

'Professor. You are seeing me now to ensure that there are no misunderstandings. I am not a patient but I am here to see your next patient. I am a very senior official in the German government and the Nazi party. It is in that capacity that I am here, and your total co-operation is required. Do you understand me?'

Nervously, the professor nodded and said, 'Yes, I do.'

'Good. If anyone, and I mean anyone, asks whether I or anyone else was here to meet with your next patient, the answer is "No".'

The professor was not used to being spoken to in this hectoring tone, and resented the lack of courtesy. He considered such behaviour to be uncouth compared to the extravagant courtesies that were observed amongst the Viennese professional class. Nevertheless, he nodded his assent.

'No, say it. Tell me that you understand and agree.'

'I understand and I agree.'

'Good. Then you and your family will be safe.'

The professor inwardly sighed with relief. The leading professionals in Vienna were almost all Jewish, and increasingly they felt that they and their families were under critical scrutiny. As yet there had been no overt physical threats or hostilities directed at them, as had happened to the Jewish community in Germany, but they were all conscious that they were at best resented and at worst loathed.

He and his friends had discussed their situation and all were of the opinion that Austria was likely to soon fall under Nazi Germany. They were realists, and recognised that if that were to happen – or, more likely when – they and their families would be under severe threat. The professor was planning to leave his beloved Vienna and take his family to England. He could not afford to fall foul of the authorities, and the man sitting in his consulting room could clearly cause him immense problems.

'I shall wait here. When your next patient arrives he is to be shown in here and you will leave us. I require total privacy and will call you in when I have finished. You can then conduct the consultation. Understood?'

'Most certainly.'

Von Ribbentrop then appeared to turn on his charm. However the professor was chilled when he asked after his wife and each of his children by name. To the professor's ears what might have been the questions of a polite visitor was a threat. The professor rang a small silver bell on his desk and the receptionist entered the room. Von Ribbentrop appraised her with the tired eye of a roué. 'Good legs and excellent figure – hairstyle too formal and rather old-fashioned – pretty face,' he thought. He flashed her one of his engaging smiles. The professor explained what should be done when Mr Windsor arrived. The young woman confirmed that she understood and left the room.

The two men sat in an uncomfortable silence that was only broken when the receptionist knocked, and put her head around the door announcing that Mr Windsor had arrived. 'Please show him in,' said the professor.

Almost immediately the Duke of Windsor was ushered into the room. He was as immaculate as ever, in a heavy tweed overcoat with a homburg hat in his hand. He was clearly taken aback when he saw von Ribbentrop, who raised his hand, signalling that nothing should be said. The professor left the room. Von Ribbentrop addressed the Duke, 'Your Royal Highness, my apology for this subterfuge but I can assure you that it is necessary.'

'Von Ribbentrop – this is a surprise. A pleasant one I hope?'

'The Führer asked that I send you his very best wishes and his admiration for your courageous action in abdicating. He also instructed me to confirm that his determination and that of the German government is to achieve a peaceful accord with Great Britain. You will then be restored to the throne with Mrs Simpson as your Queen.'

'Well thank you. Please give him my greetings, and I look forward to when I can visit him in Germany with Wallis there as my wife. It is a long frustrating wait for both of us , not least because the lawyers have insisted that we do not meet until after her divorce is finalised, which should be at the end of May.'

'It must be very trying for you both.'

'It is. Thank God for the telephone. At least we can talk to each other. She has Celia and Johnny Johnstone staying at the villa in Cannes for a few more days. Unfortunately they have to be back in England for Christmas, which will be a depressing time for us both I fear.'

'I have checked and the crowns are safe and secure.'

The Duke smiled. 'Thank you.'

'Very well, your Royal Highness, I should let you carry on with your consultation with the good professor. If there is anything that I can do to be of assistance, you only have to contact me.'

'That is greatly appreciated. Since I left England it is as though a drawbridge has been lifted. I cannot even speak to my brother the King, thanks to his wife. She is like a lioness guarding her cubs so far as he is concerned.'

'That must be very difficult for you. I am informed that the Prime Minister, Mr Baldwin, has indicated that he wishes to step down in the New Year and is likely to be replaced by Neville Chamberlain.'

'None of my business now, but I shall not be sorry to see the back of Baldwin. He did nothing to help me. I have met Chamberlain on a number of occasions. He is like a sanctimonious clergyman and pretty ineffectual so I am told.'

'I shall take my leave then.'

Von Ribbentrop rose as did the Duke, who shook him warmly by the hand. 'And a happy Christmas to you and your family, von Ribbentrop, and please pass on my greetings to the Führer.'

'Thank you, and I shall'.

Von Ribbentrop left the room. He put his head into the waiting room where the professor was idly flicking through a well-thumbed magazine. 'Your patient awaits you, professor.'

The elderly professor nodded and went into his consulting room. Von Ribbentrop was feeling a in a good mood and was looking forward to spending the day in Vienna. He was not due to return to Germany until the following morning. As he was about to leave the consulting rooms with his hand on the door handle, he paused, and turned back towards the receptionist.

'What is your name?' he asked, smiling warmly.

'Helga,' she replied looking slightly puzzled.

'I am a stranger in your beautiful city. Would you care to join me for dinner this evening? I am sure that you can show me things that I otherwise would not see.'

After a moment's thought she replied, 'Yes, I should like that.'

'Excellent. I am staying at the Hotel Residenz Palais Coburg in the Victoria Suite. May I suggest that you come to my suite at 7 o'clock?'

'You have chosen a wonderful hotel. I shall be there. Will

we be dining formally – I am just thinking of what I should wear?'

'As I am travelling I shall be wearing a lounge suit, so definitely informal. Until later then. Good bye Helga.'

'Goodbye. . .I don't know your name,' she laughed.

'Joachim, Joachim von Ribbentrop.'

Von Ribbentrop had a spring in his step as he strode along the pavement. He was now satisfied that both the Duke and Wallis were committed to the grand plan, as he liked to think of it. He knew that the Führer would be pleased. Admittedly he had not seen Wallis, but what he had learned from Bernard O'Reilly was totally in character for her. He stopped at a taxi rank and asked the driver to take him to his hotel. He was amused at the thought that the hotel in which he was staying was formerly the palace of the princes of Coburg–Gotha – the Duke of Windsor's family.

After a light lunch which he took in his suite, he ordered a bottle of vintage Louis Roederer Cristal champagne to be put on ice in his suite at 6.15pm precisely, and a second bottle to be put on ice and delivered at 10.00pm.

Next, he telephoned the German Embassy and giving his name, asked to be put through to the ambassador. After a few moments delay the ambassador was on the line. 'Joachim, my dear fellow. How are you enjoying Vienna?'

'I have to confess that I have not seen very much of the City since I arrived last night, but thank you for booking me into such a splendid hotel.'

'Delighted that it suits you. Is there anything else that we can do?'

'Two things, actually. First I must send an encrypted message to the Führer so I shall need to come in to the Embassy. Second, I should like to dine in an historic Viennese restaurant this evening. Do you have any suggestions?'

'I shall send a car for you in, say half an hour to bring you here. It will remain at your disposal until you leave tomorrow.'

'Thank you, that is most thoughtful.'

'I suggest that you dine at the Greichenbeisl. It is one of Vienna's oldest inns and reputedly first opened its doors in the 15th century. It was in its time frequented by Beethoven, Strauss and Brahms, and politicians such as Graf Zeppelin. I shall give you details when we meet later.'

'That is excellent, and I thank you again. I shall see you shortly.'

Von Ribbentrop drafted his report to be cabled to the Führer in positive terms, making the point that he had met the Duke and had a face-to-face conversation with him. That was definitely something that Himmler could not manage.

The ambassador was extremely affable when they met. On a personal level he regarded von Ribbentrop as a jumped up lightweight with no real diplomatic pedigree. However, he was all too aware of his standing as a confidante of the Führer, so it paid to be charming and accommodating. He also arranged for his protocol secretary to book a table for two in the restaurant. He handed a note to von Ribbentrop with its address and telephone number but confirmed that the driver would know it.

On returning to the hotel, von Ribbentrop shaved for the second time that day, bathed and then put on a fresh suit. The champagne arrived promptly, and he nervously paced the living room of his suite which was on two floors with the bedroom and its bathroom on the upper level. 'Ridiculous being nervous about the girl.' he thought to himself. He could think of no rational reason, except that the morning meeting with the Duke and sending the cable to the Führer had had the usual effect on him, and he was desperate to have a woman.

Promptly on the dot of 7pm, Helga was shown into the suite. She looked totally different out of her white uniform. The attributes which had attracted him in the morning were even more evident but she had also changed her hairstyle which was now modern and fashionably styled. 'Helga – you look ravishing – and I love your hair like that!'

'Thank you, Joachim, or should I call you Your Excellency now that I know who you really are – Herr Schmidt indeed,' she said with a broad smile.

'Hands up – I have to confess that on occasions it is appropriate to be incognito, but certainly not between friends – and we are going to be friends are we not?'

'I am sure we shall be,' she replied, with a knowing look that implied a closer relationship than her words indicated. They chatted comfortably over a couple of glasses of champagne then left the suite.

On arrival at the restaurant which was in an attractive old building with a stone portico, it was clear that the ambassador's protocol secretary had done her job thoroughly. The head waiter greeted them effusively and then led them to a corner table in one of the various vaulted rooms that made up the restaurant. The conversation never faltered, and von Ribbentrop realised that he was greatly attracted to Helga as a person and not just the subject of his now rampant lust. Their hands had touched many times as they talked animatedly.

Then von Ribbentrop decided that the time was right to test the water and placed a hand on her knee under the table. Her expression did not change but she moved her leg so that his hand was on her thigh. Her eyes gave the game away. As he grew impossibly hard he recognised a look of pure lust in them. Their conversation continued unabated as their hands met under the table. He shuddered as she stroked him. His voice thickened as he suggested that they should not bother with dessert or coffee.

Looking him straight in the eye, she said, 'Joachim, darling we both want the same thing badly and it most certainly is not an infernal pudding. It's time to go.'

They were in each other's arms the moment that they entered the suite. The second bottle of champagne was never opened.

# Chapter 14

Leonie and Wallis were lying entwined on the large bed enjoying a smoke. They were both smiling lazily like contented cats. Leonie was highly skilled and the two women had reached the heights together. Wallis now knew where she would be coming to let off steam.

Leonie was perceptive and intrigued by the story that Wallis now told her. It was at least based on fact even if it was embellished and edited. Wallis naturally came out of her story in a very favourable light. She omitted any mention of von Ribbentrop or the information that she had passed to him. Also, she did not mention what she now regarded as the done deal with the Nazi government.

Leonie had known Didier as one of the hangers-on around the vulnerable rich. She said that she did not despise him, how could she as a call girl. However she did not trust him.

'Well the little rat seems to have walked out on his job with me,' complained Wallis.

'I think I shall be seeing more of you, Leonie, just as soon as I get myself a new driver. It's a cushy number. Free accommodation and food, good salary and very little work.'

'I'll have a think. I may know somebody. Given what I know that Didier is good at – all of us working girls do!' – she and Wallis laughed. 'I cannot guarantee to find you someone so well-equipped but possibly a better person.'

'That suits me. Now, I want you to show me that little trick of yours again, you naughty girl. It might come in handy one day.'

The following day Tar had reported to Sir Vernon that von

Ribbentrop had been seen in Vienna. He had been followed to the consulting rooms of the ear specialist that the Duke was attending. It appeared that they had had a meeting there. Whether it was by prior arrangement was not known, but von Ribbentrop seemed very pleased with himself when he left.

'The sooner that man is out of the way the better,' muttered Sir Vernon. 'Thank Heavens that he is no longer on the throne.'

'I'll say amen to that,' said Tar who continued, 'my guess is that Ribbentrop was there to give him a morale boost and confirm that the Germans are not resiling from their deal.'

'I would agree with you Tar. I shall appraise the Prime Minister although he has now clearly lost focus.'

'I suppose he feels that the job is done?'

'Yes, he does, and on every count, well done. The Duke of Windsor's strongest supporters have been left with nothing to hang their hat on.'

'No, but they are still out there,' responded Tar.

'I know. At some point knowing what we know, he must be neutralised. My only hope is that whoever succeeds Baldwin as Prime Minister has the strength and determination to put the Duke out to grass where he cannot cause more trouble.'

'I can also report that Mrs Simpson has found a new diversion in Cannes. She is a beautiful bisexual prostitute.'

'Good God, is the woman insatiable?'

'It would seem so. Billy Brownlow has befriended the prostitute, who was tortured by Bernard O'Reilly. She is a friend of Mrs Simpson's new plaything. Apparently the girls are very gossipy amongst themselves. Brownlow believes that he will have an inside track on what Mrs Simpson is up to. She will need to take on a new driver to replace the Pascal boy. I doubt whether the Germans can infiltrate another sleeper agent.'

'O'Reilly is a dangerous man, Tar. We are going to have to deal with him one of these days.'

'I agree. Apart from being a total sadist he is still an ardent supporter of the Irish Nationalist cause. He certainly hates the British. I am instructing our people in Cannes, including Johnny Johnstone, that if he crosses their path and demonstrates hostility he must be neutralised. I am working up a plan with Maxwell Knight to discredit him with his German paymasters. Hopefully they will do our dirty work.'

'Keep me informed, won't you.'

Bernard O'Reilly had not travelled far when he left the Carlton Hotel in Cannes. He had the taxi take him to the Hotel Du Cap Eden Roc where he was a regular visitor and valued guest. He had not made a reservation, but he was sure that at this time of year they would be able to accommodate him. He was talking to one of the receptionists when the proprietor Andre Sella, who was the son of the hotel's founder, recognised him. 'My dear Mr O'Reilly. What a pleasure it is to welcome you.'

He turned to the receptionist and gave a simple instruction. 'Please be so kind as to arrange for Mr O'Reilly to be accommodated in one of the grand suites.'

'Yes Sir.'

'Thank you so much, Monsieur Sella. You are so kind.'

'It is always a pleasure to welcome a regular and valued guest, I can assure you.'

Later when he was settled into his suite and a maid had unpacked his bags, he decided to let von Ribbentrop know where he was now staying. He went to the concierge's desk and gave an anonymous telegraphic address in London. The message was simple. *"I have moved to the Eden Roc. Regards, Bernard."* The telegram would go directly to von Ribbentrop's office in the German Embassy.

Almost at the same time as O'Reilly's telegram was sent to London, Tar received a call from an old friend in the French Deuxieme Bureau. 'Tar, my good friend. It is a long time since you have been to Paris.'

'Yes, I know, but things have been rather busy of late. I shall try to get over in the early New Year.'

'Excellent. We can have dinner together. Now, I thought you would wish to know that the Irishman, Bernard O'Reilly, has moved from the Carlton to the Eden Roc on Cap d'Antibes. With so many prominent international guests there we have people on the inside, so we shall keep a watch on him.'

'Thank you, that is appreciated. He probably decided it was politic to leave Cannes. Apparently he tortured one of the working girls.'

'We heard about that, and also that his contact and low level agent, the man Didier Pascal, who was employed by Mrs Simpson, has disappeared.'

'I can help you there. The Germans, not the Abwehr, for whom O'Reilly is working, had orders from Himmler to pull Pascal in, sweat him for information then to kill him.'

'Thank you for that – I shall pass the information to the Chief of Police in Cannes, to the effect that they should waste no time on investigating his disappearance. Naturally I shall not reveal what you have told me.'

'Thank you Antoine, and I owe you a fine dinner. Au revoir.'

'And to you, my friend.'

Celia and Johnny were walking in the grounds of the villa. It was cold, and they were muffled up in coats, hats, scarves and gloves. 'Are you OK now Celia?' Johnny asked, looking at her with concern.

'Yes, actually I believe that I am. The fact that it was self defence is important to me. I am not sure that I could otherwise kill someone in cold blood. '

'It does make a difference. I expect Wallis will be looking for a replacement. She will want to be seeing her new friend in Cannes when we have left.'

'Yes, and probably continue her French lessons,' laughed Celia. She tucked her arm into Johnny's and shrugged up to him. As she turned to look at him she smiled. He tipped her chin and kissed her on the nose.

'Billy Brownlow has confirmed that the Irishman we saw in the Carlton Hotel bar has moved up the coast a short distance to the Eden Roc. I have ordered Billy to steer clear of the bastard. The trouble is that Billy is sweet on the girl that was tortured and he is out for revenge.'

'Well, what he did was vile,' said Celia.

'Yes, it was but personal feelings do not play a part in espionage. They are a danger both to the agent and his colleagues.'

'You wouldn't do that to a girl would you?'

'In this game you can never say never. It's one of the golden rules.'

Celia shivered. At that moment there did not seem to be

much glamour in this spy lark.

When Billy Brownlow left Lisette in her apartment, he felt like a coiled spring. The poor girl was terrified after her ordeal at the hands of O'Reilly and she was still in pain. He had tried to soothe, and for some time had simply sat next to her and held her. As he gently rocked her like a child in his arms, she confirmed that a doctor who looked after many of the working girls in Cannes had been to see her, and prescribed some ointment that was supposed to be soothing and lessen the pain. It did not appear to be making much difference.

He decided that he would go to Cap d'Antibes and scout around. He realised that he must be careful – O'Reilly was too much of a professional not to recognise him from the Carlton bar, and put two and two together. He walked to the nearest taxi rank and gave the driver his destination.

Arriving at the Eden Roc, he knew that the time of greatest risk would be when he entered the hotel. He was in luck. Two limousines had just pulled up at the entrance in front of his taxi. When the two groups of passengers who were all obviously one party entered the hotel, he was shielded from the direct view of anyone in the reception area. He walked through to a sitting area, took off his overcoat and placed it with his hat on the chair next to the one he had chosen to sit on.

The ever alert concierge sent a busboy over to ask if he could take Billy's hat and coat. Billy declined with a smile. He ordered a coffee and picked up a newspaper from the low table in front of him. He did not have to wait long before O'Reilly got out of the lift and approached the concierge. Billy could not hear what was said but noted that money changed hands.

When O'Reilly had left, Billy went to the concierge and asked for a taxi to take him to Nice. When the concierge had made the call he told Billy that it would be there in less than five minutes. Billy slipped a thick roll of notes discretely into the concierge's hand. 'I am a private detective working on a divorce case. If I call again will you let me have access to a guest's room? I would have a photographer with me. You would be well paid.'

The concierge looked down at the notes in his hand. Obviously satisfied, he looked Billy in the eye and without any change in his facial expression, gave an almost imperceptible nod. Just then the busboy came back into the hotel to report that the taxi had arrived.

Whilst it was not an ideal arrangement, Billy was confident that he had paid the concierge more than O'Reilly, and when the time was right would have the use of a pass key. It was a cover that he had used in the past. The concierges that Billy had dealt with over the years knew everything that was going on within the hotel, and could be relied upon to provide any service or thing that a pampered guest might wish for – at a price. Divorce amongst the rich and famous could be a messy affair and in the mind of a concierge, why should he not profit?

Wallis was restless. She had just had a long conversation with David who had given every indication yet again that the German element of their plans was secure. Wallis had asked whether the Germans were going to arrange to meet her and provide similar reassurance. David simply did not know. She decided to contact von Ribbentrop in London. As he had instructed, she left the coded message and now must wait to be contacted.

Bernard O'Reilly had received a coded telegram from von Ribbentrop prompting him to telephone. He had done so immediately, using the line to von Ribbentrop's suite at the Grosvenor House Hotel. No names were used. His orders were brief.

'The lady is concerned that all previously agreed arrangements are in place. Reassure her on my behalf. She will be warned to expect your call as an old friend inviting her to lunch at your hotel. Report back'

'Understood.'

Wallis waited for a call impatiently. When O'Reilly called the villa to speak to Wallis he exaggerated his normally minimal Irish accent. 'My name is Brendan O'Reilly and I met Wallis Simpson on the Aurora. I am staying at the Eden Roc Hotel for a few days and would love to see her. Is she there to speak to?'

Katherine covered the mouthpiece with her left hand and turning to Wallis, asked whether she wanted to speak to the charming Irish sounding gentleman who said they had met on the Aurora. The name Aurora was one of the code words agreed with von Ribbentrop. Wallis took the call and said just how delighted she was to hear from him.

'Of course I remember you,' she gushed, whilst smiling broadly at Katherine. She listened for a few moments then replied, 'That is just fine.I shall see you at your hotel at 12.30pm tomorrow.'

She finished the call. 'Oh Katherine, no offence meant, but I am really looking forward to my little outing.'

'You will love the Eden Roc – it is such a shame that it is not summer. It is a beautiful setting and exquisitely managed.'

Johnny and Celia joined them with Herman, and Wallis told them her news.

'Excellent, Wallis. It will do you good. Charles will drive you of course.'

'Oh Johnny darling, you are so kind. Now Celia my dear, you look so much better after your tummy upset.'

'Thank you, Wallis – I am feeling my old self again.'

Brendan O' Reilly knew nothing about the Swiss bank account that von Ribbentrop had set up, just as Celia had yet to tell Wallis and give her the papers. Wallis felt that she was out on a limb and would press von Ribbentrop's man very hard. She wanted answers, and by jingo she would get them.

# Chapter 15

Johnny had spoken to both Tar Robertson and Billy Brownlow. He now knew that Wallis was to meet a German agent who was the man he had approached in the bar of the Carlton Hotel. The shared assumption being that the plan was to give her the same reassurance that they believed von Ribbentrop had provided to the Duke. He briefed Charles, who would be remaining outside the hotel in the car.

He also briefed Billy who was to try and observe from within. Billy told him of the cover arranged with the concierge. He would go to the hotel in the morning and make arrangements well in advance of the time when Wallis was due to arrive. Billy was instructed that he was to observe only, and in no circumstances become directly involved whatever might transpire. He reluctantly accepted the order. He had a score to settle. Tar had contacted his friend Antoine in the Deuxieme Bureau and warned him of the planned meeting. He asked that the couple be discretely observed.

Wallis was at her elegant best when she entered the Eden Roc Hotel. As she crossed the reception area with her heels clicking on the marble floor, heads turned. Some recognised her, to others she just looked very familiar. Whichever, there was no doubting that this was a powerful woman. Quite apart from her elegant clothes, her jewellery flashed as it caught the light.

Bernard O'Reilly had warned the owner, Andre Sella, who considered Wallis important enough for him to extend a personal welcome. 'Madame, welcome to the Hotel du Cap Eden Roc. I am Andre Sella, the owner.'

'Thank you, Monsieur Sella, it is most elegant,' she drawled.

'Mr O'Reilly, who is a valued customer, has asked that you be shown to his suite.'

He nodded to a uniformed busboy, who hurried over and then led Wallis to the lift. The busboy was not relishing seeing Bernard again after the previous night's still painful activity, but at least he had been paid handsomely.

When she entered the suite Wallis could not quite suppress a gasp. The drawing room was magnificent, but it was the view that even on this winter's day was breathtaking. 'Oh my!' she cried out, as Bernard O'Reilly walked towards her with outstretched hand. 'Mr O'Reilly, you have a most beautiful view – I am forgetting my manners, I am Wallis Simpson, how do you do.'

'Mrs Simpson, I am enchanted to meet you,' he responded. 'Your pictures in the newspapers and magazines do not do you justice.'

'Why thank you, Mr O'Reilly – you are so kind. Shall we dispense with the formality? Do feel free to call me Wallis, and I shall call you Bernard.'

'Delighted, Wallis.' He smiled broadly. 'Now, I believe that a perfect Manhattan is your favourite.'

'That would be wonderful, Bernard.'

She appraised him with a practised eye as he skilfully mixed her cocktail. He did not disappoint her. Beautifully dressed, good looking and debonair, with definite charm. She also sensed an undercurrent of cruelty, or was it danger? Wallis considered him very attractive indeed.

He in turn studied her carefully as he brought her cocktail over. There was something about her that caught his interest. He was surprised that even he found himself drawn to her sexually. There was something in her looks and manner that was not truly feminine. He wondered what this luncheon might lead to. Considering that they had only just met, the atmosphere between them was already highly charged.

After they had sipped their drinks, Bernard went straight to the point. 'Von Ribbentrop has instructed me to give you his absolute assurance that the arrangements with regard to the future, in respect of the Duke of Windsor and yourself, are unchanged and endorsed at the highest level. He apologises that he could not give you the assurance personally, as he did to the Duke in Vienna, but he cannot be seen to travel to the South of France.'

'Thank you and I understand.'

'Now then, I have taken the liberty of ordering our luncheon to be served here away from prying eyes, if that is acceptable to you?' He raised an eyebrow.

'But of course, Bernard.'

After further consultation with Tar, Johnny informed Celia that the time was right to pass on the compromising papers from von Ribbentrop. After some discussion, they decided that Celia would go to see Wallis in her suite just before pre-dinner drinks with the Rogers. Celia would make an excuse to touch up her make up and do her best to get the requested photographs using the miniature camera hidden in her powder compact.

Johnny also wanted to leave for England earlier than planned, and drive back to London. He believed that with them all taking turns to drive, they could be at Calais comfortably in two days on the road. He had an important extra message that he wanted Celia to give to von Ribbentrop, hopefully to neutralise O'Reilly permanently.

At the Eden Roc, Wallis and Bernard were getting along famously. Wallis was subtly flirting, and more and more appeared to Bernard as vaguely masculine in an almost unsettling way. He was full of Irish charm. 'You know Wallis, I am not much of a ladies' man, but I sense something very special about you.'

'Really – do tell me just what,' she laughed in reply.

He reached across the oval table, at which they had enjoyed their light but delicious lunch of warm lobster with freshly made mayonnaise and salad. He took her hand in his and turned it over. Looked at it closely and realised that Wallis' hand was not much smaller than his. She looked him straight in the eye and said with a smile, 'Are you thinking what I am thinking Bernard?'

'And what might that be, I ask myself?'

Now they were both laughing as Wallis riposted, 'We are one of a kind, I believe. C'mon, let's see.'

She stood up from the table as did he, and they moved into an embrace. They did not kiss. He then led her into his bedroom and closed the door. Wallis undressed but kept on her brassiere and drawers, just as Bernard did not remove his undershorts. As they lay together Wallis pulled back a little, then leaning on her right elbow looked him frankly in the eye and said, 'I think that you may like men and women, but really you are interested in boys. Hah?'

'You are right, Wallis. And you?'

'My dear, I like anything attractive with a pulse, so not much different. Now, we are wasting time.' She reached down and wriggled out of her drawers as Bernard slipped off his shorts.

'I shall have to do something about this,' she chortled as she reached for him and he for her.

'Oh yes' he said as her mouth closed on him.

Billy had obtained a pass key from the taciturn concierge who had palmed another substantial roll of notes, and taken along a local agent who carried a camera bag. They were both armed.

When they reached Bernard's suite they drew their pistols, which were both Lugers. Billy quietly and carefully inserted the pass key, and heaved a silent sigh of relief that Bernard had not left his key in the lock. He turned the key gently and felt the tumblers move as he did so. With the faintest of clicks the door was unlocked. He opened it a crack and looked into the grand drawing room. There was nobody in it. Opening the door further, he stepped in signalling for his companion to stand guard.

He padded silently across the room. As he passed a closed door he heard what sounded like a woman's exclamation of pain. His anger roiled and he was about to burst in when he heard the woman's voice which had a distinctive American accent blurt out, 'Yes! Yes! Oh my God – do it again – again, now!' Another exclamation of pain was followed by the same request.

Billy had heard enough. Whatever Bernard O'Reilly was doing to Wallis, and however painful she was relishing it. Time to go he decided. Time to leave this sick place.

Early that evening, Celia knocked on the door to Wallis' suite.

In her hand she held the envelope sealed by von Ribbentrop.

'Wallis, Joachim asked me to give you this. He said that you must read it carefully because it is very important.'

Wallis did not tear open the envelope but went to her escritoire and picked up a paper knife, with which she carefully opened it. She appeared to study the inside of the envelope very thoroughly before pulling out the few sheets of paper it contained. She sat at her desk and then started to read.

'My Gawd! That's just marvellous! Your Bubbles has set me up a Swiss bank account with a substantial deposit in recognition of the services I have rendered. Here, look.'

She passed the papers to Celia, who feigned surprise and excitement at her friend's good fortune. Celia returned them, saying, 'You must think of somewhere very clever to hide them. Have a think about it while I freshen up my make-up.'

As Wallis held the papers in front of her, still staring at them in disbelief, Celia manoeuvred herself so that she would have a shot of Wallis in three quarter profile gazing at the papers in her hand. The bank statement of the deposit was the document on top and her name was in bold type. Wallis seemed mesmerised by the papers which she then shuffled. Celia took another shot of Wallis, this time with the boldly typed confirmation that the payment was for intelligence services rendered clear to see.

As Celia snapped her compact shut she said, 'Come along now Wallis. For now, put the papers in your make-up case. I suggest that you open a checking account where Herman and Katherine Rogers have theirs, and rent a deposit box. The papers will be safe there.'

'Good idea, Celia. I feel quite overwhelmed – I did not fully realise how lousy it is to be broke in a foreign land. David suggested that I open an account at that bank too.'

'Wallis, Joachim stressed that you must not tell David about these funds under any circumstances. He hopes that there will be more to follow.'

Wallis laughed happily as they left the suite.

Billy had visited Lisette after Wallis had left the Eden Roc. She was in much better spirits, and he was delighted when she told him that she was almost out of pain. As had now become a habit, they sat close to each other and Billy held her protectively in his arms.

He was becoming worried as the more time he spent with her, the stronger the attraction and his feelings for her. Inevitably he would be posted back to London. He earnestly hoped that that would not be for a long time. As he kissed the top of her head he thought again of what he would like to do to O'Reilly.

As dawn broke the following day, Celia and Johnny left the villa with Charles at the wheel. The bulk of their luggage was to be sent back to London as express freight. Once they were on the open road their spirits rose, as did a weak dawn sun. 'Wallis seems to have cheered up a tremendous amount,' commented Celia.

'Well, so she should. She has a stack of money in the bank, and the promise of more where that came from. She has a new sophisticated girl to play with in Cannes, as well as her maid. She has the odious and perverted Bernard O'Reilly in Cap d'Antibes, and heaven only knows what they got up to.

'She has the Duke panting after her in Austria, and reassurance from the Nazis of their intention to crown she and the Duke, King and Queen of a united Britain and Germany. I would call that pretty impressive, for a woman who many regard as a shameless adventuress – eh?'

'Put like that it is,' laughed Celia.

'On a serious note,' interrupted Charles, 'Billy Brownlow is smitten with the girl that O'Reilly tortured. He wants revenge.'

'I know,' replied Johnny, 'I have told him that O'Reilly is strictly off limits and will be dealt with another way. I made it a direct order which he will obey, however hard he finds that to stomach.'

They made very good time on the first day, and the great car seemed to eat up the miles nearly as fast as it drank petrol. The Route National was excellent. The only concern was the French rule of priorité à droit, by virtue of which any farmer with his tractor or cart could simply pull out in front of the speeding car.

'It's crazy!' cursed Celia, after a particularly hair-raising incident when she was driving.

'French perfect logic,' was Johnny's laconic reply.

They pressed on in the evening to Chagny in Burgundy, where they checked into the Maison Lameloise. Charles had changed out of his uniform shortly after they had left Cannes and they checked in as three friends.

'My old man is keen on this place, and it may cheer you up to know that the cuisine of Chagny attracted the likes of Phillip the Bold and John the Fearless – whoever they were,' chuckled Johnny.

The three laughed as they followed a porter and maid, who were struggling up the stairs with their luggage. 'They work them hard in France,' commented Charles, 'I lay you evens that we shall have these two serving us in the dining room tonight and for breakfast too.'

'Not at breakfast, Charles – we can stop on the road later on. For us it's a 5am start, with coffee by courtesy of the night porter.'

'You beast!' joked Celia.

After dinner and a quick cigar for the men they all retired to bed. Celia and Johnny snuggled up together in her room. They were both bone weary after the long day's drive. The next thing they knew was her travel alarm clock trilling on the bedside table. As she reached to turn it off Johnny laughed and grabbed her arm.

'Old army trick Celia. Only ever turn off an alarm clock when your feet are on the floor and you have thrown off the bedclothes. Come on sleepy head, we want to be on the road in half an hour. I shall tell the porter to collect your bags in 20 minutes. Chop chop!'

'You are a brute!' she laughed, as she pushed him out of the door.

'Bubbles, I am back. When would you like to see me?'

'Celia, my dear. I am supposed to be going to Germany tomorrow. Is there any possibility of this evening?'

'Yes, I could, but it would be a brief visit because my parents are in their London house, and I am to have dinner with them. I could be with you in half an hour?'

'That's fine. The usual place then.'

'Jolly good, see you then.'

'Johnny, did the boffins get the copies of the photos?' Celia enquired.

'They have taken out the film that you used, and then taken a couple of bodged pictures which will be indecipherable. You must tell von Ribbentrop that you doubt whether the pictures will be any good because Wallis was so excited that she would not keep still.'

'Very well. Everything else is as agreed?'

'Absolutely. Let me know how it goes.'

'Of course I shall. Dinner will not be a late one so do come here for a nightcap at, say 11.30pm. Perhaps you could stay over.'

'Love to, darling.'

Celia had reported to von Ribbentrop as briefed by Johnny, and handed over the miniature camera. Von Ribbentrop was delighted to hear about the reaction when Wallis received the papers. He assured Celia that the lack of the pictures would not be a problem immediately Wallis transferred funds to Cannes. Celia then told him another piece of news that whipped him into an incandescent fury. He ranted in German then appeared to regain control. 'You are telling me that Bernard O'Reilly, who was working on my instructions, is actually working for Heinrich Himmler's gang? And he murdered Didier Pascal and had the body disposed of?'

'That is what I understood from Wallis. She was initially upset about it. It seems that O'Reilly has calmed her down. She is having some sort of sado masochistic affair with him and, well, not to put too fine a point on it, I think that she rather enjoys all the cloak and dagger stuff. O'Reilly had previously tortured a French girl that Didier had become sweet on as well so he had corroboration of what Wallis had told Didier after one of their so called "French Lessons".'

'Celia – you must go now. I have some calls to make.'

Celia left, her mission accomplished.

Later in the evening when Celia was curled up at Johnny's feet with her head resting on his knee, she reported her conversation with von Ribbentrop in full. Johnny was gently stroking her thick blonde hair.

He thought to himself that whilst this time she would have no actual blood on her hands, she had just ensured the death of her second victim. Bernard O'Reilly was as good as dead.

# Chapter 16

As soon as Celia had left his suite, von Ribbentrop, who was still fuming, picked up the telephone and asked for a number in Cannes which he read from his small pocket book. 'Heinz. I am glad that I caught you. You and Willi are still keeping tabs on the Simpson woman at the villa in Cannes?'

'We are, as ordered.'

After a pause von Ribbentrop continued, 'Good, because we have a local problem that I wish you to deal with. Our Irish friend has turned bad and killed one of our own local assets. It was possibly sexually motivated but also, importantly, he is working for others. He is to be eliminated. Make it public and very unpleasant. That is an order. You must ensure that you are not seen to be implicated.'

'The gentleman has homosexual tendencies. That will make it easier. There will be no connection with us I can assure you.'

'Good, keep me advised. I go to Germany tomorrow but return in two days, and I expect the matter to be resolved before then.'

He put the telephone down. His mood was improved by the fact that Heinz and Willi were themselves sadistic killers, and Mr O'Reilly could be guaranteed a most unpleasant death. He smiled as he poured himself a glass of champagne. Things were looking good for him, and tomorrow evening he would be dining with the Führer. He was sure that his star was in the ascendant.

Heinz, like Bernard O'Reilly, looked anything but a killer. He could have passed as an academic, not only with his wild grey hair but in his style of dress which was best described as careless. His clothes were clearly of the best quality but they hung awkwardly from his gangling frame. He wore spectacles that he was constantly pushing up his prominent nose. He might have been gangling but he was by no means weak. His hands were huge. He was utterly fearless.

Willi, with whom he usually worked, was a much younger and clearly very fit, blonde-haired young man with the grace and elegance of an athlete at his peak. In contrast he was well dressed in an understated way. They made a strange couple.

Until they had received their last order from von Ribbentrop they had regarded Bernard as a competent and effective colleague. They were not close friends but they showed respect for each other. They decided that whilst killing Bernard in his suite at the Eden Roc might be high profile, it was too risky. They were sure that the French intelligence service would have a presence there. They needed to lure Bernard away from his luxurious bolt hole. Heinz, who was himself homosexual, had divined Bernard's proclivity for younger men and boys very quickly after they had met. He devised a simple plan.

Bernard was passing through the reception area of the hotel when his eye caught a strikingly good-looking young man sitting by the window. He judged him to be in his very early twenties. He decided to delay his walk and went over to the young man. 'Good afternoon,' he smiled broadly. The young man looked at him from under impossibly long eyelashes and returned the smile.

'I am Bernard O'Reilly and I am a resident here – and you are?'

'I am Jacques and I live in Cannes. I am waiting to return there now. A friend is due to pick me up.'

'That is a pity – I would have liked to get better acquainted.'

'That is not a problem if you wish to visit me.'

'Splendid. When would suit you?'

'I will give you my address. Would you like to come to me later today – perhaps at 6 o'clock?'

'Yes, that would be most agreeable.' replied Bernard, as he took the piece of paper on which Jacques had written his address.

'You do understand, Bernard, that I expect you to be generous.'

'Of course,' replied Bernard with a smile, thinking that it was excellent that Jacques was a prostitute and would do as Bernard wanted. As if on cue a slightly older man came into the hotel and waved to Jacques, who immediately stood up and shook Bernard's hand. 'Until later then,' he said, holding Bernard's hand for a little longer than strictly necessary. Bernard abandoned his plans for a walk and turned back towards the lift.

The world weary concierge had watched the little scene unfold with little surprise. As was the custom the busboy had given him 10 percent of the money that Bernard had paid. That he had entertained the notorious and rather plain American woman who had brought down the British King did not really surprise him. The housekeeper had confided in him that there was clear evidence of sexual activity on the sheets and some blood after the American woman had left.

Mr O'Reilly might have some strange tastes, but then, so did many of the guests in this most exclusive of hotels. Whilst he thought to himself that it was really none of his business, he filed away the information as always.

Bernard telephoned the concierge and asked for a taxi to Cannes. The concierge asked for the destination address which he noted down in the ledger that he meticulously kept. Like everybody else whom he favoured, the taxi he called would owe him a commission and he had to keep a record.

When Bernard arrived at the address in Cannes, he noted that the villa was in a respectable middle class area. The garden was neat but a little unkempt.

He paid the taxi and walked up the pathway to the front door. As he approached it, the door opened. Jacques did not show himself. Bernard entered a square hallway with a mirrored mahogany hat and coat stand on the right hand wall. Jacques was wearing revealing figure-hugging ballet tights and a sleeveless singlet. He was barefoot.

Not a word was spoken as he led the way to a door on the far side of the hallway. He opened the door and gestured for Bernard to enter ahead of him. As Bernard stepped into the dimly-lit room, he noted with interest that there was a wooden frame from which ropes hung. His interest was pricked by this, and he started to turn to speak to Jacques.

That was when Willi, who was behind the door, delivered a crushing blow to his head with a sand-filled sap. Bernard collapsed in a heap without a sound. Jacques closed the door. His work was done for now. Heinz and Willi were just starting theirs.

Bernard regained consciousness in great pain, and would have cried out except for the foul-tasting gag in his mouth. He now realised the significance of the frame and the ropes. He was naked, and suspended by his ankles and wrists about four feet above the ground. There was another rope around his neck, also attached to the frame. He could not see but he could feel a ligature tied tightly around his private parts.

He was not frightened yet. He had indulged in these games before, and assumed that Jacques and a friend were going to give him a hard time. 'Just wait until it's my turn,' he thought.

It was then that Heinz appeared. 'Bernard, you may wonder why I am here. We are going to kill you slowly and painfully so the gag has to stay. I can see from the look in your eyes that you wish to speak. You will not. I shall be carrying out orders. Young Jacques will be paying you back just a little for what you did to his good friend Lisette. As they say, Bernard, "What goes round comes round" – OK Jacques, he is all yours. Goodbye Bernard.'

Bernard heard the door open and twisting his head would have screamed if he could.

Billy was on the telephone to Johnny. 'They found Bernard O'Reilly. He was in a surburban house in Cannes. He was naked and trussed up. The police surgeon cannot tell whether he died of shock, asphyxiation or a mixture of both. Someone had used a blow torch on him very selectively. Strange, but the burns were almost a mirror of those inflicted on Lisette except for his backside.'

'Nasty way to go, but it sounds as though the Germans did a thorough job.'

'Yes, they did. The owners of the house have gone away for Christmas, visiting family in the north. The French in the Deuxieme Bureau have apparently told the local police enough that they are not going to actively look for the perpetrators. So far as the press are concerned, O'Reilly died as the result of an exotic and perverted sex game.'

'Thanks Billy – well, good riddance .The man was an animal. You must be happier now?'

'Yes I am. I shall only tell Lisette that he is dead. I shall spare her the details.'

'Well Celia, Wallis has lost her latest playmate. Mr O'Reilly has been found dead.'

'Oh, knowing her she will probably find another pretty quickly although possibly not as versatile.'

Johnny was a little shocked at Celia's reaction, given that she must be aware of her part in the man's death and the lie that she had told. 'Well Johnny, where are you taking me to dinner, and after that I rather fancy a bit of dancing.'

Wallis was shocked when Herman Rogers read the short piece in the local newspaper:

*Wealthy Irish businessman Bernard O'Reilly, who was staying at the Hotel du Cap Eden Roc, was found dead at a house in Cannes. Police are not treating his death as suspicious. The owner of the hotel told our reporter, "Mr O'Reilly was a regular and valued guest in our hotel. My staff and I are deeply shocked. He was a true gentleman".*

'Is that the fella that you went to see, Wallis?'

'It must be. How awful. I feel really upset. I think I shall go and lie down. Katherine, would you be a dear and ask that Laurenne be sent to me?'

Wallis left the room visibly shaken. She had had no concept of the chain of events her affair with the then Prince of Wales would trigger when it started. Neither did she comprehend then, nor ever, the impact would it have on so many lives.

# Chapter 17

Johnny was reporting to Tar and Sir Vernon on his latest visits to see the Duke of Windsor in Austria, and then accompanied by Celia, Mrs Simpson in Cannes. Celia was with him, and Billy Brownlow also.

'I'm afraid that it was all rather depressing. The Duke has now arranged for Fruity Metcalfe to join him to dance attendance, but the poor chap will get little thanks for his efforts. The Rothschilds are at the end of their tether with him. He seems to blame them for the death of his dog Slipper, even though the vet carried out a post-mortem and confirmed that the dog simply died of natural causes.

'He trails after Kitty Rothschild like a lost child. The poor woman cannot have a moment's peace except when he is on the telephone, out of the castle or asleep. He is constantly moaning about being poverty-stricken, and yet he and they know damn well that he is a wealthy man.

'He hates that his income is derived from his brother, the King, rather than the Civil List voted by Parliament. He will not accept that Parliament would not vote for him to receive a penny of public funds. The payment through the King is a sleight of hand for his benefit. He overlooks that his brother has to purchase the Sandringham and Balmoral estates from him – that will be a tidy sum in itself, and he has his accumulated Duchy of Cornwall income.

'He is obsessed with Wallis being granted the title "Her Royal Highness", even though Monckton spelt out that the grant of such a title is entirely in the hands of the King. He would not be able to conceive that many people believe that he should be known simply as Mr Windsor, having given up his

Royal responsibilities. The only time that he is reasonable is the half hour before he speaks to Wallis.'

'Well Johnny – it sounds pretty damned depressing. Do you think that in reality he has no personal emotional resources to draw on?' asked Sir Vernon.

'I'm sure of it. So long as he is getting his way and doing what he wants when he wants, all is well. Otherwise he is like a petulant bored child.'

Billy Brownlow reported a pretty similar situation in Cannes, where the Rogers were being driven to distraction. Lisette was friendly with both Leonie and Laurenne who shared their gossip with her. In turn, Lisette passed it on to Billy. Wallis amused herself with Leonie in Cannes and, occasionally, Laurenne in the villa. She was still garrulous after sex, and Laurenne additionally picked up the below stairs talk.

The new driver that Leonie had found for her was good-looking enough, and Wallis set about seducing him. Unfortunately he was a disappointing lover and most afternoons she was actually having French lessons from him.

As the weeks wore on, she complained that friends like Celia were too busy to visit her. She considered that it was her right to have them keep her company. Herman and Katherine Rogers were at their wits end. When Wallis had stayed with them in China, at the time of her separation from her first husband, a part of her attraction was her dynamic personality. Now, she was petulant and always finding fault. She made it clear that she expected to be treated with a level of respect normally accorded to royalty.

She had decided to resume her maiden name, Wallis Warfield. In part, this was to signify the absolute end of her marriage and relationship with Ernest Simpson, and in part she sought a degree of anonymity. Her feelings for Ernest were expressed in her letters to him that belied the finality she professed to want. Anonymity was a naive wish. Wallis was notorious, and had featured in the world's press for so long that she was recognised wherever she went.

Wallis was genuinely excited when she telephoned the Duke. 'My darling, our exiled separation is ending. I have heard from my solicitor, Mr Goddard, that the Decree Absolute should be granted next week, and then we can be together.'

'Wallis – that is truly excellent news!' responded the Duke enthusiastically, with a tear in his eye. 'When can we meet?'

'I think the 4$^{th}$ May. We are invited to stay at the Chateau de Cande in Mont. It is owned by a dear man, the very rich industrialist, Charles Bedaux. He has also said that he would be delighted if we were to be married there. Charles has invited me to go and stay there now, and I am sorely tempted.'

'That sounds a splendid idea. Fruity has agreed to stay with me indefinitely, so he will be in our party.'

'I am sure that that will be no problem,' responded Wallis rather coldly – she did not like Fruity Metcalfe. She was jealous of anyone who was close to the Duke, and especially long-standing friends. She found their closeness unsettling.

'Wallis, I have never heard of this Charles Bedaux. Tell me about him.'

'Well, he is a larger-than-life character, David. You will like him and his American wife, Fern. I hardly know where to start,' said Wallis with a little laugh.

'Well, anyhow, here goes. He was born in Paris where he admits to living by his wits. When his mentor was killed, he left Paris, and I think that he may have been in the army, the French Foreign Legion, or some such. Then he moved to America. He developed some sort of scientifically-based business management system, and now has a huge consulting business all over the States, Europe, Africa and the Orient. He can tell you all that.

'He is fabulously rich, and has now settled back in France in the Loire area – you know, where all the fabulous Chateaux are. They have modernised their chateau from top to bottom, and there is even a proper golf course in the grounds.'

'It sounds excellent. Is he a political animal?'

'Oh yes. He was fascinated when I told him of my friendship in China with Count Cianno, who is Mussolini's son-in-law and Italy's Foreign Minister now. He is very impressed with Hitler and the Nazi party, and says that they are running Germany just as he would advise.'

'Well darling, he sounds like an interesting cove and I shall look forward to meeting him. He'll like Fruity too – he's a great admirer of fascism.'

'We had better start planning the wedding sooner rather

than later, David.'

'Yes, I shall have to get busy. I very much doubt that Bertie will come, and I am damn sure that Elizabeth will not. I expect that brothers Henry and George will be there, as will Dicky Mountbatten – Perry Brownlow can help me with my side of the organising, as can Fruity.

'David, do you think that von Ribbentrop will come? Perhaps even the Führer himself – he was guest of honour at the Mosleys' wedding earlier in the year, wasn't he?'

'I doubt whether Hitler will venture into France, Wallis, and the same may apply to the other senior types in their government. The Mosley wedding was held in the house of Dr Goebbels as I recall.'

'Well, we can but ask.'

'Of course, my darling. We must both put together lists and then compare notes.'

At dinner that evening, Wallis told the Rogers of the plan to have the wedding in the Loire.

'I have not been there but Charles tells me that it is like a fairy tale castle. You will be coming won't you?'

'Of course Wallis – we would not miss it for the world.'

'I am going to get out of you good people's hair .You must be sick and tired of me. I shall leave next week. I shall go by train to Paris and then to Tours. My baggage can be sent by freight. My driver can bring the car – it is a tedious journey I understand, and then he can come back by train.'

'We shall certainly miss you Wallis,' responded Katherine Rogers, perhaps a little too enthusiastically she realised, but Wallis clearly did not notice.

'Herman, dear. I shall need to draw a substantial amount of cash before I go. Will you introduce me to your bank manager in Cannes so that I can open the account we talked about, and then wire some funds into it from Switzerland?'

Without waiting for an answer she continued, 'I shall need him to set up an arrangement with a bank that is local to the Chateau de Cande. I have a few papers that I want to keep safe so a safe deposit box is also required.'

'No problem, Wallis. I shall call him in the morning and arrange for us to go in immediately and set it all up.'

Katherine joined in the conversation. 'When is David

going to join you?'

'Just as soon as my divorce is made absolute and that sure can't be soon enough. I know it's probably ridiculous but I even suspected David of having a fling with Kitty de Rothschild!'

'Oh, Wallis dear, that is absurd. He is besotted with you, and she is very happily married.'

'I know that, but such a long separation has made me paranoid. She is very attractive and vivacious.'

'There is no question of such an affair,' responded Katherine.

She and Herman were no fools, and were very well acquainted with Wallis' drives and urges from when she lived with them in China. They were not deceived by the French lessons, and Katherine was under no illusions that the pretty little maid Laurenne was the object of Wallis' attentions. She decided not to point out to Wallis the utter hypocrisy of her voicing concerns about Kitty de Rothschild. She felt a little disloyal as she realised just how relieved she was that her dear friend Wallis was soon to be out of their home.

Celia was on the telephone to Johnny. 'I have received an invitation to David and Wallis' wedding. At least it's to be in the Loire and not all the way down to the Cote d'Azure.'

'So have I. Are you planning to go?'

'Oh yes I think so – and you?'

'Yes, and I think that in any event we both must from an intelligence point of view. I shall check with Tar but I am sure that he will want us there. We can motor down, which will be fun anyhow – make a bit of a holiday .What do you say?'

'Sounds a splendid idea. Now, shall I pick you up this evening on the way to Freddy's dinner party?'

'Yes and then you could stay over afterwards.'

'Righto, that would be lovely. By the way, if we drive to the wedding do we have to take Charles? It would be lovely to be alone for once.'

'Unless Tar wants him there I see no problem. It should be rather a jolly drive.'

Tar had asked Johnny to meet him at Sir Vernon Kell's office.

'Sir Vernon, with your permission, may I brief Johnny on

the activities of Charles Bedaux?'

'By all means Tar, you press on.'

'Bedaux was born in Paris. As a young man he was poor and lived by his wits. He became the right-hand man of a well-known pimp in the Pigalle area. When the pimp was killed in an underworld dispute, Bedaux wisely upped sticks. He claims that he then joined the Foreign Legion. There is some doubt about his serving in the Legion but it was a popular haven for men who wished to disappear. By the time that he left the Legion – he claims to have been a corporal – he went to America.

'Once in America, he found work in New York as what was known as a 'sand hog', digging the East River subway tunnel. Tough and dangerous work. During this time he formulated his ideas for speeding up processes in manufacturing and construction, cutting out wasted motion and generally improving efficiency. He pooled his savings and published a booklet setting out his concept. It caught on, and he became very wealthy extremely quickly.

'His concept was successfully adopted by many of America's largest corporations, and he became on intimate terms with the great and the good of American industry. He has supplied his time and motion applications to, for instance, IG, ITT, Standard Oil, General Motors, Ford and others. His concept is regarded as brutal from the workers' perspective and there have been many strikes.

'Where things become interesting to us is that he has reportedly been working in Paris with Nikolaus Bensmann, who is an avowed Nazi and that party's contact with Torkild Rieber's Texas Corporation. It is no coincidence in our view that a number of major American corporations have strong European subsidiaries, particularly in Germany. The unofficial nickname that these people have adopted is "The Fraternity". We have picked up a rumour that Bedaux has volunteered to bring the Duke of Windsor and, shortly his wife, into the circle of The Fraternity.'

'Sorry to interrupt, Tar, but how did he establish contact with the Duke of Windsor?' asked Johnny.

'He did not.' Tar smiled at Johnny's puzzled expression. 'He married a "Daughter of the American Revolution", Fern Lombard. That put him on the New York Social Register, and through Fern, contact was established with Wallis Simpson.'

'And you say his contacts generally in the USA are very powerful?'

'Oh yes, most certainly. His office is in the Chrysler Building. He had it designed to resemble a medieval monastery refectory. That is his New York base and he is often seen with the likes of Du Pont and Rockefeller in the Chrysler's Clouds Room at lunchtime.'

'So Wallis has swallowed the bait for the pair of them?'

'She most certainly has. And to think that the old saying was, *'beware Greeks bearing gifts',* laughed Sir Vernon.

Tar continued, 'On a serious note, this is a very delicate situation. Johnny, you and Celia are to be there in your private capacities as friends of the happy couple. What you observe will be of great value I am sure. It will be of particular note if Charles Bedaux offers any help, by way of facilitating a trip by the Duke and Duchess to Germany.'

'That's no problem Tar. Who else need we look out for?'

'Metcalfe, or Fruity, appears to be a pretty harmless sort. However he has strong Nazi sympathies. You know him Johnny?'

'Yes I do, and so does Celia, through his wife's family initially.'

'That's right,' interjected Celia, 'her father Lord Curzon is rather unworldly to say the least. You have heard the story of his getting on to a London bus and giving the conductor his home address.'

Tar continued, 'We have looked Metcalfe over closely. He has flirted with Mosley's blackshirts and was pictured in uniform at a fascist do in a London hotel a couple of years ago. I cannot recall the details but he will just go along with what the Duke wants.

'Lord Louis Mountbatten described him as – "The nicest fellow we have. Poor, honest, a typical Indian cavalryman." I think that is a misguided view. The Rogers you know and likewise the Rothschilds. Cecil Beaton will be there, as will Walter Monckton.'

Sir Vernon leant forward. 'Johnny my boy, the former monarch is going into a viper's nest. He will be upset by the King's dictat that neither of the Royal Princes, nor Lord Louis Mountbatten may attend. He will relish flattery and attention and we are satisfied that this Charles Bedaux is a master in that game.'

'I understand, Sir Vernon. I shall use my art business as an excuse to court Monsieur Bedaux. With luck he will have an ego which I can massage.'

The Duke of Kent, Prince George, was fuming.

'Bertie, for Heavens sake, why should I not attend David's wedding. I can understand that neither you nor Elizabeth would consider it proper so close to the Coronation, but I suffer no such constraint.'

'B b bb ut yo you do. I I I I f f forbid it. He h h has only ar arr arranged i it fo for P P P Papa's b b birthday!'

'That may be so, and I agree that it is insensitive, but I still do not see why I should not attend. It is after all a private affair.'

'M m m my f f f final w w w word is NO!' shouted the King, who had flushed alarmingly, then collapsed into the chair from which he had risen when the disagreement had flared. His whole frame was wracked with coughing.

The Queen, who had been in an adjoining anteroom and listening to the argument, burst into the room, and the two tall double doors crashed back as she dashed to her husband. She poured a glass of water which he took from her with shaking hands. As he slumped back in his chair when the coughing fit subsided, the diminutive Queen drew herself to her full height and fixed George with a ferocious stare. 'I will only say this once, George. Do not ever again contradict or argue with your brother over matters which fall to him to decide as monarch. Please convey that message to Henry also.'

Much chastened, the Duke of Kent left the room in no doubt as to who held the power within the Royal Family now. 'She might be small and normally rather sweet looking,' he thought, 'but by God she is tough, through and through!'

# Chapter 18

Celia and Johnny were in a carefree mood as they left Paris behind them, and motored south. The weather was fine and sunny and the Route National comparatively quiet. Celia was at the wheel of the Hispano-Suiza that was surging along. She was relishing its sheer power as she swung out and overtook a heavily laden lorry.

'I say, old girl, we are not in a race you know.'

'Don't be a spoilsport. Johnny darling – I am going no faster than you were earlier. Anyway, your beautiful car likes it.'

'Utter tosh my dear, utter tosh.'

'Do you think that someone is following us?' she asked after looking in the mirrors again.

'I cannot think who would want to,' replied Johnny, as he twisted round in his seat and peered out of the rear window. The only vehicle now in sight behind them was a black saloon. It was quite a way back – Johnny could not see what make of car it was.

He felt his Webley Bulldog pistol in his jacket pocket almost as a reflex. It would be no use unless he were to be extremely close to an attacker. That in itself would increase the risk significantly, depending on how many were in the following car if they intended harm.

'Just keep going as you are, Celia.'

Johnny kept looking back and noted that the following car seemed to be keeping station. 'Slow down, Celia – down to a steady 40 miles per hour. They are definitely following – they have slowed down as well. They might be friendly French but I doubt it. We'd better flush them out.'

Johnny was dry-mouthed and much less confident than he sounded. At that moment he wished it were Charles at the wheel and not the untried Celia.

'Right, Celia. At the next village stop right in the middle when I tell you. Hopefully there will be some people around. You can never tell – some of the places we have been through today looked totally deserted.'

'I'll do that – then what?'

'It depends on what they do. If they are innocent they will probably drive straight past us. If not, they may stop well back from us and wait for us to move on. Of course, they may drive past us in any event, assuming that we shall be sticking to this road and that they can pick up our tail further on. In any event, we shall turn off this road after we leave the village. I'll have a look at the map later.'

Celia slowed down as they approached a village of grey houses, occasional small shops and a petrol station flanking the road. There seemed to be nobody around as they burbled slowly along.

'This will have to do, Celia – just pull over by the baker's shop. Stay in the car, open your window and keep the engine running. Get your Beretta out of your bag and check that it is loaded – remember to take the safety catch off. Keep it out of sight. If you are threatened with a weapon, do not hesitate. Shoot first.'

'Righto, darling,' she replied brightly, and without the slightest hint of nervousness or concern.

Johnny was a little nonplussed by Celia's matter-of-fact reaction to what might be a deadly encounter. He knew from personal experience that she was a fearless rider when hunting, but surely she must realise that this was so much more dangerous. Perhaps killing that creature in Cannes had had more effect than she had shown.

Johnny stood just outside of the car with the door wide open. His revolver was in his right hand and obscured by the door. The black Citroën Traction Avant saloon slowed as it came through the village, and Johnny could see that there was a driver and two passengers. He guessed that if there were to be an attack the driver would stay in the car with the engine running.

It looked as though the Citroën was going to simply pass through the village, but as it drew close to Johnny's car it screeched to a stop. The two passengers leapt out. The one who had been in the front seat moved straight towards Celia. The other moved towards the back of the Hispano-Suiza. Johnny turned so that he would be facing the man as he came round the back of the car. The door shielded Johnny to chest height. Johnny ignored what might be happening with the other man – he was Celia's responsibility.

As the man came face to face with Johnny he started to withdraw his right hand from the left side of his jacket. Johnny caught a glimpse of grey metal and raised his revolver. As he squeezed the trigger he heard the crack of Celia's small calibre pistol, which was drowned by the roar of his own much more powerful weapon. His shot took the man in the chest and the large calibre bullet flung him backwards violently. A Luger pistol flew out of his hand as his arms flailed. Johnny ran to the man with his pistol at the ready. He was dead. His eyes stared blankly.

The black front wheel drive Citroën's tyres scrabbled to get a grip as its driver frantically left the scene. Johnny ran around the car and saw Celia standing over a man doubled up on the ground clutching his stomach. A Luger 9 milimetre pistol was on the road about three yards away. The man was groaning.

Johnny went up to him, and none too gently pushed his shoulder with his foot, rolling the groaning man onto his back where he stared at Johnny and his wicked looking revolver with terror in his eyes. 'Who are you and who do you work for?' asked Johnny, in a tone of voice that Celia had never heard. The man just shook his head and groaned.

Johnny stepped back half a pace and then kicked the man hard just above his hands. There was a scream. Johnny asked again. Still no answer. 'If you will not tell me, I am sure that the Deuxieme Bureau will sweat it out of you.'

At the mention of the French Secret Service, the man looked even more terrified, as well he might. They were not noted for their gentle handling of suspects, and rumour had it that many of their interrogators had gained their expertise in North Africa. A small crowd was now gathering.

In his impeccable French, and masking his nervous reaction to the encounter, Johnny asked who had a telephone that he could use. Knowing the rural French way of thinking, he added that he would pay handsomely.

A middle aged man in dirty overalls who was trying to wipe black grease off his hands with a rag said that he had a telephone, and gestured for Johnny to follow him to the garage on the other side of the street.

'Celia, do not let anyone touch anything and keep a close watch on this bastard.'

The telephone was in the dusty and cluttered office on a paper-littered desk. Every piece of paper seemed to have grease marks and stains. The telephone itself looked no better. Johnny gingerly picked it up, and after using the pre-arranged code was put through to his nominated contact in the Deuxieme Bureau in Paris.

He reported that there had been a shooting with one surviving but wounded assailant who would not speak. He confirmed where they were, and was told that the local police would be notified immediately. He was instructed that they should stay where they were and await the arrival of the local police.

Johnny suggested that an ambulance should be sent, and was told that everything would be in hand. He paid the garage owner the exhorbitant amount requested, and returned to the car. Celia confirmed that she was fine, and still covered the groaning man with her small pistol. Johnny went to the dead man and went through his jacket pockets. There was nothing that identified him. Johnny was in no way squeamish, but even he was shocked when he rolled the corpse over to search the trouser pockets. The exit wound created by the soft-nosed, large calibre bullet was huge.

The effort paid off. In the right hip pocket Johnny found a folded piece of paper. On it was the name and address of the hotel in Monts near the Chateau de Cande, where he and Celia were to stay. On an impulse, Johnny held it up to the light. The paper had a German water mark.

As he walked towards the other attacker, three police cars screeched to a halt – there were now 10 police officers at the scene. The officer in charge, resplendent in knee-high polished boots, cord jodphurs, a bemedalled tunic and and a silver braided kepi, went straight to Johnny.

He explained that the orders from Paris were that Johnny and his passenger should leave immediately and continue their journey. The officer asked for a description of the assailant's car. When Johnny asked whether or not formal statements would be required he was told that they would not, and the matter was closed. The invitation to leave immediately was more of an order than a suggestion. The small crowd of onlookers had been dispersed by the police, and as Johnny accelerated away he saw an ambulance arriving.

'Rum do Johnny?'

'Yes. Who in Germany would want to kill us and to what end. I just cannot work it out at the moment. The only thing that crosses my mind is that, according to what Billy Brownlow picked up from Lisette's friend, the gay prostitute, O'Reilly was killed with the assistance of German intelligence agents.

'We know that there is a turf war between the Abwehr of Canaris and the SD of Himmler, so perhaps doing away with us was an SD plan to scupper von Ribbentrop's plans. Remember Celia, you have played a part in setting up the German arrangements with David and Wallis. The SD must have known that we were travelling together.'

'Perhaps I know too much in someone's opinion,' replied Celia.

'The French will be very tough with the fellow that you shot – and well done my dear, by the way – but they were just foot soldiers, and not very good ones at that. The likelihood is that they would not have a clue where their orders originated.'

'Thank you for the compliment. You make it sound as though I have just won a challenging tennis match. Actually, I did not feel squeamish at all until you kicked him. Not for long though, when I remembered that he was out to kill me.'

'Do you want to stop for a drink or anything?'

'No, let's press on and get to this auberge that you rave about. Are you still going to turn off this road?'

'No, we turn off anyway in about 20 kilometres and head for Barbizon. I think that the Citroën driver will be a long way away now.'

Tar Robertson was reporting to Sir Vernon Kell.

'Sir Vernon, I thought that I should advise you immediately. Our French friends advise that Johnny and Celia have survived an attack south of Paris. They killed one gunman and seriously wounded another. The assailants' driver, who fled the scene, has been stopped and is also in custody. He is co-operating, after what was delicately described as some intense persuasion.

'They were a German team receiving orders from the Paris Embassy. It is believed their orders were given by a German international secret service officer, which means Himmler's lot. The dead assailant had details of the hotel where Johnny and Celia intended to stay in Monts.'

'This is a rum do, Tar. Surely the Germans view Celia as an asset, or is this another example of their extraordinary internal rivalries?'

'I would hazard a guess that it is precisely that. The fact remains that Celia is a target. I think that they will be safer in the Chateau, and I suggest that without divulging why, you put it to Monckton that he has a word with the Duke. I would have suggested Perry Brownlow, but he is in a funk about Royal disapproval, and is now having nothing to do with the wedding or the Windsor faction.'

'Very well, I shall speak to Walter Monckton immediately. Keep me posted. Billy Brownlow is already in Monts, I believe. Send some extra cover and make sure that the French do likewise. I do not like the smell of this at all.'

'Very well, Sir Vernon.'

As they pulled into the courtyard of the Auberge des Templiers at Les Bezards, Celia commented, 'Johnny darling, it looks so comfortable with the ivy-clad walls and thatched roof. It's the very opposite to a dramatic Loire chateau.'

'That's why we are here. There are plenty of classic chateaux around here, but nowhere as comfortable, actually comforting, as this old inn, surrounded by the vineyards of Sancerre and Pouilly.'

'It's far too big to be an inn.'

'Well, to be precise, it was a post house.'

When he turned off the engine, all that could be heard was the ticking of the cooling metal and some birdsong. They sat in silent companionship. This was the first opportunity to contemplate the events earlier in the afternoon and what might have been.

Down the steps from the large entrance doorway came a jolly-looking, rotund man with a broad smile. Behind him there were two young men in dark blue, ankle-length, bibbed aprons with white shirts and black ties. Johnny stepped out of the car, and the Frenchman rushed forward with arms outstretched. 'Johnny, Milord!' he cried, as he embraced Johnny in a bear hug and kissed him noisily on both cheeks.

'Phillippe, my dear old friend!' replied Johnny, 'may I present my dear friend, Lady Celia Ffrench-Hardy.'

Phillippe released Johnny and scuttled to Celia. Taking her hand, he bowed low over it and she felt his luxuriant moustache brush the back. 'Enchanté!' he cried, 'And so beautiful! You are a lucky man, Johnny, and God looks after you.'

Johnny caught Celia's eye and, with a smile twitching the corners of his mouth, said reflectively, 'Amen to that.'

He came to attention and saluted.

# Chapter 19

The view from the dormer windows, snug below the thatched roof of the old auberge, was over the large park-like but informal garden. Gravel paths wound amongst majestic trees, and in the distance a lake shimmered silver. Celia was splashing in the deep bath and humming to herself.

Johnny was still amazed that she seemed so totally unaffected by the afternoon's dramatic events. From his conversation with her when they had sat down in their large bedroom, it was clear that she was fully aware of the danger they had faced. Somehow, she had simply taken it all in her stride. He, on the other hand was feeling quite shaken. He called out to her, 'Celia darling, I am going to pop downstairs and telephone Tar.'

'Okey dokey, but don't be too long, I'm feeling a bit frisky.'

'Oh my God!' exclaimed Johnny, laughing as he left the room. His conversation with Tar was brief.

'Johnny. The thugs were Heinrich H's men. Low-level Sicherheitsdienst – SD – instructed out of the Paris embassy. One gone and two in custody. Currently receiving memory therapy. Change of plan. You are invited by the groom to stay at the chateau. More secure. Heavy local guard, plus theirs and our security agents.'

'Excellent. That will make it easier to get to know the owner. How did you spring it?'

'No problem. 300 invitations were sent out and total guests amount to 16. You are expected there tomorrow at lunchtime.'

'That's fine – we are in the Loire now.'

'How's Celia?'

'Extraordinary. Totally relaxed and calm. I'm more shaken than her!'

'Hmm. Thought she was a natural. Well, cheerio.'

'And you, Tar.'

When Johnny went back into the bedroom, Celia was reclining on the bed, naked. 'Get those clothes off Johnny, and come here. I need you now.'

Later, as they sat in the garden under a large plane tree sipping champagne cocktails, Celia slipped her hand into Johnny's and looked at him directly in the eye. 'You know, Johnny, I really needed that. I was bloody well aching for it after this afternoon's little escapade.'

'Well darling, you were certainly enthusiastic,' he smiled. 'Are you fine now?'

'Oh yes, absolutely top hole, thank you, and starving! I am dying to taste the sander in Sancerre sauce that you recommended.'

'My father and I always have it when we stay here. It is fabulous.'

After an easy drive the next morning they arrived at the gated entrance to the Chateau de Cande. There were a large number of police there, and as many reporters and cameramen. There were also cine cameras, including one clearly bearing the logo for Pathe News. After an immaculate gendarme with a clipboard had checked the registration on their car, inspected their travel papers and the letters of invitation that they had been asked to bring, the gates were opened and they started along the long and winding driveway.

It meandered through beautiful countryside. After a few minutes, through the trees they caught their first glimpses of the many-turreted chateau. Then suddenly, it was there before them. It was a romantic's renaissance dream. 'Oh Johnny, Wallis must love this. It's the stuff of fairy tales!' exclaimed Celia, laughing.

Johnny laughed, and said, 'She most certainly will – and it comes with all mod cons. I gather that Bedaux has installed all the latest comforts, from plumbing to even a telephone – that's as rare as hen's teeth in the French countryside. He has to have his own operator on site. Bear that in mind – nothing will be private.'

Wallis and David were, as always, the picture of elegance, and seemed totally at home in their surroundings where they had been together for almost four weeks. Wallis introduced Celia and Johnny to Fern and Charles Bedaux.

Fern was striking and elegant. In contrast, Charles was physically stocky with the bandy legs of a jockey, but he was powerfully-built and exuded confidence. He had prominent ears, and his hair was black and oiled. Nevertheless, his was a formidable and magnetic presence.

Johnny could now understand the rise to wealth, power and influence of this man, who had been taught street fighting and even how to dress by the successful pimp, Henri Ledoux, in the lawless Pigalle district of turn-of-the-century Paris. Bedaux went straight to the point.

'Johnny – I may call you that, I trust – David tells me that you are a big wheel in the international art market. Just to say that I am always in the market.'

'That's good to know,' answered Johnny rather offhandedly. He considered it extremely bad form for Bedaux to bring up matters of business at this time. Nevertheless, it would give him an entree to talk to Bedaux.

Wallis turned to Celia. 'Celia my dear, you must let me have all of your news. After luncheon we shall go and find a quiet spot in the grounds and have a fine chat. David, are you boys going to have a round of golf this afternoon?'

'Actually, I thought it would be rather fun. How about Fruity and I take on you and Johnny, Charles – a fourball?'

'That's fine by me,' replied Charles, looking at Johnny, who nodded and smiled in agreement.

'Very well chaps, we'll tee off at 2.30pm. I suggest that we don't bother with caddies but just carry short sets of seven clubs?'

'Agreed,' the others muttered.

Fruity Metcalfe joined the group before lunch with his wife, Lady Alexandra. She was still known as Baba, her nickname in the household of Lord and Lady Curzon, her parents. She was attractive and vivacious. Although her family was old British aristocracy and her father had been Viceroy of India, the family money was American. She got on well with Fern, but there was a distinct reserve with Wallis. She and

Celia had known each other for many years and were close friends.

The Duke's drive off the first tee was topped and the ball scuffled along in the rough for about 50 yards. He was clearly furious and did not comment when Fruity hit a clean straight drive up the fairway. Johnny and Charles Bedaux also had decent drives. The Duke hacked his ball out of the rough and onto the edge of the fairway. His next shot was excellent, and his equanimity returned.

'Charles,' said the Duke, 'explain to Johnny what you do, and your vision for the future of great international business. Fruity and I have heard you explain it but it bears repeating.'

'Pleased to, David. Johnny, my vision and that of The Fraternity, of which I am honoured to be a member, is that the world has shrunk and large corporations prosper, regardless of national boundaries and local regimes and laws.

'Inevitably there will be another great conflagration between nations. The purpose and aim of The Fraternity is to ensure that whatever happens, whatever the outcome, a New Order is established. It will be buttressed by police power, and with the peace will come a new era of social justice. Gold will be a mainstay of the New Order. We are convinced that Nazi Germany provides a living blueprint for the New Order. In Britain, you have the organisation The Link, which embraces the vision and ideals of The Fraternity.'

'Well Charles, that is quite something to digest,' said Johnny thoughtfully, 'such a vision must require great sources of funding?'

'But of course. The beauty of it is that those at the heart of some of the most powerful international businesses are actively involved already. For instance, Standard Oil of New Jersey, General Motors, Ford,and ITT, are all members and major investors in their German-based operations.

'We also have the Bank for International Settlements which was the brainchild of Herr Schacht, the Nazi Minister for Economics Economics, and Montagu Norman, the Governor of the Bank of England, no less. Added to that, the Rockefeller family control Chase Manhattan Bank as well as Standard Oil.

'In Germany itself, the Reichsbank has to approve all

international dealings by German-based businesses. This is to ensure that the dealings are in accord with the national master plan. That is the sort of management that we wish to see internationally and are working towards.'

Johnny decided to tackle the main issue head on. 'What you describe, Charles, is in effect international totalitarianism governed by powerful, but unelected businessmen.'

'Absolutely,' replied Charles enthusiastically. 'Unlike the politicians, they have proved that they can run empires.'

'I think it sounds excellent. Britain and Germany are perfectly placed to form the European core for the vision, and America has strong established links with both not least in bloodlines,' chimed in the Duke.

Johnny was not totally surprised by what he had heard. In his dealings with the international rich he had heard similar philosophies, but never had he heard the chilling reality spelt out so clearly.

'Charles, I still come back to the funding element. Who by, and how will that be achieved?' asked Johnny.

'Well, there are some interesting arrangements already in place. I hope that I am not boring you?'

'Not in the slightest, do go on,' smiled Johnny.

Charles continued with the relish of a true enthusiast. 'The Rockefellers entered into an agreement with the J.Henry Schroder bank of New York earlier this year. The partners in the bank which they formed are Avery Rockefeller, Baron Bruno von Schroder in London, and Kurt von Schroder in Cologne. He is a member of the Gestapo, which provides an excellent high-Flevel link into the German Governmental machine. Standard Oil's Paris representatives are directors of the Banque de Paris et de Pays-Bas, which also has close links with the Nazi Government of Germany and Chase Manhattan.

'You must remember that Standard Oil is the largest petroleum company in the world. Its chairman is Walter Teagle, a good friend of mine. We often lunch together in the Cloud Room in the Chrysler Building. Only recently he and I had lunch there and cemented close relationships with Hermann Schmitz of IG Farben, and Sir Henri Deterding of Royal Dutch Shell, who is strongly pro-Nazi. So you see, we are well on the way to establishing the infrastructure of our vision.'

'Apart from doing business together internationally, has active financial support been given to any government?'

'But of course, Johnny. Chase Manhattan, through its contacts, has effectively funded the Berlin – Rome Axis.'

'I say chaps, this is all fascinating stuff, but we have a round of golf to play,' interrupted the Duke, who clearly found the detail tiresome.

'I apologise, David,' said a smiling Charles, 'but you know what I am like when I am on my hobby horse.'

There was no more talk of world affairs, politics or business for the rest of the round. Johnny's concentration was poor and he played badly. His partner Charles was enthusiastic but erratic. The Duke and Fruity won easily. The Duke returned to the Chateau in high good spirits.

Johnny kept up an amiable facade but was deeply troubled. He could not shake off the feeling that he had just been shown a developing and virulent cancer at the heart of democracy.

# Chapter 20

After the round of golf Johnny excused himself, and went to the suite which he was sharing openly with Celia. She was already there, and greeted him with a warm embrace. 'How was the golf darling?'

'Actually, frightful. I was totally thrown off my game by our host. He is either totally mad or an evil genius. I fear he's the latter,' Johnny replied quietly. 'I cannot wait to report what I have heard to Tar and Sir Vernon. It's potentially dynamite, and happening under the noses of not only the American but also the British and other European governments.'

'You must tell me about it when we have more time. Poor Walter Monckton is looking very long-faced and worried. He arrived just after you chaps left for golf. He says that he has to see the Duke as a matter of urgency.'

Johnny responded, 'Well, David is in reasonably good humour after winning convincingly. I am surprised that he is so cheerful, at least outwardly .He was counting on his brothers Henry and George being here and Dickie Mountbatten, but of course they have been forbidden to attend. That, coupled with Perry Brownlow ducking out, must have hurt badly.'

After a moment, Celia commented, 'I'm not surprised about the Princes or Dickie, but it does seem a poor show by Perry.'

'Not really, darling. Perry is a courtier, and the King has made it clear that David has put himself beyond the pale. For Heaven's sake, David even talks about going back to live in Fort Belvedere. Talk about wishful thinking. His own mother, Queen Mary, summed up the Royal family's views when she wrote to him castigating him for his failure to do his duty, when so many had died doing theirs in the Great War.'

'He is childishly naive in so many ways, Johnny. You know that as well as I do. He is like a child who has no concept of consequences. I really think that he cannot understand that, after sending over 300 invitations to people they carefully selected as friends, there are only going to be a handful at the wedding.'

'We had better get ready for dinner, Celia. I think that everyone is here now except for the Rothschilds. Cutting it a bit fine, I'd say.'

'They have probably had enough of the David and Wallis show over recent months,' laughed Celia.

'I am sorry to be the bearer of this formal letter, Sir, but I must ask you to read it.' Dudley Forward, the Duke's personal secretary, was standing next to the desk.

Walter Monckton knew the content of the letter and the effect that it would almost certainly have on the Duke. Just then, Wallis burst into the room excitedly waving some photographs. 'Oh Walter, how good to see you! David, darling, I am not interrupting am I?' she asked in a way that clearly ruled out any denial.

'No, no, Walter has brought me a boring letter. What have you there?'

'Cecil, that's Cecil Beaton, Walter, the Vogue photographer you know, is here as a guest and has taken some pictures of me. Just look at this one in my Schiaparelli waltz dress with dear Salvador Dali's lobster brooch.'

'By Jove, Wallis my love, you look lovely with the sun dappling your floaty white dress. You look radiant with happiness.'

'Oh but I am, I am! Now I shall let you get on. The Rothschilds have just arrived and have immediately gone to change for dinner.'

The moment Wallis had gone, the Duke picked up the letter and with a silver-bladed paper knife slit the envelope open. Unexpectedly, he handed it to Dudley Forward. 'Here Dudders, read this for me.'

'Yes, Sir,' he replied, as he took the letter from the envelope. He read its contents with growing concern, as the relaxed and happy Duke chatted with his old friend Walter Monckton. He then turned to a grim-faced Dudley Forward. 'Well what does it say then?'

'Sir, I cannot put this in any other way. The King, by Letters Patent ratified by the Cabinet and Parliament, has confirmed your status as a Royal Prince of the Blood and entitlement to the style "Your Royal Highness", but expressly excludes your wife from such style or rights. I am sorry Sir.'

The Duke leapt to his feet. 'The bastard, the weak, utter bastard! He cannot even stand up to his bloody wife on this and gives in to her spite and bile! As my wife, Wallis legally becomes entitled to the same honour as me.'

Walter Monckton knew that he must now explain and endorse the advice given to the King which he and many senior lawyers considered to be deeply flawed. He was very uncomfortable doing so, but it had been made patently clear to him that there was no circumstance where Wallis would ever be given the style of "Her Royal Highness". He had to nip any such notion in the bud now.

'David, I am afraid that that is just not true. There was a legal study carried out by a committee of the most eminent constitutional lawyers. They unanimously advised that, on abdication, you forfeited all titles and honours. In effect, you became Mr Windsor. It was your brother, the King, who exercised his personal prerogative and appointed you a Royal Prince with the title "Your Royal Highness" by the Letters Patent that he issued. However the Letters Patent preclude your spouse from that honour, and by their terms neither she nor any offspring have any inherited rights.'

'It's not fair. Leave me now, Walter, I wish to be alone.'

Walter Monckton could not have been more relieved to leave the room. The Duke had sounded like a child when he said, 'It's not fair.' The Duke then broke down in tears, and sobbed on Dudley Forward's shoulder.

Outside the chateau where the gates were firmly closed, there was now an even greater police presence. Apart from the press corps and cine photographers, crowds of sight seers had descended on the little town of Monts, where the local people were avidly cashing in on the occasion by letting rooms to visitors.

The police were also having to patrol the extensive grounds of the chateau to intercept the curious who were seeking out ways to sneak up to it. They were mindful of the warning issued to Mrs Simpson by the Scotland Yard officers, who had guarded her whilst she had first stayed with the Rogers in Cannes. They had written to her, urging caution and that she should not return to England in any event. They were concerned that amongst the many death threats she had received, there might be some that reflected a real risk.

Armed French and British Secret Service Agents also mingled with the crowd outside the gates and were in hiding within the grounds much closer to the chateau.

The following morning was bright and sunny, and the mood of the guests was defiantly upbeat in the face of so many doubts and uncertainties surrounding the event, and the future of the couple who were about to be married.

Johnny had remarked to Celia that he wondered whether the Duke had picked the birthday of his late father for the wedding as a deliberate sleight to his family. Celia did not think so, and chose to see it as a reflection of the Duke's selfish preoccupation with Wallis to the exclusion of all else.

The British Minister in Paris was there, and took his seat in the salon, next to Walter Monckton who was listed as Sir Walter Monckton, KC, the Chancellor of the Duchy of Cornwall. Celia and Johnny were extremely conscious of the very few guests.

The other guests were Edward ('Fruity') Metcalfe, former aide-de-camp when the Duke was Prince of Wales, and his wife, Lady Alexandra Metcalfe, Mrs Elizabeth Merryman, aunt of the bride – always always known to Wallis as Aunt Bessie, Baron and Baroness Eugene de Rothschild, Mr Dudley Forward, Mr and Mrs Herman Rogers, and their hosts Mr and Mrs Charles Bedaux. Cecil Beaton was a guest, but was also singing for his supper, and would be taking some formal photographs after the ceremonies.

Five members of the press were also permitted to attend the ceremonies as witnesses.

The Mayor of Monts, Dr Mercier, stood before the seated guests with his red, white and blue gold-tasselled mayoral sash of honour. Fruity Metcalfe left his seat and then returned with the Duke. As were all the men with the exception of the Mayor, they were in elegant morning dress.

The Duke was wearing a yellow waistcoat beneath his black tail coat and had a white carnation in his buttonhole. Whether he knew that in the "language of flowers" the white carnation means *"alas my poor heart"* will never be known, but talking about it afterwards, Celia and Johnny decided that he must have been unaware of this on the happiest of days. He was carrying a prayer book that had been a gift from his mother, Queen Mary.

Herman Rogers had left his seat at the same time as Fruity Metcalfe. When he returned with Wallis on his arm, the Duke's face lit up with delight. She was wearing a floor length Mainbocher dress with a matching long sleeved jacket, all in crepe satin. The colour was pale gray-blue – "Wallis blue" as the designer called it – and she wore a matching small veiled hat of coq feathers. On her wrist was a Cartier bracelet of nine gem-set crosses with an engraved inscription on the reverse in the Duke's handwriting. Nearly all the jewellery that he showered on Wallis was inscribed with personal messages in his writing.

The short ceremony proceeded without a problem. The Duke's response was loud and clear when asked if he took Wallis as his wife. Wallis' voice shook a little. The Mayor, relishing the occasion, then gave a short address and declared the ceremony complete. Preceded by the Anglican priest who was to officiate at the religious ceremony, the couple led their guests through the library into the music room that had been converted into a chapel for the occasion.

A large ornately carved antique chest had been brought in to serve as an altar. When it was realised that the carvings were of an erotic nature, Wallis had set off and found a silk table cloth. A Protestant cross was fetched from the village, but Wallis had ordered that two candlesticks brought from the dining room should be returned there as they were required for the wedding breakfast.

The famous organist from Notre Dame in Paris, Marcel Dupre, struck up a wedding march that he had composed, and later they all sang the hymn, *"Oh Perfect Love"*. The Anglican priest who officiated was the Reverend R Anderson Jardine from Darlington, County Durham. He had flown in the face of doctrinal objections, and those of his Bishop and the Church of England establishment, to marry the couple.

By 12.30pm the ceremony was finished and the wedding party, after individually congratulating the couple, retired to the dining room for the wedding breakfast.

'I say, this looks rather spiffing,' said Fruity to his wife.

'Yes, it does rather, darling, but don't make a pig of yourself,' she responded as she surveyed the buffet with a five tired wedding cake at its centre.

'Don't fret. I shall confine myself to the foie gras, caviar and langoustines.'

'Just think of your waistline.'

'Nothing that a bit of sharp exercise won't take care of, old girl,' he laughed as he fondly touched her arm.

Charles Bedaux joined them. 'I have a local man with a rotograveur copying the Duke and Duchess's signatures and carving them into the wood panelling in the library, with today's date of course'

'Oh what a charming idea,' chimed Fruity's wife, who could hardly hide her disdain for the French-born, American multimillionaire.

After Charles Bedaux had moved on, Lady Alexandra turned to her husband, Fruity, and said quietly, 'What a perfectly ghastly little man. You know, it is really sad that here we are in rural France, just a small group witnessing the marriage of the man who only a few months ago was the King Emperor.'

The newspapermen who were allowed to witness the wedding breakfast described it as a friendly and informal affair. At 2 o'clock everybody went outside, so that Cecil Beaton could take the formal wedding photographs. Lady Alexandra also took photographs.

The patient crowd at the gates to the chateau had become restive as the morning wore on. When the news that the ceremony had concluded was telephoned to the Lodge, an old concierge was persuaded to smash a bottle of champagne on the gates to give the newsreel cameramen something to film. As the bottle smashed a cheer went up. She rather spoilt the drama of the moment when she disappeared into the lodge, only to return with a dustpan and brush to clear up the broken glass.

The Rothschilds were the first guests to leave just before 6 o'clock. The Duke thanked the Anglican priest, and presented him with a pair of gold cufflinks. Wallis gave him a small box containing some wedding cake.

To the side of the chateau, the 226 pieces of luggage that the couple would travel with and the sculpture entitled 'Love', given to them by Charles Bedaux who had commissioned it from Anny Hocken-Hempel, were being loaded into a large van. Then there was a steady stream of departures.

Herman and Katherine Rogers were staying on at the chateau and stood with Fern and Charles Bedaux as they bade farewell to their guests. Fruity Metcalfe was taking his wife to Paris where she would be staying with friends. He would shortly be joining the Duke and Duchess in the Austrian castle that they had rented for three months. Since Fruity had joined the Duke in Austria, where he had been skiing in Kitzbuhel when summoned to the Rothschild castle, he had become the Duke's constant companion.

Celia and Johnny were leaving as soon after David and Wallis as they could, on the first leg of their journey to Lyon, and then on to Geneva. Billy Brownlow was to join them for dinner at the hotel where they were to stay that night.

At six o'clock, David and Wallis climbed into their car and waved goodbye to the group gathered in front of the chateau. As they left through the gates of the chateau, the Duke and his Duchess leant forward and waved to the crowds, who had waited so long for a glimpse of the couple just married in the fairy tale romantic chateau.

The road from flag-bedecked Monts to Tours and Poitiers was lined with police every 15 metres for the first 4 kilometres. The cavalcade was led by two police cars and motorcycle outriders. Following the Duke's car was a luggage van, cars for the seven servants accompanying the couple and their two dogs. More police motorcyclists brought up the rear. Both British and French Secret Service agents followed in their cars.

'David, will we always have this much attention when we venture out?'

'I really do not know, Wallis my love,' he said, as he took her hand and brought it to his lips.

'I really do not know, but we have each other.'

The Duke delved in his Hermes baby crocodile Sac á Depeche and withdrew an elegant, engraved gold box. 'This is jolly pretty, Wallis, isn't it?'

'It sure is. When you write and thank Herr Hitler you must tell him that we intend to visit Germany in the autumn after our honeymoon.'

'Oh, I most certainly shall, and I shall also explain that I wish to see the working and living conditions of his people. I think that England has much to learn from Nazi Germany. Charles Bedaux thinks it a capital idea. I shall ensure that the German methods are brought on to the British Statute Book.'

And so the newly married couple, whose romance had shaken the foundations of a great nation and empire, were driven off together into what later came to be described as "that tarnished sunset of exiled royalty".

# Chapter 21
## Part 1

*PRESS RELEASES ISSUED FOR AND
ON BEHALF OF THE DUKE OF WINDSOR
3rd June 1937
Chateau de Cande, Monts, Loire, France
(Issued by Mr Herman Rogers)*

*The Duke of Windsor was married today to Mrs. Wallis Warfield at the Chateau de Cande. The French Civil ceremony was performed by Dr Mercier, the Mayor of Monts. This was followed by the marriage service of the Church of England performed by the Rev. R. Anderson Jardine, Vicar of St. Paul's, Darlington. Mr. Herman Rogers gave the bride away and Mr. Dudley Metcalfe supported the Duke.*

*"The Duchess and I wish to thank all those who have so kindly sent us presents and good wishes on the occasion of our wedding. We shall never forget their friendly messages, which mean so much to us on this day. After the trying times that we have been through, we now look forward to a happy and useful private life and that measure of peace that we hope will be granted to us."*

*The Duke and Duchess of Windsor wish to take this opportunity of expressing to journalists their appreciation of the courtesy which has been for the most part shown them in unprecedented circumstances. They would like it to be recorded that, although inaccurate statements and reports seem to have been unavoidable during these months, which have been trying for all concerned, there has been an evident willingness to contradict them.*

*As regards the future, the Duke realises that any atmosphere of secrecy is unsatisfactory and will always be prepared to supply any news of importance concerning the Duchess or him. At the same time the Duke and Duchess, while fully understanding the difficulties, want on this day to appeal to the press of the world to give them that measure of consideration and privacy which they feel is now their due."*

# Part 2

The Duke and Duchess were heading towards Tours and Poitiers, their destination the railway junction at Laroche-Migennes, where they and their entourage would join the Simplon-Orient Express. In their private carriage they would travel to Venice overnight.

The Duke took Wallis' hand.

'Now we are truly as one, and our pet name of 'WE' is a reality. It just goes to show that our motto "Hold Tight" was on the button, eh? It's wonderful, and we have our whole lives ahead of us together. I am so happy.'

'And so am I, my love,' replied a smiling Wallis, 'I am looking forward to seeing Venice, if only for a few hours. The Italians are so warm, charming and just elegant. When I was in China I was friendly with Count Cianno, Mussolini's son-in-law and Italy's Foreign Minister. Who do you think will meet us in Venice?'

'As this is a private visit, Wallis, there will be no official Government reception for us. There may be an informal welcome and I expect some local dignitaries will be in on the act. They are usually keen to have the association – they are politicians, after all.'

'Changing the subject, David, I am amazed that Perry, Lord Brownlow, chose not to join us. I thought he was a real friend.'

'I assume that he was precluded by his relationship with the King and the Court.'

'Pshaw, David! Look at the way he was sacked as the King's Lord-in-Waiting. Mrs Queen obviously had a hand in that.'

'I agree that he was ill treated. It was a cheap trick, announcing in the Court Circular that the King had reluctantly accepted a resignation that had never been proffered. He was with me at the Rothschilds' Schloss Enzesfeld in Austria when he heard about it. He was very cut up.'

'Well, we know what her game is, don't we, David. Is it true that she also tried to get rid of Alexander Hardinge, yours and then your brother's private secretary?'

'Yes, so I believe. Rum do that, because she is very friendly with his wife Helen. Shows her ruthless streak. I gather that Clive Wigram, who agreed to come out of retirement, decided that it was too much of a burden to shoulder the tasks of two courtiers, so Hardinge stayed in post. Quite right too, he is a good and honest man.'

'Walter Monckton was saying that the prude Baldwin stood down as Prime Minister on 27$^{th}$ May, after chairing the Cabinet meeting where your Letters Patent were approved?'

'That's correct. Spiteful business on Bertie's part, denying you the right to the style 'Your Royal Highness' – that will be the Queen's influence, no doubt supported by Baldwin. Well, good riddance to him.'

'David, don't become upset on this happy day.' Wallis leant closer and took both his hands in hers.

Celia and Johnny had left the Chateau shortly after the Duke and Duchess. They were heading for Lyon where they would be meeting Billy Brownlow. He would bring them up to date on the investigation into the armed attack that Celia and Johnny had fought off on the way to the wedding. The meeting would also enable Johnny to brief Billy on what he had learned from their host at the Chateau de Cande, Charles Bedaux.

Celia could sense that Johnny was disturbed and decided to lighten the mood. 'Johnny darling, tell me what you have planned for Lyon – oh, and a bit about the city – I have only ever driven through and never stayed.'

'Lyon itself is actually the second city of France. However its inhabitants are firm in the belief that it is the first city. They are proud and independent. With some justification, they claim that their gastronomy far surpasses that of any other city.

'We are going to stay in one of the oldest hotels in Lyon, the Grand Hotel Des Terreaux. It is in the heart of the city on the left bank of the River Saone. It's very comfortable. Tomorrow we shall have lunch with Billy at the Restaurant Larivoire. It has been owned and run by the family Constantin since it opened – the food is sublime and the cellar truly magnificent. To cap it all, it is in a lovely building surrounded by trees.'

'Is that cellar the reason we are staying for two nights in Lyon?' jossed Celia.

'Absolutely, my dear – it would be an awful act of sacrilege if we were to fail to pay due homage to the fine wines.

Actually, our next stop is Geneva, well actually Glion, where we are to stay at the Grand Hotel Victoria near Montreux. It has the most fabulous views across Lake Geneva.'

'You are making this into quite a trip, Johnny.'

'Well there is some method in my madness – I have to meet a wealthy client in Geneva, Jean-Claude Sachs. Fascinating fellow, with fingers in all sorts of pies. He was originally from the Lebanon and is married to a very beautiful, but rather fearsome woman who is Persian. You will be meeting them. Apart from being a client, he keeps his eyes and ears open and has provided some very good intelligence over the years. You will like him – I suppose best described as a loveable rogue.'

'With that name, is he Jewish?'

'He says not, and that he is a non-practising Christian, but I really could not say. I think money is his only belief, in all fairness,' laughed Johnny.

'Probably better than religion or politics – they only seem to start wars.'

Johnny's face was suddenly serious again, 'I think that you are wrong there, Celia. There are powerful men who would not regard the horror and misery of war as unacceptable, if they believed that their ultimate goal of even greater profit were to be achieved. I am afraid we are back to Mr Bedaux and his cronies.'

The former British Prime Minister, who had played a significant role in engineering the now Duke of Windsor's abdication whilst keeping his own part and the government's out of the public domain, was at Sir Vernon Kell's house in Eaton Terrace.

He and Prime Minister Baldwin had always got along well, and during what was now known as the Abdication Crisis had worked closely together. Although she had no official role, his wife was actively involved in the affairs of the Service and was sitting with the two men.

'I should think that it is sweet sorrow to be out of Downing Street, Stanley.'

'Well, I cannot say that the past months have been easy. It was a great relief that on my last day in office as Prime Minister, and in my final Cabinet Meeting, we approved the Letters Patent for the Duke of Windsor.'

Sir Vernon chuckled as he commented, 'Yes, a neat piece of work.'

'On the one hand, the new Duke of Windsor is a Royal Duke, but on the other hand neither he, his spouse or issue can enjoy or inherit that style or title. I have only met him a handful of times over the years and then on purely formal occasions. What do you make of him as a man?'

In a thoughtful tone Baldwin answered, 'Do you know, I have puzzled over that question. Childish, selfish, petulant, amoral – I could say a resounding 'yes' to all of those things. And yet there is more to him than that. The undoubted lack of full emotional and intellectual maturity described by Lord Dawson, the Royal Physician, is a major factor. Do you know Vernon, to answer your question as succinctly as I can I would describe him as "an abnormal being, half man and half genius". Does that answer your question?'

Lady Kell interjected, 'I cannot help feeling sorry for the man – I do not think that he, and consequently she, will ever find happiness.'

'Time will tell, my dear, time will tell. How do you think that Neville Chamberlain will fare as Prime Minister, Stanley?'

'He is a thoroughly honourable fellow who does not have the devious and ruthless streak that is sometimes essential in politics. He is not confrontational, and I know that at heart he would always rather seek a compromise than face a confrontation. If Herr Hitler flexes his muscles again, I believe that decisive action will have to be taken. I am not sure that Neville would accept that.'

'As you know Stanley, our intelligence indicates that Nazi Germany is nowhere near as prepared for war as they would have us believe. Their propaganda and showmanship show the world that they are, but we are sure that they are not. If their bluff is called soon enough, another war might well be averted.'

'Vernon – you are taking the same line as Winston Churchill. Unfortunately he has made too many mistakes in the past to be much more than a lone, albeit vociferous voice. Given his way, I think that we would already be embarked on full rearmament and pulling Herr Hitler's moustache.'

'Back to intelligence, Stanley. From what I have read, if Hitler and his gang were tackled now they would fall.'

'Probably so, but what then? We chose not to intervene when the Nazis reoccupied the Ruhr. Neither did the French, for the same reason, although they could not admit it given that they have an 'accord' with Russia. That reason being a strong Germany is a bulwark against the westward spread of bolshevism. Now, I should like to thank you for a most enjoyable interlude and be on my way. We have an early start tomorrow. We are off to Waterwynch House near Tenby, my parents-in-law's family place. Of course I am forgetting, you visited me there, Vernon.'

'Yes, I well remember, a beautiful and tranquil spot. I envy you.'

Benito Mussolini, the fascist leader of Italy, gave detailed instructions that the Duke and Duchess were to be given a spectacular welcome in Venice. He was eager to do so and let the world see that the Italian people held the Duke in high esteem. It would also convey the message that the former monarch did not disapprove of the fascist regime. The British Government had prevented the Duke from visiting fascist Italy but had no power to do so now. In addition, the Duke had provided significant support in relation to the Abyssinian war.

When the deposed Emperor had gone to London to plead for British intervention, on behalf of his people, King Edward VIII, as the Duke then was, refused to receive him at Buckingham Palace. Instead he had sent his brother the Duke of Gloucester to the Emperor's hotel. A very public snub.

## Chapter 22

At Schloss Wasserleonburg, preparations for the Duke and Duchess' three month visit had become feverish as the deadline for their arrival was reached. Stone masons were completing some essential repairs to the ancient fabric of the Schloss, and the swimming pool that had been found to be leaking. The white lines were being painted on the tennis court that had been newly constructed, and the gardeners were frantically carrying out the final planting of the many multicoloured beds.

In the nearby small village of Noetsch there was excitement when the Duke's large car from France, driven by his Austrian chauffer, and Chief Inspector Schober of the Vienna police arrived. The Chief Inspector had looked after security on the Duke's previous stay in Austria, and was placed in charge of security again at the Duke's specific request.

The roads around the great estate were now heavily patrolled, and in some cases closed to the public. An extra draft of police had arrived from Vienna. Extra staff were taken on in the local post office, including an English-speaking liason clerk. Over 200 telegrams had already arrived. The Duke may have abandoned his British throne, but the Austrians were determined that his stay should reflect his status within the Royal Houses of Europe.

When Johnny and Celia arrived in Lyon they were exhausted. It had been a long day at the Chateau, followed by an exhausting drive into the evening then night. Celia had shared the driving, but Johnny had driven most of the time, particularly after night fell.

As they pulled up at the hotel, Johnny heaved a sigh of relief. He switched off the ignition and the big engine rumbled to a stop. The sudden, almost startling silence was broken only by the ticking of hot metal as Johnny rubbed his eyes, after stretching to ease his arms and shoulders.

As the concierge appeared in the doorway and two bell boys ran down the steps, Johnny turned to Celia and smiling warmly said, 'Do you know what I fancy, darling? A darned big gin and tonic, then bed?'

'That sounds damn fine to me,' laughed Celia in reply.

When they moved to leave the car, the bell boys in their smart navy blue brass buttoned uniforms leapt forward and opened the doors. As Johnny and Celia entered the hotel, the elderly concierge, who was holding one of the wide brass-bound doors open, smiled broadly and said, 'Welcome, Milord, it is a pleasure to see you again, and with so elegant a lady.' His heavily-accented English was perfect.

'Thank you, Jacques, you old charmer. How are your families?'

'They are all thriving and well, Milord.'

Celia was puzzled by Johnny's use of the plural and made a note to ask for an explanation later.

Johnny handed the car keys to Jacques and told him that they would not require the car until their departure. He asked if, whilst it was in the hotel's care, oil and fluid levels could be checked along with tyre pressures.

'Of course, Milord, and of course the car will be washed and polished.'

As they walked across the thick carpeted foyer, the fussy-looking reception clerk, who sported a pencil-thin black moustache and gold-rimmed spectacles, fiddled with the blotter and pen on the mahogany counter. After a fawning welcome he handed a large key to Johnny, and gestured for yet another bell boy to escort the new guests to their suite.

'Oh, it's delightful!' exclaimed Celia, after they were shown into their suite and the bellboy had left, palming the modest tip that Johnny had given him. She dashed into the bedroom and dramatically threw herself backwards onto the bed. 'Spiffing!' she cried out,'it's just right, darling!'

'Glad to hear it, and I hope that you have not broken all

the springs!'

'Oh, later darling, later,' she laughed. At that moment, Johnny felt every one of the years' age difference between them.

'Right, my girl. G and T time. Here, or shall we rustle someone up downstairs?'

'Let's go downstairs. I'd like a poke around. You know how nosy I am.'

When they were settled with their drinks and cigarettes, Celia asked Johnny, 'Why did you ask about Jacques' 'families'?'

Johnny laughed at her earnest enquiring expression. 'Jacques may be an unlikely Casanova. His virility is a legend in Lyon. He has three families, each with a bevy of children. When he is off-duty he rushes from one to the other. He assured me that each family is unaware of the existence of the others, but that must be a fiction. In England his behaviour would be frowned upon. Here in France it is the subject of admiration.'

'We English and the French are like chalk and cheese. We are much more akin to the Germans,' mused Celia.

The Duke's secretary, Dudley Forward, was becoming very worried. The cavalcade had travelled much more slowly than he had anticipated. For the first few kilometres, there were cheering crowds lining the road in every village and hamlet they passed through – this was to be expected. However, when they reached the open road they speeded up only slightly. The cavalcade's speed was dictated by the pace of the furniture van carrying the couple's massive amount of luggage.

His heart sank when the Duke said, 'Righto Dudders – picnic time.'

'Sir, I do not think it wise. We are already behind schedule and the train may not wait.'

'Wisdom be damned. A picnic we shall have. The train will wait for us.'

The cavalcade drew to a halt and the group went into an adjoining field.

'This'll do,' called the Duke. He handed Dudley Forward the leads of the two terriers that he and Wallis had recently acquired. 'Let 'em off Dudders, so they can stretch their legs and have a pee.'

'Sir, I fear that they will run off. They are untrained and young.'

'I agree with Dudley,' interposed the Duchess.

'Oh very well, take them into the next field on their leads. Raise your leg regularly to give the little blighters the right idea.'

Dudley Forward was not sure whether the Duke was joking, but determined that in front of all these staff and gendarmes, let alone the group of British detectives, this was one instruction he would ignore.

Picnic tables had been set up with canvas-seated director's chairs. There was horror when Monsieur James, the household comptroller, found that the picnic baskets only contained peaches. There had been a misunderstanding in the kitchens of the chateau, and the remainder of the food had been sent ahead to be put on the train.

'I said we would have a picnic, and a picnic we shall have! Ah Dudders – have they done their business? Come and sit down, and have some peaches.'

'Thank you sir, and yes, they have.'

'Capital, capital.'

The Duke's almost feverish determination to enjoy the picnic was on the verge of being embarrassing. Dudley Forward was feeling queasy after eating three of the admittedly delicious peaches. 'Dudders dear fellow, come on now – another peach.'

'Sir, I really couldn't. They are marvellous, the best peaches I have ever tasted, but I have had my fill and must decline.'

The others all indicated that they had eaten all the peaches that they could. The Duke's mood changed. 'Right then, we have a train to catch, so no more loitering here. We must get back on the road. Dudders, be so kind as to advise the gendarmes that we must go hell-for-leather.'

'Sir.'

As Dudley walked quickly towards the senior gendarme who was smoking with his colleagues as they stood by their car, he could not avoid what he felt was a disloyal thought, that marriage was unlikely to temper his master's unpredictable mood swings.

The cavalcade now raced to the station. The Duke seemed to be enjoying the excitement. Wallis was not. 'David – this is damned crazy, we'll all be killed at this rate!' she exclaimed, as she looked at the Duke through eyes made huge with fear.

'Don't worry, old girl – damned good drivers and the gendarme motor cycle outriders are clearing the road.'

They pulled into the station yard to find that as the Duke had predicted, the train had been held for them. As the recognisable couple were escorted to their private carriage, other passengers who had gone onto the platform to catch a glimpse of them mostly watched in angry silence. There were a few desultory handclaps. Neither the Duke nor the Duchess acknowledged their fellow passengers whose journeys they had selfishly delayed. A flustered Dudley Forward entered the private carriage.

'I am afraid that there will be a further delay, Sir. Some of the luggage has yet to arrive.'

'No harm. I am sure that it will not be long.'

'Yes Sir, but I understand that some of the other passengers are becoming very agitated at the delay.'

'My dear fellow, they have seen us. That should be sufficient. Don't forget that the trunks and cases with the red labels are to be placed in this carriage and not the luggage van.'

'Are you sure Sir – there are 50 of them I believe – they will take up an enormous amount of space?'

'No matter, we shall manage,' replied the clearly-irritated Duke.

At last, the final pieces of luggage were loaded, and the Duke and Duchess' entourage of staff were on the train in the carriage adjoining the private car. The guard stood on the platform and blew his whistle, warning of impending departure. Before he could raise his illuminated baton to signal for the driver to move the train out of the station, Wallis' head appeared out of a carriage window. She shouted in her horribly-accented French, 'Wait! Hold the train!'

Having heard her shout, Dudley Forward bustled into the carriage. 'Oh Dudley,' Wallis said, bestowing a beaming smile on him, 'I left my hat in the car, and I must have it.'

'But the train is leaving and already over an hour late. It will be forwarded to you.'

'No Dudders, go and get it now, Wallis must have her hat,' ordered the Duke, in a harsh high-pitched tone.

Dudley could sense the hostility of other passengers as they looked to see what the latest delay might be. He was out of breath when he returned to the train, hat in hand.

'Thank you so much, Dudley,' gushed Wallis, 'what would we do without you.'

Try telling that to the hundred or so other passengers who had paid to travel on an express that had the reputation of always being on time. 'Thoughtless,' was the word that came into his mind. He returned to his compartment, manoevering his way around the mountain of the Duke's French-made luggage, distinctive with the maker Goyard's chevron symbol.

The following morning, Celia and Johnny woke, thoroughly refreshed after a night's deep sleep. They moved into each other's arms and Celia murmured into Johnny's ear, 'Now darling, it's time to test those springs I think?'

She reached for him, 'Oh yes, that's a good enough answer for me.'

She sat up and pulled her nightdress over her head, throwing it to one side. She drew back the bedclothes and reached for the waistband of Johnny's shorts, which he preferred to pyjamas. 'Mmmmm – that looks inviting,' she said as she lowered her head.

'Damnation!' she cried out as the telephone on the bedside table rang stridently. Johnny rolled onto his side and picked up the receiver. He listened for a short while and then simply said, '45 minutes. See you there.' When he turned back, he had a look of concern on his face.

'Who, and what, was that?'

'Billy Brownlow. He and his boys have spotted some people shadowing us and keeping the hotel under watch. He is concerned that they may be more of the same lot that attacked us the other day. C'mon, young lady, wash, brush up and get dressed. We are meeting him in the Musee des Beaux Arts in 40 minutes from now. A couple of his men are going ahead to establish a protected area where we can talk safely.'

'Excuse me, but bugger! I was really in the mood for a damned good gallop,' laughed Celia, as she leapt out of bed. 'Bags the bathroom first,' she called over her shoulder, as she pulled the door closed behind her.

As they left the hotel, Celia could not help having a good look at Jacques. They walked casually arm-in-arm, and leaning close to Johnny, Celia asked, 'Do you know the secret of the unlikely Lothario?'

'I have no idea, but possibly his enthusiasm, and of course energy. Now this is serious. Listen carefully in case something goes wrong and we are separated. The rendezvous with Billy Brownlow is on the second floor of the museum, in front of the famous Degas picture, *"Café-Concert at Les Ambassadeurs"*. When we get to it I shall tell you about the picture, as I would any visitor with me, until Billy joins us. He has picked that spot because his chaps can cover any access. He will join us when they are in place. OK?'

'Crystal clear. I have my little Beretta in my pocket. Fully loaded, safety catch on.'

'Good girl. Now look relaxed, we are on holiday!'

'Well Celia, there it is,' Johnny pointed to a large and imposing building as they entered Place des Terreaux.

'It's huge!' exclaimed Celia.

'It was a major Benedictine convent for centuries and then reconstructed in the 17th century, hence the architectural style. It's a bit heavy and brooding for my taste, but magnificent all the same.'

They walked through a huge stone arch and came into a vast courtyard garden. It was formally planted with low-cut shrubs and bushes, intersected by paths. There were some deserted benches.

'Good choice,' muttered Johnny, almost to himself, 'no cover for any ambush. Right Celia, over here and through the cloisters to the grand staircase. There is no lift so access is very limited.'

After climbing the stairs and still resisting the natural urge to look behind them, they walked along a long stone-floored passage with rooms displaying artworks to either side.

'Here we are, Celia.' Johnny led her into a side gallery which was dominated by a single painting that seemed to glow. Celia's eye was immediately drawn to a woman in a red dress at the centre of the picture.

'Some history I think?'

'Yes please, Johnny.'

'Degas, like Toulouse-Lautrec, liked to paint scenes from the clubs and meeting places of Paris in the late 19th century. This picture, which is pastel on paper, was probably drawn, or rather sketched live during the performance. The singer in the red dress is believed to be a Victorine Demay. You will see that he has placed you, the viewer, in the audience by the orchestra pit and. . .ah, here's Billy.'

'Right, Johnny, a quick situation report. The men who attacked you on the way down from Paris were members of the Sicherheitsdienst des Reichfuhrers – SS, the SD, Himmler's outfit. Unfortunately, none of them survived.'

'What do you mean?' asked Celia, looking shocked, 'the driver escaped without a scratch.'

'Apparently he tried to break out of custody after interrogation, and was hit by a train. At least his remains were found on the track.'

'Convenient way of disguising torture,' commented Johnny wryly.

'Quite so. Anyhow, the story that the Sûreté have given me is that orders from very high up – for that read Himmler or his pal Heydrich – were relayed through the Paris Embassy. You two were to be eliminated. It seems that the internal rift in the German intelligence services is even greater than at first thought. I have had a talk with my Abwehr source, who interprets what happened as you two being seen as assets of von Ribbentrop and/or the Abwehr. For the moment, Himmler and co do not feel strong enough to mount an attack on German agents. On the other hand, you would be regarded as fair game.

'The Sûreté and Deuxieme Bureau are furious that this turf war has been brought onto their patch. As I speak, they should have rounded up the watchers who were at your hotel, and the two who followed you here.'

Celia was shocked by the matter-of-fact report. 'But what will they do with them? Surely they will not kill them?'

'Probably not,' interposed Johnny, 'I expect that they will hold them incommunicado for a month or two, and then let the Abwehr apparently rescue them. That will really upset Himmler. In the meantime, Celia, we are at great risk. Billy, if you are satisfied that the French will have achieved a clean sweep of the goons then I think we should leave Lyons straight away.

'We will go back to the hotel now and I shall warn them that I may want the car very shortly. Well done, Billy, that's a good job. I shall have to give my report to Tar and Sir Vernon face to face when we get back to London. I am sorry, Celia, no fabulous lunch here, and no trip to Geneva.'

'Don't worry about that. I would rather stay in one piece. We can do it another time.'

'One last thought, Billy, before we split up. How safe are the Duke and Duchess of Windsor?'

# Chapter 23

Through the night, the great express thundered through the lush vineyards of Burgundy towards the Alps, crossing the Swiss border just after dawn. The driver and his crew had strained to make up the time lost in the delay caused by the Duke and Duchess' party. They succeeded, and arrived in Milan at precisely 10am, the scheduled time.

From Milan, the train sped cross-country to Venice, where a large crowd awaited the arrival of the newly-weds at the station. As the train pulled in, the cheering of the crowd reached a crescendo. The patriotic throng raised their arms in the fascist salute as the Duke and Duchess stepped down from the train. The Duke drew himself up smartly and gave a crisp fascist salute in return.

On the direct orders of Mussolini, a fleet of gondolas escorted the highly-decorated large launch that bore the Duke and Duchess to the Lido, where they disembarked at the Hotel Excelsior. The haunt of the internationally rich and famous, the grand hotel, with its Moorish design, was the obvious destination of choice. During the now-famous annual Venice film festival, it was the hotel of preference for the most well known international stars. Dr Goebbels, who was a regular attendee, also always chose to stay at The Exelcsior. A suite had been reserved for the Duke and Duchess to freshen up after their overnight journey.

'Well Wallis, Venice is certainly beautiful – and romantic,' said the broadly-smiling Duke, as he turned away from the view over the Lido. 'That was a grand welcome, my dear, and something you will become used to as my wife.'

'It sure was, and thank you for bringing me here. We must come again – we only have just under three hours left today. Are you ready for lunch?'

'Most certainly.'

As the Duke and Duchess were shown to their table in the huge arched dining room, everybody present rose to their feet and applauded loudly, to the accompaniment of some cries of "Bravo". The Duke was more used to crowds than Wallis. She looked a little awkward as she gave a weak smile and a wave of acknowledgement. He, on the other hand, smiled widely, and was careful to take in the whole room as he turned slowly and waved. His was practised showmanship, learnt over his years of royal apprenticeship.

After a lunch of a light risotto Milanese and green salad that had been pre-ordered, the couple left to more applause to which Wallis responded more effusively, although afterwards some commentators still felt that she looked a rather cold fish.

They embarked again on the highly-decorated launch which, with a growing escort of other vessels took them down the Grand Canal. The canal sides were lined with cheering people. The Duke acknowledged enthusiastically, smiling and waving his straw hat. 'I say, Wallis, this is quite a welcome, eh?'

'It sure is. Just look at those palaces!' cried Wallis, 'some of them look mighty shabby to me.'

'Ah, but Wallis, in Venice you cannot judge a book by its cover. You should see the inside of some of them. Quite magnificent.'

They alighted at St Mark's Square. They had been warned that the press would be looking for a photo opportunity. Feeding the pigeons provided ideal shots of the elegant couple. 'I hate bloody pigeons,' muttered the Duke as they walked on. The flamboyantly uniformed and sword-wearing caribinieri officers held the press back to afford some privacy to the couple.

'I am afraid that there is no time to have a proper look at St Mark's Cathedral or the Doge's Palace. Yes, we must come back. I love it – do you, Wallis?'

'Most certainly I do. It is so romantic. I agree, we will return.'

Dudley Forward approached the couple as they continued

their stroll. 'Sir, we have been asked whether you would both go onto the balcony of the Doge's Palace and acknowledge the crowd. Would that be acceptable?'

'Most certainly – it's the least I can do after such a magnificent welcome. Lead on.'

The Duke and Duchess appeared on the palace balcony a few minutes later. Again, he gave the fascist salute in response to the cheering crowd doing so. At last, Wallis was smiling broadly as she waved an elegant gloved hand. They were prompted by Dudley Forward after a few minutes, and reluctantly the Duke stopped waving to the crowd, bobbed a brief bow and gave another salute. He then led the Duchess off the balcony.

'Absolutely splendid! You know, I wanted to visit Italy before, but that stuffed shirt of a foreign minister, Anthony Eden, forbade it. He maintained that it could be construed as a British government endorsement of Mussolini. I should have ignored him.'

'Don't worry David darling, we can come back soon.'

'Absolutely, my darling. We are now free to do as we bloody well please!'

They returned to the Excelsior where they had tea. It was soon time to leave for the station, and they climbed back into the launch which took them there, where an even greater crowd had gathered. They were behind another cordon of dashing caribinieri.

Just as the Duke and Duchess were approaching their platform, a small girl in a white dress was presented to them. She was almost weighed down by a huge bouquet of a hundred carnations. The child curtsied and then went to present the flowers to the Duke. He smiled, and stepped a little to one side, indicating that they should be presented to the Duchess. She had to bend forward to receive them. At the same time, an Italian Bersaglieri officer, his distinctive wide-brimmed hat decorated with cappercaillie feathers, handed an envelope to Dudley Forward.

As they reached the door to their private carriage, the Duke stopped and turned again to wave at the still cheering crowd, and return the stiff-armed fascist salute given by so many of the well wishers. As the train noisily pulled away from the platform and then the station, the Duke could be seen at the carriage window again with his right arm in the now familiar salute.

Johnny and Celia had made good time once they had cleared the traffic of Lyon.

'If you are game, old girl, I would like to press on and drive straight to the Channel. If we have a good run we should be able to reach Calais late this evening. If there are no ferries until the morning, I am sure that we can put up at Le Meurice or one of the other hotels in the town. Le Meurice suits well because it has a garage, and I am sure that they will be able to rustle up some dinner.'

Celia looked up from the road map that she was studying, smiled, and replied, 'That's fine by me.'

'Good girl. Have you picked out our route on the map?'

'Yes, I think so. At Dijon you are going to turn off and head to Reims, and then to Calais from there. Is that right?'

'Yes, I want to give Paris a miss. As soon as we reach London, I would like you to contact von Ribbentrop and arrange to see him. I shall go straight to Tar and then I expect a meeting with Sir Vernon.'

'You would like me to find out what von Ribbentrop is up to, with regards to the Duke and Duchess and, importantly, whether they are at any risk from a German agency?'

'That's correct. Also, try to find out what lines of communication von Ribbentrop has established with Wallis.'

'I shall have to go and see him in that damned suite of his in the Grosvenor House. I find that rather depressing and not a little sordid. I hate to think what the staff say about me.'

'I am sorry that you have to do this, but it is the only way we will find out what they are planning. You must also mention Charles Bedaux, and find out what role he is playing. I think that he is going to turn out to be a very interesting link in all this. You and I may have to take him up on his standing invitation to visit them in one of their estates. I recall that he mentioned one in Hungary with some good shooting.'

'If we must – he gives me the willies!'

Von Ribbentrop was on the telephone to Helga, the receptionist to Professor Newmann, the ear specialist in Vienna who had been consulted by the Duke earlier in the year. Von Ribbentrop had seduced the very attractive younger woman on his last visit to Vienna. He had found her to have a robust and voracious sexual appetite. Just as he would greatly relish seeing her again for that reason alone, he believed that Wallis would find her irresistible.

'Helga, listen carefully. I shall be coming to Vienna in a few days and will be seeing you then. I shall stay in the same hotel. I am going to visit Professor Newmann, and advise him that he should close his practice and emigrate with his family as soon as possible. He must be near retirement age anyhow.

'I hope to have you appointed as a secretary to the Duchess of Windsor, who is going to be based at Schloss Wasserleonburg for the next three months. All being well, she will make it a permanent appointment. In that role you will be an important link between the Duchess and me. Do you understand? More to the point, would that suit you?'

'Yes Joachim, it sounds exciting. Much as I respect and like the Professor, I am finding the work ever more boring. Tell me, why do you think that the Professor should leave Vienna, his home?'

'He is Jewish. Soon it will not be safe for Jews in Austria, just as in Germany now. It is as simple as that.'

His tone changed and became much lighter. 'Enough of business. I vividly remember the wonderful night we spent together and I look forward to many more. I shall let you know when I will be arriving and we can be together. We shall enjoy each other's company fully, yes?'

'Oh yes, and I send you a big kiss, Joachim. . .and much, much more. I must go now, there is a patient due. Goodbye.'

'Good bye, Helga – until we meet soon.'

After taking the first ferry from Calais to Dover the following morning, having stayed in the slightly run-down but comfortable old Hotel Meurice, Johnny and Celia drove up to London where he dropped her at her house. He drove to his home and immediately telephoned Tar Robertson, arranging to be at the headquarters of the Security Service in an hour. Tar would arrange for Sir Vernon Kell, head of the Service to be in the meeting.

As arranged, Celia had contacted von Ribbentrop. He had been delighted to hear from her and invited her to join him for dinner that evening. She enthusiastically accepted the invitation, giving no hint of her personal reservations in doing so.

She gave instructions to her lady's maid both as to when she required her bath, the particular scented oil the she had decided upon, and the clothes that she would be wearing. She also gave instructions for a hairdresser and manicurist to come to the house in the afternoon, and for her driver to be ready with the car at 7.15pm.

Celia informed her butler that she would be lunching at 1pm, would not require dinner, but might wish for some light refreshment on her return home in the late evening.

Sir Vernon and Tar welcomed Johnny. They were joined by Charles Harvey. Sir Vernon uncapped his fountain pen, and looking at Johnny over his half-moon reading spectacles, invited him to report. 'Johnny, it will be simplest if you take us through the whole thing.'

'Sir Vernon. I shall start with the armed attack shortly after we had left Paris '

Johnny described what had happened and the part played by Celia. Her small calibre pistol had not killed the assailant that she took on, unlike the one who had been killed with one shot from Johnny's Webley Bulldog.

'It's a good thing that she had that crash course in pistol shooting from Billy Brownlow at the Bishopsgate Police Station range,' commented Tar.

'You can say that again – she was as cool as a cucumber throughout, and did not seem shaken by the experience at the time or later. She's a natural.'

He then went on to describe the action taken by the French security service. He outlined the information they had gleaned from the surviving wounded gunman and the driver, who had sped off from the scene only to be captured shortly afterwards. He mentioned the extreme methods of interrogation used, and that the two German agents who had lived after the shooting were dead.

'On the subject of German agents following Celia and me, I assume that Billy has reported what happened in Lyon yesterday morning?'

'Yes, he has,' replied Tar, 'the four agents that the French picked up are reckoned to be of higher calibre than the others. The last report was that they were not co-operating with their interrogators. I do not envy their chances. The French are satisfied that they too are German SD agents, and therefore under Heydrich and Himmler.'

'Celia is going to mention the first attack to von Ribbentrop, who may bring up the issue with Hitler.'

'Well, he certainly swallowed the bait in Cannes and dealt with that Irish sadist O'Reilly,' commented Tar.

Johnny continued, and described his alarming conversation with Charles Bedaux, the owner of Chateau de Cande and the host for the wedding of the Duke and Duchess.

Sir Vernon paraphrased this part of Johnny's report and then added, 'I shall see the Prime Minister on this. He flatly refuses to see Germany under Hitler and the Nazis as the threat that they truly are. It is alarming.I asked him the other day to have our budget increased substantially. I pointed out that we only have 35 full time agents, and have to rely on part-timers and co-operative locals. He flatly refused, and told me that there was no threat that justified any increase in intelligence resources.

'I digress. I shall contact J Edgar Hoover in America. I find him odious on a personal basis, but from what you say he will have one of his sinister files on your Mr Bedaux, just as he has on the former Mrs Simpson.'

Johnny was asked about the other guests and the wedding service itself. At the mention of Fruity Metcalfe, Tar interrupted, 'Metcalfe is a lightweight. He has toyed with fascism like so many of the officer class and aristocracy, but I do not think that he holds any great convictions. Above all, I am sure that he is an unswerving patriot. However, his wife has strong fascist leanings and she definitely wears the trousers.'

'Be that as it may,' said Sir Vernon, 'I have seen that picture of him at that fascist dinner. It appeared in Tatler. The organisation to which he belongs is the January Club, which is fervently pro-Hitler. The Duke has been infatuated with this rather silly and shallow man for many years, unhealthily so it has been said. Added to all this, his wife, Lord Curzon's youngest daughter, is ardently pro-Hitler. He has the ear of the Duke of Windsor. He is worthy of keeping an eye on.

'Mind you, whether the new Duchess will look favourably on their relationship is another matter. I doubt whether that lady will tolerate a third person in the marriage, even though she will probably continue with her sexual escapades.'

Johnny responded, 'Sir Vernon, I am inclined to agree with Tar. I think his position with the Duke is as a playmate, and no more. Wallis can't be bothered with him, and on that score I think you are right, she will try to keep him at a distance. Speaking of Wallis, Celia is having dinner with von Ribbentrop this evening and will find out whether he has managed to open a further line of communication with the Duchess.'

The meeting drew to a close, with Johnny agreeing that he and Celia would accept any invitation to join the Duke and Duchess if invited by Mr and Mrs Bedaux.

'Good work Johnny, and thank you my boy,' said Sir Vernon, as Johnny and Charles left the room. 'Please let me have your written report as soon as convenient.'

After Johnny and Charles had left the room, Sir Vernon turned to Tar. 'This unholy alliance of international big business and the fascists alarms me deeply, Tar. I only hope that the Prime Minister will bite the bullet and speak to President Roosevelt. I am not sure that he will.'

# Chapter 24

The train bringing the Duke and Duchess of Windsor pulled into the station in the little Austrian town of Arnoldstein, after over four hours. Wallis stood up as the train squealed to a halt, and as she leant forward, straightening her pencil skirt, smiled at the Duke, 'Well my darling, I just cannot wait to climb into a bed that is not shaken and rattled. That private carriage was mighty plush, but a train's a train, when all is said and done.'

The Duke laughed and replied, 'I couldn't agree more. Having stayed here in February when the Schloss was one of those recommended for us, I found it most comfortable indeed. I am sure that you will.'

When they alighted from the train, they were greeted by the Mayor and the station master. Inspector Shoher stood behind them. Chief Inspector Storrier, Inspector Attffield of Scotland Yard and Dudley Forward stood slightly behind the Duke and Duchess. Dudley Forward held the leads of the two terriers. The Duke acknowledged the mayor's formal welcome in German.

'We are delighted to be here after a long and tiring journey, and thank you for attending us. I see that there is no welcoming crowd as in Venice,' he observed, with a hint of petulance.

The mayor turned towards Inspector Shoher, who stepped forward and said, 'Your Royal Highness. A large number of the town's young people in national costume were here to greet you. I decided that in the interests of security, and in view of your long journey, they should be turned away. We have allowed only the six journalists who you see there.' He pointed to a small group of men further down the platform, outnumbered by the police who surrounded them.

He continued, 'I also took the liberty of forbidding any photographers because that would have been an intrusion.'

The Duke's good humour appeared to have been restored. 'I see Shoher, well done, and by the way, I am glad to see you again. Right, let's be off then.'

The Count and Countess were not there to greet them but she had sent her Mercedes. The Scotland Yard officers were to follow in Inspector Shoher's car. When the Duke and Duchess were settled in the back of the Mercedes and Dudley Forward in the front, the two cars set off for the climb up to the Schloss. The remainder of their staff and the baggage would follow a little later.

'Now Wallis, you must not be nervous. I know that you hate heights. The road up to the Schloss is winding and climbs very high. The Schloss itself is partly up the mountain, as you know. Anyway, we are in good hands and there is no snow to contend with, unlike there was on my last trip.'

The Duke hoped that cloaked in darkness, Wallis would not realise that the road was flanked by some terrifying sheer drops. He kept talking to distract her. 'Well, after we have settled in we have a few friends who will be coming over to join us. The first to arrive will be Fruity Metcalfe.'

'Oh, your lapdog,' laughed Wallis. 'Thank goodness he took that snooty wife of his to Paris and given us some time together.'

'I say, that's a bit harsh, Wallis, he is a fine chap and a good friend. As you saw with the wedding, my – sorry – *our* circle of friends is sadly diminished as a result of Baldwin and the Queen's efforts. Look at Perry Brownlow's position.'

'David, don't mention that man. He will never be welcome in our home again. Is that a deal?'

'If you say so Wallis, but it is such a shame to find one's circle dwindling.'

'Don't you worry about that. As soon as we are settled I shall get to work. You will see, my dear. I have plans. You mentioned that some of your German and Austrian relatives might come and stay. Who were you thinking of?'

'Well, I am in touch with quite a few – we have always kept in contact, except of course in the Great War. I believe my cousin, who is a big wheel in the Nazi Party, will be coming shortly. It's a rum old story. He was born and brought up in England, where he was Prince Charles Edward with all the English titles and honours that went with that.

'He was a sixteen year old Eton schoolboy when Queen Victoria decreed that he shoud go to Germany, and take the title of Duke of Saxe-Coburg and Gotha. That's the family and principality that her Consort, Prince Albert had come from. He was packed off to Germany – she was after all head of the extended family. The poor chap spoke not a word of German.'

'Gee, she could really do that?'

'Of course. Our family is represented in all of the Royal Houses of Europe. Anyhow, when the Great War came, he had to join the German army. Kaiser William was his first cousin, as was the Tsar, and my father King George. He fought with distinction and was awarded the Iron Cross for gallantry.

'After the war, my father ordered that he be stripped of all his British titles and style – up until then he was still entitled to be addressed as 'Your Royal Highness'. He was also stripped of his chivalrous title as a Knight of the Garter, and treated like a traitor. My father ordered that his name was never to be mentioned by the family or at Court.'

'That's a really sad story. You think that he will come?'

'I'm sure of it. He is now President of the Anglo-German Fellowship, and for an age has been pressing me to meet Herr Hitler. My cousin, Prince Christopher of Hesse-Cassel, is also likely to come. He is a Colonel in the SS and on the staff of Herman Himmler.'

As they came around what was to be the last bend, the headlights lit the entrance to the large gothic castle that was to be their home for the next three months.

'Just wait until tomorrow when you will see the views, Wallis. Breathtaking, truly breathtaking.'

As tradition demanded, the Duke picked up a protesting Wallis and carried her through the massive entrance. The large staff were all lined up in their uniforms to greet the couple. As the Duke put Wallis back on her feet, the men servants bowed. The women and girls curtsied.

'There Wallis, that ensures good fortune and a long and happy marriage for us,' said the smiling Duke, as he acknowledged the servants.

Wallis was only half-listening. It seemed that every part of the walls of the great hall was taken up with hunting trophies, some of which were snarling menacingly. She shivered as she thought, 'They are coming down in the morning.'

The following morning, the personal staff of the Duke and Duchess took over the private duties concerning the couple. The Duke had been delighted when Dudley Forward had shown him Mussolini's personal note of congratulations and good wishes addressed to the Duchess and himself. It was in the envelope which had been delivered at the same time as the carnations, as they were leaving Venice. Mussolini expressed the hope that they would return shortly.

'Wallis, what say you that we go to Venice after our trip to Vienna? We could go at the end of next month for a few days – I should think that July at the Excelsior would be first rate.'

'That sounds just dandy, darling. Now then, about our circle of friends. One couple that I am sure will come and stay is Johnny and Celia. You and he can play some golf and go off shooting, so long as you don't drag ghastly trophies back with you. Which reminds me. . .'

'Topping idea! I was also thinking of an old shipmate, Commander Colin Buist, and his wife Gladys. What about your old friend Josephine Gwynne?'

'Well, she is great fun, and a dear friend since childhood, but of course she is single.'

'No trouble, I can ask Hugh Molyneux, the Earl of Sefton's son. He was one of my Lords-in-Waiting when I was King. Great man of the turf, rather dashing and single too. You never know.'

''We must get in touch and make arrangements.'

'We have another problem. There have been so many telegrams and letters that I really do not know how we shall be able to respond. Dudley tells me that another 300 letters arrived this morning. We shall need more help.'

Celia had arrived at von Ribbentrop's suite on the dot of time the previous evening. She knew that she had to appear enthusiastic and pleased to see him, despite her misgivings.

'Celia, my dear, you look ravishing.'

'Thank you, Bubbles darling, you are looking very chipper yourself.'

They embraced briefly, and von Ribbentrop gestured for Celia to take a seat. As she sat down and opened her handbag to take out her cigarette case and holder, he poured her a glass of champagne. 'So, you must have so much news, where would you like to start?'

'Gosh! Well Johnny and I were travelling alone, and we were followed when we were south of Paris.' She and Johnny had agreed that the facts of the shoot-out, and subsequent involvement of the French Security Service, should not be mentioned. He would tell Tar of their decision which was contrary to what had been agreed in the meeting with Tar and Sir Vernon.

'Johnny was brilliant. Thank goodness he has that Hispano-Suiza. He left the Route National and took to the country roads where he lost them. We do not know who they were, but it was very uncomfortable. We changed our plans for the wedding itself, and stayed in the chateau where the ceremony took place. It was crawling with policemen, so we felt safe.'

Celia went on to describe the wedding ceremonies and then the departure of the Duke and Duchess for Venice. 'Do you have any contact with Wallis at the moment, Bubbles?'

'Not directly. She can contact me, but until she is in Austria I could not risk contacting her. I want to talk to you about that. The young man, Didier, was my contact in Cannes until that sadistic pervert Bernard O'Reilly, who was his controller, murdered him. Another one of Himmler or Heydrich's stunts. I made sure that O'Reilly got his due desserts. He was supposed to be loyal to me. '

'What happened to him?' asked Celia, the picture of innocence.

'He had tortured a young prostitute with a cigarette end applied to her most sensitive places – he was a pervert. One of her closest friends, a homosexual prostitute, lured him to a deserted house where two of my men overcame him and tied him up. He probably thought it was a sex game, until they left him at the mercy of the young homosexual friend who repaid him with a blow torch.'

'In the newspaper it merely said that he was a prominent businessman, and had been found dead with no foul play suspected. Tell me honestly, Bubbles. Do you think that the

Duke and Duchess are at risk from Himmler and his cronies?'

'I do not think so. They are cards which the Führer sees as his own. I do not think that Himmler would risk such a move, although he hates the aristocracy and sees them as the old order. Now, what I want you to do is call Wallis in the morning and ask how their journey went. Tell her that I have found her the perfect secretary to augment her staff and keep contact with me. She speaks and writes fluent English, German and French. She is an Austrian, currently in Vienna.

'Her name is Helga. At present she is the secretary to the ear specialist whom the Duke saw earlier in the year. That job is finishing. I wish Wallis to persuade the Duke to go and have a check up. She must accompany him. She must then engage her in conversation in English. Helga will indicate that she will be shortly looking for a new job. Wallis must then ask her a few more questions, and then, when she sees the Professor in the presence of the Duke, ask him for a reference for Helga. He will readily give it, I can assure you. You can also mention to Wallis that Helga is not only beautiful, but very enthusiastic. You know what I mean?' von Ribbentrop had a twinkle in his eye as he looked at Celia.

'Shall we have a spot of dinner?'

After a delicious but light dinner, Celia felt much more relaxed with von Ribbentrop, who stood and held out his hand to her. Celia took it and he led her to the bedroom. Celia had forgotten how von Ribbentrop could match her sexual needs, but soon remembered as they slowly undressed each other.

He was naked before her and was fully aroused. Celia was still in her provocatively tailored underwear made for her by Madame Bertrand in Paris. As they kissed deeply, she could feel him against her and within moments her need matched his. She pushed him on to his back, and still wearing her silk knickers, straddled him.

'My God! I thought only tarts wore underwear like that!'

'Shut up, Bubbles!' she panted, as she began to gyrate her hips. 'I bet you'll buy some for Helga!'

Late the next morning, after speaking to Johnny and reporting her conversation with von Ribbentrop, Celia telephoned Wallis. After some difficulties she was connected. They discussed their respective journeys and Wallis described her first impressions of the Schloss, extending a warm invitation for Celia and Johnny to join them. Celia confirmed that they would be delighted. Celia then explained about Helga exactly as requested by von Ribbentrop. Wallis not only took the bait – she almost snatched it.

# Chapter 25

After Celia had reported her conversation with Wallis to Johnny, she called von Ribbentrop. 'Bubbles, I have just spoken to Wallis, who is very keen on the idea of Helga joining her staff. She will make arrangements for the Duke to see Professor Newmann. They are driving to Vienna, and will arrive at the Hotel Bristol on the 20$^{th}$ June. She is very excited about the Vienna trip – she was one of the Duke's party when he stayed there in 1935.'

'Right, Celia, I shall change my plans and also book into the Bristol. There is no reason why I should not meet the Duke and Duchess. We still need to go through the charade with Wallis meeting Helga at Newmann's consulting rooms; I do not want the Duke or his "minders" having any suspicion that she is a plant. Do you understand?'

'Yes, I certainly do. She suggested that I join them in Vienna with Johnny Johnstone, but he definitely cannot go then, and I am not sure.'

'Oh, Celia – don't be what you English call a spoilsport. It could be fun.'

'Well, I'll see. I must dash now, Bubbles darling.'

'Very well, goodbye then, and as you English say, "Jolly well played!"'

Celia called Johnny back. He then spoke to Tar Robertson, who felt that Celia should definitely join the Duke and Duchess in Vienna. She decided to go and contacted Thomas Cook and asked that the appropriate bookings and reservations be made. She would fly to Cologne to visit an old friend from finishing school, and then take the overnight train to Vienna. She would be flying out of Croydon Airport, south of London, on the Friday morning Lufthansa flight. She would then catch the Saturday evening train to Vienna, arriving on Sunday morning, the same day as the Duke and Duchess.

She then called Wallis, and told her of her plans to be at the same hotel and that von Ribbentrop would also stay there. She stressed that bumping into von Ribbentrop must be seen to be a surprise.

'Of course it will be a total surprise,' replied a laughing Wallis, 'excellent, Celia – we should have quite a party!'

The Duke and Duchess were enjoying an early evening cocktail on the terrace of the Schloss.

'By Jove, Wallis, the views are stupendous – I love the contrast of the dark green pine forests and the stark mountain tops behind. This area of Carinthia is so appealing!'

'It is wonderful. Changing the subject, how is your ear that was troubling you last winter?'

'Well, it seems fine now, but I still use an ear plug when I am swimming, just in case.'

'I think that you ought to see your professor when we are in Vienna. You want to be able to enjoy the sea when we go to Venice, don't you?'

'Rather, that's part of the reason for going. But that's a good idea – I shall have Dudley make the arrangements.'

'I will keep you company, darling.'

'Thank you, Wallis.'

'That was easy,' thought Wallis.

Celia's driver dropped her outside the modernistic, white terminal building in Croydon Airport. A porter loaded her luggage onto his trolley. As usual, the drive from Mayfair had been rather tedious. London seemed so depressing when you crossed south of the river, she thought to herself. It could not be the fault of the River Thames, but the people looked so drab and miserable. So much looked run down and ill-kempt.

She walked into the smart terminal, and quickly spotted the Lufthansa desk. When she presented her travel papers, the charming and handsome young clerk welcomed her, and checking her name on the passenger manifest for her flight gave instructions to her porter, who wheeled away her luggage after she had given him a shilling tip. A tall, blonde girl in a smart Lufthansa uniform asked Celia to follow, and led her into a comfortable lounge, where she asked whether Celia would like a coffee.

'That would be lovely, thank you.'

The attendant returned shortly, and placed a round tray with a fine white bone china coffee pot, cup, saucer and sugar bowl, all bearing the Lufthansa name.

'Thank you. Are you able to tell me what aircraft I shall be flying on today?'

'Of course, Milady. It is a Junkers JU-52 tri-motor named *"Emil Schafer"*, with capacity for 17 passengers and crew. The flight will not be full today – in fact, I think there will only be 5 passengers. I shall be one of the two flight stewardesses and Herr Schmidt, who is at the desk, will be travelling as a passenger.'

'Thank you. I have flown on a JU-52 before. With so few passengers we will certainly have excellent service.'

The stewardess flushed, and with a forced smile replied, 'Milady, if you will pardon my saying so we believe that the service on Lufthansa, our German national airline, is always excellent.'

'But of course, it was only my little joke. And now, if you will excuse me.'

Celia wondered whether staff like that were brainwashed. She reached in her small travelling valise and took out her book. It was a paperback published by Penguin, with the familiar orange cover denoting a work of fiction. She found Ernest Hemingway's *"A Farewell to Arms"* hard work, but was disciplining herself to read it. She had a couple of Agatha Christie mysteries in her luggage to dip into, once she reached Vienna.

On Friday 18th June, von Ribbentrop presented himself in Professor Newmann's consulting rooms. 'Good day to you, Helga,' he greeted the uniformed receptionist, as he came through the door. She had her hair in the unflattering style that she adopted when working, but von Ribbentrop knew what she really looked like when off-duty. Helga beamed at him.

'And to you, Herr Schmidt, if I am not mistaken,' she responded, as she smiled mischievously. 'The Professor is ready for you.'

'Excellent. I feared that I might be early for him. I changed my mind, and I am staying at the Hotel Bristol. It really is most comfortable – I have a beautiful suite on the fifth floor, the President's Suite, but I doubt he has need of it,' he said with a laugh, handing her an embossed visiting card bearing the German crest and with his rank and full name. He held up both hands indicating the number 7 with his fingers, looking at her questioningly, and she responded with a broad smile as she mouthed the number seven. He nodded in confirmation.

She stood up from her desk and walked slowly over to the door to the Professor's consulting room. She had a magnificent figure and legs which were not disguised by her uniform. Von Ribbentrop felt himself stirring just looking at her and anticipating the evening they would spend together. She knocked, and opening the door wide beckoned von Ribbentrop to enter as she announced him as Herr Schmidt. Von Ribbentrop sat down opposite to the Professor who welcomed him warily.

'Professor, first I must thank you for your co-operation with regard to my previous visit. Second, I am here to give you a warning. Soon you and your family will not be safe in Austria.'

The professor visibly stiffened. Von Ribbentrop continued, 'However determined the Austrian Chancellor Schusnigg may be to stay independent of Germany, his endeavour is doomed to failure. The Austrian Nazi party is rapidly gaining power and influence. Soon – and I believe within a year at the outside – Austria will become a part of the greater Germany. You are a prominent Jew. I need not say more. You must close your practice immediately and leave this country with your family whilst you are free to do so. To support my knowledge of the matter, here is my card.'

The professor took the proferred card, and seemed to stare at it for longer than necessary to simply note its content. He looked up, and clearing his throat asked quietly, 'How could I possibly just shut my practice and take my family away from the city where I was born, trained, taught, and practised medicine for my whole career?'

'Easily. Inform your receptionist that you are unwell and are cancelling all appointments. Give her the name of a colleague who will take over your patients. She can then telephone and duly cancel all appointments. That will take a few days, so I suggest that you close down next Thursday. You will of course see the Duke of Windsor on Wednesday, and inform him of your decision.'

'You have it all planned for me, it seems.'

'Yes, Herr Professor, I have. You will need to consult your lawyers and complete the documents giving them power of attorney to dispose of such property that you do not take with you.'

'Do I have a choice, Herr von Ribbentrop?' he asked, in an even fainter voice.

'No, you do not, of that I can assure you.'

'I have been giving the matter some thought, as it happens, and I shall do as you say. My wife and I wish there to be a future for our children, grandchildren and, indeed, children of generations to come. We cannot bear the thought that if our family were to cease to exist now, it would bring a total stop to the blood lines of which we are only the present. Those bloodlines stretch back to time immemorial over countless generations. They must not be stopped in this way. We shall go to England.'

'You are very wise, Herr Professor, very wise. I would suggest that you leave discreetly and travel through Switzerland, then France. Under no circumstances enter Germany or Italy for any reason.'

'But we have family in Germany and wish to say goodbye to them.'

'I know that you have one brother who is a dentist in Berlin, a second who is a professor at Heidelburg University, and another who is a banker in Frankfurt. You know as well as I do that to go and visit them and their families, you risk everything, and I mean everything.' Von Ribbentrop fixed the professor with a cold hard stare.

'I understand – I am ashamed to say that I heed your warning and we will not go to Germany. Thank you for clarifying the issue. I shall tell Helga, my receptionist, now, if I may?'

He rang the small silver bell on his desk and Helga entered the room. He then told her of his decision, and gave her instructions as suggested by von Ribbentrop.

Von Ribbentrop paid a courtesy call on the German Ambassador and accepted his invitation for lunch in the Embassy. They discussed the unification of Austria and Germany, and the steps that must be taken to fully implement it efficiently.

'I have a team working flat out, Joachim. Their brief is the Nazification of every aspect of Austrian life. We are even looking at the way they manage their horse racing. That is the level of detail we are setting ourselves. When the Führer brings Austria into line it will be totally absorbed.'

Von Ribbentrop was pleased with the progress that was obviously being made, and mentioned that he would be informing the Führer. He knew full well that the Ambassador, an aristocrat and professional diplomat, despised him and their leader, but was too much of an old hand to give himself away.

He was then provided with an office and a secretary so that he could go through and deal with his messages. After signing the typed communications that need not be encrypted and passing the secure communications to the Embassy encryption clerk for processing, he took his leave of the Ambassador and was driven back to the Hotel Bristol.

Billy Brownlow's spirits were at a low ebb. He had always known that his period of duty in the South of France would end when Wallis Simpson moved on. Any new posting would take him away from Lisette, the beautiful former prostitute who had been tortured by the Irishman Bernard O'Reilly.

There had been some satisfaction in O'Reilly's tortured death, but that could not make up for being indefinitely separated from the vulnerable girl that he loved. His family fortune meant that he had been able to help her start a new life, and she now lived in a large apartment which he regarded as his home also. After the events in Lyon he had been granted his leave request, and rushed back to Cannes to spend two idyllic weeks with Lisette. He was now in Vienna awaiting the arrival of the Duke and Duchess of Windsor. His role was as back up to Celia if there should be any trouble.

He had already observed von Ribbentrop, and followed him to Professor Newmann's consulting rooms. He was aware of the role that Helga was to play. He was staying in the Hotel Bristol, and he permitted himself a smile at the thought that the hotel would be like a live setting for an Agatha Christie mystery. On reflection, he hoped not. He had not stayed at the hotel before, but could now appreciate why it had such an outstanding reputation.

His cousin, Perry Cust, Lord Brownlow, had been one of the then Prince of Wales' party who had stayed at the Bristol after a winter sports holiday at Kitzbuhel, in February 1935. The Prince's party had taken a whole floor of the hotel. According to his cousin it had been a raucous time. Cousin Perry was unusually depressed at the moment. It was because two powerful women wanted him out of their husbands' lives. Wallis, the Duchess of Windsor, was slighted that he had not attended her wedding to his old friend the Duke.

Elizabeth, the Queen, had effectively had him banished from Court after procuring his apparent resignation as the King's Lord-in-Waiting and making it clear that neither she nor the King would receive him. The Queen considered that when the Duchess, as the married Mrs Simpson, had fled from England, Lord Brownlow had given her too much assistance and support. She chose to ignore that he was one of the then King's Lords-in-Waiting and acted on his orders to do so.

As Billy settled down to do the crossword in the previous day's copy of *The Times,* he thought to himself that whilst people talked of the fickle finger of fate, they overlooked the fickle nature of the world of royal favour.

# Chapter 26

Von Ribbentrop had been amused when, on arrival at the hotel, he found that he had been allocated the President's Suite. After checking around the suite and noting the view of the Opera House just across the road, he instructed the two maids to unpack his luggage and put it away in the second of the two large walk-in wardrobes in the dressing room. As he walked back to the sitting room along the marble floored corridor, he planned his evening. He sat at the desk in the corner of the opulent sitting room, and and picking up the telephone, dialled the hotel reception.

He booked a table in the Grill Room for two at 8.30pm, and said that it must be a prime corner table. He also ordered a supply of Louis Roederer Cristal champagne to be placed in the refrigerator in the suite's small kitchen, and for ice buckets to be brought at 6.45pm and 10pm. He gave instructions that the bedroom was to be prepared by the maids after he and his guest had gone down to dinner. He was not to be disturbed.

He was humming to himself as he had a long, hot shower which he finished with a minute under shocking cold water. He towelled himself vigorously, savouring the tingling afterglow as circulation returned to normal. He smiled at his reflection in the mirrored wall of the bathroom. 'Pretty good for a man of my age, pretty damned good,' he thought.

He finally splashed on cologne. It was created by the old, established Parisian perfumier Creed. It had been specially created for the Duke of Windsor when he was King. Wallis had extolled it and had arranged for a quantity to be sent to von Ribbentrop in London. The fresh, but masculine combination of juniper, jasmine, lime and Scottish pine appealed to him almost as much as the irony. After dressing with care he realised that his excitement at being with Helga again was making him edgy. He told himself to get a grip but he felt like an eager teenager. He would have to do something about it before dinner or it would be sheer hell.

Shortly before Helga was due to arrive, a messenger from the Embassy was shown into his sitting room. He handed an officially sealed envelope to him, and then retired to the hallway whilst von Ribbentrop went to the desk and opened it. He read it quickly, and then penned a response which he sealed into one of the hotel envelopes, signing it across the sealed flap. His face was expressionless. He summoned the messenger.

'This is to go directly for encryption and despatch. Nobody, absolutely nobody else, is to have sight of it. Do you understand my order?'

The nervous messenger, addressing him in his official rank of Oberführer, confirmed that he would do so. He was well aware that von Ribbentrop far outranked the German Ambassador to Vienna.

'Very well, you are dismissed.' The messenger came to attention and gave an impeccable Nazi salute. 'Heil Hitler!'

Von Ribbentrop echoed him and also saluted in a rather more relaxed manner, as befitted their respective ranks. After the messenger had left he cursed gently. The message from Admiral Canaris, head of the Abwehr, courteously informed him that amongst the Duke and Duchess of Windsor's visitors in Vienna, there were to be two of the Duke's cousins. The Duke of Saxe-Coburg was a former senior member of the British Royal Family who had been an ardent Nazi for a number of years. He was not a problem.

However, the other cousin could well be. Prince Christopher of Hess-Cassel was a Colonel in the SS, attached to Himmler's staff. The last thing that von Ribbentrop wanted was Himmler's interference in his plans. He would have to engineer a meeting with the Duke and spell out caution.

In his reply to Admiral Canaris, he merely thanked him, and asked that he be informed when the visits were to take place and the venue. He needed to think. For the moment, the interruption had driven thoughts of Helga out of his mind.

Billy Brownlow was contemplating the tedious side of being an intelligence officer, as he apparently relaxed in an armchair in the lobby area of the Hotel Bristol. The lobby, like so much of the hotel, was decorated and furnished in an ornate and heavy old-fashioned style that made him think of his grandmother's Victorian taste.

Compared to the fashionable lighter styles to which he had become used, it felt oppressive. The owners clearly had not taken the opportunity to thoroughly modernise the whole hotel when it was refurbished and updated in 1928. Perhaps the many members of Royal families and fashionable people who chose to stay at the Bristol indulged in a nostalgia that he could not share.

To the casual observer he was engrossed in his newspaper and coffee. An unopened book with a tasselled bookmark lay on the low table in front of him, next to the tray with the coffee pot. The concierge was aware Billy was a British security agent, tasked with protection of the Duke and Duchess. Billy had informed him of this in confidence, adding that there was no specific threat. Nevertheless, the couple were considered to be generally at risk, and he was keeping an eye out for known terrorists.

Given the number of members of Royal families and dignataries of all nationalities who stayed in the hotel, the legendary concierge, Hekkel, who at his own insistence was only ever addressed by his surname, was totally at ease, and would not have expected anything else. He was quite sure that there would be other watchers, including Austrian agents. Nevertheless, he would mention it in his handover at the end of his long shift.

Just before 7pm, Billy's attention was caught by the entry into the reception area of an utterly stunning young woman. She was above average height, and a picture of understated elegance from top to toe. Her high heels clacked a rapid rhythm as she walked across the marble floor and approached the concierge's desk.

In response to Hekkel asking how he might be of assistance, she asked to be directed to the Presidential Suite occupied by Oberführer von Ribbentrop. Hekkel turned towards the page boy who was standing rigidly to attention at the side of the high mahogany desk. 'Kollar, escort this lady to the Presidential Suite.'

The boy clicked his heels, and with his white-gloved hand gestured that Helga should follow him. He led her to the ornately-decorated doors of the two lifts at the end of a short corridor off to the right, between the reception area and the adjacent lobby where Billy was sitting.

Hekkel dialled the extension number of the suite from memory. The call was answered almost immediately.

'Von Ribbentrop.'

'Your Excellency, Hekkel here. Your guest is being shown to your suite.'

'Thank you.'

Hekkel noticed that the elegant, self-confessed British agent had shown a close interest in the young woman. The famous long case clock that stood against the wall, separating his desk from that of reception, chimed the hour of 7pm.

'There's a young lady who values punctuality,' he thought. 'Unlike so many of the fashionable Viennese who relish an elegantly louche approach to life,' he continued his reflection with some distaste, 'so different to our German cousins – I admire their efficiency.'

He wondered whether the now Duke of Windsor would give his security people the slip as he had done when he stayed in the hotel in 1935. On that visit, at the Prince's personal request, Hekkel had arranged for a driver to be waiting at the rear porters' entrance with a Daimler limousine, which took the then Prince of Wales to a so-called mystery destination on a number of occasions. On each occasion he had been unaccompanied. The destination was no secret to Hekkel, to whom the driver had reported.

The Prince, who had travelled as the Earl of Chester, was visiting a powerful man. He had been one of the supporters of the right-wing President Dolfuss, whose fascist views survived his assassination in July 1934, and were still popular in Austria. Those views were not shared by the strongly pro-German Austrian Nazi party. They would have no truck with the current President Schussnigg who was supported by Benito Mussolini. Schussnigg was striving to contain the increasing German Nazi threat and maintain Austria's independent neutrality. The British Security Service was unaware of the meetings that the Prince of Wales, the future King, had attended.

Billy had checked with Hekkel, who had skilfully palmed the notes that were slipped into his hand. Billy was now aware that von Ribbentrop was to dine in the Grill Room of the hotel. He asked that a table be reserved for himself which would afford him a good view of the restaurant. He thanked Hekkel and left to get changed into his dinner jacket. He would then have a pre-dinner drink in the Anglo-American Bar.

Von Ribbentrop had decided that he should not greet Helga in his dressing gown even though that would have been more appropriate, given his intentions. As she entered the suite he noted with pleasure that she had adopted a fashionable hair style, rather than the severe and rather unattractive one that she had for work. 'My dear,' he cried out, 'you look ravishing!'

She smiled broadly in response to his enthusiasm but then gave him a coquettish look, as she started to peel off the long, soft kid glove on her left hand.

'Champagne?' he asked, still smiling.

'But of course, Joachim darling.'

She was now peeling off her other glove equally as suggestively and still holding his gaze. As he poured the two glasses she began to unbutton her tailored suit jacket. Von Ribbentrop found her every movement erotically charged, almost to the point of distress. He went to hand her the champagne but then put the glass down, and holding her eye he started to move towards her. She simply raised her right hand, and extending her finger slowly, moved it to and fro in front of her. He stopped moving towards her but gave an involuntary groan.

'Take off your clothes,' she ordered. He pulled an end of his bow tie and then shrugged out of his jacket and his black silk waist coat. He slipped the straps of his braces off his shoulders.

Helga continued to slowly undress, moving ever more sensually as she did. As von Ribbentrop eased out of his patent leather evening dress slippers, Helga, who had now removed her silk blouse, was slowly undoing the side fastening of her skirt. She signalled for him to remove his trousers and then his shirt. He was now standing naked except for knee length silk Sulka shorts, his black silk stockings and their suspenders. In any other circumstances it would have been a comical sight. The loosely-cut shorts did nothing to hide his state of arousal.

Helga now dropped her skirt. He gasped as it pooled around her ankles. She was wearing only her bustier from which the suspenders were fastened to her stockings. The bustier was cut so that her bare sex was exposed. She turned away from him, and on her high heels stalked across the room, looking over her shoulder, staring into his eyes. Her eyes burned with a hunger, a lust.

He followed her as she reached a high backed armchair. She gave him one last fiery look and then bent forward over the chair back. She then reached back with both hands and drew on each cheek. Von Ribbentrop's groan turned into a growl as he tore off his shorts and leapt forward.

Promptly at 8.30pm, Billy noted that a very relaxed von Ribbentrop ushered his attractive companion into the Grill Room. The Maître d' bustled forward, and fussily led them to a corner table that was secluded from much of the room. As he and Helga were seated, von Ribbentrop looked at the Maître d' and with a broad smile said, 'Most satisfactory, and thank you.'

'Your Excellency, we are honoured '

As the Maître d' turned away, a broadly smiling Helga said, 'And I could say the same.'

'Thank you, my dear, indeed, so could I.' They both laughed.

Even across the room it was clearly apparent that they were lovers, and that they had slaked their thirst for each other before coming down for dinner. Billy felt a strong pang of envy. If only Lisette were here, perhaps they would have that look. He thought that she would have enjoyed the dimly lit Anglo-American bar, which was darkly panelled with plenty of alcoves and corners, where discrete conversations or assignations could be carried on. The bar had an air of mystery and intrigue.

The Grill Room was opulent, but Billy found the fact that it was a copy of the Grill Room on the ill-fated RMS Titanic strangely depressing. The exquisite meal passed uneventfully, and after von Ribbentrop and the girl had left, Billy was at something of a loss as to what to do. He decided to ask Hekkel to recommend a typical bar close to the hotel. He had rather taken to the outwardly-forbidding figure of the concierge. 'I am sorry to trouble you, but can you direct me to a typical Viennese bar close to this hotel. You know, the sort of place that you would go to?'

'Of course, Sir. I can go one better if you wish. I am finishing in 10 minutes if you do not mind waiting that long. I am happy to take you. The bar I have in mind is hard to find.'

'I say, that's most awfully kind of you. Of course I am happy to wait. There is no rush!'

'Very well, sir. When I am ready I will have you shown to the rear service entrance to the hotel. It might be useful in any event. If you would be so kind as to wait in the lobby I will send a page boy when I have changed.'

Only a few minutes later, the same page boy who had escorted Helga earlier appeared, and asked Billy to follow him. They passed through an unmarked service door, and after the glittering crystal chandeliers and opulence of the public rooms it was hard to believe that the drab and ill-lit corridor was in the same building.

Their footsteps sounded loudly on the dark brown composition floor, and Billy was glad when they turned a corner and entered a better-lit hallway where Hekkel was waiting. Out of uniform he still cut a smart figure in a dark double breasted suit with a homburg hat in his hand.

'Well then, Herr Hekkel, lead on. The drinks are on me.'

'Hekkel, Mr Brownlow, Hekkel. That is my name, and that is what all call me, even my dear wife. We shall see about the drink.' He laughed.

'You do not think that I will look out of place in my evening dress?'

'Absolutely not. The Opera House is our neighbour and members of the audience are required to dress accordingly. We go down this alley which leads to a small square – and there is the bar.' Hekkel pointed at an unprepossesing looking bar which had no tables outside.

As they pushed through the double doors they were assailed by a total fug of tobacco smoke and heat, overlaid by the sound of many men's voices and laughter. Hekkel led the way straight to a small marble-topped round table opposite the beginning of a very long bar. 'That was lucky!' commented

Billy. The huge bar was packed.

'No luck, Sir, this is my table. Actually, it is my bar. I am going to have a beer and schnapps. Does that suit you?'

'Most certainly, but you must allow me to buy the drinks.'

'No, you are my guest and that is the end of the matter.'

Their drinks arrived with the pale lager in tall misted glasses and the schnapps chasers in small tumblers.

'Well, what do you think of the back way out of the hotel?'

'I can see its uses. Do many guests use it?'

'Very few know about it. Your Duke when he was Prince of Wales did though. I organised for him to use the back service stairs and have a Daimler and driver waiting at the kerb.'

Billy fought hard not to give away either his surprise or his excitement. 'Did he do it often? I mean, who went with him?'

'Oh, he went three times and always alone. He was gone for just over an hour the first two times, then on the last occasion almost three hours.'

'Where on earth was he going? Mrs Simpson was in his party, so I doubt that it was an assignation with another woman?'

'The house that he visited on each occasion was that of Arthur Seyss–Inquart. He was a member of Dolfuss' cabinet, and then after the assassination that of the present Chancellor Sshussnigg. I have heard him speak at my club. I was a keen mountain man in my youth, as is he. He is President of the German-Austrian Alpine Club. He is now a member of the National Socialist Party, and has become a follower of Heinrich Himmler and a believer in racial purity, as am I. He has personally sponsored various expeditions to Asia to prove the truth of the assertions of Aryan superiority.'

'That's interesting. Did the Prince of Wales ever comment?'

'No, nothing at all, except when I asked him whether everything had run smoothly, he responded, "Swimmingly Hekkel, absolutely swimmingly". He was in a very good mood.'

This was dynamite in Billy's opinion. If true, and there was no reason to doubt what he had been told, the Duke of Windsor, almost a year before his father's death and his accession, was having secret discussions with an Austrian politician who had recognised sympathies towards not only Germany, but also holding extreme Nazi beliefs. There may never be proof positive, but at this stage of the game the information was of great importance. It begged the question "Could the Duke of Windsor be a traitor who would have been crowned"?

# Chapter 27

The following morning, Saturday, Billy sent an encrypted message to Tar Robertson in London from the British Embassy. He explained what he had been told, but did not draw any conclusions. They would be self-evident to Tar and Sir Vernon. He also reported that he intended to find out more about Arthur Seyss-Inquart. The Duke and Duchess were not due to arrive until the following day so he might as well do a little investigating.

After a leisurely breakfast he set off to Rengasse, where on the corner with Wipplingerstrasse he entered the Cafe Louvre. It was directly across the street from Vienna's telegraph office and next to Radio Austria, where radiograms could be sent all over the world. It was the haunt of nearly all the foreign journalists in Vienna. The cafe had long been a home from home for radical thinkers, and the foreign correspondents had flocked to it since American journalist Robert Best made it his unofficial office, his Stammtisch, in 1923.

Vienna was the hub where information was gathered from the new democracies that had emerged in Central Europe after the collapse of the Austro-Hungarian Empire. News from Czechoslovakia, Poland, Hungary and the Balkans was collated in Vienna. The Cafe Louvre was the unofficial 'bourse' where the information was offered, tested and traded amongst the foreign correspondents.

Billy's entree to this goldmine of information and gossip had been his friendship with William 'Bill' Shirer, a brilliant young American journalist. They had met by chance at a literary party in Paris, where Ernest Hemingway was the unofficial guest of honour. The acerbic Shirer had commented to Billy that personally he thought Hemingway a clever writer, but full of bullshit. They had had a spirited argument which totally failed to resolve the issue, notwithstanding a large number of cognacs. They had left in the early hours unsteady and arm-in-arm, and set out to find somewhere they could have a coffee. When they had met the next day, their crippling hangovers may have precluded serious conversation, but a bond had been formed. They had recovered a little after a 'hair of the dog', and that had since become their catchphrase greeting.

Billy pushed open the door into the crowded cafe. It was not particularly comfortably furnished, with the ubiquitous violin-backed hard chairs and small tables. There was one longer table with an uncomfortable bench on one side and chairs on the other. Billy spotted his friend in one of the chairs, pipe in mouth and arms stretched as he held a newspaper open. 'Bill,' he said loudly, so that he could be heard over the steady rumble of voices, 'hair of the dog, you old devil?'

'Billy, my man, and a hair of the dog to you too, sir. What brings you to this charming city of contrasts on the Danube. Is it Strauss and Franz Lehar, or the delicious pastries and women?'

'Oh, just a bit of research work. Mostly boring. Hang on a minute, I'll just get a coffee. Anything for you?'

'No thanks, I'm awash with the stuff.'

When Billy sat down again on the bench opposite, they exchanged inconsequential information and gossip about mutual friends and acquaintances. Bill had long before surmised that Billy was an intelligence officer in some British agency.

'Bill. What do you know about the chap Arthur Seyss-Inquart?'

'Well, let me see.' Shirer was blessed with an encyclopaedic memory. He looked at the ceiling for a moment or two, tapping the stem of his pipe on his teeth.

'Yup. He qualified as a lawyer and set up his own practice that was successful. He was very active politically, but careful to keep a low profile. He was rumoured to have pro-German leanings, but nothing proven. He joined the Cabinet of Dolfuss in 1933. He manouvered his way through the mess of the Dolfuss administration and assasination, and popped up again as a State Councillor under Kurt von Schussnigg. He holds that post now.

'He is an enigma. Everybody says that he is politically too smart for his own good. He is reckoned to still have strong German leanings, and has voiced support for the most extreme Nazi views on race. A very dangerous man indeed, I would say, albeit masked by his charm, erudition and prowess as a mountaineer. Mountineering is a big deal in Austria, remember. He is President of the German-Austrian Alpine Club. It's said to be a front for discrete Austro-German unification.'

'But that is expressly banned by the treaties at the end of the Great War, isn't it?'

'Of course, my dear fellow, but mark my words that is what will happen. Probably sooner than later.'

'Do you think that he is a Nazi?' Billy asked.

'He could not be in Schussnigg's government if he were openly, but frankly, I am sure that he is. The Nazis are determined to see all of the "German Peoples" – and that includes the Austrians – within one nation. You have heard Herr Hitler's cry, "Ein Volk, ein Reich, ein Führer!" There you have the blueprint for his dream, his goal and Germany's goal.'

'My God!' muttered Billy, who was visibly shaken. He could not mention the intelligence that the Prince of Wales, as he then was, had visited this man alone on a number of occasions in 1935.

'Come on, I owe you a drink. Here, or somewhere more comfortable? Why don't we splurge and go to the bar in the Hotel Sacher – it's on my expenses, by the way?'

'No sooner asked than accepted. I might even have a slice of the divine torte – I haven't had breakfast. What are we waiting for?'

The two friends left the Cafe Louvre apparently without a care in the world.

Billy could not wait to report to Tar. What he had learned would indicate that the Duke of Windsor was far more enmeshed in Nazism than had been suspected, and, alarmingly, from before there was any significant suspicion concerning his beliefs. What seemed clear was that he was no innocent pawn. Was he up to his neck in a dangerous political intrigue?

■ ■ ■

'We should have a fine time in Vienna, Wallis. Apart from two of my cousins visiting us, we have dinner at the Brazilian Legation with George Messersmith, the American Ambassador – you have met him, haven't you?'

Wallis nodded, smiling. The Duke continued, 'Sam Gracie, the Brazilian Minister in Vienna, has an English wife – for the life of me I cannot recall her name – remind me to have Dudley find out – and there will be an Italian chap as well. It should be pleasant.'

'Have you anything else planned? '

'Nothing specific. I want this to be a very private visit. If we leave tomorrow really early we should be there in the late morning. Inspector Shoher is insistent that we have an armed escort. Apparently there has been some trouble in this area, Carinthia, you know. He's a good chap and we can rely on him.'

'What sort of trouble, David?'

'Not quite sure dearest, but I think that it was some fighting between rival fascist factions. Austrian President Schussnigg – dreadful name – is right-wing and a fascist, but not a total supporter of the German model. He has leant towards Mussolini and the Italians. One of my meetings will give me a better picture. I am going to be seeing a member of his government. A good chap. Very cultured and a mountaineer. I met him before, you know, when we were here in '35 – Arthur Seyss-Inquart.'

'Don't forget that we are going along to se Professor Newmann on Wednesday to check out your ear. You want to be able to swim in Venice, don't you?'

'Do not fret, my dear – I shall not forget, and Dudley will keep me on the right road – he has management of the diary. I'm looking forward to Venice. This will be a wonderful break for us. Now, Wallis, are you sure that you want to celebrate your birthday tomorrow in Vienna, and not here on the actual day?'

'Quite, quite sure, my darling – I just love my present – it looks just fine, doesn't it?' Wallis turned her shoulders to emphasise the diamond and sapphire-encrusted brooch pinned on her left side. 'You clever man, David, you know how I love animal jewellery.'

'Well, it was tricky. I had placed the outline order with Cartier when I was in London, but could not finalise the design until I reached Austria. Thank goodness for the telephone, I was able to discuss the detail of the panther after they sent me sketches and a mock-up picture. It is grand, I have to say.'

Wallis left her chair and moved quickly to the Duke, and leaning forward whispered in his ear, 'We must have a very early night tonight, my love. We have to be up early in the morning and I want to thank you properly.' He shivered as she blew into his ear.

'David, this really is an absurdly early hour to be on the road. It feels like the middle of the night!' Wallis grumbled.

'Oh, it's not so bad, old girl – I was often on the go by this time when I was hunting. Actually, it gives one a wonderfully long day.'

'I suppose so. I may have a nap after luncheon.'

'But of course. We are on holiday, and you must do just as you please.'

The Buick was following a police car and two uniformed motorcycle outriders. Behind it came another police car, with four more armed officers. The little convoy was able to set its own pace with no other traffic on the road.

The Duke turned to Wallis, and smiled broadly. 'I really cannot wait for breakfast tomorrow! I know that I always have the same thing, but in Vienna I also have those wonderful, fresh, warm Viennese rolls – Kaisersemein – delicious.'

'Well, David, in my view anything would be delicious as an addition to your unsweetened grapefruit, toast with hardly any butter or marmalade, and black tea.'

'Well, I do have Earl Grey occasionally.'

'Hardly exciting, my dear – at least not in my book.'

'Well, it's no worse than your black coffee and dry crispbread.'

'Now, David, a girl has to watch her figure just as you watch yours.'

'Touché,' he laughed, 'now then, shall we play patience or enjoy the beautiful dawn in this picturesque countryside?'

'Oh, the view I think. It is beautiful.'

In the late morning, they drove through the outer suburbs

of the romantic city and had their first sight of the mighty Danube. Nearing the centre, the traffic became much heavier even though it was a Sunday. As they drew to a halt outside the Hotel Bristol, the doorman, in his pink frock coat, moved to open the rear door of the car. He raised his black top hat with its black cockade. Uniformed police formed two cordons on the pavement either side of the entrance. The armed officers from the two escort cars leapt out and took up defensive positions.

As first, as the Duke, and then Wallis left the car, there was a smattering of applause from the small crowd. A loud voice rang out, 'Bloody British – that's what you are! Heil Hitler!' The Duke, who was smiling broadly and had raised his hat in his now-customary wave, didn't pause but cried out his reply in perfect accentless German, 'I am a German and an Austrian first. Long live Austria!' The small crowd now cheered louder and with much greater enthusiasm.

Three of the police guards from the cars dashed into the crowd, and as the smiling Duke and Duchess entered the hotel, the crowd parted. A man who apparently could no longer walk was dragged to the second of the cars, where he was bundled into the back. His face was bloodied and ashen.

'I say, Wallis. Rather topping of them to put us in the Prince of Wales Suite, eh?'

'It sure is, honey. Where shall we have lunch? I'm famished after our journey.'

'I asked Dudley to make a booking at the elegant Restaurant Eckel. Hans Eckel is something of a legendary chef and will give us a warm welcome. The wine cellar is superlative.'

'Whatever you say, my treasure.'

Dudley Forward entered the sitting room. 'Sir, Your Royal Highness, I apologise for disturbing you. Ma'am, I have here a note for you, apparently from another guest.'

He handed Wallis a hotel envelope addressed to 'Her Royal Highness the Duchess of Windsor'. Wallis immediately went to the writing desk in the corner of the sitting room to look for a paper knife.

'Dudders – did you make the luncheon reservation at Restaurant Eckel, old chap?' asked the Duke.

'I most certainly did, and Eckel will be delighted to

welcome you both. I have alerted your chauffeur and the good Inspector Shoher. He said that he would be taking precautions.'

'Actually, Dudley, as we came through the lobby I noticed that concierge Hekkel is on duty. Ask him to have one of the hotel limousines at our disposal. Our driver will be tired and the car is in need of a clean.'

'Very well, Sir. I shall go and speak to him now.'

'David!' Wallis called out excitedly, 'von Ribbentrop is here, he is staying in this hotel. Do let's invite him for dinner. It would be such fun to see him. We can have it served in the dining room here in our suite?'

'Capital idea.'

The Duke called out, 'Dudders, will you invite von Ribbentrop for supper in our suite, please. 7.30pm for 8pm drinks, then a simple supper with just the three of us.'

'Certainly, Sir, and I shall order supper.'

Von Ribbentrop was delighted to accept. Helga had left earlier in the morning. Von Ribbentrop was relieved but pleasantly exhausted. The woman was extraordinary. Until last night, he believed that he had experienced every form of lovemaking. Now his aches and pains told him that until he met Helga, he most certainly had not. 'Heaven knows what she and Wallis will get up to,' he chuckled to himself.

Billy had asked Hekkel to inform him when Lady Celia Ffrench-Hardy arrived, and he received a call from the lobby at 12pm. Hekkel was speaking very quietly. 'Lady Celia has arrived, sir, and she is to stay in the Rubinstein Suite. The Duke and Duchess are to lunch at the Restaurant Eckel in Sievering and will be travelling in one of the hotel limousines. They have invited Herr von Ribbentrop to have supper with them in their suite.'

'I say, Hekkel, thank you so much.'

'My pleasure.'

Billy lost no time in calling Celia's suite.

'Celia, it's Billy here. Good trip?'

'Hello Billy, lovely to hear from you. Super, actually. I had a fine time in Cologne with my old friend Lotte von unprounceable – that's what she was known as at our finishing school. Lots of gossip and suchlike.

'The overnight train was pretty comfortable, but there was some sort of hold-up at the border and German police came right through the train, waking everyone up to inspect their papers before the train could leave Germany. Very odd, and rather annoying. I had hoped to arrive in time to go to Demel and have the violet blossom and champagne sorbet that Empress Elisabeth used to have with her morning coffee.'

'Well, Celia, depending what else is going on, there is always tomorrow. Do you fancy lunch with me here in the hotel – we can catch up and so forth?'

'That would be super. I need to freshen up and change after the journey, so shall I meet you in the Anglo-American Bar at 1.30pm?'

'That's perfect. I shall book lunch in the Restaurant Korso – I tried it the other evening and I prefer it to the Grill Room.'

'That's fine then. I shall see you later.'

Celia felt refreshed, and ready for a drink then lunch as she entered the dark bar. It was almost empty, and with heavily-shaded wall and table lights and heavy oak panelling, broken only by large sombre portraits, it was quite dark. 'More of a place for a discreet assignation,' she thought as she paused, and then saw Billy rising from his seat in an alcove.

'Hello, Billy. Just the place for some intrigue, I'd say,' she laughed as he took her hand, drawing her closer as they brushed cheeks.

'I think that it is marital intrigue rather than the espionage variety, Celia, but mind you. . .'

Celia settled into the chair that the immaculately-dressed Billy pulled out for her. A white-jacketed waiter materialised next to them. 'I would adore a champagne cocktail, Billy.'

'Good idea,' He turned to the waiter, 'two champagne cocktails please.' The waiter nodded, almost in a bow.

'Rather sinister, Billy. Are all the staff mute?'

'Certainly not, and, by the way they nearly all speak, and more importantly understand, English. Now, first news, von Ribbentrop is staying here and is having supper with the Windsors tonight.'

'Gosh! How should I play that?'

'I have spoken to Johnny who referred me to Tar. He suggests that you call Wallis this afternoon and let her know that you have arrived. They are going out to lunch by the way.

She may invite you to join them for supper. If so, Tar suggests that you accept and see how things unfold.'

'Right, I shall do that. Ah, here are the drinks.'

'That's good, Billy,' said a smiling Celia as she took her first sip, 'in fact, quite, quite divine.'

# Chapter 28

After a splendid lunch in the hotel's ornate Restaurant Korso, Billy and Celia agreed that she would have a rest and then contact Wallis. Billy had decided to return to the Café Louvre on the off-chance that Bill Shirer would be there. He and Celia would speak again in the late afternoon.

Billy collected his hat from the cloakroom, and decided that after the fine, but substantial lunch it would be best to walk. The pavement was crowded with window shoppers strolling along enjoying the sunshine. There was a pleasant and friendly atmosphere, and compared to Berlin on his last visit a pleasing lack of uniforms.

When he entered the café, he was greeted by an almost identical sight as on his last visit. There was the same fug of tobacco smoke, and the all male clientele was either engrossed in reading newspapers or in earnest conversation with each other. He spotted Bill again, engrossed in a newspaper and went over to him. 'Bill, my friend – how are you? A hair of the dog?'

'A hair of the dog to you too. You betcha – I'll have a Jack Daniels and branch water.'

'Never heard of "when in Rome"?'

'I'm an American, and don't forget it! I can't hear you asking for a pint of that warm stuff you Brits call beer!'

'Ok then, let's leave it at that. I'm going to have a large glass of bone-dry Austrian Grüner Vetliner white wine.'

When Billy had returned with the drinks, Bill Shirer folded his newspaper and asked whether Billy had seen the Duke and Duchess of Windsor, who were staying at the same hotel.

'No, I haven't – I doubt if I shall there seems to be quite a bit of Austrian security surrounding them.'

'Billy, I think that it is time you levelled with me,' Bill Shirer had fixed him with a gimlet stare, 'I think that you are involved in security and intelligence work. Are you?'

'Bill, I cannot answer that.'

'Fine, now I know. I don't mind sharing hard-gleaned information with you, provided you are not a journalist.'

'I most certainly am not – you should have seen my school reports!'

'I believe you. I was thinking about your question regarding Arthur Seyss-Inquart.That led me to other prominente whose political beliefs are becoming very hard to fathom here in Austria.'

'What do you mean?' asked Billy, his interest pricked.

'Right. Let's start with the Church. The Austrians have historically been a strongly religious people. Take the case of the Archbishop of Vienna, Cardinal Theodor Innitzer. He is an undoubted political animal, and after being Rector of the University of Vienna he became the Minister of Social Affairs in the government of Johann Schober. He became Archbishop in 1932 and was made a Cardinal in 1933.

'So far so good, but then he became an ardent supporter of Dolfuss, who became Austro Fascist dictator after effectively having the parliament dismissed. After the assassination of Dolfuss he has continued to support Shuschnigg, his successor. Dolfuss pulled it off by having the President Wilhem Miklas pull the same stunt as Hitler did, with the German President Paul von Hindenburg. He, and now Shuschnigg, effectively rule by so-called "emergency decrees".

'Their successive governments have been supported throughout by massive police presence, and the paramilitary Heimwehr troops. That's the Austrian way of getting around the armistice treaty restrictions. Sounds familiar, eh? The Archbishop has openly said that the future of Austria lies with Germany.'

'Which in its Nazism practices a different form of more secular fascism, where it differs from the Italian model?' asked Billy.

'That's right, Billy. But this is the nub of the question – the enigma as I see it. A few days ago, he made what has been described as a 'deeply moving speech', and I quote the British

*Catholic Herald*, in which he condemned the "monstrous campaign of calumny against the Church" by the Nazi regime.'

'So how does one fit with the other? You cannot advocate getting closer to Nazi Germany and at the same time decry Naziism, can you?' By now Billy looked confused.

'Precisely the point I am trying to make, Billy. What are his beliefs in truth?'

'I can see the dichotomy, Bill, but what relevance do his conflicting beliefs have to Austria generally?'

'Well, I am coming to the view that Austria is a country riven by contradictions, and therefore greatly weakened. I think that the impossible balancing act that the Cardinal is attempting, is one and the same as that of men like Seyss-Inquart on the secular side, probably even Schuschnigg himself.'

'If I am getting the drift, Bill, what you are saying is that Germany will effectively take control of Austria, if necessary by force of arms.'

'Precisely. However, I would lay a bet with you that there would be no bloodshed, provided Il Duce, Benito Mussolini, sees which side his bread is buttered on, and withdraws Italy's support for Austro-Fascism and the so-called independent Austria.'

'For the sake of discussion, I can accept that. But I still have a burning question. Why did you bring this up in the context of the Duke and Duchess of Windsor?'

'As the report has it, when a man in the crowd shouted at the Duke as he arrived at the Hotel Bristol, "Bloody British – that's what you are! Heil Hitler!' and the Duke unhesitatingly responded, "I am a German and an Austrian first. Long live Austria!"'

'So you think that he is positioning himself with a foot in both camps, as it were?'

'Precisely. And that, my friend, is exactly what I am becoming convinced Arthur Seyss-Inquart is doing.'

Billy decided not to tell Bill Shirer that the Duke had had secret meetings with the Austrian politician in 1935, but he could now see how the Duke's mind was working. The Duke was clearly much more politically astute than his detractors had believed.

■ ■ ■

The Duke and Duchess were escorted to their table in the brightly-lit restaurant by its founder and owner, Julius Eckel. The chef had built his reputation as the finest chef in Vienna during his time at the Hotel Bristol. With his kitchen brigade numbering 40 chefs, he had regularly produced meals of stunning quality to over 1,000 diners after they crowded the hotel's tables following a first night at the opera.

The Duke, who was as elegant as ever in a double-breasted, light grey Prince of Wales check suit, cream silk shirt with cutaway collar, and tie with his signature broad knot, thanked Herr Eckel. Referring to the famous book which Eckel had published to wide acclaim a few years previously, he asked, 'What shall you cook today?'

Eckel laughed, and replied, 'Aha, you mean, *"What Shall I Cook Today?"*. As I recall, Your Royal Highness, you greatly enjoyed my minced veal schnitzel with potato puree. May I suggest that you both have that as a main course, and either a warm lobster cocktail or goose liver terrine to start with.'

'What say you, Wallis? I have had both the lobster and the veal, and they are superb – memorable.'

'That sounds fine by me, David, but do please ask for small portions.'

'Of course, my dear.'

The Duke ordered, and asked that Eckel choose appropriate wines. 'Herr Eckel keeps a fine cellar. I promise that we will not be disappointed. Now then, we have a few days and need to settle our plans. I have one or possibly two meetings that I must attend, quite apart from the good Professor with my ear.'

'Well, David, I have been looking at the Baedeker Guide whilst we were at the Schloss. I would like to see the cathedral and the Spanish Riding School.'

'Yes, of course, the Riding School – I would love to see those magnificent Lipizanner stallions and the wonderful dressage display again. I shall pull a few strings so that we can have a look around behind the scenes if possible. The cathedral is no problem. We should be seen at the opera I think as well.'

'Yes darling, I cannot say that I am a great fan, but I agree that it would be a rather fine showcase for us. You must be missing the razzamatazz, I imagine?'

'Yes, to an extent, but I do not miss the tedious stuff, oh, you know, all those damn papers that I was supposed to plough through. I tried telling the stuffed shirts that unless what I said carried some weight as King, what was the point of my bloody-well reading all their outpourings. Well, now, I can do something. I had some very interesting chats with Charles Bedaux, and he is going to fix up a fact-finding mission to America for us. Also, he agrees that we should go to Germany as soon as possible. I want to see how their working people live, and importantly, the way they work and their conditions. Same thing in America.'

'That all sounds exciting, sweetheart – will we meet Herr Hitler?'

'Of course, my dear. He recognises our rank even if my bloody brother and his poisonous wife don't.'

Wallis could see that the Duke was becoming agitated. She reached across the table and rested her bejewelled hand on his. Looking at him with a sympathetic smile, she said, 'Darling man, we now have our own lives, can make our own rules, have our own friends and can go where we wish. We will create our own Court. Remember the crowns – I think of them every day.'

'Did you mean what you said in your Cannes press release – you know, that you were stepping aside?'

'If that had been what you wanted then, I would have, but I knew that you were determined that we should marry. I just wanted to hit back at the hateful rumours about me being a gold-digging adventuress put about by Prime Minister Baldwin and his cronies.'

'And you did, dearest, you did. Ah, here is the lobster – it looks delicious.'

Von Ribbentrop was with Hans Friedrich von Wedel, an aristocratic senior Abwehr officer who, earlier in the year, had married a beautiful but mysterious agent, Vera Ignatieff. She was thirty years younger than him. She was a woman of great allure, and her background was shrouded in mystery.

Her first husband, whom she had married in 1930 when she was only eighteen, was Count Sergei Ignatieff. Although of a noble Russian family, he had a bad reputation. He was a ruthless double agent, and she only managed to live with him for a year, but worked with him for longer as his courier.

Not only the Abwehr was aware of his activities, but also MI5. The report that had landed on Sir Vincent Kell's desk described him as, "A cocaine addict, a pervert and actively engaged in espionage for the White Russians". Vera came to the attention of the Abwehr when in Brussels, her husband tried to stab her for threatening to stop spying on Communists. Von Wedel then engineered a meeting with her, and as well as recruiting her into the Abwehr, fell in love with her. She was a beguiling creature.

In the course of recruiting her he realised that some of her history, as she told it to him, was almost certainly untrue. That she was ideal material as a double agent was proved, when she tipped off the Russian Bolshevik spymasters, who believed that her husband only worked for them, that Ignatiev was in fact an agent of the hated and forever-plotting White Russians.

He was arrested in Moscow, tortured and then shot. She was free to marry, and her credentials with the communist rulers of Russia were impeccable. She was the perfect double agent. She was the object of von Ribbentrop's interest. He had met her in Paris shortly after his marriage, when he was enjoying the fruits of his father-in-law's great wealth. He was no longer just a charming but impoverished champagne salesman. He was now wealthy, and determined to enjoy himself. He and Vera had a short, intensely physical affair. It was with fond memories that he had learnt of her recruitment and marriage to von Wedel.

'Joachim, Vera tells me that you and she met in Paris before she married that swine Ignatieff.'

'Yes, that is true but. . .'

Von Wedel raised his hand, interrupting von Ribbentrop, 'I need to know no more than that. All that I wanted to say is that I have been less than frank about her history and origins to Admiral Canaris, and even the Führer. Apart from loving her she is a great asset in espionage terms, since the Russians trust her. We learn a lot simply from the tasks that they set her.'

'I can see that, Hans. You may rest assured that her past is of no interest to me either, and I would not dream of mentioning anything. Now, she is here in Vienna with you?'

'Yes, and she is staying after I leave this evening.'

'Good. I have a task that I should like her to undertake, with the Abwehr's agreement of course. I understand that there is a British agent staying in this hotel. He is not one of the goon squad that is naturally shadowing the Duke and Duchess of Windsor, who are of course assets of ours. His name is Brownlow, and I think that he is a part of an elite team that works directly under the head of the British Secret Service, MI5, Sir Vernon Kell. We need to know what he knows. He is susceptible. In Cannes he fell head over heels with an upmarket prostitute, who was unfortunately tortured by a German agent.'

'Not Abwehr, I hope?'

'He was an Irish national – a fenian rebel – ostensibly working for the Abweher, but in fact Himmler.'

'My God! What happened to him?'

'He was a pervert, and found dead after a sex game went wrong, or so I believe.'

'Good. Of course Vera will help.'

'Thank you, you are most considerate,' smiled von Ribbentrop. He had not needed to threaten to expose Vera's past after all. 'We understand each other perfectly, Hans.'

Billy and Celia were in her suite. He had told her of his conversation with Bill Shirer and the implications with regard to the Duke and, by association, the Duchess.

'You want me to find out what their plans are?'

'Put simply, yes. I was in on Johnny's briefing report from the Chateau de Cande and the revelations about Charles Bedaux. I have also seen the dossier on him that Tar obtained from the Americans. We need to know whether Bedaux and the Duke are planning anything together.'

'Righto, Billy. I will call Wallis now.' Celia went and sat down at the desk. She picked up the telephone and asked to be put through to the Prince of Wales' Suite. 'It's Celia Ffrench-Hardy here – oh it's you Dudley – how are you?'

'Fine form Celia, fine form. Would you wish to speak to Wallis?'

'Yes please.'

'A moment if you please.'

'Celia, my dear, how are you and more to the point, where are you?'

'Tip top Wallis, and I am here in the hotel – the Rubinstein Suite.'

'Excellent, David will be so pleased. Is Johnny with you?'

'No, he couldn't manage to come, more's the pity.'

'Well, don't worry, von Ribbentrop is also staying here – they have put him in the Presidential Suite.'

'He'll love that,' laughed Celia.

'He sure will. Now, he's coming to us for a light supper this evening – how about you joining us to make up the party?'

'I'd love to. Thank God you said something light. The food here in Vienna is fabulous, but oh so rich. What time?'

'7.30pm for drinks.'

'I shall be there.'

When she had replaced the telephone receiver, Billy smiled and said, 'Well done Celia, and good hunting. I had better be off now. Talk in the morning?'

'That's fine. I feel mean leaving you on your own.'

Oh, don't, I am sure that I can amuse myself. I rather like the American Bar – it has a wonderful air of mystery and a hint of decadence. It really needs a writer like Graham Greene to describe it.'

Billy had changed into a more formal suit and taken himself and his book to the American Bar, which was set in the middle of the hotel. The lighting was so subtle and the shadows so deep that he doubted whether he would be able to read but he always liked to have a prop. He settled into an alcove and looked around. There were very few people in the bar which probably was not surprising on a Sunday evening.

His eye was drawn to a striking dark-haired woman who was sitting on a stool by the bar. She looked to be in her late twenties or early thirties. His heart might belong to Lisette in Cannes but that did not prevent him enjoying looking at a beautiful woman. She looked around the bar slowly, and for a fleeting moment they caught each other's eye. She turned away and finished her drink. As she stood up to leave, her handbag fell to the floor and its contents spilled out. Instinctively Billy jumped up, and reaching down beside her said in German, 'Permit me to be of assistance, Madam.'

The woman flashed him a grateful smile. The task was soon complete. They stood up, and looking at each other laughed. 'Would it be forward of me to offer you a drink by way of my thanks, sir?'

'Absolutely not, but thank you. Please allow me to invite you to join me.' He gestured towards his table, and inclining her head, smiling, she followed his gesture and walked to his table. She picked up his book.

'Goethe, no less. Serious stuff for a Sunday evening.'

'No, not really, it is a good discipline for my rusty German.'

'Which is excellent, by the way. My name is Vera von Wedel, and yours?'

'William Brownlow, but everyone calls me Billy. Now, what will you have?'

Billy found Vera fascinating. Apart from her looks which were striking, almost exotic, she had an extraordinary accent that he simply could not place. Her voice was low and vibrant, and her dark eyes were expressive, even in the shadowy bar.

'Vera – I am puzzled. Please do not be offended, but I cannot place your accent.'

She laughed, and raising her eyebrows a little, responded almost archly in heavily accented English, 'You are permitted to guess.'

'I think that there may be a hint of Russia – certainly the East – but there is more to it than that. There is a little Scandanavian, and also French influence. I give up!'

'You are right to the extent that I was born in Siberia, have lived in Denmark and then was taken to Paris when I was twelve. I have also lived in Germany and Belgium.'

'Well, you have certainly moved around.'

'I travelled a lot also with my late husband's work.'

'Oh, I am sorry.'

'There is no need to be sorry, it was not a happy marriage.'

'What sort of work did he do that you could help him – that is not meant to sound like a rude question by the way, just curious?'

'Oh, he was a gatherer of information.'

Billy was struck by the strange response but decided not to pursue the matter for now. 'I was going to dine alone with Goethe as my companion. Would you care to join me?'

'If you are implying that I am only being asked because you find Goethe heavy going. . .'

'Absolutely not, I think that you will be delightful company.'

'Then I shall be delighted.'

Billy felt strangely excited and not a little guilty at the prospect of dinner with this mysterious woman.

# Chapter 29

Wallis had asked Dudley Forward to let von Ribbentrop know that Celia was joining them for supper. After his activities with Helga he was not sure that he could handle any physical activity with Celia if the opportunity should arise. He decided to simply let the evening develop as it might.

When he arrived at the Prince of Wales' suite he was shown into the large sitting room by the butler, who formally announced him. 'His Excellency von Ribbentrop, Your Royal Highnesses.'

Wallis and the Duke both stood and smiled their welcome. 'Welcome my dear fellow,' said the Duke, extending his hand, which von Ribbentrop shook.

'Joachim, how divine to see you,' gushed Wallis, as he took her hand and bending forward, kissed it.

'The honour is mine,' he responded.

'Champagne, I believe?' asked the Duke.

'Thank you, that would be excellent.' The butler poured him a glass from the heavily frosted bottle of Krug.

'Now then, sit yourself down and make yourself comfortable .Tell us about your visit to Vienna – is it business or pleasure?'

'Whilst it is always a pleasure to visit Vienna, I am afraid that it is business that brings me here. I have meetings with the Chancellor and others in the Austrian Government.'

'It is difficult to define Austrian politics – I have tried since I arrived back in December but everything seems to be somewhat contradictory,' commented the Duke.

'You are right in that. Fortunately there are some men of real vision in the Government here who can see how the future interests of Austria will best be served.'

'And how is that?' enquired the Duke.

'By embracing its place in the greater Germany. That is the vision of the Führer and I can assure you that before very long, that will be achieved.'

The Duke responded, 'Yes, I for one, having relatives in both Germany and Austria, can appreciate the logic of such a joining. What on earth is the point of having so called national boundaries that separate people who should by nature and heritage be as one?' asked the Duke.

Before von Ribbentrop could answer, the butler again entered the room and announced Celia. As the men stood, Wallis dashed forward, and taking both of Celia's hands, drew her into an embrace, touching cheeks in a symbolic make up preserving kiss. 'My goodness, Celia – you look so well!' cried Wallis.

'And you too, Wallis. David, Joachim, hello.'

'Enough of politics for now, I think,' said Wallis, with a hint of finality. 'How long are you staying in Vienna, Celia, and of course you too, Joachim?' Von Ribbentrop made a gesture of deferral to Celia.

'Well, I am not sure but certainly until the end of the week.'

'I am afraid that I shall be leaving Vienna on Tuesday morning if my meetings go to plan,' said von Ribbentrop.

'Well, let's plan a few diversions, shall we? That really is rather soon for you to leave, Joachim,' was the firm but smiling response given by Wallis.

Celia responded enthusiastically, 'I say Wallis, what have you in mind? I really must visit the Spanish Riding School. Dressage was never my strongest discipline but I have heard that it is a wonderful display.'

'It most certainly is an amazing display. I was taken there in 1935 when I was Prince of Wales – unfortunately you could not join us, Wallis. The actual performance used to be much shorter, but now is expanded. It starts with the young stallions, then leads onto ever more complex movements, culminating in the twenty minute School Quadrille, which is reputedly the longest and most complex in the world.'

'Can you fix it for us, David?' asked Celia.

'Most certainly. Dudley can tackle arrangements in the

morning. I shall ask him to seek the Royal Box. I say, would anyone care for a top up?' asked the Duke as the butler noiselessly entered the room. In response to their nods he gestured for the further drinks to be served. Von Ribbentrop asked about their time in the Schloss Wasserleonburg and how they were enjoying the stay.

'Well,' said Wallis taking a long rather dramatic pause, 'the drive up to it is frankly terrifying. Thankfully it was dark when we were travelling, but even then I was absolutely petrified.' She paused and gave a theatrical shudder. 'I can tell you when I saw it in daylight I nearly fell in a faint!'

'Oh Wallis, don't be so melodramatic,' laughed the Duke.

'Well, David, you may have not been upset but I sure was. Anyhow, when we entered the castle, David was a true romantic and carried me over the threshold!'

'Bravo!' interrupted von Ribbentrop.

'Well all the staff were lined up, about 30 of them, and of course, we had our own following. I can tell you, I thought to myself that this sure ain't going to be a private little honeymoon. It was then that I noticed the hunting trophies. My God, the walls were covered in these beastly grinning or growling faces of animals slaughtered over the years. They were all bared teeth and horrid glinting eyes. My first words to David were, "Those grisly things have got to be put into store".'

'Well, there were rather a lot of them, I have to admit,' laughed the Duke.

'Once they were removed, we settled in very quickly, and have really enjoyed our time so far, haven't we, David?'

'Oh yes, most certainly, my love. Ah, I believe supper is served.' As the Duke stood, he looked at the others and asked the rhetorical question, 'Shall we?' The light supper was excellent and conversation ranged over many topics but with politics scrupulously avoided.

'Wallis, given that this is so informal and intimate an occasion, unless you wish to do otherwise, I suggest that you and Celia stay at the table with us whilst we have a cigar. Is that acceptable.'

'Most certainly, David – Celia, are you happy with that?' asked Wallis.

'I most certainly am, and if I may, I should love a cigar.'

The butler presented the burr walnut humidor first to the Duke who directed him to Celia. Celia carefully selected a small Monte Cristo which she sniffed carefully and then rolled in between thumb and fingers by her ear. 'Perfect,' she declared, as she picked up the onyx handled gold cutter that the butler had placed on the table, and expertly cut the end of the cigar. She then lit it from the long taper held by the butler, and quickly drew on it to ensure that it was burning evenly. She inspected the glowing tip and nodding towards the Duke said, 'Excellent, David, perfect condition.'

'Thank you, Celia – that was awfully proficient, I really have to say.'

'Oh well, Papa has allowed me to choose and light his cigars for yonks.'

'I apologise, Celia, but what is this "yonks"?' asked von Ribbentrop.

'Oh, it means "ages" – there you are, you have learnt something tonight! Now, tell me, David, have you seen or heard from Charles, you know, Charles Bedaux?' Celia had decided that she might not have another opportunity of finding out about the rather sinister host of the wedding, and she thought this a perfect opportunity in the presence of von Ribbentrop.

'Well, we are in touch, of course. I probably mentioned, when we were in France, that I wish to visit Germany and the USA to see working and living conditions, and of course efficient practices at first hand. With his amazing connections, Charles has agreed to facilitate both trips, and hopes that the Führer will receive us.'

'Gosh, is Charles really that powerful, David?' asked Celia, feigning a surprised expression.

'He most certainly is. His connections in the USA with major industry, bankers, and politicians at the highest level, stretch into Germany. As he puts it, "International business, organised efficiently with appropriately focused and strong governments in support, transcends all matters of nationality and all borders".'

Von Ribbentrop then spoke, 'That philosophy accords with Germany's aspirations for not only the greater Germany, but also the free world, rid of the canker of bolshevism. And, yes Celia, Charles Bedaux is very well connected in the

German Government, and, of course, industry. I shall make a point of contacting him and will assist in planning the visit. Wallis, might I suggest that Celia accompanies you?'

Before Wallis could answer, the Duke who was smiling excitedly said, 'Bravo!' He clapped his hands excitedly. 'Take it from me, Celia, Bedaux is the man to make it happen in business and banking, just as Germany, brilliantly led by Adolf Hitler and his team, has created the perfect political and economic environment.' The Duke had delivered this little speech with fervour. Wallis had paid rapt attention.

Conversation then drifted back to social and more trivial matters. 'I hate to break things up,' said Celia, stifling a yawn, 'but my night on the train has left me rather tired – will you all excuse me?'

'Actually, I should leave now also, I have to run through my briefing papers for tomorrow's meetings before I sleep,' said von Ribbentrop.

'That is no trouble – Wallis and I were up before dawn for the drive here. I suggest that those who are able, join Wallis and me at Demel for coffee and some pastries in the morning at 11.30am – fearfully indulgent but irresistible, eh?'

'I would love to,' responded Celia, 'and whilst I am in Vienna I wish to visit the Cafe Sperl – was that not a favourite of Adolf Hitler, Joachim?'

'Yes, so I believe.'

After suitable thanks and goodbyes, Celia and von Ribbentrop left at the same time. When the butler had closed the double doors behind them, von Ribbentrop stopped, and taking Celia by the shoulders, looked into her eyes, then leant forward and kissed her gently. 'You are so beautiful, Celia, my dear. I know that you are tired, but can we not have a little time together?'

'Of course, Bubbles, please come to my suite – here, we can use the stairs, it is only one floor down.'

They walked down the grand marble staircase arm-in-arm.

Billy knew that Vera had deliberately picked him up, and he guessed that some arm of German intelligence was behind her interest. According to the rules, unless he had reason to think that something specific were to be gained, he should break off the contact. On the other hand, he found her almost alarmingly attractive. She was fascinating, and the more time he spent in her company the more he felt himself falling under her spell.

That she was a skilled operator he was in no doubt. No questions were intrusive and nothing specific put him on his guard. Nevertheless, he could tell that she was working on building a picture of him, his experience, and current assignment. He started to play the same game in reverse. She gave every impression of being frank and open, even hinting that she had been involved in some mysterious goings on when with her late husband.

She made no bones about his drug habit, or his obsession with the White Russian cause. She mentioned his violence, and alluded to his sexual perversions that had driven her from his bed and home after only a year of marriage. So why did she carry on working with him? That was the question foremost in Billy's mind. 'Earlier on Vera, you mentioned that you were born in Russia – Siberia, I think you said. Have you been back?'

'Not to Siberia, but I have been to Moscow a few times. I do not really like it there – it is so grey, not just the place but the people.'

'Was that a problem, being married to an aristocrat and White Russian?'

'No, in Russia you can do pretty much as you like if you have the right contacts.'

'Yes, contacts, always contacts. It's the same all over the world, I think.' As he said this, Billy thought to himself that in Russia those contacts would have had to be the intelligence service. The beautiful Vera was a dangerous lady of that he was sure. If she was not lying about Moscow she must have been a double agent. And now she was married to a high-ranking, well-connected German officer. Did that mean that she was spying for or against Germany, Russia, or both? This was not only interesting but certainly had potential. Billy decided that he would not be breaking the rules by enjoying her company. He knew that he would sleep with her this night.

Celia gasped when she saw von Ribbentrop's chest criss-crossed with angry scratches. He did not demur when she turned him around and saw that his shoulders, back, and buttocks were similarly scarred. His buttocks bore heavy, scabbed horizontal lines that would indicate a vicious beating with a cane or riding crop.

'Oh my God, Joachim, what have they done to you?' she gasped when she turned him around facing her again, and her eyes travelled down over the whole of his body.

'Let's just say that things got a little out of hand, Celia.'

'A little out of hand – this is the handiwork of a maniac! A woman, I suppose?'

'Yes – in fact Helga, who will become one of Wallis' secretaries and be my eyes and ears.'

'Are you mad?! The woman is bordering on a homicidal maniac and you are putting her in the same house as Wallis?'

'Don't worry. Wallis likes pain and I can assure you that she can look after herself.'

'God, I hope that you are right.'

'I am sure that I am. Now then. . .'

'There's no "now then" tonight, Bubbles. Put on your clothes and let's chat.'

He looked relieved as Celia fetched her dressing gown. When they had settled down at either end of the large and softly upholstered settee Celia took the bull by the horns. 'Does Charles Bedaux really have the influence that he claims; you know, the Duke's trip to Germany, meeting the Führer, and all that?'

'In a word, no. Oh, we are playing along and letting him think that he has, but the actual arrangements are being made by Fritz Wiedermann on the direct instructions of the Führer. Wiedemann is a senior member of the Fuhrer's personal staff and a very old friend. Details will be tied up when the Windsors are back from their Venice trip. So, in reality, Bedaux is a blind.'

'But he is sorting out the American trip, isn't he?'

'Yes, he is, but we have good intelligence that feelings in the American trade unions are so strongly opposed – they hate the 'Bedaux Method' with a vengeance – it just will not happen. I am afraid that he suffers from little man syndrome, and even worse, has come to believe his own publicity. However, his business and banking connections are highly valued. Now, should I stay over for a few extra days?'

'Not if Helga's on the loose, if I were you!' laughed Celia.

'I think that you are right. You can bring me up to date

when we are back in London.'

'Righto, Bubbles. The Land of Nod for me, and a good night's rest for you too. Now, shoo, and sweet dreams – and not of Helga.'

'Where the hell is this all heading?' she muttered to herself after he had left, and she headed for the bedroom.

Billy and Vera were lying together like spoons after making love. It had been delicate, almost tentative at first as they explored each other, but gradually their hunger had taken over and their true natures were revealed.

'Vera – that was very special you know,' he whispered into her ear.

She half-turned her head, and he could just see the corner of a smile as she replied, 'Yes, I know. The same for me too.'

She wriggled around in his arms so that she was facing him, their bodies pressed together. 'Is it too soon for us to be totally honest with each other?' she asked, looking deeply into his eyes.

'It would be easy to say 'No' at this moment, but I think we both might regret it in the cold light of day. Let's keep things as they are for now. We have a few days before we go our separate ways. Let's not push it.'

'I can live with that, Billy,' she replied, as she burrowed her face into his neck and started to gently lick him.

'Oh God, Vera, that feels good.'

'So does something else,' she laughed as she slipped her right arm from around his neck, and shifting a little away from him, reached down. That they were agents of foreign governments who might be in conflict was the last thing on their minds as they surrendered – to each other.

# Chapter 30

The hotel director, Felix Primus, had remembered the detailed instructions that he had received from the British Embassy when the Duke had previously stayed at the Hotel Bristol. Once again, two limousines were on permanent standby. He had remembered the instructions, but refreshed his memory by re-reading the original confidential Embassy Memorandum.

Prior to the arrival of the Duke and Duchess, he had contacted the British Embassy and requested guidance on the protocol to be adopted. He had been informed that the Duke and Duchess held no official position and were to be treated as any other well-known guest, but without any formal recognition. They would not be accorded any recognition of Royal status by the Embassy or Austrian Government. Naturally their privacy should also be respected. The terms of the response seemed to indicate an almost hostile official attitude towards the couple.

Whatever the Embassy said, so far as he was concerned, the Duke and Duchess would be given the respect and service that his hotel afforded to all of its royal patrons. After all, following the Great War and the brutal armistice terms, many a crowned head was deposed including that of Austria. In his eyes that made them no less royal.

He had been informed that the Duke and Duchess were to leave the hotel at 11.20pm and be taken the short distance to the grandly titled Imperial and Royal Court Confectionary Bakery, Demel. He was waiting in the foyer in his formal morning dress, flanked by Mr Gabriel, the general manager, and concierge Hekkel. As the Duke, Duchess and Celia exited the lift with its art deco doors, the attendant pageboy bowed.

'Ah, Primus, Gabriel, Hekkel – good day to you,' smiled the Duke, as the trio bobbed their heads.

'And to you, Your Royal Highnesses. I trust that you are finding our hotel comfortable and to your liking?' asked Felix Primus.

'Oh, rather. Capital!'

The little party, with Dudley Forward bustling behind, swept out of the doors and into the black limousine parked at the pavement. Again, uniformed police had stopped pedestrians and Chief Inspector Shober's men waited by their car. The little cavalcade drove off.

Earlier in the morning, Celia had invited Billy to join her for a light breakfast in her suite. 'Well, Billy, how was your evening of solitude?'

'Actually extraordinary, quite extraordinary, but I shall tell you later. How did you get on?'

Celia recounted the conversation about Charles Bedaux between the Duke and von Ribbentrop, and then his telling remarks to Celia in her suite.

'Excellent. Tar will be pleased with that, particularly that Hitler himself is taking the initiative. Tar will also have words with our American cousins – he always complains that doing so involves him in a long and rather liquid lunch at his beloved Reform Club. Methinks he protests too much,' laughed Billy.

'Now Billy, why was your evening so extraordinary?'

He told Celia the whole story, only omitting the most intimate details.

'Oh my God!' exclaimed Celia when he finished, 'you have been hooked by a femme fatale, a Mata Hari, no less.'

'Not quite, but I am pretty sure that she is a double agent. I think that we might be able to turn her.'

'Is that a dangerous game?'

'Of course, but Tar and Maxwell Knight – you haven't met him yet – are determined to perfect the art of creating double agents. Sir Vernon agrees with them, that a person who is happy to be a spy is rarely driven by pure ideology. Generally, spies relish the constant danger and the intrigue you know, the cloak and dagger stuff. The plan is to capture the foreign spy and give him or her a stark choice. Death or work for us. Surprisingly, spies have a strong survival instinct. Tar and

Maxwell are confident they should achieve a pretty good success rate.'

'Billy, whilst I remember, von Ribbentrop has recruited a woman called Helga to be his eyes and ears and contact with Wallis. She is going to be one of her secretaries. Judging by the state of von Ribbentrop, she is also a sadist. I'll keep you in the picture – Wallis is bound to confide in me.'

'What do you mean by "the state of him"?'

Celia described von Ribbentrop's body. Billy visibly blanched when Celia added her final observation.

'That's downright perversion, for God's sake – perversion on the part of both of them. Will the Duchess be safe?'

'Von Ribbentrop thinks she can handle the situation.'

'I hope he's right.'

'I must go now – we are off to the legendary imperial bakery, Demel, for some coffee and pastries. I have only read about it but it sounds divine, and I can't wait.'

'Well, off you go and enjoy yourself. I must send in a report, which means a trip to the Embassy.'

Tar Robertson and Maxwell Knight were discussing Billy's telegraphed report that had just been de-encrypted.

'Strikes me, young Billy is rather taken with this Vera. Nevertheless, let's pull up the Ignatieff file – I'm pretty sure I remember the name.'

Tar picked up the telephone and asked to be put through to the Registry, where he asked for the file on Count Sergei Ignatieff and any file concernin his wife.

'Right Max, we have this Vera who sounds as though she has already been turned once. Now, what about the apparently sadistic Helga? She is going to be close to the Simpson woman – sorry, the Duchess – and reporting to von Ribbentrop. I assume that she will do so directly, which whilst the whole crew are in Austria, should not be too difficult.'

Maxwell Knight added, 'The odds are, Tar, that she and the Duchess –let's just call her Wallis – will end up in a close relationship. From what we know, Wallis is partial to a bit of rough stuff and von Ribbentrop normally is the one who dishes it out.'

'What a motley bunch, eh?' mused Tar.

'I would not disagree but we need to test whether Helga is

susceptible to being turned. I think that we shall have to wait until Helga is on the strength so to speak and then re evaluate.'

'In the meantime, Max, I am instructing Billy to carry on and see how far things go with Vera.'

An orderly in a brown dustcoat knocked on the door which was ajar, and came straight in with two files, handing them to Tar, who signed the proferred docket. 'Thank you, sergeant.'

'Sir.' Although the Secret Service was technically outside of the armed forces, its origins meant that military ranks and manners were still observed.

'Right Max, you take the wife and I will start on the Count.'

They read in silence for some minutes, both smoking. Tar put down the thicker file which told the unappetising history of the late Count. 'Well Max, the Count was an utter bastard on any basis. Vera was only 18 when she married him in 1930. He came to the attention of our chaps when he started peddling cocaine to the Second Secretary in our Paris Embassy. I doubt whether the poor girl knew what she was getting herself into.

'He had some powerful friends in France. The Deuxieme Bureau wanted to pull him in as a communist spy, but his White Russian cronies leant on some very senior politicians and the matter was dropped. The behind the scenes gossip was that he had supplied heroin to some of the French elite and threatened exposure. That is of course, hearsay, as is the other gossip that he was also the purveyor of children for senior members of the government, church and military. Apparently it stayed on his file, as did some pretty unpleasant stuff concerning his sexual predilictions. She obviously alluded to this to Billy, but I fear that she might be damaged goods. What comes up on her file?'

Max pushed his half moon spectacles up his nose and spoke slowly, 'It bears out what she told Billy. Yes, probably born in Siberia and, most interestingly, possibly of Jewish extraction. However, there appears to have been a Danish connection. She may have been illegitimate – anyhow, it is not clear whether she was adopted. The family escaped to Denmark at the time of the Russian Revolution when she was five.

'That may account for her brother's activity – he is a big wheel in the Danish Nazi movement, and is even tipped as a future leader. The family stayed there for seven years and then moved to Paris. I assume that the adoptive or natural brother, whatever he may be, stayed in Denmark.

'She claims to have danced in the Folies Bergères, but there is a margin query, given her age. However, the file has her having had training as a ballerina, and then ending up in the nightspot from the age of sixteen. Conversely, even whilst with Ignatieff she appears to have also danced with the Russian Ballet. The fact that she was not only beautiful, but multilingual, would have appealed to the Count, as would her tender years. He preferred younger fare but he couldn't marry them.'

'That all fits,' said Tar, 'he appears to have hooked her on heroin, and in recent years used her as a courier. His file concludes, although without evidence, that she shopped him to Russian Intelligence and they did away with him.'

'And now she has married von Wedel, a senior Abwehr officer reputed to have links to the highest level in the Nazi hierarchy,' said Max quietly, 'that is even more surprising, as earlier this year her name appeared on a Gestapo black list.'

'I am going to look into von Wedel some more. There is more here than meets the eye. You know Max, I think by accident, Billy has hit on a possible agent for us. Beautifully placed, eh?'

'She certainly is, but you know this is all becoming very convoluted – don't forget we have von Ribbentrop slap-bang in the middle.' 'I am going to call for von Wedel's file.'

'Oh my Good Lord!' exclaimed Celia as she and Wallis entered the baroque ground floor shop of Demel, the former Imperial confectioner and baker. The mirrored walls reflected the extraordinary confections that filled the counter tops and round-tiered mahogany display stands.

'A kind of confectionary paradise, huh?' laughed Wallis.

'Now, straight ahead, ladies,' ordered the Duke, and directed them towards a staircase at the side of the large shop. 'Up we go.'

He followed Wallis and Celia up the fine sweeping staircase which opened out onto a salon with crisp, white, linen-covered tables. A white-capped waitress gave a small curtsey and led the trio to a round table, where the Duke fussily settled his companions in their chairs before sitting down himself. They were each handed a stiff white card which bore a menu of delicacies named in elegant script.

'I have taken the liberty of ordering for you ladies,' laughed the Duke, as a waitress came to the table. The young woman looked first at Wallis and asked, 'Has the lady already made a selection?'

Wallis smiled and gestured to the Duke. The same question was then addressed to Celia, who did likewise. As the waitress turned to him, the Duke raised his hand and spoke clearly, indicating that he had already ordered for his party, and thanking her. She bobbed again and moved away.

'My language skills are limited,' said Celia, 'but that was a rather strange way in which to put that question to us, wasn't it?'

'Well, ladies, the origin lies in history. The waitresses in Demel were always convent-educated and became known as the Demenlinerinnen. The formal, impersonal construction of the question was designed to avoid offensive familiarity with the aristocratic clientele. The tradition remains.'

'Gee, that's extraordinary!' exclaimed Wallis, 'it's living history!'

'Ah, here come our indulgences. The Empress Elizabeth, known as Sissi, with her treasured 20 inch waist, might not have approved, I fear.' As the three-tiered round stand bearing a selection of pastries was placed in the middle of the table by one of the waitresses, another laid hand-painted, flowered porcelain plates, cups and saucers.

'They are beautiful!' exclaimed Celia, as she looked closely at the Wiener Rose and green-edged crockery.

The Duke smiled and responded, 'That is Augarten porcelain, or so I was informed when I was last here. Fruity Metcalfe was with me – he insisted on tracking the manufacturer and buying a tea service for his wife. Ladies Slipper was the design that he chose.'

'It really is beautiful – it is so delicate. I must remember that when we are setting up our home, David.'

'Of course, Wallis. Now then let's savour Mr Demel's offerings, eh?'

'Oh my God!' said Wallis as she tasted her first forkful of Sachertorte, 'it is so darn rich, but still light as a feather.'

'Mmm, I agree. If I lived in Vienna I would be the size of a house,' laughed Celia.

Before they left Demel, they were presented with small painted tins of candied violets. 'These are what the good Mr Demel used to regularly deliver to Empress Sissi at the Hofburg Palace,' said the Duke.

'Now Wallis, we must have a very light lunch – we are dining with Sam Gracie, the honarary Brazilian Minister here, and his wife, at the Brazilian Legation. She is British. George Messersmith, the American Ambassador, will be there, as will a senior chap from the Italian Embassy.'

'David, I hardly think that I could manage any lunch at all,' said an unsmiling Wallis, as she patted her ironingboad-flat stomach.

The formal dinner party had proceeded smoothly, but Wallis had chosen the occasion to complain bitterly to Ambassador Messersmith about the way in which she considered herself to have been shabbily treated in the American press. The Duke paid close attention.

'Your Royal Highness, you and I know that the so-called Fourth Estate, as the press like to style themselves, stoop low to dramatise any story. There are some exceptions, but sadly few.'

'Yes, Ambassador, but that is no excuse for muck-raking and downright lies, surely?'

'Of course not, but I am afraid that with the high profile such as you have enjoyed and continue to enjoy, comes the downside of public interest. The public is rarely interested in good news or stories regarding happiness of public figures.'

'I am sure that Herr Hitler would not permit the sort of trash that has been printed about me in America.'

'No, Ma'am, he probably would not.'

'Then I know who has it right.'

Wallis, with uncharacteristic rudeness, turned away from the Ambassador and addressed her host on her right. 'Are you enjoying your time in Vienna?' she asked with a smile.

A few minutes later, their hostess suggested that they retire to the salon for coffee in less formal surroundings. The party was mingling when Austrian Chancellor Schussnigg's Private Secretary was ushered into the room and formally announced.

The room fell quiet. The Secretary went straight to George Messersmith and handed him a sealed envelope bearing the Austrian crest. The Secretary left. Messersmith tore open the envelope and quickly scanned the contents of the note from the Austrian Chancellor. He stuffed the note in his pocket.

The Duke of Windsor was now standing next to him. Speaking quietly, he asked, 'What could be so urgent that the Chancellor sends you a note here?'

'In confidence, it is rather worrying. There has been a train crash in Austria, and it turns out that the cargo was not as stated on the manifest but is naval shells. The train was running through neutral Austria from Germany to Italy.'

'So why should that cause a flap?'

'Because, Sir, it is proof positive that Germany is supplying Italy, contrary to League of Nations rulings, thereby compromising Austria's neutrality. Importantly, it appears to signal that Italy's support and succour for Austria can no longer be relied upon.'

'Oh well, it is probably a storm in a tea cup, eh?'

The American Ambassador then made his excuses and left. The Duke went and sat next to the Italian diplomat. 'I have not had an opportunity to talk to you – I trust that you do not think me rude. I think that you should know what was in the message delivered to the Ambassador.'

'Not rude at all, I can assure you. What was the message?'

'In confidence, of course, there has been a train crash in Austria today.'

The Duke then related what he had been told. When he had finished, he looked quizzically at the Italian diplomat and said, 'Well then, what do you make of that?'

'It is not for me to say.'

'Do remember that I told you in confidence.'

'Of course.'

Early the following morning, Ambassador Messersmith was at his desk when his secretary announced that the Military Attache wished to see him. 'Send him in, Miss Jones. Ah, Colonel, good morning, and what may I do for you this fine day?'

'Trouble, I am afraid, Ambassador. I have here a decoded version of the intercepted message sent by the Italian Embassy here in Vienna to their Foreign Office in Rome last night. It sets out the content of a conversation between the Duke of Windsor and one of their diplomats when he repeated a conversation you and he had last night including your conclusions.'

'Damn and blast. I spoke to the Duke in confidence, which he acknowledged. Here, let me read it.' He took the flimsy and quickly read it. 'Essentially, it is accurate. Well, we know one thing – the Duke is not to be trusted. I assume that he shares the political beliefs of his wife. I shall send my report to the State Department immediately. It makes you wonder whose side the Duke is on, in reality.'

# Chapter 31

Wallis and the Duke arrived at Professor Newmann's consulting rooms, and were greeted by Helga. On this occasion she had abandoned the plain and unflattering hairstyle she normally affected for work, and looked unashamedly glamorous. Her crisp white uniform perfectly complemented her figure, and the skirt was just short enough to show off her fine legs. Wallis' attention was instantly focused.

'David, I shall not join you in the consultation. I shall wait for you here.'

'Very well my dear.'

Wallis appraised Helga further as she showed the Duke into the professor's consulting room. 'Well, my dear – Helga, I believe – would you be interested in working as a member of my personal staff?' Wallis had subtly emphasised the word *personal*, and noted the flicker it brought to Helga's eyes.

'Yes, I certainly would be honoured. My employment with the professor concludes after the Duke's appointment this morning. I believe that we have a friend in common – Gruppenführer von Ribbentrop?'

'Yes, so I understand, but of course, in my position that is a matter for discretion.'

'Naturally. I am fully aware of the need for total discretion and confidentiality with regard to your affairs, and the part that you wish me to play.'

'Excellent. I believe that we understand each other. Will you come to see me this afternoon at my hotel – the Bristol?'

'Of course, as you wish, Ma'am.'

'Good – say 3 o'clock then.'

'I shall be there.'

The professor ushered the smiling Duke out of his consulting room.

'I say, Wallis, excellent news, the professor is satisfied that my ear is totally healed, so swimming is no problem.' He was oblivious to the sexual tension between his wife and the beautiful blonde receptionist.

'Oh my dear, that is just such good news – thank you, Professor.'

The professor smiled and acknowledged the thanks.

'My Secretary, Mr Forward, will be in touch with regard to your account, Professor,' said the Duke.

'There will be no account. As of now I am retired. You were my last patient and I am delighted that the treatment worked. That pleasure is sufficient reward.'

'That is damned decent of you, and I thank you. I trust that you have a long and happy retirement.'

When they were back in the car, Wallis told the Duke that she had agreed to take Helga on to her staff. 'We just cannot cope with all the correspondence. She is a bright girl, and multilingual, with no ties. She is ideal.'

'Good. Do you mind if Fruity and I go for a round of golf this afternoon? It's a beautiful day and I need to stretch my legs.'

'I think that is an excellent idea, my darling,' replied a smiling Wallis, who felt a familiar tightening in her groin. 'I have a slight headache. After luncheon I shall lie down. The staff can have the afternoon off – I do not wish for any disturbance. Please have Dudley make that arrangement.'

'Of course, my dear – I am so sorry. Hopefully a good rest will do the trick. We are supposed to be at the opera this evening.'

'I shall have to see how I feel.'

Billy was in the hotel reception lobby when he noticed the dramatically attractive young woman, who had previously visited von Ribbentrop, approach the concierge's desk. She was given directions, than walked to the lifts. Billy waited until the doors had been closed behind her, then approached Hekkel.

'Ah, Hekkel. Where was that young woman going?'

'She asked for the Duchess, Sir.'

'Thank you.'

Billy knew that his patience had been rewarded. Von Ribbentrop had clearly made a move.

After the Duke had left with Fruity Metcalfe, and the staff had all gone from the suite, Wallis had had a quick bath, then slipped into one of her Chinese-style silk gowns. She waited impatiently for Helga to arrive, and was sitting drumming her fingers on the arm of her chair when the telephone rang. It was the concierge, informing her that her guest was on her way up.

Wallis sneaked a quick check in the gold-framed mirror over the fireplace, and then walked along the marble-floored corridor towards the doors to the suite. She was standing in the hallway when there was a gentle knock on the door, which she promptly opened The pageboy stood aside as Helga thanked him, and smiling confidently, entered the suite. Wallis closed the doors and then turned towards Helga. She wasted no time on conversation but reached forward and drew the younger woman towards her, and into an embrace.

As they kissed, Wallis instinctively knew that in Helga she had met a soul mate. She silently thanked von Ribbentrop as her hands slid down Helga's back and onto her firm buttocks. Wallis held Helga tightly to her, pelvis to pelvis. The younger woman groaned, and Wallis, taking this as a cue, released her hold and led her into the bedroom. Without another word being said they both undressed and then resumed their embrace. As Helga's hand felt Wallis' engorged sex her eyes flew open for a moment, then breaking from their kiss, she smiled broadly as Wallis gave a throaty laugh.

They lay on the bed, and as Helga started to stroke and tease Wallis, it was clear that she was a sensual expert. Wallis reached under one of the pillows and produced a silver-mounted, curved ebony dildo. Helga firmly took it from her, pushed Wallis back on the bed, and then lifted her knees. Wallis gasped, realising what was intended as she felt the head of the dildo pressing firmly against her resistant muscles.

As Helga worked the dildo into Wallis, with her other hand she continued to stroke with her thumb whilst her fingers were sliding in and out, picking up the same rhythm as the dildo. Wallis was gasping as she felt her first climax building.

'Oh My God!' she cried, as she lost control in a series of convulsions.

Helga gave Wallis no time to recover as she continued bringing Wallis to a seemingly endless series of climaxes. Almost an hour later, Wallis gripped Helga's wrists and said hoarsely, 'That's enough – I'm spent!'

It was something she had never said in her life before.

Billy was in the lobby when the immaculate visitor came out of the lift, and confidently walked to the hotel entrance, apparently oblivious to the stares she attracted from every man and woman she passed. She had been with Wallis for just over three hours.

He went back to his room and dialled Celia's number. She answered almost immediately and agreed that he should join her. He was soon telling her about the glamorous visitor.

'I'll find out what the score is, Billy. We are going to the opera tonight, so Wallis will be in an expansive mood; if not then, certainly over dinner afterwards. I think that David has the Royal Box, so Wallis will bask in the attention. You know, everyone here in Vienna is addressing her as "Your Royal Highness", which was of course expressly denied to her. Neither she or David corrects them, and now her own staff are picking up the habit. I think she loves it!'

'I'll tell Tar when I report on the identity of her visitor tomorrow morning.'

'I am told, Wallis, that the Imperial Box in the Opera House here is rather fine, and gives a marvellous view of the stage. Quite unlike the Royal Box at the Royal Opera House in London. That's tucked away at the side.'

'How do I look, David?'

'Absolutely splendid, my dear – that oyster-grey silk suits you so well, it sets off your jewellery magnificently, and the tiara complements your hair perfectly.'

'Thank you, David – and you look every inch my dashing prince.'

'Celia – I really must apologise – you look splendid as ever. We are quite a fine party, eh? Right, time for the off I think – Dudders?'

'Yes, Sir, the motors are at the front of the hotel. I have

given instructions for the drivers to go aound the block so that they can draw up at the entrance in a suitable manner. There will be a police guard of honour on the pavement, and nine motorcycle outriders. The security chaps will be following in their cars, although I understand that there will be a full complement on the ground and inside the Opera House.'

'Very good, Dudders. Come ladies.' The Duke offered an arm to both Wallis and Celia as they crossed the hallway to the lift.

When their car drew up outside the entrance to the Opera House, the Duke noted with satisfaction that a wide red carpet had been laid across the pavement, and gleaming brass upstands supported the dark blue thick silken ropes on either side. A line of smartly-dressed police officers in their ceremonial uniforms was drawn up on either side of the ropes. They saluted with their swords as the Duke and Duchess left their car, with Celia and Fruity Metcalfe following.

There was quite a crowd on the pavement, and as the party walked towards the entrance the Duke and Duchess were smiling and waving graciously to them, acknowledging the loud applause that accompanied their arrival. At the entrance, they were greeted by the director of the Opera House who then led them past a further guard of honour across the foyer, where other members of the audience, also wearing formal evening dress, were straining to see the couple. There were more uniformed guards flanking the grand staircase.

The director explained that the intention was that the Duke and Duchess and their party would first wait in an anteroom until the audience had taken their places. They would then be escorted to the Imperial Box. As they waited in the ante room they could hear the buzz of conversation from the auditorium and then the sounds of the orchestra tuning up. A hush fell, and then the sound of loud applause. The director explained that the conductor was now in place, and they should make their entrance.

As they stepped through the arch leading from the anteroom onto the gallery, which ran to their box, the audience rose, and loud applause greeted them. Neither the Duke nor Duchess waved, but both smiled and nodded, acknowledging their welcome.

Celia and Fruity Metcalf followed five paces behind, and

in turn Dudley Forward and the director of the Opera House followed them. As they reached their seats, the conductor bowed in their direction then, turning to the orchestra, raised his baton. As he brought it sweeping down there was a mighty drum roll, and then the orchestra played the British National Anthem. Both the Duke and Fruity Metcalfe stood smartly to attention. As the last notes died, the audience again applauded, and there were many cheers and cries of "Bravo".

The Duke and Duchess sat down and with a rustling the audience followed suit. As the orchestra started the overture, the Duke leant sideways and whispered to Wallis, 'That's more like it, eh?'

'David,' she replied, smiling, 'that is something I will never tire of.' She took his hand and gave an affectionate squeeze. Celia noted that Wallis had an expression bordering on ecstatic. It was not lost on Fruity Metcalfe or Dudley Forward.

When the first interval came, the party were again escorted to the anteroom where drinks were served, and they could avail themselves of washroom facilities.

'Well, Wallis, how has your day been?'

'Good, Celia, very good. I went with David to see his ear specialist this morning, and quite apart from his being given a clean bill of health, I had a piece of luck. The specialist is retiring – today in fact – and his receptionist, who is multilingual, has agreed to join my staff as a secretary, to help with the mountain of letters I am receiving every day.'

'That certainly is a bit of luck – and she will travel?'

'Oh yes, that is one of the attractions from her point of view. I have no doubt that you will meet her. She is a very capable young woman – about your age, my dear.'

'Poor Wallis had a headache at lunchtime, so Dudders kindly got rid of the staff in order that she could have an uninterrupted rest this afternoon, whilst Fruity and I had a rather good round of golf.'

'Better for you, David – you soundly beat me,' laughed Fruity.

'Ah, there is the second bell, Your Royal Highnesses. It is time to return to your seats, please,' fussed the director.

Von Ribbentrop was in bed with Helga, in a suite that he had taken in the former Royal palace where they had first spent the night together. He had explained that she must be careful not to leave any physical signs of their sexual activities on his body. She had understood.

'Now, Helga, tell me everything that you discussed and did with the Duchess today.'

'Everything?' she asked coyly.

'Yes, every detail.'

As she did, he felt himself growing hard again. She felt it too. 'Joachim. Do you want me to do something a little special for you?' she asked, the picture of innocence. His mind ran riot at the thought of what she might intend.

'Yes, of course, but remember what I said,' he replied, with a coarsening voice. He admired her figure as she left the bed and went to her handbag. When she turned around, he was puzzled by what she had in her hand.

'Now Joachim, just lie back and close your eyes. This will hurt a little at first, but then you will find that it was worth it.'

He did as he was told.

The following morning, Celia and Billy were having a coffee in her suite. 'Right then, Celia, piecing together what we know. At the instigation of von Ribbentrop, Wallis has taken on this beautiful, but sadistic personal secretary who is keen to travel. We know that he has had a fling with the girl, Helga – you reported that she had given him a severe thrashing.'

'And more, remember, Billy...'

'Yes, of course. So now von Ribbentrop has his spy in the camp again.'

'That is the only conclusion. She, of course, has a new playmate, which will ensure that her new secretary will soon be privy to all hers, and of course, the Duke's secrets. Wallis hinted that I would get on with the girl – from what I saw of von Ribbentrop, I don't relish that one iota.'

'Romantic place, this Vienna, Celia.'

'Don't you start! You are getting into quite a game with your lady of mystery.'

'That's true, but I don't think that she is quite as lethal as your Helga. Right, I had better go to the Embassy, get a signal to Tar and give him an update.'

'I am off to the Spanish Riding School, and guess what –

the Duke has been put in the Royal Box yet again. Wallis will be preening.'

# Chapter 32

The Duke and Duchess, Celia, Fruity Metcalfe and Dudley Forward were settled into their seats in the Royal Box of the Spanish Riding School, beneath a large portrait of Emperor Charles Vl. The crystal chandeliers of the indoor Winter Riding School were alight and sparkling, even though the comparatively small fifty metre-long rectangular arena was brightly sunlit.

The audience in the two pillared galleries of the white, grey and beige painted hall had also settled down, after standing and applauding the small party as it had entered the Royal Box. Celia had duly noted, as she had anticipated, that Wallis was again revelling in the attention they were receiving. By contrast, the Duke looked slightly wistful. Celia mused for a moment or two that Wallis might be enjoying something she had craved for, whilst David was contemplating something that he had lost.

Her thoughts were interrupted when the first riders came into the arena, and riding forward from the entrance opposite the Royal Box, stopped and saluted. The display was breathtaking in its elegance, and the skills of not only the wonderfully trained stallions, but also their riders. As the performance reached its long finale, the School Quadrille, accompanied by the orchestra playing classical music, Celia found herself near to tears. It was a time to treasure.

She glanced at Wallis, and noted that unlike the others in their party who were clearly similarly moved, Wallis had a set, fixed smile. Her expression showed no real emotion. When the display finished, and as the riders left the arena, there were some moments of silence before the applause started, and then mounted to a crescendo as the audience rose to its feet.

The riders re-entered the arena and drew to a halt before the Royal Box. As they saluted, the orchestra played the British National Anthem. Celia stole a glance at Wallis. She was now smiling warmly, again clearly basking in the attention.

'What is the picture that we are building up, Tar?' asked Sir Vernon Kell, as he laid his fountain pen on the foolscap sheets where he had been making notes, and leant back in his desk chair. Tar Robertson and Maxwell Knight were with Sir Vernon in his office.

'We have something of a vipers' nest in Vienna, Sir Vernon. I know that I am repeating myself, but it really is turning into something quite extraordinary. We have the Duke of Windsor, who is either blithely ignorant of his actions, or knowingly giving away critical confidential intelligence. I had lunch with Chester Harris, the American Embassy's so-called Legal Attaché. He heads up their intelligence in the United Kingdom, you will recall.'

Sir Vernon nodded in confirmation.

'They are hopping mad the Duke tipped off the Italians that the arms supplies from Germany had been rumbled. Apparently there was even talk of recalling Ambassador Messersmith from Vienna. Harris also briefed me on the Duke's great friend, Charles Bedaux. He is not only a Nazi sympathiser, but an activist. He undoubtedly has very powerful friends – allies even – the likes of Henry Ford and Rockefeller in America, and Sir Henry Deterding here.'

'Deterding – he is the chairman of Shell, and reputedly the most powerful and richest oil man in the world?' interrupted Sir Vernon.

'That is so, Sir Vernon. Apparently, J Edgar Hoover has pressed President Roosevelt to allow him to arrest Bedaux next time he sets foot in America, but the President doesn't want to rock any boats. That seems to be Bedaux's modus operandi. He gets so cozy with the powerful that it is very risky for any politician to sanction action against him. Harris described it as an invisible shield of influence. The other thing is that Bedaux never threatens, but instead relies entirely on his relationships being recognised.

'Bedaux is working on two immediate projects involving the Duke – a trip to Germany, where he will meet Hitler and the Nazi top brass, and a trip to the USA. Ostensibly, these are fact finding trips to study working methods, conditions and the like. The Duke, and again, is he being cleverer than we give him credit for or just naive, apparently thinks that, armed with first-hand knowledge of the way these nations run industry so efficiently, he can come back to Britain, and make good the empty promise that he made in Wales.'

'But Tar, how can he contemplate returning to Britain in any active role? The King has made it abundantly clear that he is unwelcome, and there is no place for him here. Prime Minister Chamberlain endorses that view, and even Winston Churchill has performed one of his political pirouettes and withdrawn his support.'

'There is only one conclusion, Sir Vernon, and I am afraid that it is not very palatable. He sees himself back on the throne, and I do not believe that he has any moral scruples as to how he gets there. What do you think, Max – you have been very quiet?'

Maxwell Knight responded in a reflective tone, 'I have to agree. In fact, I would go further. I believe he has a genuine conviction that Britain and Germany share a heritage and ethos, which should not be sullied by their going to war again.'

'I am inclined to agree,' interposed Tar, 'he sees Hitler's Germany as the strong bulwark against the Bolshevik threat. He may not have read *Mein Kampf,* but in my view he embraces Hitler's vision.'

'I have read it,' said Sir Vernon, 'it's a hard slog, particularly with rusty German. Nevertheless, it spells out the plans of Herr Hitler as clearly as night follows day. I wish more of our politicians would read it. They might have a better understanding of the threat we, and Europe, face. I certainly do not think that the British ethos embraces the genocide that he advocates, or at least does not shy from. There might be mistrust of the Jewish community, and gypsies are at best unliked, but the Nazi "solution" would be unthinkable in Britain.'

Tar then continued, 'The Duke's views were formed by what he saw first hand in the Great War, and his reaction to seeing so many crowned heads – indeed relatives – deposed, and even executed. His father, the old King, had a constant fear of revolution, and it stands to reason that he passed that on to his sons. For all that he is a dilettante who permanently lives on the edge of public scandal, almost disgrace, Prince George, the Duke of Kent, has forged close links with the Nazi government.

'I am not implying that he has done so with any traitorous intent, but we know from our surveillance that he has been visited by William de Ropp on a number of occasions, and we strongly suspect that those visits were ordered by Herman Goering, if not Hitler himself.'

Maxwell Knight spoke again. 'Tar, if I may add, the Duke of Windsor has nobody close to him taking a balanced view. Certainly not his wife. Wallis has no scruples, Sir Vernon, and is a self-professed admirer of the Nazis. I believe that she is a ruthless adventuress – his "Lady Macbeth", if you like.'

'Now – Tar, Maxwell – keep Shakespeare out of this!' laughed Sir Vernon, ' but I agree. I am no prude, but by Jove, she certainly doesn't hold back.'

'No, and we now have von Ribbentrop's new "dove" working for her, and as a consequence, a part of the household.'

'Let's not beat about the bush: they are also bound to become lovers if they are not already. Billy reports that she was placed by von Ribbentrop, and is very striking to look at.'

'Yes, Maxwell, and he also reports that she is a vicious sadist. Whilst we look at the menagerie currently in Vienna, we have Billy Brownlow's new friend, the mysterious beauty Vera. . .'

'If I may interpose here, Sir Vernon?'

'Of course, Maxwell, fire away.'

'I have been doing some digging and spoken to our friends in the Deuxieme Bureau who keep close tabs on the Russian émigrés. Paris has a very large émigré community, and many see themselves as anti-communist activists. Much of what they spout is pure self delusion and in reality harmless, but nevertheless, they are seen as a threat.

'Anyhow, the sweet Vera is more of a deadly nightshade than a pretty flower. She has operated in various countries against the Soviets for the White Russians, and vice versa. That, of course, provided her with the means to dispose of the disgusting husband, Count Ignatieff, or rather have the Soviets do the dirty work. She is now working with the Germans – ostensibly the Abwehr – but with a direct link to von Ribbentrop.

'I am sure that it was was he who instructed her to investigate Billy Brownlow. As you know, I have very good connections in the Abwehr, Tar likewise. It is clear that young Vera – and remember that she is still only 25 years old – is a survivor, and likes to hedge her bets. I think that we can turn her, and if you are in agreement would like to pursue that avenue.'

'Very well, Maxwell, I agree. How about you, Tar?'

'I am content, Sir Vernon. In my opinion, in Billy she may realise that she has at last encountered a truly decent man who nonetheless understands, and is a part of the world of espionage.'

'Then am I right, gentlemen, what you are proposing is that Billy Brownlow sublimates. . .no, actually prostitutes his feelings for this girl, and becomes her controller?' asked Sir Vernon, with a raised eyebrow.

'Yes, that is precisely what we propose.'

'Thank you, both. You may brief Brownlow accordingly.'

'Now, Helga, we are all off to Venice on Sunday – we had such a wonderful welcome there after our wedding. We shall all be staying at the Excelsior on the Lido. You will of course have some work to do, but I am sure that there will be plenty of time for swimming and sunbathing.'

'It sounds wonderful, Your Royal Highness – sorry, I meant Ma'am.'

'Oh it will be. Now, when we are in private like this just call me Wallis. Ma'am is fine the rest of the time, unless we are in formal circumstances. Come here.'

The Duke had asked Dudley Forward to arrange for a car to take him to the Jockey Club. He was ostensibly paying an informal courtesy call on the President of the club, but his real purpose was to meet Arthur Seyss-Inquart.

'Sir, do you wish me to accompany you?'

'No, Dudders, it will not be necessary – Fruity is coming with me. It is a private visit. Please advise the good Inspector

Shober I would appreciate it if he would restrict my escort to a single following police car.'

'I shall do that, but he will not be happy. He is concerned for your safety in the present, unsettled political climate here.'

'Typical policeman. The Austrians have an inbred fear of assassination attempts – I think that it goes back to Sarajevo,' said the Duke, with a wry smile.

'Well, Sir, more recent than that, given the murder of Doctor Dolfuss.'

'Point taken. Ask him all the same, will you please.'

'As you wish, Sir.'

As the Duke and Fruity Metcalfe were driven to the Jockey Club, the Duke turned to Fruity and said, 'When we get there, Fruity, we shall be shown to the Reading Room. I will then be taken to my private meeting, but I would wish you to stay in the Reading Room. I anticipate that I shall be gone for an hour or so.'

'Understood, David – I am sure that they will have some English periodicals.'

'Of course – as I recall from my last visit to the club, or to give it its full title, The Jockey Club für Oesterreich, I saw *Country Life* and *Horse and Hound* for sure. Whilst the club is the authority for the turf, it is the happy hunting ground of the Austrian nobility who make up the majority of its members.'

When they arrived at the club, a liveried servant, who had the look, gait and stature of a former jockey, led them up the Turkey-carpeted grand staircase with equine prints lining the walls, and then into a large and comfortable room. There were clusters of red leather-covered armchairs and settees, and low mahogany tables. In the centre of the huge Persian rug stood a large mahogany table, on which was set out an array of newspapers and magazines. There were also some writing desks set against the walls. There were only a handful of generally elderly gentlemen sitting reading. One or two of them appeared to be asleep.

'Could be any London Club,' whispered Fruity, as they approached the table.

'Ah, there you are, Fruity – some English magazines and yesterday's *Times*. Take your pick and settle down. I'd order a coffee if I was you.'

As Fruity was looking around deciding where to sit,

another elderly club servant entered the room and, bowing to the Duke, in a hushed voice asked His Royal Highness to follow him. The Duke was led along a broad corridor where the cream-panelled walls were hung with pictures of racing scenes. Many were clearly from an era long before the club was founded in 1867. The servant knocked on a heavy mahogany door, and after a moment's wait opened it wide, and stood aside to allow the Duke to enter an elegant office.

As the door clicked shut behind him, the Duke strode towards the desk and stretched out his hand to the tall and trim dark-suited man who came around it, smiling as he extended his hand. 'Your Royal Highness – it is a delight to see you again.'

'State Councillor – I am delighted to be re-acquainted with you. It is my earnest wish to hear what is happening in this, our beautiful country.'

They sat in the leather armchairs in front of the desk. Seyss-Inquart, who was of a similar age to the Duke, was a studious-looking man, with dark hair receding at the temples. He wore tortoishell-framed, round-lensed spectacles.

'Well Sir, that is an easier question to ask than to answer.'

'Ah Inquart – I detect a lawyer's answer,' responded the Duke with a smile.

'Whilst I was a lawyer by profession before I entered full time politics, I can assure you that my answer is a reflection of the truth. To give you an answer I must go back to the end of the Great War. At that time, the majority of the Austrian people wanted to unite with the new German Republic. Both nations had lost their monarchs, and Austria had been divested of the provinces that had provided almost all of the industry of the now-dismantled Austro Hungarian Empire.

'The Treaty of Versailles expressly forbids a union of Germany and Austria. Just as in Germany under the Weimar Republic, there was great poverty, so there was in Austria. The power struggles here have resulted in the creation of what some have described as "private armies". They are the physical manifestation of various political parties and factions.

'The Austrian National Socialist Party, of which I am a prominent member, is ideologically fascist, but follows the same path as the Italians, as led by Benito Mussolini. The Austrian Nazi Party, which on the other hand espouses the secular fascism of Hitler's Germany, is officially banned in Austria, but remains a powerful force with growing influence.'

The Duke, who had been listening intently, then asked, 'Is it not correct that Mussolini has committed to supporting Austrian fascism and independence?'

'Oh yes, indeed – the Italians actually mobilised troops on the Austrian border. That was when we almost had civil war in the south of the country, when the Nazis there took to arms. The Nazi view is in fact expressed on the very first page of Hitler's book, *Mein Kampf*, and I quote:

*"German Austria must return to the great German Reich. Identity of blood demands a joint Reich."*

'Under the terms of the Treaty of St Germain, Austria may not have an effective army – men under arms including police and the gendarmerie may not exceed 30,000. Consequently, the private armies have developed and we have the Heimwehr, the Heimatschutz of Major Fey, the Ostmärkische Sturmscharen, loyal to Doctor Schussnigg, and the illegal Nazis who also have a paramilitary arm.'

'Last year, Doctor Schussnigg signed the "Treaty of Friendship" with Germany, and maintains it is a guarantee that Austria will retain its independence. He also believes that the trading relationship with Germany does not conflict with the continued illegality of National Socialism in Austria.'

'If Herr Hitler believes what he wrote in *Mein Kampf*, surely that cannot be?' asked the Duke.

'I have come to that conclusion. Austria is becoming more and more economically dependent on Germany, and from a military point of view I do not think that Mussolini's Italy will again threaten war with Germany to preserve our independence.'

'Are you saying that unification is inevitable?'

'I am saying that I believe Austria will find itself swallowed up by its vastly greater neighbour. It will not be a partnership – the high-minded David could never have lived with the brute Goliath. An independent Austria is an economic and military myth now, and its people will best be served by unification with Germany.'

'Austria borders Czechoslovakia, Hungary, Switzerland, Italy and Germany, if I am correct?' asked the Duke.

'That is correct.'

'When do you think that Hitler will make his move?'

'Within months, within months. In my view, he flexed his muscles last year, when his military reoccupation of the Ruhr went unopposed by France, Belgium and the British. Why should he heed treaty restrictions that stand in the way of his vision?'

'May I assume, from what you have just said, that you would wholeheartedly support a German Nazi unification with Austria?'

'Absolutely. It is not only inevitable, but essential.'

'As my family's heritage is rooted in both Austria and Germany, I can assure you that it would please me to see not only a political union, but a true union of the people, who will then share the Führer's wise governance and vision. Thank you for sharing your views with me so frankly. I appreciate that they are private, and I shall treat them as absolutely confidential.'

That evening, as the Duke and Duchess were sitting with Celia, Fruity and Dudley, enjoying cocktails before dinner, the Duke told them of his conversation with a very senior member of the Austrian Government, Cabinet Member Arthur Seyss-Inquart. He left out no detail.

After dinner, Wallis complained of a headache, and making her excuses left the Duke and Fruity to their cards. Celia announced that she too felt like an early night and also left. As soon as Wallis was in her dressing room, she telephoned Helga, and asked her to come and join her. Helga was there in minutes. Wallis asked her to make a note whilst matters were fresh in her head. She then repeated what the Duke had told them earlier, virtually verbatim.

'Now, Helga, can you get that to Herr von Ribbentrop?'

'Of course, Wallis – I shall do it first thing in the morning.'

'Good girl. Now put that notebook in your hand bag and come here.'

Celia had likewise called Billy who had joined her in her sitting room. Celia reported the Duke's remarks.

'So that means that within hours, that opinion will be with von Ribbentrop, and then Hitler. Either Seyss-Inquart is a fool trusting the Duke, or he wants his position recognised in Germany – always assuming he knows of the Duke's attitudes and sympathies. I assume the latter – he will have made enquiries, and, of course they had those secret meetings in 1935. I will keep an eye out and follow Helga in the morning, before I go to the Embassy to send an encrypted message to Tar. Well done, Celia – this just the sort of thing we need.'

'Well, it's hardly difficult when the Duke is so casual with confidences, is it?'

# Chapter 33

The following morning, Helga came to the Hotel Bristol and reported to Wallis in her suite. Gone was the rather frumpy hairstyle she had affected when working for the professor, and she was smartly turned out in a slightly severe, but still flattering business suit.

'Helga, my dear. The Duke decided to go out for breakfast, back to Demel for some of those hot Viennese rolls he so loves. I would like you to go to von Ribbentrop's rooms – he is in the Presidential Suite – and relay to him all that I told you last night, about what was said to the Duke by the State Councillor. You had better go immediately, because he is planning to return to Germany today.'

Helga left straight away. Wallis did not know the precise location of von Ribbentrop's suite, and she instructed Helga to take elevator down to the ground floor then have a bellboy escort her. Helga was not sure whether she should reveal that she had previously visited von Ribbentrop in his suite, and decided that it was best to obey the instruction.

Helga approached the concierge's desk where Hekkel was on duty, and asked him if she could be directed to the Presidential Suite. A bell boy was summoned, and led the way back to the elevator. Hekkel telephoned the suite, and informed von Ribbentrop that a young lady visitor was being shown up. Von Ribbentrop was delighted to greet Helga, and swept her into a warm embrace.

'Joachim, I cannot be long, I am expected back with Wallis. I am here because I have a report for you.'

'Very well, please come over here and sit down. Now, tell me.'

Helga then repeated the comments made by Arthur Seyss-Inquart to the Duke. Both she and Wallis had excellent memories, and her report was totally accurate.

'That is very interesting, Helga. Now, you have memorised the telephone number I gave you?'

'Most certainly – I have an excellent memory for such things. I had better be going.'

'Very well, you are right, of course. I am leaving for Germany shortly. Please convey my very best wishes and thanks to Wallis.'

He stood, and took her to the door, where he embraced her again before she left. He was delighted with what he had been told and knew that his Führer would be also. As he left his suite shortly afterwards, he had a spring in his step.

This should definitely be one over Himmler.

Sir Vernon was sitting in the Prime Minister's office in 10 Downing Street. Try as he might, he could not warm to Neville Chamberlain. He had served a number of Prime Ministers in his time, and his years of experience gave him an insight into their personalities, their strengths and weaknesses.

'I must stress, Prime Minister, that the intelligence that we have received from Austria provides an important insight into the way in which Herr Hitler and the Nazis regard not only the independent integrity of their neighbours and their treaty obligations, but importantly, their cynical disregard for agreements into which they may enter.

'The German Ambassador in Vienna is reported to have said that the Führer is eager to sign a so called "Treaty of Friendship" with Dr Schuschnigg's government, and quoted Bismarck, who was adamant that Germany and Austria should live alongside each other as close, but independent friends.'

'Sir Vernon, I hear what you say, but I must tell you that I have no reason to doubt the sincerity of Herr Hitler.'

'Prime Minister, I must point out that by standing back when the Nazis re-occupied the Rhineland, an opportunity to destroy the canker of Nazi government was lost. We are satisfied from our intelligence that the apparent German military might was a huge bluff. I sincerely hope that neither you nor the British people will have cause to regret that lost opportunity, or any trust placed in Nazi Germany.'

'Thank you, Sir Vernon. I would ask that you refrain from opining on political matters. They are the preserve of the politicians. Now, I am afraid that we must conclude, I am due in the House. Thank you.'

Sir Vernon was displaying a rare irritability as he discussed his earlier meeting with Tar Robertson. 'The man is living in a rarified cloud cuckoo land! Heaven help us if he ever goes into bat against Hitler. Surely he cannot be as naive as he appears to be?'

'Well, Sir Vernon, we have heard politicians in the past come out with that same line; effectively that they know best regardless of intelligence reports. I call it "convenience thinking" – a selective process where they deliberately ignore that which is contrary to their views. He cannot be blind to the Non-Intervention Agreement, when 27 countries, including the Soviet Union, Germany and Italy, expressly agreed not to intervene in the Spanish Civil War. Germany and Italy have totally ignored it, providing equipment, and even troops, to General Franco's Nationalists, as indeed have the Russians helped the Republicans.

'He has now been warned of another likely cynical breach of an agreement by Hitler's Germany, in defiance of Treaty obligations as well. He clearly will go on ignoring the warnings until matters blow up in his face.'

'You are right, Tar, I am afraid to say. Wolfgang zu Putlitz, the First Secretary at the German embassy in London, who continues to provide us with first rate intelligence, reported that von Ribbentrop was delighted at Chamberlain becoming Prime Minister for two reasons. First, he regards him as strongly pro-German, and secondly, he will not allow Anthony Eden to get on with his job as Foreign Secretary – Eden is of course, anti appeasement.'

'Yes, and zu Putlitz has actually said that Britain is letting the trump cards fall by not calling Hitler's bluff, because the German military is not yet ready for war. What next, Sir Vernon?'

'I believe that it would be helpful if Celia could discreetly try to explore German intentions with von Ribbentrop. She need not be too detailed – in any event, I think that he is too wily a fox for that. However, she can perhaps pick up the drift of their thinking – he is after all, a confidante of Hitler. That will help me focus the efforts of our chaps on the ground; for instance, Hugh Christie in Berlin. He is pretty close to Goering, who gives away a lot of information when he is in one of his expansive moods, particularly over a good lunch or dinner.'

'Very well, Sir Vernon. As soon as she is back from Vienna, I shall brief her. We also need to decide how to play it with Vera Ignatieff – or Schalburg, as she now calls herself. She and Billy Brownlow have formed a good bond, but he is a cool enough customer not to become too emotionally entwined. At any rate, for the moment his heart belongs to Lisette in Cannes.'

'Very well, Tar, I think that is all for now. Young Billy seems to have a talent for falling in with very beautiful but totally unsuitable women, doesn't he?' laughed Sir Vernon, as Tar stood and left the room.

It was obvious to Celia that the arrival of Helga had virtually negated the interest that the sexually predatory Wallis had previously shown in her. Whilst it was a relief in many ways, it did make it more difficult to garner any snippets of intelligence that she could report back. Celia was also becoming rather tired of the endless round of activities that the Duke and Wallis were determined to pursue in Vienna.

The Duke was playing a role that he had been accustomed to for many years, and if anything found the endless attention rather irritating on occasion. Wallis on the other hand, was relishing every minute of it. Before the marriage, she had been out of the direct spotlight, certainly in Britain. Now she was centre stage in the full glare of publicity. She did not even see the irony in the British National Anthem *"God save our gracious King"* being played so often when they appeared in public, when David was the King no more.

Wallis had invited Celia to visit her for an early evening cocktail before they all went out for dinner, and then a visit to a club which had a long established reputation as being decadent. Wallis had decreed that short skirts were to be worn, and the men would be in black tie and not evening dress tails. Celia's lady's maid was helping her into one of her Parisian dresses that, by its very formality, added to her sexual allure.

After inspecting herself in the full-length mirrored wall of her dressing room, Celia collected her coat hat and gloves, thanked her maid and told her that she would not require her services again that night. Wallis looked as polished as ever, and was sitting ramrod straight on a sofa next to the Duke. Fruity Metcalfe was there, as was Helga, who was clearly not dressed for joining them. Celia wondered why she was present, and did not have to wait long for an explanation.

'Celia, my dear, I asked Helga to stay and join us for a cocktail after we finished dealing with some of my correspondence. I have decided, and she has agreed, to be as much a companion to me as my secretary. I feel that we think so alike.'

Wallis smiled warmly at Helga, and reaching forward in an uncharacteristic show of affection patted her knee.

'What a good idea, Wallis – you must become lonely when David is playing golf or shooting.'

'Quite so. Now, Helga has been telling me about Der Nachtfalter, the club that we are going to later. Apparently it is one of the oldest clubs in Vienna – Helga, my dear, tell Celia about it.'

'I have only been once, but it was explained to me that it opened about sixty years ago, and was known as the Casino de Paris until the turn of the century, when it changed to its present name. It then also changed the nightly show, from what I think was called music hall, to what it is now. It is very different and exotic in a decadent way.'

Wallis interrupted at this point. 'Inspector Shoher was very disapproving when the Duke told him that we were going there. It was Hekkel, the concierge, who suggested it to Dudley Forward. David had sent him with Fruity to ask where we could find something really unusual. I apologise Helga, I interrupted you. Do carry on.'

'I do not wish to spoil your surprise by telling you too much,' laughed Helga, 'when I was taken there, I was quite shocked at some of the performances. Nothing is quite what it seems at first. There were transvestites, burlesque dancers, striptease – both men and women – I shall say no more. I am surprised that the police have not been ordered to close it. I think that it must have some very powerful patrons.'

Just then, the Duke and Fruity Metcalfe came into the room laughing like a couple of happy schoolboys. 'Wallis, my dear, we have just had a severe whigging from the good and righteous Inspector Shoher. He is shocked that we should even contemplate going to Der Nachtfalter. He is concerned about our security, and also thinks that the show is totally unsuitable for ladies. I told him that we were not worried about security there, our ladies were made of stern stuff and would not faint.'

Wallis clapped her hands, and laughing loudly, responded with a resounding, 'Bravo David, bravo!'

The Duke looked at his watch and said, 'It's time to go, everybody. Goodnight Helga, no doubt you will be here in the morning.'

'Yes, Your Royal Highness. I trust that you all have a very enjoyable evening.'

She bobbed a half-curtsey, and with a smile to Wallis and Celia, left.

'A very capable girl, eh, Wallis?'

'Most certainly, David. I think that she will be a great asset in every way.'

Dudley Forward was not accompanying the Duke's party that evening.

When they arrived at the Restaurant Drei Husaren, there was the by now familiar double rank of smart police forming a secure corridor from the small party's limousine to the doors of the restaurant. They were ushered into the smaller of the two dining rooms after admiring the wood panelled curved alcove, which framed the painted statues of the heavily-moustached three mounted hussar officers who had founded the restaurant.

The silver haired Maître d', who had the air of a senior diplomat, supervised their being assisted into the green velvet-upholstered seats and welcomed them formally in impeccable and only very slightly accented English. 'Your Royal Highnesses, Milady and Major, may I welcome you to the Restaurant Drei Husaren. You are seated in the library, as you can see. I trust that you are content for our sommelier, Maître Louis, to select appropriate wines to accompany your choice of food.'

'Most certainly, but whilst I recall from our previous visit in 1935 that you have a magnificent cellar of French wines, I would appreciate it if we might enjoy Austrian wines this evening, apart from some champagne, with which we wish to pique our palates.'

'That will be his pleasure, Your Royal Highness. After a small amuse bouche of warm lobster bisque with a beluga caviar accompaniment, may I suggest that you each make a choice from our trolleys of hors d'oeuvres. After that, I suggest some poached sole fillets with a secret stuffing, served in a champagne sauce. To follow, my suggestion is breast of pheasant braised in a red wine sauce, accompanied by cabbage-filled ravioli, roast endive and duchesse potatoes.'

'That suits me very well, how about everyone else?' The Duke looked at the others enquiringly, and they all agreed that the menu would suit them well.

The meal lived up to expectations in every respect, served under the eagle eye of the maître d', who kept a discreet distance from their table as the waiters in their striped waistcoats served them. The Duke praised the choice of wines made by the sommelier, and complimented him accordingly.

'Maître Louis, thank you for your splendid choice of wines this evening. The ice wine which you served to accompany my foie gras, was in perfect balance, the Wachau Riesling was bright and fresh, and the red wine again a perfect accompaniment.'

'Hear, hear,' echoed Fruity.

A piano had been playing quietly in the background throughout the meal. The Duke summoned the maître d'and asked him if the pianist could play *As Time Goes By*.

As the pianist started to play the song, Wallis commented, 'Thank you, David.' Looking at the others, she said quietly, 'This song is something of an anthem for me, and now for David as well. I first heard it in New York on Broadway in 1931, in the musical *"Everybody's Welcome"*. The words and music are by Herman Hupfeld.

Taking the Duke's hands in hers, and staring into each other's eyes, Wallis paused, then said, 'The verse which sums up our view is:

*"It's still the same old story*
*A fight for love and glory*
*A case of do or die.*
*The world will always welcome lovers*
*As time goes by."*

# Chapter 34

The Führer was pacing behind his desk in his vast and ornate Berlin office. As was his habit since being confined in a prison cell, he took only three paces in each direction before turning around sharply. His chin was cupped in his right hand with his left hand supporting his right elbow.

Himmler, the head of the SS and its intelligence agencies, knew better than to interrupt the Führer when he was deep in thought. He was sitting in silence. Whilst outwardly showing no emotion on his unhealthy and pasty face, he was inwardly fuming. The Führer had summoned him after concluding a meeting with Ribbentrop.

He had openly mocked him for the failure of any of his agents to obtain the important piece of intelligence that Ribbentrop had obtained via the naively garrulous former British King. He had been furious when Hitler had laughed, and sarcastically said that he was minded to promote von Ribbentrop and put him in charge of all intelligence services in his place.

The Führer abruptly sat down, and after a moment's silence, spoke. It was as if he were thinking aloud. 'I have my plan. I shall lure Chancellor Schuschnigg into a sense of false security, emphasising our friendship agreement, or at least assurance. I shall take steps to ensure that State Councillor Inquart secretly totally shifts his allegiance to the Nazi party, which is growing in strength in Austria by the day. I shall offer him fine positions in our government as a reward for delivering up his country. He was, after all, born and brought up in the German-speaking area of Austria.

'I shall then deal with Schuschnigg, who will resign. There

must be no assassination. Seyss-Inquart will immediately become Federal Chancellor in his place, and invite Germany to enter Austria with its forces to ensure stability and peace. He will revoke the illegality of the Austrian Nazi party by emergency decree, with immediate effect. Mussolini will squeal but do no more – until that moment, Seyss-Inquart is nominally his man as leader of the Austrian fascists.

'The Austrian Nazis will ensure that our troops receive a warm welcome, and the world at large will see the joining of two peoples who never should have been separated. Goebbels will have a well-prepared campaign, and I shall make a speech, as an Austrian, welcoming another step in recreating the true Germany.'

'Is there not a risk that the French and British will seek to intervene, Mein Führer?'

'I believe that there is no such risk, provided our planning and timing are perfect. I shall personally supervise the operation. Heydrich must carefully review our blueprint for the Nazification and total absorbtion of Austria into the Greater Germany. I shall deal with Mussolini when the time comes. Please instruct Heydrich without delay. His plan must encompass all aspects of Austrian life, do you understand? It must effectively change the whole fabric of society; root and branch.'

'I fully understand, Mein Führer. I shall start drawing up plans for appropriate SS and Gestapo units to accompany our forces.'

'Very well, Heinrich, to work then. I must speak to von Ribbentrop now. Thank you.'

Himmler's stomach was churning as he stood, snapped a salute and cried out, 'Heil Hitler!' His Führer gave him a casual acknowledgement, and sitting down, stared at his desk top, deep in thought.

Himmler's thoughts were dominated by his hatred of von Ribbentrop, whose intelligence coup had not only impressed the Führer but provided the key to his achieving his ambition bloodlessly.

After a noisome session with his Turkish masseur, the pressure in his gut was greatly reduced and he returned to his office, where he began to plan.

The source of von Ribbentrop's intelligence was the

dilettante former British King. It now seemed plain that he and his wife, the American whore, were still a valuable intelligence asset. Rather than continuing to try to thwart von Ribbentrop, perhaps it would be better to try and develop his own links to the former King. He was aware that Fritz Wiedemann was actively organising a trip to Germany by the Duke and his wife.

Wiedemann was a career diplomat, fiercely loyal to the Führer, but was no admirer of Himmler whom he saw as an extremist within the Nazi party. He had been chosen for the task because he was a staunch royalist, who believed that the status quo of the European royal houses swept away at the time of the Great War should be restored.

Wiedemann had met Hitler during the Great War, when he was the Adjutant of the regiment in which the future Führer was a corporal. He recommended Hitler for the Iron Cross First Class on a number of occasions, ultimately being successful in 1918. He became Hitler's adjutant and close aide in 1934, having worked with Rudolf Hess and had joined the Nazi party then. His responsibilities included arranging meetings for the Führer. It was in this role as a high level go-between that he liased with, and became friendly with von Ribbentrop.

Whilst in London visiting the German Embassy, Wiedemann was introduced by von Ribbentrop to the almost-mesmerically attractive Princess Stephanie von Hohenloe, who was a German agent. She was half-Jewish, but her value as an agent and her impeccable connections in international high society were sufficient cause for that matter to be ignored, even by the Führer and Himmler.

She had been forced to leave France in 1932, being suspected of spying. It was then that she came to London, and settled into the fashionable Dorchester Hotel on Park Lane. She was one of von Ribbentrop's many lovers whilst he was in London, and ironically, it was he who introduced her to Wiedemann, whose mistress she became almost immediately.

Sir Vernon and his team were alerted to her activities by a report from the French Secret Service in 1933, saying that they had found incriminating documents in her Paris apartment. They alleged that she had been contracted by the German Government to persuade newspaper proprietor, Lord

Rothermere, with whom she was on very close if not intimate terms, to campaign for the return to Germany of lands taken over by Poland at the end of the Great War. Her reward for success was to be a very substantial fortune. It was not a difficult task, because Rothermere, like so many of her circle of friends in London, was strongly sympathetic towards German interests.

Ironically Rothermere, who had become a strong advocate of the Nazi regime, agreed to pay her a generous annual retainer to persuade influential friends and acquaintances to actively support and promote closer links with Germany. When Himmler had realised that the Princess was regularly summoned to meet and discuss policy with the Führer – who had started referring to her as "My dear Princess", he decided that it was prudent to befriend her, as did Hermann Goering.

Following some disparaging remarks about her Jewish blood, made by Heydrich, Himmler decided to nip that matter in the bud, and declared her an Honorary Aryan. The British Secret Service was well aware of the reasons behind her German trips, and had formally noted and reported that "the Führer appreciates her intelligence and good advice. She is perhaps the only woman who can exercise any influence on him."

Such was her status, that it was she who instigated the meeting in Germany of Lord Halifax, later to be British Foreign Secretary, and Hermann Goering. The Duke of Windsor had mentioned in a letter to his friend, the 7th Marquess of Londonderry, that he was very much hoping the visit to Germany being arranged by Charles Bedaux would also serve the purpose of giving Wallis a taste of what a State visit would be like. The Marquess immediately spoke to the Princess and she in turn arranged to go to Germany the following day to meet the Führer.

After leaving the restaurant, the Duke's small party was driven the short distance to the nightclub, Der Nachtfalter. Two uniformed doormen were on the pavement outside the entrance, and as usual, the Inspector had two lines of police on the pavement. When they entered through the doors they were greeted by a fussy, rather short man in a dinner jacket. He bowed, and then welcomed their Royal Highnesses to the club.

Two pretty blonde women in modest black dresses took the party's hats and coats, and led them along the short corridor to the foyer, which was plush in a slightly shabby style, evoking the turn of the century. There were red velvet drapes floor to ceiling, and gilt detailing around the double doors that were thrown open by two more burly doormen as they approached.

The first impression was of a cross between a night club and a theatre. In the centre of the dark room there was a stage, only about a foot higher than the floor, on which there were round tables with red shaded lights. The air was pungent with an almost decadent mixture of cigar smoke and perfume, and the room was crowded with elegantly dressed men and women in evening dress. Diamonds glittered at throats and on wrists. Formally dressed waiters flitted about with silver ice buckets and bottles of champagne. There was a hum of polite conversation.

A small orchestra were seated playing quietly in a far corner, illuminated only by the reading lights attached to their music stands. The conductor was on a low rostrum, his heavily brillianteened hair glistening when caught in the light. After settling at a table in the front row next to the stage, waiters brought a silver ice bucket frosted with condensation. A bottle of vintage Krug was opened and poured with great panache and elegance.

A cigarette girl, wearing very high heels and a short skirted skater's dress, came to the table, and despite the size of her tray upon which a humidor sat in the centre, bobbed a short curtsey. She was a pretty, fresh-faced young woman, and Fruity ogled her generously revealed bust when it was his turn to select a cigar. Celia and the Duke had decided to have cigars, but Wallis said she would stick to her cigarettes.

'Well, Wallis, this is all very civilised, isn't it – we could be in almost any London night club.'

'I sure expected the place to feel and be a lot more decadent than this. I guess if we want to dance, we go onto the stage.'

'I suppose so – anyhow, there is a cabaret which might be fun.'

After a drum roll, a single spotlight flashed onto the stage and the orchestra struck up a jaunty melody. A compere in full evening dress stepped into the spotlight, and the orchestra quietened, but continued playing as he announced first in Austrian and then in English, 'Our first performer tonight is a beautiful young English rose – Ladies and Gentlemen, I give you Burlesque Dolly!'

As he stepped back into the darkness, his place was taken by a strikingly pretty, long-legged blonde woman in her twenties. She was heavily made-up and wearing a gold short skirted costume with bare shoulders, and long matching gloves reaching above her elbows. Her peep-toed gold shoes were high-heeled.

She began to dance, moving ever more seductively, and occasionally appeared to flick up her skirt accidentally, each time looking wide-eyed at the audience, her bright red lips forming a shocked moue. She slowly and suggestively peeled off one glove and then the other, never missing a beat as she continued her dance. She gave a questioning look at the audience, then started to fiddle with the side of her dress as she continued her dance.

Then in gradual stages, she inched her dress down, gradually revealing the tops of her pert breasts. The men in the audience were spellbound. There was not a sound until, with a flourish, she threw her arms out wide, and the top of her dress fell away revealing that she was left with gold-tasselled nipple patches. Apparently in shock, her hands flew to cover them, and then looking coyly at the audience, a broad smile slowly appeared, and taking her hands away she started to gyrate so that the tassles were soon whirling.

'Bravo!' cried out Fruity, and soon other men were calling encouragement.

After placing a finger over her lips and wagging an admonishing hand at the audience, she mimed having an idea, and taking the top of her skirt in both hands, introduced a wriggle into her dance until her skirt fell around her feet. She was now left wearing very brief sequinned knickers that were transparent, except for a tiny centre panel preserving her modesty.

There was another gasp from the audience as she turned around, revealing that she was in fact wearing a g-string. Then, with feet planted well apart and her hips still gyrating to the music, she bent from the waist and slowly picked up her dress.

There were louder and louder cries of "Bravo!" as she continued her dance, and after miming yet another idea, twiddled with the side of her knickers – one more wriggle and they fell to the floor. She was totally shaved.

The audience gave a huge cheer as she leapt in the air and landed back on the stage, having done the splits. She raised one arm in the air and then gracefully bowed to the audience. The spotlight went out.

Fruity was the first to break the silence, and said excitedly, 'I say, David, what a little cracker, eh?'

The Duke replied, 'Rather – quite an act!'

'Yeah – I sure hope for her sake there were no splinters on that stage,' added Wallis sardonically.

'Amen to that!' was Celia's response.

The orchestra started to play a little louder, as four stage hands totally dressed in black, with hoods covering their faces, placed a dark-painted wooden structure in the centre of the stage. The stage hands left, and then with a crash of cymbals the orchestra began to play a vigorous march. The hum of conversation had died completely.

From the back of the stage strode a tall man in black evening dress, with his face masked in stark white make-up, contrasting with vivid red lipstick and black rimmed eyes. He stopped at the front of the stage, and gave an exaggerated theatrical bow before spinning around and striding to the back of the wooden structure. He was out of sight for a moment, then he appeared at the top, standing behind the front of what was now clearly recognised as a low tower.

He turned towards the conductor and gave a slow nod. The music abruptly stopped, and there was total silence. Then a bass drum began a slow marching beat. The four black-hooded stage hands appeared, bearing what could only be a black coffin on their shoulders. They slowly carried it in front of the tower, where they carefully lowered it to the ground. At a single clash of cymbals, they reached down in unison and removed the coffin lid, which they conveyed off the stage.

A woman in high heels, black stockings, suspenders and a basque, wearing a black mask, strutted onto the stage, and with strangely mechanical movements went to the coffin. Out of it she took what appeared to be wooden rods, to which long cords were tied. She reached up, and the white-faced man took them from her. She left the stage again with the strange movements of an automaton. The audience was spellbound.

The orchestra started to play a sombre dirge as the man held out his arms and the cords taughtened. As he slowly raised his arms, a creature was apparently drawn out of the coffin. When it stepped out of the coffin, the shape of a shrouded woman was discernable. The tempo of the music increased, and the creature seemed to begin a slow dance with the slightly jerky movements of a puppet. The puppeteer suddenly gave a loud cackling laugh, and to the clash of cymbals the shroud fell away.

The audience gasped.

The creature that was revealed, with its whitened skull mask, was clearly a young woman. Of that there could be no doubt, given that she now stood before them with her thigh-booted legs apart and red leather-laced basque which stopped below her breasts. That was all she wore.

Wallis seized Celia's hand, and squeezed painfully hard as the girl bent her knees and began to gyrate her pelvis in time to the music The puppeteer untied the cords from his frame and threw them down. He disappeared from his stage. The audience hardly noticed until suddenly, he appeared again naked, apart from his white gloves.

He approached the still-gyrating girl, and squatting down, undid the cords from her feet, then standing again, those on her wrists. He stood behind her, and then as one white-gloved hand reached into her sex, the other took hold of one of her full breasts. He was gyrating against her, and the music became ever faster. When he released her from his grasp and stepped out from behind her, he was fully and impressively aroused.

He stepped off the stage, and stopping only to caress the chin of a heavily bejewelled member of the audience, fetched a chair which he took back onto the stage. He led the girl to the chair and directed her to kneel on it facing away from the audience. He then bent her forward over its back.

At this point, the strange automaton woman appeared dressed as before, but wearing a large gleaming black strap-on dildo. She crossed the stage and took the man's penis in her hand, and led him around the girl in the chair until he was facing her skull face. He moved forward, and the girl on the chair took him in her mouth. The automaton then stalked back around the chair and, standing behind, slid the long dildo into the girl on the chair, beginning to move vigorously.

After only a few minutes there was yet another clash of cymbals, and a monstrously erect, naked, but masked negro strutted across the stage, pushed the automaton aside, and with a loud grunt took her place. There was now a single spotlight on the little tableau where both men were moving strictly in time to the music. Another clash of the cymbals, and both men withdrew and left the stage.

The automaton now reappeared, having shed everything but her shoes, stockings and suspenders. The black bush of her pubic hair was in stark contrast to her pale skin. She was wearing a top hat. Again, she moved jerkily to the chair and helped the kneeling girl off it.

They both crossed the stage and stood right before the Duke's table. The automaton swept off her top hat, and then they both performed full curtseys, much to the amusement of the Duke and Fruity, who stood up and gave a small bow in acknowledgment. As they sat down, the girls stepped off the stage. The girl with the skull mask went up to the Duke and sat on his knee, and the automaton, after placing her hat on his head, sat on Fruity's lap, where she started to squirm as she stroked his cheek. Celia could see that Wallis was fuming, but impotent in the face of the rousing applause of the audience.

The strange encounter was brought to an abrupt end when, after a rousing drum roll, the orchestra started to play the British National Anthem. The Duke and Fruity quickly divested themselves of their companions, and stood to attention as the rest of the audience also stood.

When they sat down again, Wallis turned to the Duke, and in a voice that left no room for argument, said, 'I think we have had quite sufficient, and should return to our hotel. We have an early start in the morning, and we must be fresh for Venice.'

Having said goodnight and goodbye to the Duke, Duchess and Fruity, whom she would not see in the morning, Celia was relieved to return to her suite and kick off her shoes. As her lady's maid was helping her undress, the telephone trilled. Celia left the dressing room and, wondering who might call her at this late hour, picked up the receiver.

'Lady Celia – I hope that it is not too late, but I was wondering whether I might come to see you as we are leaving in the morning.'

'Of course you may, Helga – I shall look forward to seeing you shortly.'

Helga arrived just after the maid had left. Celia was in a plain ivory silk dressing gown. Helga was in a business-like suit.

'It is so kind of you to see me, Lady Celia.'

'Not at all, and from now on it is Celia, please. What is it you want to talk about? Would you like some champagne?'

'No, thank you, we have an early start and a long day. You are a close friend of the Duchess and von Ribbentrop, I believe?'

'Yes, I am, and I have fulfilled the same role as you in the past – acted as their contact. I have also been lover to both of them, as I imagine you are?'

'Thank you for being so open. I do hope that we can be good friends. I like the Duchess – she is, how do you say, "smart" – but both she and Joachim are so much older.'

'They are both very broad-minded. So long as you do not flaunt it under her nose, Wallis will turn a blind eye to you having affairs, and Joachim is in no position to judge or criticise. I think he has seduced every woman who has ever worked with him. Of course we shall be friends, I shall be a frequent visitor, I am sure.'

'Thank you for saying that. May I speak with you by telephone when you are in London?'

'But of course. Now, off to bed with you, and have a wonderful time in Venice before you return here to Austria.'

'Thank you again, Celia, goodnight, and au revoir.'

As Celia climbed into bed, she thought to herself, 'Helga isn't as tough as she appears, and I can probably use her quite effectively. I must tell Johnny and Tar.'

As she drifted off to sleep, she smiled at the thought that she was planning how she would turn her first agent.

# Chapter 35

The Führer's face broke into a smile, as his aide announced that Her Serene Highness, the Princess Stephanie von Hohenlohe had arrived.

'Kindly arrange for some coffee and water to be brought in immediately, and then show Her Serene Highness in to me. I do not wish to be disturbed, and that includes telephone calls, whoever it may be. Understood?'

'Yes, mein Führer. Heil Hitler.' He snapped the customary salute, turned about smartly and marched out of the huge office. After only a minute, the coffee and water were brought in by a military steward and laid on a low side table, flanked by classic French-style gilt-framed armchairs.

There was a moment's pause. The 14 foot-high double doors swung open again, and standing to one side, the aide ushered a striking woman with vivid red hair into the room. The Führer did not give the aide time to make the formal announcement as he strode towards his visitor, with arms outstretched. 'My dear Princess, this is an unexpected delight! Come sit with me.'

'Mein Führer, it is my delight to see you.'

They took their seats, Hitler still smiling with obvious pleasure. 'And how are things in London, my dear?'

'Much the same. I fear that Lord Rothermere may be wavering a little. He still fervently supports an Anglo-German accord, but he is concerned about ugly rumours with regard to your government's treatment of minority groups – the Jews in particular. I am doing all that I can to reassure him. However, I believe that Doctor Goebbels should devote some more energy into countering such propaganda.'

'Point taken, Stephanie – I shall speak to him immediately after you leave.'

'Churchill continues to rant about your territorial intentions, and to urge full and urgent rearmament. The influential Cliveden set – you know, Cliveden is the Astors' place – ridicule him, but, nevertheless, whatever his faults, he is a man to be watched. I am close to Lady Margot Astor and I am also one of that set – indeed, I am invited to Cliveden this coming weekend. I shall no doubt pick up quite a lot of inside track political gossip then, which I shall of course report to you.

'My unexpected visit to you today was prompted by Charles, the Marquess of Londonderry, approaching me. He told me that the Duke and Duchess of Windsor are very excited about their forthcoming visit to Germany, when they will be meeting you. However, the Duke also mentioned that everything is being arranged through Charles Bedaux. Adolf, my dear, that would be a mistake. Brilliant though Bedaux may be, please do not let him take this credit. The Duke hopes that the visit will be on the scale of a State visit. He wants the Duchess to experience the glamour and the drama.'

Hitler looked thoughtful, then said, 'I have already instructed Fritz Wiedemann, my adjutant, whom you have met, to discreetly sideline Bedaux. We have to be careful, because Bedaux is in very close with the foreign – particularly American – bankers and industrialists, who have major interests in Germany. They are of vital importance to the Reich. However, we shall step up the profile of the visit and put on a grand show.'

'I think that would be wise, and of course the Duke still has a large following in Britain, a significant one. His tacit approval of your government will go quite some way towards providing counter-publicity to the ugly rumours that I mentioned.'

'Wise counsel as ever, my dear. I shall send for Wiedemann before you go, and you can run through arrangements with him.'

'I would also mention, Adolf, I have been made an honorary member of the Anglo-German Fellowship, where I have become very close to Lord Elibank and Lord Sempil. They are providing some excellent insights into the matters discussed in the House of Lords.

'The mood of the British aristocracy can be hard to gauge, but many, whilst not necessarily supporting National Socialism, strongly feel that Britain and Germany should work together to ensure that the spectre of bolshevism remains just that, and is defeated utterly in due course. Your policy, dear Adolf. Now, I had better get together with Fritz Wiedemann. I can only stay in Berlin tonight and must return to London in the morning.'

'Very well, I quite understand.' Hitler rose and went to his desk, where he pressed the bell summoning his aide, and instructed him to send for Adjutant Wiedemann immediately.

Hitler was unaware that the Princess and Fritz Wiedemann were already lovers, having met previously in London. They had both agreed that, notwithstanding their close personal relationships with the Führer, it would be best if he were unaware of the affair. This was especially important in the case of Stephanie, who rightly surmised that Hitler harboured a deep sexual attraction to her.

'Ah, Fritz – this is Princess Stephanie von Hohenlohe; but of course you have met.'

Stephanie rose from her chair and formally shook hands with the handsome Fritz, who smiled politely, and said, 'Yes Princess, I remember meeting you at our embassy in London when Ambassador Ribbentrop introduced us.'

Hitler then outlined his conversation with Stephanie, and suggested that she go to Fritz's office so that they could review the plans he had prepared so far, saying, 'Stephanie, as always, a pleasure seeing you, and your efforts are greatly valued.'

Stephanie thanked Hitler, and he then kissed her on both cheeks.

When Stephanie and Fritz approached his office, he addressed the three secretaries and uniformed aide who were seated at desks by the doors. 'No interruptions, please.'

His palatial office was on a grand scale, but much smaller than Hitler's. After closing the doors he turned to Stephanie and gathered her into his arms. 'It is so good to see you, and now we have an excuse for meeting openly.'

'Yes, my dear, but we must be circumspect. I have a suite at the Adlon and we can be together tonight, so for now, to business.'

'You are right, as ever,' he replied with a wry smile, and led her to an ornate side table on which there were neatly arranged small stacks of papers.

'Right, Stephanie. Each set of papers represents one day of the planned visit. They are arranged chronologically, and record the measured timings for each event: travel times, rest periods, security, guards of honour, menus, table and seating plans, orders of precedence, content of official speeches and photographic opportunities.

'Herr Strack, the Chief of Protocol, has the final say on everything of relevance to his office, and I shall advise him of the Führer's instruction that the visitors are to be accorded the highest status. Doctor Goebbels is personally dealing with the press communiqués for national and the international press, newsreels, filming and broadcasting generally. Doctor Robert Ley, the official leader of the trade unions, is helping in the selection of sites for visits, and identifying the best people for the Duke to meet.

'I will not trouble you with detail of the background checks that are being carried out on everyone the Duke and Duchess will meet. They will all be individually briefed as to what they are to say, answers to questions and so forth.'

'That is good, Fritz – nothing must be left to chance. Now then, what opportunities are there for some grand occasions?'

Over the next five hours they reviewed the work already done, and Stephanie made copious notes. Stephanie then raised a rather delicate matter.

'Fritz, may I suggest that the Reich meets all the expenses of the trip? Charles Bedaux may have assured the Duke that it is a private visit, and not a propaganda event for this government. Nevertheless, the reality is that as the Duke wants it to have the trappings of a State visit, it will provide an excellent international showcase for Germany. There must be some mechanism to do this?'

'That will not be a problem. The personal expenses of the Duke and Duchess will be very little, in comparison with the overall expense, in any event. There are of course what is best described as "special funds" held in the Reichsbank, which we control. I shall formally have the Führer give his approval tomorrow, and confirm it to you as soon as you next contact me.'

'Excellent. The Duke is always complaining that he has been left a poor man. According to Lord Rothermere, that is simply untrue, but the Duke uses that line unashamedly so that others feel obliged to extend their hospitality. It is an aspect of his character that I find particularly unattractive.'

'That is probably a consequence of his upbringing.'

Stephanie looked at her wrist watch and concluded, 'When the Duke and Duchess return from Venice in a week or so, I shall telephone the Duchess and give her an outline brief so that she can start planning her wardrobe. Would you like me to do likewise with the Duke?'

'That would be most helpful. Shall I have a car take you to your hotel now?'

'Thank you, dear Fritz, and I shall look forward to seeing you at about 7.30pm.'

'I cannot wait. Until later, my darling.'

He summoned his aide, and gave instructions for a staff car to take the Princess to her hotel. The aide was to accompany her.

Charles Bedaux had just finished a telephone conversation with Doctor Robert Ley. It was Ley who had masterminded the effective destruction of the German trade union movement, and now headed the German Labour Front which had replaced them. He was an alcoholic with a speech impediment, which in itself made it impossible to tell whether his slurred words were the result of his being drunk, or merely his impediment.

When Bedaux had negotiated a facilitation payment, to enable his business in Germany to be restarted following its suspension, he had dealt with Doctor Hjalmar Schacht. He was the brilliant economist who had manipulated the German economy, enabling not only the growth of the Reich, but its rearmament. As well as the substantial cash payment, Schacht added an additional pre-condition to annulment of the business suspension. In Germanyu, Bedaux could in future only operate in partnership with Doctor Ley.

Doctor Ley was obsessed with the notion of uniformity in all activities, and it turned out that he and Bedaux had much in common. He was also very close to the Führer, who placed great trust in his judgement, even thaough at times it proved totally flawed. Bedaux was delighted that Doctor Ley had readily agreed to not only facilitate the visit of the Duke and Duchess, but also accompany them on many of the visits that were being planned.

Bedaux's next move was to invite the Duke and Duchess to visit his castle in Hungary – Castle Borsodivanka. He would extend that invitation in a cable to the Duke and Duchess.

Their second trip to Venice was a great success in the eyes of the Duke and Duchess. Once again, their arrival was marked by cheering crowds at the station. Their launch made slow progress down the Grand Canal, as hundreds of gondolas, filled with cheering and clapping people, crowded around it.

Their arrival, at the Excelsior Hotel on the Lido, was witnessed by another large crowd. The smiling Duke enthusiastically returned the fascist salutes of the onlookers, and Wallis waved and smiled with animation.

The weather was wonderful and during their stay they swam and sunbathed to the delight of the many photographers. The Duke had watched the launch of catamarans with oars with interest. 'I say, darling, that looks rather fun – how about I take you out for a row?'

'David, dearest, it doesn't look very safe.'

'Oh, it'll be fine – the sea isn't rough, and I was in the Navy, you know.'

'No, David, as you would say, it is not my cup of tea, but you have a go.'

'Righto, dearest, I shall.'

The Duke, in his usual dark blue shorts, approached the deeply-tanned, colourfully dressed attendant, who was wearing white shorts, a loose red shirt and a boater. He asked how much the hire would be. The boatman understood the question and told him. The Duke turned to Fruity, who had accompanied him and said, 'Fruity, be a good fellow and pay, will you?'

'Of course, David. Shall I come with you?'

'No, I think not, but you could always hire one for yourself. You will have to wait until he has launched me.'

Fruity paid, and the Duke watched impatiently as the attendant put the money in his purse, then heaved and pushed the strange vessel into the water. He then gestured for the Duke to climb aboard. Once he was seated on the plank rower's bench, he took the oars, which were in fixed rowlocks, and the boatman ran the vessel into deeper water as the Duke took his first stroke.

Fruity joined him a few minutes later, and was clearly having difficulty in getting the measure of handling the strange craft.

'I say, Fruity, let's have a race – out to the second marker post and back to the beach, eh?'

Fruity was not keen. The vessel seemed flimsy, and there were some white-capped waves that they would have to handle.

'Come on, Fruity – ready, steady, go!' cried the Duke, bending to his oars.

The Duke had completed the course, and arrived back at the beach by the time Fruity had reached the second marker post. As the boatman steadied the craft, he jumped off into the knee-deep water and, laughing gaily, ran up the beach to where Wallis, who was now wearing a wide-brimmed, black straw sunhat, had been joined by Helga.

'Did you watch me, Wallis darling?' he cried out excitedly, 'I beat Fruity fair and square!'

'Of course I did – congratulations! Now, Helga has brought me some messages. One is a cable from Charles Bedaux, inviting us to go and stay with them at their castle in Hungary.'

'Do you want to go?'

'Of course, David – I think it is high time for a change. Shall I have Helga reply on our behalf and accept?'

'Yes, my dear, rather. It should be fun. Good boar hunting there, according to Charles, but I am not sure what the season is.'

Wallis turned to Helga, who was wearing a sundress that did nothing to hide her beautiful figure, and said, 'Helga, please be so kind as to cable a reply that we are delighted to accept.'

'Yes, Ma'am. I shall go and do it now.'

'Efficient girl that, Wallis – a good find.'

'Well, darling man, you know me, I sure know how to pick 'em!' responded a chortling Wallis.

# Chapter 36

En route to their castle, Charles and Fern Bedaux stopped over in Budapest. Charles had arranged a meeting with Howard Travers, the United States Charge d'Affaires, in the US Embassy. Before the meeting, Travers had consulted with the State Department in Washington who, by way of response, had sent him a lengthy report on the highly suspect activities of Charles Bedaux.

Travers was taken aback to read that this prominent and influential international businessman was considered to be guilty of espionage, but that there was insufficient proof to justify his arrest and prosecution. J Edgar Hoover, the head of the Federal Bureau of Investigation, had personally supervised a full in-depth enquiry into Charles Bedaux, and as a consequence he was rated as a high-security risk to be barred from any governmental contracts. He was also to be the subject of close surveillance at all times if visiting the United States.

The State Department instructed Travers that a detailed account of his meeting was to be passed to George Messersmith, and the meeting should be recorded verbatim by a stenographer. Messersmith had returned to Washington as Assistant Secretary of State responsible for the Balkans.

When Charles Bedaux was shown into Travers' office he was surprised to see that a stenographer was sitting in the corner with his machine. 'Mr Bedaux – it is a privilege to meet you.' Travers greeted him as he stood, and extended his hand across the standard-issue desk.

'And to meet you, Mr Travers, thank you for your time. I know just how hard you guys work for us taxpayers.'

It was all that Travers could do to refrain from commenting that he was given to understand Charles Bedaux was being pursued by the Internal Revenue Services, for a fortune in taxes that he and his businesses had illegally evaded. 'It is no trouble, Mr Bedaux – now, how may I be of assistance?'

'I am representing the Duke of Windsor. When he was Prince of Wales, and later King, he took a great interest in the plight of the working man and, indeed, the unemployed. One could say the poor in general.'

'Yes, so I believe from press reports that I have read. Do carry on.'

'He intends to visit a number of countries to study working conditions, methods and even housing. I am arranging for him to visit Germany, where he greatly admires the progress made in recent years under the Government led by Herr Hitler. He also wishes to make a similar study in the USA, and I have agreed to arrange that as well.

'It is fair to say that he is an admirer of my systems, and, for instance, would wish to meet Henry Ford, along with others who have embraced them. His ultimate aim is to return to England as a champion of the working classes. I am here today to give advance notice that such a visit will be taking place later this year.'

'I see. Well, in principle I can see no problem, but you will appreciate that I shall have to refer the matter to the State Department. In fact, it will be George Messersmith, who knows the Duke extremely well from his time in Austria.'

'Excellent – then he will know what a good and sincere fellow he is. I shall not take up any more of your time, and thank you again for this meeting.'

'It has been a pleasure, Mr Bedaux.'

The transcript was encrypted and telegraphed to the State Department that afternoon. Unwittingly, Charles Bedaux had, in a single sentence, changed the entire future course of the lives of the Duke and Duchess.

Their exile would now be permanent.

Chester Harris, the head of United States Intelligence in Great Britain, had telephoned Tar Robertson, and requested an early meeting. As it happened, he was free for lunch that day, and

Tar invited him to the Reform Club in Pall Mall – a favourite with Chester. Sitting in the grand saloon where the bar table was situated, Chester came straight to the point.

'Look, Tar, what I am going to tell you has not yet filtered through the diplomatic channels in the maze that is the State Department, so your Government has not been informed. Please keep it within the Security Service for now, or my head will roll. OK?'

'Understood, Chester. You had better spit it out, I am all ears,' laughed Tar.

Chester then described the meeting in Budapest between Charles Bedaux and Howard Travers. When he finished, Tar was aghast. 'Chester, you can have no idea just how grateful I am, and indeed Sir Vernon will be, for this information. What is staggering, is that the Duke's wedding should have been permitted to be held at the castle of a man who is striongly suspected of being a Nazi agent at the highest level. If that had been known, it simply would not have been allowed.'

'How could it have been stopped?'

'Oh, there are ways and means. A threat to stop the Duke's allowances paid through his brother, the King, would have done the trick, I think.'

# Chapter 37

'Charles, my dear chap – how are you?'

Charles Bedaux took the Duke of Windsor's hand and shook it warmly as he and his wife Fern welcomed their guests to Castle Borsodivanka. Fern Bedaux embraced Wallis. 'How was the drive?'

'Excellent. No problems, and such beautiful scenery. This is a wonderful spot,' said the Duke, looking around, 'it is most kind of you to invite us.'

'Not at all, David, and I know that you enjoy the hunt so we can get in some boar hunting.'

'Capital – are we in the permitted season?'

'Yes, there is no closed season for boar, but of course the usual protection for sows and piglets. Although the red stag is the king of the forests here in Hungary, I am not so keen on hunting them. They are in rut around here – actually started a few days ago, but I prefer the more dangerous wild boar for sport.'

'I am happy with that, Charles. I see that you have adopted local traditional dress.'

Charles, who was as short as the Duke but of a much heavier build, laughed as he looked down at the loden-green, silver-buttoned jacket and matching shorts that he was wearing. 'Well, David, "when in Rome", as they say. I bet that you have something similar.'

'But of course. I shall change later after my valet has unpacked. Fern, you must forgive me – how are you?' the Duke asked, as he placed his hands on Fern Bedaux's shoulders and kissed her on the cheek. Fern, who was a good few inches taller than her husband or the Duke, was also wearing traditional dress with a rakish, small-brimmed, dark green, trilby-style hat, white embroidered blouse, long dark green skirt and stout ankle boots. She was rake thin and the outfit suited her.

'I am very well, thank you, David – we have so looked forward to your visit. Now, come into the castle and have some refreshment.'

The little group entered the castle through its great oak double doors. Wallis was relieved to note that the stone walls of the great hall that they had entered were covered in tapestries, mostly of hunting scenes and not grisly trophies. 'Thank God, Fern, you do not have the walls covered with trophy heads – I had to have them taken down as soon as we arrived at Schloss Wasserleonberg. They give me the willies.'

'I couldn't agree more,' laughed Fern, as Charles led them to a long refectory table upon which there was an array of snacks and crystal flagons of red wine.

'Now, David, Wallis, we do have whatever you fancy in the way of drinks. The locals are keen on their beer, and of course the Hungarian traditional red wine, known as Bull's Blood. I find it too heavy to drink during the day, but it is a good warmer if you are hunting in the winter. Champagne?'

'That would be fine with me,' answered Wallis, and the Duke nodded his agreement. Charles turned to one of the servants who had been standing by the long table, 'Please fetch champagne – the Louis Roederer Cristal. Thank you.'

'Now that you have stretched your legs a little after the long drive, shall we go and sit?' asked Charles, gesturing towards two giant sofas flanking the stone fireplace that dominated the far end of the hall.

'That would be fine,' responded Wallis. As they sat down, she commented, 'Is that a whole tree smouldering in the hearth?'

'Just about, Wallis. This time of year we only need it to keep off the chill, but in winter we burn a tremendous amount of timber – thank goodness we are surrounded by our own forests. It was not possible to install proper central heating here as we did in France.'

Helga had not travelled to Hungary – instead, at von Ribbentrop's request, she had gone to Vienna and checked into the Hotel Bristol where he had booked a suite for two nights. He wanted an update on the Windsors, and was very excited at the thought of what he regarded as some bonus time with the sexually inventive Helga.

Concierge Hekkel had recognised the elegant young lady as the friend of von Ribbentrop when she had registered, and a quick enquiry of the receptionist confirmed that it was to the suite reserved for him that she had been taken. Ever alert to earning a little more, he tried to reach Billy, but he was not responding.

Hekkel had not seen him leave the hotel, and rightly guessed that he would be in the room of the slightly mysterious, but very alluring Vera von Wedel. He had seen her husband, who was undoubtedly a distinguished-looking man, but he correctly surmised at least thirty years her senior. He doubted if he would be able to satisfy the smouldering lady. Hekkel quickly penned a note for Billy, and summoning a bellboy, instructed him to take it to the room service servery and ask that it be placed on the next tray to be delivered to the room of Frau von Wedel.

Billy and Vera were lounging in armchairs chatting about their childhoods when a waiter arrived with coffee and pastries. He placed the tray on the low coffee table. They noticed the envelope propped against the silver coffee pot. She reached for it and then laughed. 'You will not believe it, Billy – it is for you! Is someone spying on you, I wonder?'

He took the envelope and tore it open. It was brief and to the point, simply saying that the same young lady as on his last visit had checked into the Presidential Suite booked by von Ribbentrop.

'What is it, Billy, who is it from?'

Billy thought for a moment, then made a snap decision that would change the course of Vera's life, and to a lesser extent, his own. 'It is from my friend, my eyes and ears, Hekkel, the concierge. Von Ribbentrop has booked the Presidential Suite, and his Austrian girlfriend, who now works for the Duchess of Windsor, is already in it.'

Vera gave Billy a long, appraising look. 'Billy, when we first slept together, you said that it was not time to be honest with each other. By your telling me that, I think that you have changed your mind. Am I right?'

'Yes, Vera, I have, but on the condition that we are utterly frank and honest – no holding back. That is the deal. Do you accept it?'

'Yes, I do, and not just because I have strong feelings for you.'

'Very well, I shall tell you who and what I am. I am a Viscount, an English Lord, and a member of the aristocracy. Another way of putting it is that I am a member of the establishment. When I left the army, I joined the British Secret Service, in which I am an officer.

'I am monitoring the activities of the Duke and Duchess of Windsor. She has a relationship with von Ribbentrop, to whom she passes information. I am not an admirer of Herr Hitler, or of his Nazi government, which I regard as a threat to peace. I abhor the activities of their secret police – the Gestapo – and their persecution of Jews and other minorities. Now, how about you?'

Vera then told her story with a surprising frankness and disarming honesty. Billy interrupted her at the point when she described her recruitment into the Abwehr. 'So, Vera, let me understand this completely – you only allowed yourself to be recruited because you had been tipped off that you were on a Gestapo death list?'

'It may seem strange, but they had found out that I had betrayed my pig of a husband, Ignatieff, to his Soviet masters. Since he was a double agent working for the Germans as well as the White Russians, the Gestapo regarded what I did as hostile to their foreign branch, the SD. I knew that von Wedel was a senior Abwehr agent – Ignatieff had told me, and warned me to avoid him. There is intense rivalry between the different German security services, but you will know that.'

'Yes, it is a great weakness, and will cost them dearly. Do carry on.'

'I made a point of meeting von Wedel. He knew who I was. It was easy to flatter him and win his affection. He had told me that he was a widower, and lonely. I quickly picked up that he had very good connections high up in the Nazi Party – right at the top; it might even be Hitler.

'We discussed marriage, and he was very honest. He is diabetic, and cannot perform sexually, but having fallen in love with me, he would happily marry me, and do whatever was necessary to get me a German passport. As his wife, I would be protected. I naturally agreed to both proposals, with the condition that I have needs, and would have discreet affairs. He accepted the condition.'

'That's quite something.'

'Billy, there is more that you should know. I met von Ribbentrop in London, and we had a little fling, as you would say. No emotional entanglement, purely physical. That means that he knows me. It was my husband who instructed me to find out what you were here for. He had had a meeting with von Ribbentrop, so it could be that it was at his request.'

'This gets complicated, Vera!' laughed Billy, 'give me some time to think. I hope that you do not mind, but I am going back to my rooms to change, then I must go to the Embassy to signal London. I was supposed to have left Vienna in the morning, as you know, but now I believe that I should stay. Will you be OK for a couple of hours?'

'Of course, I understand. I shall have a long bath and see if a hairdresser is available. If you are not rushing off too early in the morning, dinner would be nice?'

'Yes, it certainly would. Right, I will be off.'

Tar Robertson, Maxwell Knight, Johnny Johnstone and Sir Vernon were discussing the content of Billy Brownlow's message that just been decoded. Sir Vernon had listened to their views and made his decisions.

'Tar, please telephone Billy, and tell him that he should enjoy his holiday and stay where he is. The locals and our "friends" will deal with the other business. There will be a message for him later. You had better go and do that now – he said that he would wait at the Embassy. Maxwell, please send an encrypted message to Billy instructing him that, One, since Vera has no ideological link to Germany and the Nazis, he should try to turn her, as you believe possible. Tell him that, if necessary, you will meet her in Vienna which is risky. The alternative is that she makes an excuse to come to London. That may be preferable.

'Two, she should make herself known to von Ribbentrop and see what he wants. Three, she should tell him that she has befriended Billy, whose brief was to look out for the Duke's safety, and no more than that. Since he will probably know, she should say that she and Billy are having a relationship, but that it is purely on a physical basis – he should understand that.'

Sir Vernon then turned to Johnny. 'Johnny. It seems certain that the Duke and Duchess are going to make the trip to Germany. I should like you to see if ideally both of you, otherwise just Celia, accompanies them. Is that clear, everyone?'

They all confirmed that it was, and left the room. Sir Vernon sat quietly puffing his pipe. He ruminated, 'Is the whole world driven by lust? Lust for power, and sexual lust?'

# Chapter 38

Vera went to the desk in the corner of her room, and taking some hotel writing paper from the leather folder, wrote a note for von Ribbentrop. She put it in an envelope which she addressed to him and carefully sealed it. She then went down to the concierge's desk, and asked that the note be given to him on arrival. After returning to her room, she ran a deep bath, and after pouring in some scented oil, climbed in and luxuriated. She was still in the bath when Billy returned.

'Hello, darling, I'm back,' he called.

'I am in the bath – come and join me, it's big enough.'

Billy needed no urging – he quickly undressed and went into the bathroom. Vera had twisted a small, white hand towel into a turban, and as he bent to kiss her, a sudsy arm appeared, and she gave him a playful squeeze.

'Ouch, you little minx –you'll pay for that!'

'Probably, but after you have washed me from head to toe – and I *mean* from head to toe,' she said, as she looked at him coyly.

'It'll be my pleasure – I am going to sit behind you.' He climbed into the bath and sat against the end, with a leg on each side of Vera who lay back against him.

'Mmmm, you make an excellent armchair,' she purred, as taking the large natural sponge, he reached around and started to gently soap her chest. By the time that they climbed out of the bath, the water had cooled, but they had not noticed.

'Oh my God, Billy, most of the water has splashed out onto the floor – it's awash!'

'Don't worry, Vera darling, I shall call the housekeeper and tell her that there is a fat tip for the chambermaid. Now, dinner. Where shall we go? Any favourites, or shall I choose?'

'Somewhere simple and typically Viennese would suit me.'

'I shall ask Hekkel – he will know somewhere off the beaten track. I will pop back to my room and change into something suitable.'

Shortly after Billy had left, a bellboy delivered a note for Vera. It was from von Ribbentrop, asking her to meet him for coffee at 11am the following morning at Cafe Sperl. The note said that the concierge would be able to give her directions.

After an excellent traditional Viennese supper, Vera and Billy had a nightcap in the hotel bar where they had first met, seemingly by accident at the time, then they retired to her room. Billy had arranged an early alarm call because he wanted to go to the Embassy and check for any instructions before Vera left to meet von Ribbentrop.

'I say, David, you sure look every inch a Hungarian gentleman,' was Charles Bedaux's reaction, when Wallis and the Duke appeared after changing for luncheon, 'and you the lady, Wallis,' he added.

The Duke was wearing an Austrian-cut fawn jacket which was just over waist length, lederhosen shorts, long thick stockings and heavy brogues. Wallis' concession to traditional local dress style was a comparatively long-skirted, short-sleeve dress in a dark green material, cinched at the waist with a black leather belt. She was wearing ankle boots. The severity of her outfit was softened by the large, jewelled brooch that she wore. Nevertheless, the overall effect, particularly with her jet-black hair parted severely down the centre and drawn tight in a bun, was severe.

'Right!' cried an enthusiastic Charles, 'this calls for a photograph.'

He dashed off, returning after what seemed like only a minute with his camera. It was obviously of professional standard. He called for one of the servants to accompany them, and then led the way out of the castle. He took the young servant on one side, and explained how the camera worked. He then fussily arranged the little group in front of some dark-stained, closed louvre shutters. The servant took four pictures as instructed.

'I shall develop these in my dark room this afternoon. Now then, since it's a beautiful day, how about a picnic. We can take one of the open carriages into the forest. There is a beautiful peaceful clearing by a small lake – a perfect spot for lunch. Well, how about that?'

'That would be fun, David,' responded Wallis with a smile, taking the Duke's arm. He did not look at all enthusiastic, and had been hoping for some rough shooting if not a boar hunt.

'Wallis, if that would make you happy, it suits me, my love.'

'Very well, if you will excuse us, I shall go around to the mews and arrange the coach – Fern will instruct the kitchens and, of course, my sommelier. Fern, please ask that they ensure that there is plenty of ice.'

'Yes dear, I had thought of that,' she replied, raising her eyebrows expressively to Wallis.

The picnic was a disaster. The traditional outfits were more suited for a cool, if not cold, day. Instead it was an unusually hot and humid day for the time of year, and the still air had a heavy, thundery feel. The pair of beautiful matched bay geldings drawing the carriage were plagued by horse flies, and were extremely skittish.

Charles had insisted that they did not need to take a coachman and he would take the reins. It soon became apparent that he couldn't cope, and after a particularly nasty moment when it looked as though the carriage might overturn, the Duke insited that he took over. The forest track was rough and rutted the ground, iron-hard after the long summer. It was hard work keeping on course, and the Duke was soon sweating profusely, something which he hated.

They reached the clearing by the lake after an hour of uncomfortable jolting and swaying. The Duke was by now furious. and very uncomfortable. Wallis was equally unhappy, and hardly consoled by the fact that therewould be the return journey to face, however enjoyable the picnic itself might be.She too felt uncomfortably hot and sticky, to the point where she wondered if her carefully applied make-up might run.

The clearing was pretty enough, but nothing spectacular,

and the small lake was weed-filled and a greenish hue. As they climbed out of the carriage, the first mosquitos attacked. 'Oh my God!' cried Wallis, 'I am being eaten alive!'

'Me too,' agreed Fern, slapping at her exposed arms.

'Oh, don't make a fuss – if we light a fire the smoke will drive them off. David, while I set up the picnic table and chairs, I put you in charge of collecting firewood and starting a fire.'

The Duke stomped off into the forest. After three foraging trips he had assembled a pile of kindling and dry wood next to the folding picnic table. 'We must have the fire close to us, Charles, or there will be no benefit from the smoke.' As if to emphasise the point, he slapped hard at his cheek.

The table was soon laid and the Duke had lit the fire. The four sat down. The fire was burning fiercely, producing a lot of heat and little smoke. Wallis picked up her place setting and moved to the other side of the table. She was closely followed by Fern. The mosquitos continued their attack on the humans, whilst the horse flies did not spare the fretting horses.

'We need green stuff on the fire to make smoke!' cried the ever-enthusiastic Charles, who leapt up, and taking the carving knife from the platter on which a joint of roast smoked wild boar rested, dashed off to the forest and started hacking off green leafed branches. He returned and threw a pile on to the fire. Nothing appeared to be happening, until some of the leaves had dried enough and started to smoulder. The thick smoke enveloped the party, making their eyes smart as they started to cough.

The Duke stood, and stepping away from the smoke, turned towards Charles. He was red-faced and clearly livid. 'Charles, in case you have forgotten, I am the ex-King of England, now a Duke, and Wallis is my Duchess. You are our host and you are a fucking multi-millionaire. What in the name of hades are we doing in this stinking hell hole?'

For a moment, Charles looked crestfallen, but then rising from his folding director's chair, looked first at Wallis, then the Duke, and said, 'Unusually for me, this was a good idea gone wrong. I apologise, and believe that we should return to the castle and have a late luncheon there.'

The journey back was every bit as uncomfortable. It did nothing to improve tempers. When they finally reached the castle they were a sorry sight. Wallis announced that before doing anything else, she needed a wash and complete change. She would also need to wash her hair to get rid of the smell of smoke. Fern agreed, as did the Duke.

Fern turned to Charles, 'Come on, darling, come with me and we can eat later. Wallis, David, please join us on the terrace in forty five minutes and we can have our picnic and a nice glass of wine there. I shall give instructions for iced water and lemonade to be taken to your suite.'

In Vienna, Billy had left Vera sleeping and taken a taxi to the British Embassy. After the usual security checks, he was shown into a plainly-furnished office and a clerk brought him a thin folder for which he signed. The instructions were clear. He must get back to the hotel and brief Vera. He was very conscious of the risks involved in turning her, but then, so were his masters in London. She still knew nothing of his real objectives and focus, but soon he would have to tell her.

As he sat back in the taxi he had a sudden pang of conscience. He had not intended to fall for Vera, but simply to use her. Now he realised that he was falling in love with her despite his affection for Lisette in far-away Cannes.'What a bloody mess,' he thought.

Back in the hotel, Billy was briefing Vera 'Before you go,I have a request to make. Please only tell von Ribbentrop that my job is to watch out for the safety of the Duke and Duchess and that is all. You can tell him who I am – he will find out very quickly in any event. Also, tell him that you and I are having an affair, but that it is a purely physical thing – he will undoubtedly find out if he has not already done so, and anyway, he knows all about purely physical relationships. Ask him what you can do to assist him. OK?'

'That's fine. Right, Cafe Sperl, here I come!'
'Good luck.'

Vera climbed out of her taxi and entered the café, which the concierge had told her was a Viennese institution. Her nostrils were assailed by the enticing smell of roasting coffee as she looked around the long, high-ceilinged room appreciatively. It was magnificent in a subtly understated style. The richly decorated ceiling, crystal chandeliers and wall lights were cleverly offset by the highly polished parquet floor, marble-top tables and wooden Thonet chairs. There were also richly upholstered, high-backed settles against the half-height dark wood panelling, which created cozy booths and privacy.

Vera correctly guessed that von Ribbentrop would be in one of these, and smilingly declining the offer of a waitress to show her to a table, walked slowly down the room until she saw him. His eye caught hers, and he stood, offering his hand which she took, and leaning forward, kissed him lightly on the mouth.

'Vera, my dear, you look more beautiful than ever – positively radiant. Married life must be suiting you,' von Ribbentrop greeted her, with a knowing smile.

'Joachim, do stop teasing me. You have not changed, or should I say improved,' she responded, giving him a coy look.

'I rather doubt that you have – always a little minx. Now, you must have coffee with a slice of the blissfully decadent Sperl torte – it is delicious.'

'What is it?'

'Oh, a confection of almonds and chocolate cream. Sublime. I have ordered some to take back to Berlin for the Führer. He loves it.'

After a waitress had taken their order, von Ribbentrop wasted no time in getting down to business. Gone was his flirtatious manner as he coldly asked, 'Have you made contact with the British agent as instructed?'

'Indeed I have.'

Vera then told him what she knew of Billy's background, and as agreed, simply that his brief was protection of the former king and his wife.

'Are you really sure, Vera?'

'Yes Joachim, I am. I started to sleep with Billy the first night we met and we are having an intensely physical affair. No strings – he has a lover in the South of France. He has been very frank with me. He knows that I am recently married, and that I have an understanding with my much older husband.'

'And he has given no indication that the British Secret Service suspects the Duke or Duchess of any, shall we say, impropriety?'

'Not in the slightest. He thinks them rather ridiculous, I think.'

'I see. Now, Vera, please continue your affair, and at the slightest indication that he has any suspicion, or has been told that his masters suspect the Duke and Duchess of any improper behaviour, you must contact me. Do so through your husband. Now then, no more work. Enjoy your torte.'

'Mmm, it is gorgeous,' murmured Vera as she savoured her first mouthful, thinking that she would bring Billy here to try it.

Having put Vera in a taxi, von Ribbentrop returned to the hotel and Helga. As he entered his suite, he heard Helga singing to herself in the bedroom. On entering the room, he saw that she was seated at her dressing table putting on mascara. She was naked and beautiful.

'Helga, my dear, you look fabulous!'

'Then come and show me that you mean it, Joachim.' She gestured to him, and obediently he crossed the room and bent to kiss her. He knew what would follow as he felt her respond. He growled with pleasure as she deftly opened his trousers, and her cool hand found him.

'A little pain, and then a lot of pleasure I think, Joachim,' she purred, as without letting go of him she led him to the bed.

# Chapter 39

Princess Stephanie von Hohenlohe was having lunch with Johnny Johnstone at L'Ecu de France in Jermyn Street.

'I always enjoy lunching here, Stephanie – it lets me pretend that I am in France for a couple of hours.'

'I know what you mean. It is not just the food and the wine, or the décor, but the way the French staff behave is just so different to any other style. I love it, and thank you for bringing me here.'

'It is entirely my pleasure to be in the company of so beautiful a companion,' responded a smiling Johnny, 'let's have a Kir Royale while we look at the menu and order, then we can have a real chin wag.'

'A what?' asked a startled-looking Stephanie.

'You know, a really good talk.'

'Oh, I now understand. You English have some really strange phrases but yes, good idea.'

After ordering two Kir Royales, Johnny studied the menu. 'I am going to have l'escargots followed by confit de canard, I think. How about you, have you made up your mind?'

'I shall have foie gras and then join you with the duck.'

'Excellent – I shall choose the wine.'

The orders were placed with a request for a good interval between courses, made necessary because the French staff had become used to the uncivilised English rushing their food, instead of savouring both it and the occasion.

'Now Stephanie, what's your news – I bet you have some juicy gossip.'

'I don't know why you might think that,' laughed the Princess. 'I have just had a quick trip to Germany.'

Johnny feigned surprise, although Tar had briefed him on the report that Stephanie had suddenly flown to Berlin to see Adolf Hitler.

'Oh, why did you go?'

'I went to see about the visit to Germany that David and Wallis are planning. David is very keen that Wallis has a really good time. Charles – you know, Londonderry – asked if I could help. There's a business consultant, Charles Bedaux, who is supposedly making all the arrangements. I went to see what was planned, and ensure that the occasion was properly organised.'

'Yes, I met Charles Bedaux at the Windsors' wedding at in his French castle. He is an absolute dynamo of a man.'

'Well, anyhow, I saw the Führer who passed me on to one of his adjutants, Fritz Wiedemann, who is handling the arrangements. I reviewed them with him. It will be impressive, and I think that Wallis will love it.'

'Who will be accompanying them as part of their party – the British element, that is?'

'I understand David's "poodle", Fruity Metcalfe. They say that Wallis cannot stand him, and is really jealous of the relationship between David and him. And there will be Dudley Forward. Beyond that, I am not sure that there will be anyone apart from staff.'

'That's rotten for Wallis. Actually, my friend, Celia Ffrench-Hardy, has met Herr Hitler more than once – she went with Unity Mitford.'

'Hah! That unbalanced Mitford girl, always mooning around the Führer. There are some wild stories about her sexual escapades with SS officers, and I am inclined to believe them. I met Celia at Cliveden earlier this year – she is a beautiful and clever girl, no?'

'Well, that she most certainly is. I know David well, as you know, so does Celia, who is close to Wallis and David. How about if we volunteered to accompany them?'

'I think that is a grand idea. Ah, the foie gras. Now that looks really pretty with the jelly and dried fruit. Fritz Wiedemann is meant to be coming to the London Embassy in a day or two, and I shall be seeing him then. I shall put the suggestion to him, but in the meantime I shall telephone Adolf this evening early, before he settles down with his films, and have him make the suggestion to Fritz in advance.'

'Will he do as you suggest?' asked Johnny with a hint of incredulity.

'Of course he will, Johnny. He often asks my opinion about things. It's really rather flattering.'

'I bet it is. Is he very keen on watching films?'

'Oh yes – he is addicted. Do you know what really makes him laugh? You will not believe it.'

'Not a clue – tell me.'

'Mickey Mouse. In July, he had five delivered, including *"Mickey's Fire Brigade"* and *"Mickey's Polo Team"*. He watches them again and again. He likes adventure too of course, but Hollywood has to be very careful. The irony is that so many of the film makers are Jewish, but he seems to be happy to overlook Jewishness when it suits him.'

Johnny put his hand on Stephanie's. 'Are you in love with Fritz Wiedemann? If not, I would like to spend more time with you.'

'Dear, handsome Johnny. I can never love any one man. Rather, as the Catholics believe in original sin, I have come to believe that all men are potentially heart-breakers. I will never allow myself to be vulnerable again, I simply will not allow that to happen, but that does not stop me fully enjoying the company of men that interest me. You interest me, Johnny. Does that answer your question?'

'I rather think that it does. Do you fancy dinner and some dancing one evening soon?'

'I most certainly do. That would be lovely. You have the number of the Dorchester don't you?'

'And you live there?'

'I most certainly do, and I love it. I have an idea – come back and have tea with me after we leave here. It is most civilised, I can assure you.'

'Very well, that sounds a splendid idea.'

Johnny realised that in the interests of intelligence gathering, he was going down the same path that Celia had to tread with Joachim von Ribbentrop. He knew that he must make a decision, probably this afternoon. It would not be easy, but there was no doubt that Stephanie presented an incredible intelligence opportunity. He realised that his mind was already made up. He would surrender himself to this fascinating woman.

When they left the restaurant arm-in-arm, the doorman whistled, and a London taxi pulled off the rank, stopping by them. As they were driven along Jermyn Street, Stephanie took Johnny's hand squeezed it gently, then laid it on her thigh. She was looking into his eyes with an intensity that was almost electric.

The day following the disastrous picnic, Charles Bedaux suggested that he and the Duke go boar hunting. The Duke was in a better mood than the previous evening, when he had been ungraciously short-tempered. 'That's a capital idea.'

'Then come with me, David, and we can draw guns and ammunition. My head gamekeeper will accompany us with some of his men to act as beaters, provide safety back up and cart the dead animals back to the castle.'

'Safety back up?' asked the incredulous Duke, 'I have shot tiger in India, and they must be a damn sight more dangerous than a wild pig. We used to go pig-sticking on horseback as well – great sport.'

'These wild boar are big, David, and they are fast. Every year, hunters are killed by them, and I cannot take that risk with an important guest such as yourself.'

'Very well, Charles, I will not argue – bad form, what?' he asked rhetorically.

After the arrangements were made, they climbed into an American Ford "Woody" shooting brake, and the head game keeper came with them. He explained that his men had gone to the chosen hunting ground on a trailer drawn by a tractor.

'This is a jolly comfortable motor, Charles,' commented the Duke.

''Yes, it sure is. Henry, Henry Ford, gave it to me as a personal gift. It was when I opened some doors for his business in Germany. He has established a big operation there, you know, and is supplying the German military with trucks in large numbers, particularly as the army expands – the air force too. Now, we are nearly there.'

They pulled off the track in an area where there was much more scrubby growth than larger trees like those in the forest that they had gone through the previous day. The scrubland covered a large area, and was flanked by rolling bare wheat fields.

'Now that the wheat has been harvested, the boar like this scrubland for cover. They are quite timid in spite of being so dangerous. There are no clearings as such, so we have to be very alert – there is little or no warning when they charge, and you end up firing and praying for a good shot at almost point-blank range.'

The head gamekeeper left the car and stood for a moment checking his rifle. Just then, some of his men appeared and joined him. They too had rifles. He and three others set themselves in a half circle about fifty yards across, with a central gap, and he indicated that that was where David and Charles Bedaux should stand.

When Charles Bedaux and the Duke were in place, a loader, with a spare gun slung on his shoulder and crossed bandoliers of ammunition, came and stood just behind each of them. Each loader also had a long lance which they stuck upright into the ground at their sides.

Shouts were heard as the beaters drew closer. The Duke checked his rifle yet again, making sure that the safety catch was off and it was ready to fire. Although with a shorter barrel, it was almost as large a calibre as the elephant guns to which he had become used in Africa, until he became more interested in photographic safaris.

Wild boars were not animals of beauty – they damaged crops, bred prolifically and were good for the pot. A very different proposition to the beautiful, endangered species that he had taken to photographing rather than hunting. Suddenly, his thoughts were shattered as there was a wild crashing directly in front of them .He saw the head gamekeeper and his men raise their rifles to their shoulders in a firing position, and he did likewise.

At that moment, a huge boar crashed out of the scrub only twenty yards in front of the Duke and Charles Bedaux. Charles fired. It was a poor shot, and at best only grazed the boar, which was now charging straight at the Duke. His loader had come almost to his side, and was crouching, with the lance pointing at the snorting red eyed beast. The Duke squeezed the trigger. The recoil was massive and punched him out of his crouch. The wild boar sank to its knees, its eyes seeming to be staring balefully at the Duke as it toppled sideways on to the ground.

'A fine shot, Your Royal Highness – just look.' The bullet had entered the animal's skull precisely between its eyes, which were now turning opaque. The head gamekeeper then turned to Charles Bedaux and said, 'It is a truly brave man who stands his ground before the charging boar so as to have the perfect shot. I estimate that this beast will weigh in at over three hundred kilos, perhaps even more.'

Charles Bedaux was clearly put out by his head gamekeeper's apparent dismissal of his own efforts in comparison to those of his guest. 'Shall we return to the castle now?' asked Charles.

'Whatever for, that was great sport! Are there more around here?' the smiling Duke asked the head gamekeeper.

'Most certainly, Your Royal Highness. We should re-form approximately half a kilometre over there.'

'Jolly good – come on, Charles, let's have another crack at the blighters.'

'Very well, David,' responded a clearly reluctant Charles.

It was hard going through the scrub. But after just over twenty minutes they were again in the same formation as before. 'Shall I leave the first shot to you, Charles old chap?' asked the Duke, adding, 'I prefer to let the blighters get in close before I fire.'

'Very well, David.'

Once again, the beaters could be heard. Whilst Charles was looking distinctly nervous, the Duke turned to his loader and gave a broad grin. He was clearly enjoying himself. 'Please make sure that that second rifle is loaded and the safety off if I need it.'

Suddenly there was the now familiar crashing sound of a large animal racing through the scrub. A boar broke through, and charged straight at Charles and the Duke. Charles fired and clearly missed. Just then another animal broke out, and it too was running towards the two men. Charles seemed paralysed with fear, and his loader leapt forward with his lance at the ready.

The Duke went down on one knee, and when the boar was only ten yards from him, fired. Again it was a perfect shot. He reached behind as he threw his rifle down, and seizing the second rifle from the loader calmly despatched the second boar as it was swerving around the still-twitching first one.

The head gamekeeper and his helpers gave a great shout of "Bravo", and the Duke stood wreathed in a broad smile of satisfaction. 'Wonderful sport, Charles, wonderful! I think that a drink is called for.' He took his silver hip flask from his pocket, and raising it in salute to the head game keeper, took a long pull. He wiped the top with his handkerchief and passéd the flask to Charles Bedaux, who was still looking pale.

'That was as fine a piece of shooting as I have seen in my forty years of boar hunting, Your Royal Highness,' said the head gamekeeper. The Duke's bravery and skill was destined to pass into local legend amongst the fanatical Hungarian hunting fraternity.

# Chapter 40

Johnny and Princess Stephanie crossed the marble floored reception area of the Dorchester Hotel and entered the long richly decorated Promenade. With a piano playing quietly in the background and the soft hum of polite conversation, the elegant clientele were taking tea.

'You know, Johnny, even though they serve the daintiest sandwiches you have ever seen and the most delightful light cakes, I really do not think I could eat a thing after our splendid lunch.'

'I am very relieved to hear that, Stephanie! I am feeling exactly the same.'

'Very well, come with me and I shall show you my suite. It has a lovely outlook – it's on the seventh floor.'

Johnny recognised that this was a moment of no return, but did not hesitate as he replied, 'Yes, I should love to see it.'

When they entered the suite, Stephanie did a pirouette with outstretched arms – a welcome that was also an invitation. As Johnny stepped forward, she brought her hands together behind his head, and drew him into an embrace that became a lingering kiss. She drew away from him, and with her arms at full stretch stared into his eyes – with a smile playing at the corners of her mouth, she said, 'Mmm, that was lovely – I would like to do it again in a minute or two. First, allow me to show you around. It won't take long.'

'It is certainly very spacious and light,' commented Johnny, taking in the contemporary, but very opulent style of the suite.

'Yes, you must know Oliver Messel, the painter and set designer. When he came here for a drink he said that he would love to be given a free hand to decorate and furnish it. He came with Harold Acton, you know, the young writer.'

'I know them both, very talented chaps, and Acton throws quite some parties. I am not sure that he is very keen on girls though.'

'Well Johnny, that goes for quite a few, it seems to me,' laughed Stephanie.

'You do not want to see the bedroom do you, Johnny?' she asked smiling.

'Well my dear, I thought you were going to show me everything,' he responded straight-faced, a look betrayed by the twinkle in his eyes.

'Then you shall, oh yes, you shall.' And she took him by the hand and led him into her bedroom.

After the Duke and Duchess had left Hungary heading for Paris, Charles Bedaux again presented himself to Howard Travers, the US legation Charge d'Affaires.

'Good day Mr Travers, and again, thank you for your time which I shall not waste. I must advise you that the Duke of Windsor will be making a public announcement on 3$^{rd}$ October, that he and his Duchess will be visiting Germany on 11th October for twelve days at the invitation of the Führer, who is placing two aeroplanes and eight automobiles at the disposal of the Royal couple for the duration of their stay. The Duke and Duchess will be leaving for the United States on the German vessel *"Bremen"* on 11$^{th}$ November, and whilst there, the Duke would appreciate being received by the President to discuss social welfare.

'The Duke has asked me to stress that the plans for his forthcoming visits will be kept entirely secret for now, but that he will telegraph the British Ambassador in Washington with his plans on 3rd October at the same time that he telegraphs the British Ambassador in Berlin. I trust that everything is crystal clear.'

'Most certainly, Mr Bedaux,' replied Travers, putting down his pen. 'I shall report accordingly.'

His encoded report reached the desk of Assistant Secretary of State, George Messersmith, later that day, and he deemed it sufficiently serious in its implications to seek an immediate meeting with Secretary of State, Cordell Hull.

'I tell you here and now, Messersmith, this promises to cause immense problems, both nationally and internationally. The US government, even the President, are being pushed into a very awkward situation. The President should not refuse to see him, but does not wish to give the man credence. His personal view is that the Duke is being manipulated by a bunch of dangerous Nazi sympathisers. However, in view of the Duke's popularity, he cannot be seen to snub him. He will have to wait to see what the British Government's line is before any decision.'

'Well, Cordell, I can help a little there. I understand that when it was known that the Duke and Duchess were to visit Hungary, orders were given to the Ambassador, to the effect that they were not to be given any official recognition. For instance, nobody above the rank of Third Secretary to greet them on arrival, no official introductions or invitations. In other words, the cold shoulder. Polite but nevertheless, just that.'

'Yes, I was in fact aware of that dictat. The British Ambassador to Washington, who is unfortunately back in Britain at the moment, tipped me off over dinner. I am going to contact Lindsay in London. Until I have made up my mind, and done some more digging, I want this whole matter kept under wraps.'

Sir Robert Vansittart had assiduously collated as much information as he could concerning the activities of both the Duke and Duchess, and their friends. He had a whole file devoted to the proven and suspected espionage of the Duchess. Quite apart from some of the Duke's actions, and the activities of Charles Bedaux, who was now considered to be a dangerous crony.

Sir Robert was the Permanent Undersecretary of State in the Foreign Office, and second only to the Foreign Minister. His action in issuing the instruction to all diplomatic missions, severely restricting the treatment to be given to the Duke and Duchess, had been prompted in part by his being contacted by Sir Alexander Hardinge, who, far from being an ongoing supporter of the former king as the new Queen had anticipated, had proved to be absolutely loyal to the Crown.

Vansittart and Hardinge were now totally convinced of the serious threats posed by the Duke and Duchess. They were powerful men to have as implacable enemies. Vansittart's worst fears were crystallised by a memorandum from the Ambassador in Washington, Sir Ronald Lindsay, who was on leave at his Dorset home. He warned that in his opinion, the Duke's planned visit to America was the first stage in a planned semi-fascist comeback to England by the Duke.

Vansittart called Sir Ronald into the Foreign Office so that he could show him his files on the Windsors. As Sir Ronald walked up the imposing double staircase in the Foreign Office, the same thought that recurred whenever he was in the imposing building crossed his mind: was the scale of the architecture and its magnificent decor intended to intimidate?. He believed so. He could well imagine the nervousness of an ambassador summoned to attend the Foreign Secretary in this mighty monument to Empire.

They had sat in silence whilst Sir Ronald read through the files.He finally looked up and said, 'Robert, this is truly shocking – that even whilst on the throne, the Duke should have been so naive to act as he did, let alone allow his mistress access to secret information of the utmost national importance. As for that woman, she is a bad lot.'

Vansittart nodded agreement, then commented, 'Prime Minister Baldwin did the nation and the Empire a great service forcing the king into abdication. Our task now is to remove him from the world stage where he continues to be such a liability.'

'I concur with that. In America, particularly the Mid-West, there is a strongly-held view that the Duke was a "Champion of the People", and was hounded off the throne by the arch-Tory Baldwin. The South Wales comments are seen as supporting that view. The workforce in America is very conscious of its exploitation for profit and lack of regulation. For instance, there is a horrific rate of industrial accidents involving fatalities in the coal and steel industries.'

'Am I right that the American Unions are powerful now?'

'They are, Robert. Yes, they are riddled with corruption and not afraid to use violence but they are strong.'

'Presumably they are hostile to this Bedaux fellow and his

methods?'

'Most certainly, and he now associates himself with the barons of big business, you know, the Henry Fords of this world. Ford is, of course, a staunch supporter of Nazi Germany, and there are ever closer links between American big business and the so-called new Germany of Herr Hitler and his thugs.'

Vansittart commented, 'My younger brother, Nicholas, works for General Motors, and I know that he is concerned about the degree of investment the company is making in Germany.'

'Well, as Ambassador, I meet all sorts in Washington, and there is no doubt in my mind that there is much pro-German sentiment in the United States. That must be coupled with a generally-held isolationist view, and a horror of ever being involved in a distant European conflict again. On that basis, business is business.'

'Well, Ronald, you were my predecessor in this job, and you well know that in that capacity I have unlimited access to government information. I am convinced that anything Hitler says is for public consumption. and the Germans will start a European conflict as soon as they are strong enough.

'As for the Duke, I have acted as I have, and base my personal assessment on not only the espionage carried out by his wife, but also his own actions. I cannot say whether he is simply naive or deliberate in his actions, but I can think of three instances where his actions give cause to think that it is the latter.'

'Well, I can guess the latest, Robert – breaking George Messersmith's confidence, and tipping off the Italians that the Americans were aware of the illegal supply to them of arms from Germany.'

'Spot on. Add to that, his tip-off that Britain would not intervene militarily if Hitler reoccupied the Ruhr, and the deliberate leaking of Cabinet secrets.'

'I don't know about those.'

'Well, Walter, Runciman attended a Cabinet meeting in the morning. That evening he was seated next to von Ribbentrop at a dinner. Von Ribbentrop proceeded to talk about matters discussed that morning in Cabinet. Baldwin had reported the content of that part of the meeting to the King, who must have told Mrs Simpson who in turn informed von Ribbentrop.'

'That really is monstrous, but having seen your file on her activities, I should not be surprised, should I? So, how would you like me to play it with regard to this proposed visit?'

'I suggest that you explore whether the American Unions would oppose the visit, given the close involvement of Bedaux. Secondly, in relation to any official reception, try to ensure that any American decision be subject to consulting us first.'

'I shall do that, and let you know the response I receive.'

Johnny and Stephanie were lying in her large bed. She was snuggled on her side facing him, and their legs were entwined.

'I think that maybe we have worked off a little of our lunch perhaps.'

'I should think so,' Johnny laughed, then continued. 'When will you be going to Germany again? Will you be there when the Duke and Duchess of Windsor visit?'

'I expect I shall have a meeting with Fritz Wiedemann here in London later this week, and then I shall fly over next week to make sure that all the arrangements are in place. I do not know whether I shall be there at the time of the visit.'

'What do you and Herr Hitler usually talk about?'

'Oh, this and that. Sometimes he asks my opinion straight out. Other times he sort of thinks aloud, then waits for my reaction.'

'Such as?'

'Oh, let me think. Ah, I know. The other week he said to achieve the world order that he envisages, the Duke must be put back on the throne.'

'But that cannot happen, if no British politician of standing is willing to form a government with the King, married to Mrs Simpson as was.'

'Ah, but there you are wrong. You know that Lloyd George visited Hitler at Berchtesgaden, and they got on very well indeed. I joined them for dinner one evening, in part to act as interpreter if needed. They talked about the Great War and their different perspectives, and then politics. They share many views.'

'That does not mean that Lloyd George would form a

government if the Duke were to be returned to the throne.'

'Oh, but he would. The Führer asked him straight out, and he said that he would, in the interests of peaceful co-existence and long term international stability.'

'So how does the Duke get back on the throne that his brother now lawfully occupies?'

'He does not believe that Britain has the wish to go to war. Nevertheless, if there is no agreement for peaceful co-existence, then there will be unification by force. He believes that Britain would capitulate in a year.'

'Well, I am not so sure of that. Anyhow, this is all a bit serious – I apologise for asking.'

'Don't be silly. Oh dear, look at the time, I have to get ready – I am out to dinner tonight.'

Stephanie turned her face slightly, and Johnny kissed her before they both got out of bed.

The Duke and Duchess had returned to Paris where they maintained a nine-roomed suite at the luxurious Hotel Le Meurice – nicknamed the "Hotel of Kings" – overlooking the historic Tuileries gardens. They were finishing their breakfast and engrossed in the newspapers, when Dudley Forward bustled into the dining room.

'What is it, Dudders – you know that I do not wish to be disturbed before noon.'

'Well, Sir, I thought you should know that a message has come through from Mr Errol Flynn, the actor. He wishes to visit you this afternoon with two gentlemen from Berlin. They are travelling incognito.'

'Gee, David, that sounds real fun. Errol is a charming man, and I would love to meet him again.'

'Then you shall, my dearest. Dudders, may I suggest 3.30pm – I shall greet them in the foyer. Better have some tea laid on.'

That morning, the overnight train from Berlin pulled into the Gare du Nord. The famous actor, Erroll Flynn, and two well-dressed men were met by a large Mercedes Benz saloon and driven to the Hotel Plaza Athenee, where Flynn had a suite, and had been staying until his apparently sudden trip to Berlin a few days before. The British Secret Service was shadowing him on this trip to Europe, as were American agents. The British were doing so because they had a tip off that he was organising the transfer of funds raised in America to the Irish Republican Army. The Americans were concerned about security issues generally after an in-depth FBI investigation.

Billy Brownlow had left Vera in Vienna with considerable regret, but they would keep in touch, and she promised to do her best to find opportunities to meet, as did he. After the tedious journey from Vienna, he was pleased to check into the Hotel Le Meurice and have a long bath. With a change of clothes he felt a new man. He contacted London and was told that there was a German trip in the near future and he should report to the Embassy that evening at 7pm for an update briefing.

As was his habit, he headed down to the lobby and found a spot where he had a good view of the comings and goings of guests and staff. He had known that the woman he now knew as Helga was travelling with the Duke and Duchess, and was not surprised when she crossed the lobby. Even in Paris she managed to look supremely elegant and attractive. 'A real head-turner,' he thought to himself. He was ordering a coffee, when to his surprise fellow agent, Charles Harvey, greeted him and asked if he might join him.

'But of course my dear fellow – what brings you here?'

'Oh, I fancied slumming it a bit, old boy – actually no, I came to see you. I know that we will be meeting this evening, but I thought you might give me something of an update.'

Billy explained that he had stayed in Vienna whilst the Duke and Duchess had gone to Hungary to stay with Charles Bedaux. He did not mention Vera, because he did not know how Tar would want to play that, even within the service.

They decided to have a light lunch and chatted amiably, then returned to the same seats overlooking the lobby. A few minutes before 3pm, three well-dressed men entered the lobby, and after going to the concierge's desk, took seats near to the bottom of the grand staircase.

'Christ, Charles, what are they doing here – if I'm not a Dutchman, that's Errol Flynn with Rudolph Hess, the Deputy Führer, and I think the other one is Martin Borman, Hitler's quiet but deadly fixer.'

'You are right, but look over by the door – there's two of our chaps, Jack Smythe and Dingo Bates, the Aussie. What the heck are they doing here?'

Just then, a slight and immaculately-dressed fair-headed man appeared on the broad staircase, and after shaking hands with the film star was introduced to the other two. They shook hands then he gestured for them to follow him back up the stairs.

''Strewth!' exclaimed Dingo, 'was that the bloody Duke of Windsor?'

'It most certainly was,' said Billy as he walked over to the shocked pair 'come and join our little party, and we can try to find out what the hell is going on here. Starting with why you are tailing a well-known randy film star and two of the most powerful men in Nazi Germany.'

'And you, Billy, can tell us just why they are meeting the man who was our King!'

# Chapter 41

'Wallis, my darling, have you met Mr Errol Flynn, the famous actor – or should I say cinema star – Deputy Führer, Rudolf Hess, and the Führer's right hand man, Martin Borman?' The Duke was smiling affably as he ushered his guests into the sitting room of their opulent suite.

'I have met Mr Flynn, but not the other distinguished gentlemen,' replied a smiling Wallis, as she shook hands with the intense-eyed, saturninely dark-visaged Hess, and the stocky, undistinguished-looking Bormann. She then turned to Errol Flynn, and taking his hand offered her cheek. He flashed his dazzling smile as he leant forward and kissed her. 'Wallis, it is such a pleasure to meet you again.'

Wallis was almost simpering as she asked him, 'Will you be staying long in Paris, Errol?'

'A few days, I expect.'

'Then you must join us for dinner.'

It was just then as the group were settling down in the comfortable armchairs, and the butler was receiving their requests for refreshment, that Helga, looking as svelte and alluring as ever, slipped into the room and handed Wallis a folded note. Out of the corner of her eye Wallis noted with satisfaction that Errol Flynn's attention was focused on Helga – his handsome features had taken on an almost vulpine look. 'Just as I planned,' she thought with satisfaction, 'he's hooked.'

'Righto then, gentlemen, to business. Before we start our discussions, I must put it on record just how delighted the Duchess and I are to be visiting Germany shortly. As you know, I regard Germany – I should say Greater Germany, including Austria and the lands cruelly confiscated by the infamous Treaty of Versailles – as my spiritual home. It is the homeland of my forefathers.'

'That is appreciated, Your Royal Highness, and of course well understood by our Führer,' responded Hess, continuing in his distinctive voice, 'the ostensible purpose of your visit is to see in person the working conditions of our loyal workforce, who have done and are doing so much to restore the Fatherland. However, our Führer wishes it to afford a far greater opportunity for you and Her Royal Highness to see our new and proud nation in the round, and to provide our people an opportunity to see you both.'

'And for that we are truly grateful – I think of the German people as my people.'

'Just so. Now, may I outline some of the arrangements which we trust will meet with your approval ? I am happy to continue in English.'

'As you wish, most certainly, but excuse me for a moment – Wallis, may I suggest that as we shall be discussing detail you have Helga by your side – she can take notes and translate for you if necessary?'

'Very well, dearest.'

Wallis picked up a silver bell from her side table and rang it. Within moments, Helga appeared with a shorthand notebook in her hand. 'Helga my dear, pull up a chair next to me, take notes and also translate anything said in German that may be of relevance to me.'

Helga drew up a chair and sat down, wriggling slightly as she pulled the hem of her tight skirt straight just above her knees. Her legs were demurely crossed at the ankle, but her apparent modesty only made the beautiful young woman all the more alluring. Again, Wallis noted the way that Errol Flynn's attention was clearly fixated on Helga. The actor had a predatory glint in his eye, Wallis was delighted to note. She had plans for him.

'Very well, Reich Minister, pray continue.'

Hess cleared his throat, and then after glancing at his notebook, began to speak in perfect English with only a slight German accent. Over the next hour, he ran through the timetable of formal events that would involve the Duke and Duchess during their visit. The programme, devised by Fritz

Weidemann and overseen by Princess Stephanie Hohenloe, was clearly demanding, and involved a considerable amount of travelling. Wallis was looking very concerned, and interrupted, asking, 'Are you sure that it is possible to do all of this in the time available?'

Before Hess or Bormann could respond, the Duke commented, 'Wallis, dearest, I spent years on Royal tours, some of which lasted months. They are no cakewalk, or picnic, as you would put it, but nonetheless, memorable. Remember, the idea is for us to see as much as possible of the German miracle, and of course, meet the leaders and be seen by the people.'

'That is just so, Your Royal Highness,' added Hess.

When the official business of the meeting was complete the Duke asked Hess, 'You were a fighter ace in the great war. Do you still fly?'

'Most certainly. I am privileged to fly all of our latest aircraft – sometimes at the factory even before our air force. I am a great believer in the concept of the Knights of the Air. There is a common bond of chivalry amongst fliers that does not exist amongst the other arms of the forces of nations. The bond, how do you say, transcends national boundaries. I have met your own brother, Prince George the Duke of Kent, and of course, Lord Clydesdale, who attended the Berlin Olympiad and dined at my house. The Duke of Kent became Grand Master of the Guild of Air Pilots and Air Navigators last year, and is greatly respected in international aviation circles.'

'As indeed are you,' responded the smiling Duke, adding, 'there is camaraderie amongst you all. My younger brother is also the Grand Master of English Freemasonry. I too am a pilot, and I am pleased to subscribe to your view with regard to chivalry between flyers.'

'Excellent. Now, Your Royal Highness, if we may get down to business. The purpose of my visit was of course to run through the formal programme for your forthcoming visit to Germany. We are also here to assure you and Her Royal Highness of the degree of welcome that you will receive from not only the people, but also the State. Mr Flynn has kindly accompanied us to likewise confirm the support that you will receive when you both visit the United States of America. Is that not correct?' He turned to the actor as he said this.

Errol Flynn smiled and inclined his head towards the Duke, then Wallis, and said, 'If I may, I should like to confirm that your visit to America is eagerly anticipated. In New York the American German Bund, of which I am a member, will ensure that you receive the welcome that you richly deserve. Other similar organisations on the West Coast in California, and of which I am also a leading member, will equally play their part. I understand that you will be presented to the President.'

'I have requested so, and of course, since I shall be meeting the Führer in Germany, it is only fit and proper that I should meet his American counterpart, is it not?' the Duke asked, almost rhetorically.

'I certainly would have thought so,' replied the actor, adding, 'but of course, I can in no way speak on behalf of the American Government. It will no doubt make its position clear to your advisers. I assume that Charles Bedaux is organising everything through his contacts?'

'That is so – and an excellent job he is making of it,' responded the Duke.

For the next hour, the planned social programme for the visit to Germany was carefully explained and the Duke and Duchess's questions answered. Helga made copious notes, knowing that her mistress would wish to select appropriate outfits and jewellery for each occasion. As the meeting was drawing to a close, the Duke made a statement which almost repeated what he had said at the outset.

'It would be appreciated if you would inform the Führer that the Duchess and I greatly look forward to meeting him. I am proud of my German blood which is my heritage. The great nations of Germany and Britain should stand united, and not a single life or a drop of blood need be lost or shed in achieving that. The Duchess and I are committed to that cause, and will do everything in our power to achieve it.'

Both Hess and Borman rose, and snapping their arms into the familiar salute, cried out, 'Heil Hitler!'

Hess was visibly moved as he then quietly responded, 'In you Your Royal Highness, the Reich has a true friend and ally. Thank you. Now, I think that the time has come for us to take our leave. We must leave for the Gare du Nord to take the overnight train to Berlin.'

'Mr Flynn, are you staying in Paris?' asked the Duke.
'Yes I am, at the Plaza Athenee.'
'Excellent – will you stay a while and continue our conversation?'
'I would be delighted.'
'Very well, I shall just accompany these gentlemen downstairs and be back shortly.'

After the formal goodbyes had been completed, the Duke and his German visitors left the suite. Errol Flynn wasted no time. 'I would consider it an honour, and indeed a great pleasure, if you ladies would visit me in my hotel one day soon.'

'Well, that should be no problem. Helga, my dear, please go and quickly check my diary – I think that I have a fitting at Schiaparelli tomorrow afternoon at 2.30pm, and if so we could come to you at say 4 o'clock?'

'Perfect.' Flynn had a glint in his eye as he added, 'It will be a perfect opportunity for us to become well acquainted.'

'Most certainly. Ah, well Helga?'
'That is correct, Ma'am, 2.30pm for the fitting.'

The Duke came striding back into the sitting roomm clearly in an excellent mood. 'That was capital, wasn't it, Wallis dearest. Now then Mr Flynn, shall we dispense with formality and use our Christian names?'

Billy and Charles had watched the departure of Hess and Bormann. They noted that the Duke had bid them farewell in the foyer after escorting them down the grand staircase. Clearly Flynn was staying on. The other agents who were tailing Flynn had briefed Billy and Charles on the reason for their doing so. The actor was known to be active in a neo-Nazi group in New York, and also a German-Japanese group in California. The FBI was concerned about these activities, and both organisations were being actively monitored.

The prime British interest was Flynn's vociferous support for the outlawed Irish Republican Army, for which substantial funds were raised in the USA. The British Security Service suspected that Flynn was a courier for such funds. That he had travelled to Berlin and then returned with two such high-ranking members of the Nazi party was baffling to those agents, and Billy did little to enlighten them. Billy turned to Charles. 'I am going to pop back to the Embassy and get a message to Tar Robertson in London. Will you hold the fort?'

'Pleased to, but there is the risk that the Duke will remember me, so if Flynn leaves I had better swap with one of these fellows and catch up with you later.

'Good thinking – I'll be off then.'

Tar Robertson rushed into Sir Vernon Kell's office with the decoded message in his hand. 'Sir Vernon, I apologise for barging in like this, but I think that you will wish to take immediate action and probably speak to the Prime Minister.'

'Not at all, dear boy – now give it to me.'

Sir Vernon's eyebrows literally shot up as he read the message. 'Good God, Tar – what is that bloody man up to now? You are right, I must warn the PM. I want you to speak to Johnny and brief him to meet up with this Princess Stephanie, prime her to find out from Herr Hitler what went on at the meeting. This also underlines that it is imperative that Johnny and Celia accompany the Duke and Duchess on their German trip.'

'Very well, Sir Vernon – I shall do so immediately. Oh, and good luck with the PM.'

'Well I can tell you I would rather be briefing Baldwin – Neville Chamberlain deeply distrusts the Duke and Duchess, but he is painfully cautious.'

The following afternoon, Wallis and Helga left the coutourier. They were in the Buick driven by her French chauffeur, and were taken the short distance to the Hotel Plaza Athenee in Avenue Montaigne, just off the Champs Elysee.

'Well Helga, it is a fine hotel, and much loved by film stars and the like. Rudolph Valentino stayed here. It's a very pretty building, isn't it?'

'I really like the little balconies with the red sun awnings, Wallis. It looks so jolly in the sunshine.'

'Yes, they give an impression of, oh I don't know – happiness, almost frivolity. Well here we are. Now, remember, this might be interesting. I'm curious anyhow,' laughed Wallis as they left the car.

When the two elegant women were shown into Errol Flynn's suite, he greeted them warmly and kissed each of them on the cheek. 'May I offer you tea, coffee or something more interesting?' he asked with a smile.

'Oh definitely more interesting, don't you agree, Helga, my dear?' replied Wallis flirtatiously.

'Oh yes, Wallis, I think so.'

'Very well, ladies, we shall have some champagne.'

After the champagne had been poured, Errol dismissed the servant, telling him that he would not be required for at least two hours. 'Now Wallis, do you have to rush back promptly, or can we take our time getting to really know each other, and you too of course, Helga.'

'There is no rush. The Duke is used to the amount of time it can take when I go for fittings, so he has gone off with his companion, Major Metcalfe, for a round of golf. I do not expect him back before 7 o'clock at the earliest.'

'Excellent. Now, do let me show you around my suite. It has quite a history. It was in this very suite that Mata Hari, the Dutch exotic dancer and spy, was arrested in the Great War. She was executed. Terrible waste. There is a portrait of her in my bedroom.'

'Oh, do show me – that's fascinating, although very sad.'

'With pleasure – come with me.'

The large picture hanging above the bedhead was of an almost naked, voluptuous woman who was only wearing body jewellery and a jewelled headdress.

'Apparently, although Dutch, she spent some time in the Far East, and learnt many of her skills there.'

'I spent a considerable amount of time in China.'

'Really, Wallis – did you learn very much there?'

'I like to think so, Errol.'

Wallis moved close to Errol and appeared to accidently brush her arm against him.

'Do you have anything up your sleeve so to speak, Errol?' she asked with a twinkle in her eye.

'Well Wallis, I am not sure about my sleeve,' he replied, gently taking her shoulders, turning her to face him directly then drawing her close. As Wallis tilted her head back to look up at him, Errol leant forward and kissed her lightly, and then moving her away, asked almost rhetorically, 'Well Wallis, shall we?'

'Oh, I sure think so, but what about poor little Helga? She will feel so left out?'

'Shucks, she needn't – come here, Helga.'

Helga moved close to Errol, and he then had an arm around the shoulders of each of the women. He gently manouvered them towards the bed, Wallis asserted herself. 'Now, Erroll – you just make yourself comfortable in that armchair and watch. Helga, it's time we were undressed.'

The two women then began to sensually embrace and gradually undressed each other. Before they could finish, it had obviously become too much for Errol, who standing up abruptly, started to frantically tear his clothes off. When he had only his boxer shorts left, the two women pounced on him and rolled him onto the bed. Wallis straddled his chest, and Helga freed him from his shorts, giving a squeal of excitement as the actor was revealed in all his glory. Wallis looked back over her shoulder, then leant over the now-grinning Errol and whispered hoarsely, 'So, the stories are true – now let's see if you can use it.'

Celia was on the telephone to Johnny. 'I say, Johnny, I have received a call from Wallis letting me know that an official invitation for us to join her and David on their German trip is to be delivered in the next day or two. It will come through the German Embassy. That should be interesting, and rather fun.'

'Yes, darling, it certainly will, and we can keep tabs on what goes on behind all the flim flam. Are you free if I were to pop over in half an hour or so?'

'That's fine – I shall see you then. Love you, darling.'

Celia then telephoned Unity Mitford. She wanted to know whether Unity was going to be in Germany at the time of the visit. She hoped not. 'Hello Unity – I caught you – I wasn't sure whether you were over here or back in Germany.'

'Celia, so good to hear from you. I am supposed to be back in England for a few weeks, but I am changing my plans. I gather that the Windsors are going to have a rather grand tour of Germany and will meet dear Uncle Adolf. I want to be there.'

'Will you receive a formal invitation, Unity?'

Unity replied breezily, 'Silly old you, I don't need one.'

'Oh, I see.' Celia was inwardly cursing. The last thing she wanted was Unity getting in the way. She would have to discuss the problem with Johnny.

'Celia, we really must do lunch in the next day or two – do you fancy Rules again?'

'Yes, lunch would be fun but I think that we should ring the changes. Now, let me think. I know – how about *L'Etoile* in Charlotte Street – it's rather fun.'

'That sounds a good idea – how about lunch on Thursday then – say 1 o'clock?'

'Righto, I'll book it. Looking forward to a good gossip. Bye for now.'

When Johnny arrived, Celia wasted no time in telling him about her conversation with Unity. 'Johnny, she will just get under our feet. I know what she is like. I am seeing her for lunch on Thursday, and I have to say rather dreading it. But I shall find out what she is up to.'

'Good girl. Leave it to me. I think that we have a way of scuppering her plans.'

Johnny felt guilty, but did not want to tell Celia about Princess Stephanie, whom he was meeting later for a drink at her hotel. 'It sounds as though the Germans are going to pull out all the stops for the Duke and Duchess – just what he wanted for her. But the extraordinary thing is that Errol Flynn turned up in Paris at the Meurice where the Duke and Duchess are staying – guess who was with him when he was greeted by the Duke?'

'I have no idea – do tell me.'

'Only Rudolf Hess and Martin Bormann!'

'No – well, I would never have believed it!' exclaimed Celia.

'Well, it's true – Charles Harvey and Billy Brownlow saw it, as did the agents following Flynn. The trouble is, we do not know what they discussed. Could you bear to go fishing and see von Ribbentrop? You must not let him know, or even suspect that anyone is aware of the meeting, of course.'

'I can have a try, but please, please try to stop Unity being there.'

'I can only do my best.'

'Now then, what's your news Celia?'

An hour later, Johnny left and went straight to the Dorchester. Stephanie greeted him enthusiastically, and then after a long embrace they sat next to each other on the sofa.

'Well Johnny, my first task was accomplished without any

difficulty. You and Lady Celia should have your official invitations in the next day or two'

'Well done Stephanie, was Fritz Wiedemann co-operative?'

'Oh, but of course,' she replied with a smug smile.

'Excellent. A couple of things. Can you find out what is understood to be the Duke of Windsor's present attitude towards Germany – in other words, what is the Führer's perception of his beliefs?'

'That should be no problem – I am popping over to Berlin tomorrow for a meeting with Fritz, so I shall be seeing Adolf.'

'Something else that's very delicate. Unity Mitford is aware of the visit, and intends to be a part of it. It would be a disaster. She is unstable, and too closely associated with her brother-in-law, Tom Mosley.'

'Who is Tom Mosley?'

'Sorry, Stephanie, that's what family and friends call Sir Oswald Mosley.'

'Ah, now I see. Yes, I can understand what you are saying. I shall have a word with the Führer on this. He is very worried about her. He is afraid that some of her fantasy games are getting out of control. He encouraged her at first. Do you know what they are?'

'No, I don't really. I can probably find out – she is hardly the most discreet of women!'

'You find out what you can, and then we'll compare notes.'

'Very well.'

Stephanie looked hard into Johnny's eyes and in a low voice said, 'Well now, my dashing Johnny, I think that you are supposed to, oh, what is it you English say? Oh I know – have your wicked way with me.' As she leant towards him, Johnny knew that he was about to do just that. She was utterly irresitable at that moment.

# Chapter 42

'Well Wallis, how did the fitting go?'

'Oh, excellent, dearest – Elsa Shiaparelli is just so clever, but with her amazing attention to detail one has to be patient. She would like to steal Helga from me and have her as one of her house models. I made it clear that so far as I was concerned, it was out of the question, and Helga, the dear girl, piped up that she would not leave my staff whatever were to be offered.'

'Good girl. You should give her a little reward perhaps.'

'Oh, I shall think of something. Tomorrow afternoon I have a fitting with Mainbocher. The time passes quickly with him – he is such a gossip, and so amusing.'

'Wasn't he a journalist?' asked the Duke, feigning interest.

'Yes, he was Editor of French Vogue before he opened his salon here in 1929. He was the first American coutourier in Paris and so original.'

'Well, my dear, you can thank Katherine de Rothschild for introducing you to him – she extolled his virtues to me when I stayed with them last winter. Eugene commented rather acidly that he wasn't sure that even his family's wealth could sustain the cost of Mainbocher creations.'

'Oh, phooey darling – what's good enough for Mary Pickford is fine by me – anyway, you only get what you pay for, and they say that my wedding dress is the most copied dress in the world. By the way, did you have a good game?'

'Yes, thank you. We played at Morfontaine, to the North of Paris in the great pine forest, the Fôret d'Ermonville. It's a lovely course and the most exclusive club in France – very akin to Muirfield in its approach. Its extension about ten years ago was funded by Edouard de Rothschild. It was through that connection that we were able to play there, as he is putting me up for membership.'

'There seems to be a Rothschild connection in everything we do, darling,' laughed Wallis.

'Well, I think that is pretty true of many things in this life – certainly in Europe. They have a fantastic network. Eugene told me that they had even helped fund Hitler's rise to power. Remarkable, given that they are so prominent a Jewish family.'

'Oh, not really – I suppose they saw it as an investment opportunity, backing a sure horse as it turned out, and from the Nazi point of view, money is money, wouldn't you think?'

'Well, you are probably right there. Anyhow, the Nazis are pretty generous – it was gratifying that they are meeting all the expenses of our trip to Germany and doing so in secret. Changing the subject, if you have a fitting tomorrow afternoon, I think that Fruity and I will go and play St Cloud. We'll probably go before lunch. Apparently they have a most imposing clubhouse with a top notch restaurant. That is, of course, if you would not prefer me to join you.'

'Oh no, dearest – that is very kind, but I know that you will be bored and Main loves to gossip away. The last time, he told me that William Bullitt, the American Ambassador here – you remember we had him to Fort Belvedere a couple of years back – is having an affair with his personal secretary.'

'Well, what's so unusual about that, Wallis?'

'Well, the secretary's name is Carmel Offie, a man, and he lives in Bullitt's residence. They are both strong supporters of Germany apparently.'

'Really. That might be handy one day. Perhaps we should invite him for dinner before our trip?'

'That's an excellent idea – I shall have Helga contact his diary secretary.'

Princess Stephanie was shown into the Führer's office by a young aide, who closed the doors silently behind her.

'My dear Princess, how delightful to see you.' The Führer, dressed as usual in the quasi-military style of the Nazi Party, came around from behind his desk and warmly embraced Stephanie.

'It is my pleasure, Adolf, I can assure you. I have come to Berlin to check final details for the Windsors' visit with Fritz Wiedemann. On paper it all looks very good.'

'Excellent, he is a very efficient chap, and I know that he has been liasing with Robert Ley. They make a formidable planning team.'

'There is a rather delicate matter that I would like to mention, Adolf, if I may.'

'But of course my dear. What is it?'

'It's Unity Mitford. I have heard a rumour she intends to join in the visit. I believe that that would be a mistake, and it would potentially devalue the visit in the eyes of the British people – it could detract from the positive publicity that I know you wish to be generated.'

'I can see that. Between you and me, I am becoming worried about her behaviour. I am very fond of the girl, but I fear that she is obsessed and showing signs of serious instability. I feel guilty in that being fond of her, I may have encouraged her extreme devotion.'

'You cannot blame yourself. She comes from a most unusual family. They are not just eccentric aristocrats, but also intensely political. You have one sister married to the leader of the British fascist party, Unity devoted to you and Nazi Germany, and another an ardent Bolshevik. You cannot imagine a stranger menagerie under one roof, can you?'

Hitler laughed, 'I know, it is very odd. Now, going back to your point, I shall take steps to ensure that she is not present at any of the events involving the Duke and Duchess whilst they are in Germany. She may not like it, but that is how it will be.'

'Thank you, Adolf, I am sure that is for the best. Have you heard whether the Windsors are looking forward to their visit?'

'As a matter of fact, I have. Rudolf Hess and Martin Bormann have visited them in Paris and it was most encouraging. The Duke stressed that he is proud of his German blood, and the great nations of Germany and Britain should stand together, be united without a drop of blood being shed in achieving that. As Rudolf put it when he summed up the visit, "The Duke and Duchess will be no problem, and are enthusiastically committed to our plans for the future".'

'That must be very heartening?'

'Most certainly it is. When the current British Royal

Family has been sent into exile, the Duke will be reinstated as monarch with the Duchess as his Queen, and Lloyd George will be our British Prime Minister.'

'Has Lloyd George agreed to that – after all, he was the British leader in the Great War?'

'Most certainly. Quite apart from his agreeing to all this when he and I met in Berchtesgaden, at my request Robert Ley has had further discussions with him recently, and all is reconfirmed. I believe that the present Royal Family will be exiled to Canada or Australia.'

'How does the Duke feel about that, I wonder?'

'Oh , he will not mind: after all, according to Charles Bedaux, the Duke considers that he has been unjustly exiled with his Duchess. He is also incensed that she has been denied the status of 'Her Royal Highness' to which he believes that she is entitled.'

'I shall note that, and mention it to Fritz Wiedemann – he can cover it in the Protocol Notes for the visit.'

'Excellent. Now, I see that it is time for me to meet a delegation of Sudetan Germans so I must take my leave of you.'

'I quite understand.'

Stephanie and the Führer stood, and after a brief, almost formal embrace, she left the room.

Billy Brownlow was with Tar Robertson, reviewing the extraordinary events at the Hotel Meurice; the visit of the film star and the two high-ranking Nazis to the Duke and Duchess.

'I would have given my eye teeth to have been able to listen to their conversation, Tar.'

'Well, Johnny has hopes of finding out the content of what Hess will have reported to Hitler. We should know in the next few days.'

'In the meantime, what is this about your little songbird coming to London?'

'Yes, Vera is being sent here, ostensibly to brush up her English and work in the protocol section of the German Embassy. Her real Abwehr job is to take the role of a "femme fatale" and infiltrate London's so-called high society, hunting out German, even Nazi sympathisers.'

'So you are really well placed then,' responded Tar with a smile.

'Yes, I suppose I am. She is to use her married name, von Wedel, and will be in an Embassy apartment in Mayfair. I imagine that von Ribbentrop will have a go at bedding her – he appears to do so with every attractive woman he encounters.'

'From what you have told me, I think that she can look after herself. Maxwell Knight has done some quite detailed background checking. The French Deuxieme Bureau were full of admiration at the way she had Ignatieff liquidated by the Soviets, and then when she realised that she was on a Gestapo death list, hooked poor old von Wedel – by marrying him she effectively neutralised that threat. Anyway, his investigation indicated that Ribbentrop may have previously had a fling with her when he was in Paris. She must be quite a girl!'

'That she is. I shall introduce her to Celia if you agree. Celia can then introduce her to her set, who fit the bill perfectly, and most of whom pay no more than lip service to real politics.'

'I see no objection to that. Celia knows the score and can play along. She obviously must not let on that she and Johnny are a part of the "Firm".'

'Vera arrives tomorrow, so I shall be taking her out to dinner. I may take her dancing later. Could you inform Johnny and Celia of their role in case our paths cross – we all tend to frequent the same haunts.'

'Creatures of habit, eh? Of course, I shall brief them now.'

Unity and Celia met in L'Etoile in Charlotte Street. Celia had requested a a table in the rear room, partially separated from the main restaurant, which was a long room with dark panelling on the photograph-hung walls and red banquettes.

''I say, Celia, there are so many famous faces – I had not realised that this place was so well established.'

'Oh yes – my father often lunches here, if not in one of his clubs. Between you and me, he is rather sweet on Elena, who sort of manages the restaurant. She is very young for the job, but lovely and welcoming. She rules the French waiters with a rod of iron. Ah, here she is now. Elena, how lovely to see you.'

'And you, Milady – you are looking lovely as ever, and how is your handsome father?'

'Oh, he's jolly well, thank you. Buried in the country at the moment, just back from Scotland. I think that he is planning to come up to London next week. May I introduce my friend, Unity Mitford – I would not be surprised if she became another of your regulars.'

'Miss Mitford – a pleasure. Milady, please give my kindest regards to you father and I hope that he has time to come here.'

'I shall. May we have two glasses of Kir whilst we study the menu – Unity, you need not look at the first courses, there is the most wonderful hors d'oeuvres trolley – Papa reckons that it's the best in London.'

'I shall order your drinks, if you will excuse me.' Elena left their table.

'Well now, Unity, what is your news?'

'I am really a bit bored here in London at the moment, so I think I shall go back to Germany and stay in Diana's apartment in Munich – I have my own room there. It's really a bit like a shrine. I have a large portrait of Uncle Adolf next to the bed. There are also big floor to ceiling Swastika banners either side of the bed. I only ever light the room with giant church candles – it is quite big, so there are lots of shadows.'

'It sounds quite spooky to me –ah, here is the kir. Thank you. Now, cheers Unity.'

'Cheers. Actually, it isn't spooky, just atmospheric. It is the essence, the soul of Uncle Adolf.'

'But he has surely never visited the apartment?'

'Heavens, no. Some of his officers do though. I'll tell you later.'

After the two young women had chosen their main courses and Celia, the wine, the large hors d'oeuvres trolley, with its array of glass dishes on different shelves, was wheeled to their table. The waiter reeled off descriptions of the dishes, and choices were made.

'Oh Celia, this Montagny is delish!' gushed a smiling Unity, as she took a sip of wine.

'Papa always has it, so its almost a ritual, but yes, it is super. Now, are you going to confide in me? What does go on in your apartment?'

'I need a bit of Dutch courage first, Celia, so let's enjoy the food and wine for now.'

After their main course had been cleared, they decided to

forego a pudding or cheese and just have coffee and finish their wine.

'Well, Unity, spill the beans.'

'Well, I often go to a little bar near the barracks of Uncle Adolf's personal SS bodyguard. Some of their officers are there usually. You know that Uncle Adolf won't sleep with me because I am not a true Aryan. I have tried and tried to persuade him, but he just will not. Anyhow, I had this idea that his personal bodyguards are so close to him, that if I slept with their officers I was in a way worshipping him.'

'Crikey, Unity, but what did he think about that?'

'He agreed, on condition that I tell him about it afterwards, and they must all wear protectives.'

'What do you mean, all?'

'Well, I decided that six was a good number.'

'At the same time?' Celia's eyebrows had shot up.

'Yes, you see it is a ceremony. They all come in full dress uniform, and I wear a long-skirted black outfit with gauntlets and boots. When we get to my room I take off gloves, boots, stockings and and skirt – I don't wear knickers anyhow, never have – and then they blindfold me with a Swastika armband and I lie on the bed. They put me in position, then tie my wrists, and sometimes my ankles, to the bed.'

'What do you mean, "in position"?'

'Well, it varies, you know, sometimes I am spread-eagled on my back or front, or kneeling – oh you can work it out. Then they put on the gramophone with a rousing Nazi marching song – my favourite is the Horst-Wessel song. Then they all have sex with me.'

Celia sat in stunned silence. There was something truly awful about this beautiful young girl calmly recounting her being a willing victim of what was little better than ritualised rape.

'Unity – do you then tell all this to Hitler?'

'Oh yes. I usually do after we have watched one of his favourite films – you know, he watches them time and time again. At the moment he adores Errol Flynn in *Captain Blood* – I've lost track of just how many times I've seen it. Then we have Wagner on the gramophone, and he has torte and hot chocolate. That's when I tell him.'

Celia had vivid memories of Hitler's eating habits from

when she had met him in his mountain lair. If that image were not repulsive enough, the thought of his listening to Unity at the same time with Wagner playing in the background was dreadful.

'Does he want all the details.'

'Oh yes, I have to tell him every little thing. He is especially delighted when I can tell him that I had more than one orgasm.'

'Well, Unity, you have certainly surprised me today, and that's for sure. I shall ask for the bill – my hairdresser is due in half an hour.'

As soon as Celia arrived home, she telephoned Johnny.

'Can we meet for dinner tonight? I have just had lunch with you-know-who, and she told me what she gets up to. You will not believe it when I tell you.'

'Delighted, and I can't wait to hear. Shall I pick you up at 7.30pm?'

'Perfect, darling, come in for a drink – big kiss until then.'

'Well, Helga – time to go and see Mainbocher for a very quick fitting, and then we are off to visit Errol.'

'That should be fun, Wallis – I was very impressed yesterday. At first I wondered if we could accommodate him.'

'Well we did and he seemed to enjoy himself for sure. We must make the best of this afternoon, he's off back to America tomorrow.'

When Johnny arrived at Celia's house, she invited him in for a drink, having decided that what Unity had told her was best recounted in private. When they were sitting comfortably in her drawing room, and as soon as the butler had left after pouring their drinks, Johnny turned to Celia. 'Right, now, darling, spill the beans – what is it that Unity gets up to?'

'Well, I thought that I was pretty broad-minded, but what she told me really takes the biscuit.'

Celia then recounted precisely what she had been told at lunchtime. Johnny sat looking stunned. 'The poor deluded little fool!' Johnny spluttered when Celia finished, 'it is utterly perverted, and the idea of bloody Hitler, lapping it all up to Wagner with his cake and hot chocolate, almost makes me retch.'

'Well, I was pretty shocked. I know that she hasn't worn knickers for years, and Tom Mosley took her virginity on the billiard table whilst he was already having an affair with Diana, but six at a time, and the ritual. It makes my flesh crawl.'

'No wonder she is so neurotic. I shall have to put this in my report to Tar. They pass this sort of stuff on to the psychiatrists who build profiles of leaders. Now, I must mention that we may bump into Billy Brownlow with a woman newly-arrived in London. She is Vera von Wedel, and is an Abwehr agent, but Billy believes that he has turned her. You and I are to befriend her – you in particular – and introduce her to our set on the social scene. She is scouting for Nazi sympathisers. Billy took up with her in Vienna, and is pretty smitten, so it's a tricky wicket for us, I'm afraid.'

# Chapter 43

The King and Queen were sitting with Alexander Hardinge, whose judgement and loyalty to her husband she had come to value, after her initial misgivings. She now wholeheartedly recognised that he was a true servant of the Crown in every sense. In fact, rather than remaining loyal to the Duke of Windsor, quite to the contrary, he now despised him.

'Your Majesties, I have asked to see you both on a matter of some delicacy which we have previously discussed; namely the intention of the Duke and Duchess of Windsor to visit Germany, and then the United States of America. A statement has today been issued on the Duke's behalf by a Mr Carter, who was the Duke's Private Secretary, but is actually believed to no longer hold that position. Nevertheless, may I read it to you?'

'B b b last that man – will there never be any respite from his ridiculous behaviour?'

'Darling,' said the Queen in a quiet, but surprisingly hard tone, 'you must accept that David is turning into a rotter, if not one already. He is up to something, so let's just hear what this statement says.'

'Oh, very well – l l l let's hear it, Alexander.'

'Your Majesties, it reads as follows:

*In accordance with the Duke of Windsor's message to the world press last June, that he would release any information of interest regarding his plans or movements, His Royal Highness makes it known that he and the Duchess of Windsor are visiting Germany and the United*

*States in the near future, for the purpose of studying housing and working conditions in these two countries.*

'If I may add, we are aware that, contrary to the impression being fostered that this is a private visit, the German visit is being organised and paid for by the German Government. There is another matter of concern. The Duke and Duchess have received the Deputy Führer and the Führer's Private Secretary, who is effectively his political co-ordinator, in their hotel in Paris. The two Germans, senior members of that Government, were in the company of a Mr Erroll Flynn, a well-known cinema actor, who is suspected of being a Nazi sympathiser and an activist in support of the terrorist Irish Republican Army.'

The King was lighting yet another cigarette with a shaking hand as Hardinge paused.

'This is monstrous.' The Queen was clearly furious, and her eyes were flashing as she carried on, 'it is bad enough his marrying that woman, and trying to drag the monarchy through the gutter, but this is just too much!'

'I must agree, Ma'am. I have spoken to Sir Robert Vansittart at the Foreign Office, and subject to my advising him of the approval of Your Majesties, he proposes he should instruct that no member of Embassy staff should act in a way that might imply the visit is at all an official British visit. He will go further, and give detailed instructions. This whole affair smacks of a propaganda exercise by the Nazi Government.'

The King appeared to have regained his composure when he commented, 'I find all this d d d d istasteful in the extreme. I speak as someone who has family in Germany, and indeed some members who are in the Nazi party. B b but I am the K k king of En nn gland and that is where my heart and duty rest. W w w hy c c c can n not D d d d david accept t t t that such is his p p position and d d duty?'

'I am afraid that it is worse, Sir. Our intelligence is that he has sent a personal assurance, through Hess and Bormann, to Hitler, effectively of an alliance between the two nations, and declares himself a German in heart.'

Again, the Queen stepped in. 'Alexander, I think that you will understand our dismay at the Duke's behaviour. It must be assumed that the German Government will make great capital of the visit and, I am afraid, so will he.'

'Yes, Ma'am, but he has already made one grave error. He has apparently put it about that this is a private visit and privately funded. With your agreement, Your Majesties, Sir Robert Vansittart proposes our ambassadors discreetly let it be known in appropriate circles that such is untrue, and the German Government is paying – it is a pseudo "state" visit, in other words. The truth will be revealed in the nature and style of events.'

'Excellent – he has always been greedy, according to the King, is that not so, Bertie?'

'Y y yes, ev vven as a b bboy. Papa called it most "unprincely".'

The Queen then spoke again. 'Alexander, we would appreciate it if Sir Robert Vansittart's instruction goes to all Embassies and diplomatic missions, and not merely those of Germany and America. I fear the Duke and his cronies are set on making mischief, and we must deny them every opportunity that we can.'

'I believe that most prudent, Ma'am. I shall ensure that you are furnished with a copy of the instruction. I also understand that Lord Beaverbrook is flying by private aircraft to Paris, to see the Duke in an attempt to have him change his mind.'

'Well, we can hope that he will succeed, but I have my doubts. As we saw with the abdication, once the Duke has made up his mind he is stubborn as an ox, or rather a donkey – especially where that woman is concerned,' commented the Queen.

'So it would seem, your Majesty. Now, if you will excuse me, I shall attend upon Sir Robert Vansittart and give him the authority of Your Majesties to act as he has suggested.'

'Our thanks, Alexander,' responded the Queen, and the King nodded his assent.

The Duke's butler announced Lord Beaverbrook. The dynamic Canadian, an old friend and supporter of the Duke, swept across the sitting room of the suite in the Hotel Meurice with outstretched hand.

'Max, it is so good to see you,' said the smiling Duke, as

the two shook hands.

'And you too, David – you are looking well, Paris must suit you.'

'In the circumstances, Max, it is the best of a bad lot. Wallis and I have received nothing but courtesy wherever we have gone since being hounded out of England. Nowhere more so than in France, but I can assure you that I am not absent from England by choice.'

''As your good friend, David, I can assure you that many in Britain regret your abdication and will always do so. Nevertheless, there are undoubtedly powerful people who did not, and do not favour your cause, and would not wish to see you return. I'm sorry to be blunt, but you know me, I tell it as I see it.'

'I have always valued your frankness, Max – I regard it as the mark of a true friend. You see, there is no law that prevents my returning to England. Initially I wanted to keep out of Bertie's way so that he could find his feet as King. That I believe he has done. Unfortunately, there are two things which I feel are serious impediments though, and they affect Wallis.'

'They are?'

'Well, Max, you know that I believe that it was unconstitutional that the style of Her Royal Highness be denied to Wallis. It was and is a petty and vindictive thing. She says that she does not mind, but I most certainly do. The second thing is the attitude towards her of my mother, Queen Mary, and Queen Elizabeth.'

'David, you are kicking against the pricks on those fronts. The Queen Mother is following your late father's line, and Queen Elizabeth will never forgive Wallis for being the cause of her husband being thrust onto the throne, unwilling and ill-suited. You cannot make conditions.'

'Damnit, Max, I am not making conditions, I just cannot accept that my wife be demeaned in this way. Why is it that other nations are willing to accord her the status to which she is entitled as my wife?'

'I cannot answer that, but as your good friend, may I counsel you to cancel this trip to Germany?'

'You can counsel me all you like, Max, but the answer will not change one iota. We are going. All the arrangements are in place. It will be wonderful for Wallis to experience a Royal visit.'

'David, David – do you not see how this will play in the world's press, and the minds of the people? You, the former King of England and Emperor, making what appears to all intents and purposes to be a State visit to Nazi Germany is highly sensitive, and will give great support to Herr Hitler and his regime.'

'Very well, so be it if that is the result. I happen to greatly admire what the Nazi government and German people have achieved under the leadership of Hitler.'

'Maybe you do, but taking a step which effectively endorses that government and its policies is surely at odds with your position, can't you see that?'

Both men were clearly becoming angry, and Beaverbrook well knew that if truly angered the Duke would become totally entrenched in his stubbornness. 'David, I have a suggestion. Why not postpone the German visit and go ahead with the American one first, see how that plays out?'

'No Max, we are going to Germany first. Now, I am sorry that you have had a wasted journey, but that's my last word.'

'Very well, how about we treat the matter as closed between us – let's go and have a good lunch at the Lucas Carton, with Wallis of course, if she can join us. Whilst we are doing that, my aircraft can return to London and bring back Winston to talk with you.'

'The answer is no, Max. It matters not who comes to see me, whether it be a friend like yourself, or Winston, or a foe like those bastards in the government and establishment that forced me into a corner less than a year ago. I shall not change my mind.'

'Very well, David, I am deeply saddened, but will press the matter no further. Now, shall we go and have that lunch?'

'I think not, Max. This conversation has opened old wounds and I would be poor company.'

After Beaverbrook had left, the Duke paced up and down then called for Dudley Forward. 'Dudders, old fellow, I think that the Duchess will be returning shortly. She was contacting the American Embassy to see whether Ambassador Bullitt would join us for dinner. I suggest that we have a light salad for luncheon, and that you join us to run through the diary to see what we have on the agenda, before we leave for Germany.'

'Very well, Sir. I shall give instructions accordingly.'

Celia was in bed with von Ribbentrop who was gently stroking her perspiration-slicked back. 'You still have the flush of a fulfilled woman, Celia, my little hellcat,' he said with a smile.

'Well, Bubbles, you are one to talk – I think your shout must have echoed around the whole hotel!'

'Touché, my dear. A cigarette?'

'Oh rather, that would be super.'

As they lay quietly relaxing and watching the smoke curling towards the ceiling, Celia knew that now was the time when she must broach the subject that had brought her back to von Ribbentrop's bed. She had not been totally unwilling – she knew that the sex would be good – but she had realised that she was falling deeply in love with Johnny, and that love would leave no room for other physical relationships. She was beginning to realise the value and strength of a deep relationship, like that of her parents.

She was also beginning to realise that what had started out almost as a game of espionage working with Johnny, was a deadly serious reality. Any doubts had been dispelled by the shoot-out in France on the way to the Windsors' wedding, and the subsequent events in Lyons. 'Bubbles, I am sure that you know, but Johnny and I have been invited to accompany the Windsors on their visit to Germany – isn't that super?'

'Naturally I knew – the invitations were delivered through the Embassy. It is going to be a showcase visit, and is being designed to show the world just where the Duke stands.'

'But Wallis told me that Charles Bedaux is organising the whole thing, and has assured them that it is to be a private visit, organised by private individuals in that capacity, and would not involve Nazi Government propaganda.'

'Ha, I cannot accept that they believe that,' laughed von Ribbentrop.

'Why not? I thought that is what the Duke's statement said?'

'Celia, let me put you straight. Bedaux is allowed to think he is in charge, but he is not. The whole thing is being organised at the top level to maximise beneficial impact politically. You cannot imagine something on this scale being handled otherwise, can you?'

'I don't know, Bubbles, but how does the German government know that the Duke, and therefore the Duchess, will go along with this?'

'Ah, but they do. Rudolf Hess, the Deputy Führer, has met the Duke in Paris, and reported back to the Führer. To roughly quote Hess, he reported the Duke is proud of his German blood, is more German than British, and is deeply interested in the development of the Nazi Reich. Hess concluded, to the effect that the Duke and his clever wife will deliver the goods.'

'So there you have it, little one. Now then, shall we have some champagne and a light supper?'

'Yes, but first I am going to have a shower, if that is ok?'

'Of course. There's a shower cap in the cupboard.'

As the warm water cascaded over her, Celia hugged herself with delight – she had found out precisely what she had been asked.

Johnny was with Tar and Sir Vernon. He had just delivered Celia's report of what she had been told by von Ribbentrop.

'Excellent work, excellent work by both you and Lady Celia,' said a beaming Sir Vernon. 'To have this corroborated is exceptional – I shall contact Vansittart and the Foreign Secretary as soon as we have finished this meeting. Are you satisfied that von Ribbentrop does not suspect that Celia is working with us?' Sir Vernon asked Johnny.

'I cannot be sure, but from all that she has told me, he is as blinded by his ego as his ambition.'

'Very well, Johnny, I think that we must accept that as a view. He will shortly be leaving London to take up post as the German Foreign Minister. A poor choice, in the opinion of Anthony Eden, you know. He thinks Ribbentrop a slick operator, but with superficial talent and no real experience of the complexities of the great diplomatic game. I would like Maxwell Knight to join us for a few minutes – Tar, will you call him in please.'

After Maxwell Knight had taken his seat, Sir Vernon indicated that he wanted to review the intelligence assets that the British Secret Service currently had around the Windsors. Tar Robertson volunteered to do so. 'Quite apart from our long established sources, by way of individual agents in place on the Continent of Europe, and our relationships with the US government and French intelligence agencies, we now have some personal assets.

'Johnny has established an excellent relationship with Princess Stephanie, which provides an insight into, and indeed an influence over Hitler's mind. It will be interesting to see how Unity Mitford is handled by the Nazis – a nice little test. Billy Brownlow is now effectively running Vera von Wedel. She is an excellent asset, having no loyalty to Germany, but a member of the Abwehr. She was sent here to infiltrate the British establishment which Billy, Celia and Johnny will organise for her. By that means, we can influence Nazi thinking about the views and beliefs of what they see as the ruling class in Britain.

'Johnny and Celia will of course be travelling with the Windsors in Germany, and will pick up the private reactions and thoughts – also what is said in private meetings which they attend. I believe that we are well placed.'

'Might I add another potential angle?' asked Maxwell Knight. At a nod from Sir Vernon, he continued, 'The Duchess of Windsor has the Austrian woman, Helga, as her personal assistant and plaything. Helga is also the mistress of von Ribbentrop, and according to Celia, indulges in extreme sadistic sexual games with him. I would mention that I have passed that tidbit onto the psychological profilers. Celia thinks that she may be able to turn her. They are of an age, and both beautiful women. Helga is undoubtedly the go between planted by von Ribbentrop with Wallis. If we can turn her, it could be very valuable. Is it acceptable that Celia should proceed in this, albeit with great caution?'

After looking round and noting assent of Tar and Johnny, Sir Vernon responded, 'Most certainly, Lady Celia is proving herself a very capable young woman – an excellent resource. Very well, gentlemen I must go and report at the Foreign Office, and I shall then arrange to see Sir Alexander Hardinge at the Palace. Thank you for your time.'

As the others left his room, Sir Vernon screwed the cap onto his fountain pen and shuffled his pages of notes into a neat pile. Before leaving to report the latest intelligence, he allowed himself a few minutes thought. 'I may be an old man nearing the end of my career and the storm clouds are gathering, but so long as Britain has young people of resource and courage such as those I know and work with, she will prevail.'

# Epilogue

The Nord Express had swept across Northern France after leaving the Gare du Nord in Paris, and then through the night until it drew into Berlin's Friederichstrasse Station at 8.50am. As the great train was gliding to a stop at the platform, lined with strings of Union Jacks alternating with swastikas fluttering in the cold wind, a military band was playing *"God Save the King"*.

Wallis was standing smoothing her severely-tailored, navy blue coat over her hips. The Duke was checking the knot of his woven, plain Macclesfield silk tie and red carnation buttonhole in the art deco-framed wall mirror of their spacious sitting room. After patting his neatly trimmed hair, he stood back from the mirror. Wallis took his place, putting on a neat velvet hat that exactly matched the colour of her coat. She then drew on fine kid gloves. 'So honey, what happens next?'

'Well, my love, the normal protocol is for a member of the Royal Family to be met first by the British Ambassador – in this case, Sir Neville Henderson. He will come to us before we leave the train and are met by our German hosts. From the level of noise, I judge there to be rather a crowd – quite a welcoming party for us.'

At that moment, the Duke's valet, as the senior manservant of his household on the train, entered the sitting room. The Duke turned to him with a questioning look, and he responded, saying, 'Your Royal Highness, I beg to inform you that a Mr Harrison of the British Embassy wishes to pay his respects.'

A look of surprise flashed across the Duke's face, and Wallis looked at him sharply. He instantly recovered his composure. 'Do please show him in.'

Harrison, the Third Secretary at the Embassy, was shown in, clearly nervous and uncomfortable. He was smartly dressed, but his overcoat folded over his left arm gave the impression of informality. If this and his junior status were a deliberate snub, it was certainly noted by the Duke.

'Mr Harrison, good day to you – I was expecting Sir Neville Henderson, the Ambassador – and you are. . .?' The Duke raised a quizzical eyebrow, and his expression was anything but friendly.

'Sir Neville has been called away unexpectedly, Sir, and I am the Third Secretary.'

The Duke now looked incredulous. 'You are the *Third* Secretary?'

'I am, Sir, and I have a letter for you from the Charge d'Affaires, Sir George Ogilvie-Forbes.'

'Ah, well, at least I know him,' the Duke turned to Wallis, 'I met him when I was Prince of Wales – a good man. Very well, give me the letter. We cannot let our hosts wait any longer. I shall read it when we have reached the hotel. Thank you Harrison, you may leave us now. Ready, my darling?'

'I sure am.'

As the Duke and Duchess stood at the door of the train before stepping down to the platform, they were greeted by the sight of a formal receiving line of senior uniformed Nazis, flanked by black uniformed SS Soldiers, and Berlin police with their traditional military style headgear. At the front of the crowd, from which they were separated by a cordon of more SS guards and police straining to hold the people back with linked arms, there was a large group of uniformed officers, possibly as many as two hundred.

It was the noise that first impacted on the visitors – the massive crowd was chanting, and it was a moment or two before the Duke and Duchess recognised the chants which were accompanied by the familiar Nazi stiff arm salute. The ecstatic crowd was chanting and screaming, 'Heil Edward!' and 'Heil Windsor!'

The broadly-smiling Duke acknowledged the rapturous welcome with a Nazi salute. Any diffidence she may have had swept away by the welcome, Wallis also smiled and waved. As they stepped onto the platform, the senior Nazis came forward to them, led by Joachim von Ribbentrop, whose appointment as Foreign Minister had just been announced. He snapped another Nazi salute which the Duke returned, to more cheering.

It was difficult for von Ribbentrop to make himself heard over the noise. He leant forward after he and the Duke had exchanged Nazi salutes. 'Your Royal Highnesses, welcome to Germany. I trust that you had a pleasant journey, and will find your visit interesting, enlightening, and of course, most enjoyable. Again, on behalf of the Führer, his Ministers and the German people, a warm and sincere welcome.'

Both the Duke and Wallis thanked him. The crowd was still as noisily enthusiastic, as von Ribbentrop ushered forward the other welcoming senior members of the party. He first introduced Doctor Robert Ley, the National Labour Leader, who was to play a major role in the tour, then adjutant to the Führer and a key organiser of the tour, Fritz Wiedemann, and a number of others.

Doctor Ley presented Wallis with a box of chocolates accompanied by a card inscribed, *"Konigliche Hoheit"*, which the Duke later translated for her as 'Royal Highness'. A visibly nervous small girl presented the Duke with a small bouquet of red roses, and after she curtsied he smiled, thanked her, and passed it to Wallis.

By now, the police and SS men were having great difficulty holding the still-cheering and saluting crowds back. An order must have been given, because suddenly, a unit of black-uniformed guards formed up in two rows, providing a corridor out of the station and through the crowds outside. Dr Ley now took charge, and led them to his massive "Grosser" Mercedes Benz limousine that was to take the Windsors to their hotel. As they walked slowly down the corridor through the crowd, which the SS guards were holding back with difficulty, Doctor Ley, who was in military uniform, walked on their left, and Ribbentrop on their right. The Duke flourished his bowler hat as both he and Wallis smiled broadly. She too waved to the crowd, but in a much more restrained manner.

Once they were settled in the rear of the gigantic limousine, with Dr Ley sitting between the Duke and Duchess, SS guards tried to clear a way through the crowds for the cavalcade of outriders and official cars, all flying Nazi pennants. As well as the black-uniformed SS driver, two SS soldiers with sub machine guns sat in the front of the car, and two more stood on the running boards.

At last, the crowd parted, the cavalcade left the station and was soon racing along the broad boulevards at speed. Wallis caught the Duke's eye, and it was clear that she was very uncomfortable and nervous. The Duke determined to have a word with Dr Ley.

When they arrived at the Kaiserhof Hotel there was another large crowd, and as the car drew to a stop, flowers and oak leaves were showered on it. They were escorted through the throng, again with some difficulty. Some of the crowd were chanting and saluting just as at the station, but the majority were singing a well-rehearsed song especially written by the Propaganda Ministry of Dr Joseph Goebbels.

Once they were in the hotel, Dr Ley introduced them to Dr Keil, the press officer for the Labour Front, which he headed. 'I am delighted to meet you, Dr Keil, and indeed with the welcome we have received. It is 18 years since I was in Berlin. I am surprised at the change in the outward appearance of the City. I am looking forward to seeing a great deal.'

'I believe that there is much that will impress Your Royal Highnesses in the course of this historic visit. We are honoured.'

'Thank you, Dr Keil. Now then, Dr Ley, if it would be possible to have us shown to our suite it would be appreciated. It has been a long journey overnight, and my wife will rest here for the remainder of this morning I think. We shall have breakfast, and I shall come down at 10am to meet you here for our first visit, if I recall the time table correctly.'

'That is absolutely correct, Your Royal Highness.'

Wallis and the Duke were shown to their suite by a formally dressed member of the hotel management staff, who insisted on showing them around the suite. Wallis had gone to the window and asked the Duke, 'David, what is the huge building opposite?'

'I don't know, but I shall ask, dearest.'

He was told that it was the new Chancellry. As soon as they were alone, the Duke turned to Wallis, smiling broadly. 'Well, Wallis, my darling, now you know what I have talked about, the true affection and respect in which we are held.'

'Well, of one thing I am sure, dear man, we sure have arrived in style!'

'As it should be, Wallis, just as has been wrongly denied to us, but not any more if I have my way. This is the beginning of our true journey, my love – a taste of our life to come.'

'Amen to that,' said Wallis, adding quietly, 'perhaps our adventure is just beginning.'

# Postscript

*The story begins and continues in*

Volume One
King or Pawn?

*Available now:*
Paperback
ISBN-13 978-149603-129-7
Kindle ebook
ISBN-13 978-1-84396-294-6

Volume Three
The Court of Knaves

*To be published Autumn 2014:*
Paperback
ISBN-13 978-1-49603-348-2
Kindle ebook
ISBN-13 978-1-84396-301-1

Printed in Great Britain
by Amazon